Dear Inmate

BOOK TWO OF THE PADDY SERIES

LISA BOYLE

Dear Inmate

ISBN: 978-1-7366077-2-5 (Ebook)

ISBN: 978-1-7366077-3-2 (Paperback)

Copy Editor/Proofreader: Constance Renfrow

Cover Designer: Rafael Andres

Dedication

This book is for my niece, Faith. I'm so proud of you. Thank you for supporting me. In my writing, in my decision to go for a third plate at the dinner buffet. All of it.

And for my sister, Megan. Thank you for always believing in me. And for creating aforementioned human.

Chapter One

T he tolling of the church bells could only mean one thing: They were coming for us. For our church. For our school. For our girls. We listened in horrified silence. They were truly coming. I looked up at the man atop the bell tower, who had been keeping watch, staring through his spyglass into the distance. He used all of his weight to pull down on the rope, his body bobbing up and down in a frenzy. I glanced to Mairead next to me. Her black curls bounced as she looked all about her in panic. Her eyes were wide and full of fear. I stepped closer to her. I tried to be steady. Confident. Strong. I hoped she could feel it in me.

"We can do this," I whispered.

She breathed loudly out of her mouth in long gusts of air. She nodded once, and I watched her focus on me, burying her fears elsewhere.

I heard scurrying feet in the distance and imagined Sister Celeste, Sister Hunna, and Sister Edith slipping out the back of the church as they had been instructed to do at the chime of the bell. They would be carrying their most personal and intimate belongings. Diaries, letters, rosary beads, undergarments. Things they couldn't bear to see picked through, looted, or destroyed.

I squinted, and in the distance, I could see the mob, very small and moving through the streets, turning this way and that, all together, like a school of fish. My heartbeat drummed loudly in my ears. I tried not to picture their faces. People who I might have seen on the street, at the bookstore, at an antislavery society meeting. Their silent disgust failed to affect me anymore. But this was not silent. This was loud and forceful and violent, and I could not ignore it.

I bent down to pick up my weapon. Mine was a stone, but next to me, Mairead held two bricks, one in each hand, and Fiona gripped a club. Beads of sweat trickled down my back. I looked at Mairead again, biting the side of her lip. I tried to slow my breathing.

Behind us were the men—Emmett, Dennis, Frank, Patrick, and Mr. Joyce. Out of the corner of my eye, I could even see Quinn nervously toeing the dirt. Emmett, Dennis, Frank, and Patrick all had weapons, too. Chains, clubs, rocks, concrete slabs. Mr. Joyce carried nothing. He stood like an oak tree, eyes focused ahead, and his thick, strong arms crossed over his chest.

This was the fourth day we had come. We came when our shifts at the mills and machine shops and canals ended, and formed a human wall of protection.

The sun was starting to set, but the heat hadn't given way. Fiona practically bounced in place. I imagined that she'd been waiting for the chance to tear these people from limb to limb. Yankee, abolitionist, Know-Nothing, it mattered not. To her, they all meant the same thing: enemy.

The mob was approaching the bridge when I heard a sound, piercing and wild. It didn't sound human, but it was coming from Fiona's open mouth. Still gripping the club, Fiona ran for the bridge. Quinn stared at her in horror.

But then, another woman yelled, "Let's get the bastards!"

More yells rose up and the barricade of human bodies began to lurch forward. At first one by one, then by groups of many more. I looked around, not sure what to do. Should I hold the line at the church? Or should I go fight? This wasn't what we had planned.

I looked to the men. Frank had shoved past me right away, but Dennis, Patrick, Emmett, and Mr. Joyce stood strong. My eyes met Emmett's, and he smiled at me. A small, secret, close-lipped smile. I knew what he meant by it, and that amazed me. That sometimes, we didn't even need to speak to understand each other. That smile was my approval. My encouragement to do what I needed to do.

Mairead was also looking around frantically. She had taken half a step forward and then back again.

"Mairead," I said, commanding her attention again. "What will we do?"

She looked at me, and I knew she heard the steadiness in my voice. She knew I was with her. No matter what.

"We fight," she said, staring straight ahead.

And then, we ran.

Chapter Two

Far ahead of us, Fiona had not slowed. I could barely see her now but knew she was still leading us. We were approaching the bridge when we heard a loud groan over the noise of our labored breathing and quick foot-steps. Mairead went faster, elbowing her way through the crowd. I followed. I could hear the Know-Nothings now. The shouting and spitting.

We were nearly at the front, the small stone ledge lining the bridge to our left. I could see only a wall of bodies in front of us. Irish on one side, Know-Nothings on the other, swinging and pushing and falling on one another. Fiona was directly in front of me now, her auburn hair tied back, but flailing wildly as she fought. She still held tightly to her club, but the man across from her had grabbed it, too. They were locked in a tug-of-war for only a moment before he ripped it from her hands. She grabbed him by his shoulders and yelled again. This time, it was a deep, vibrating yell. And then, she threw the man with all her might, and he fell, stumbling over the ledge and into the canal.

A wave of water followed, splashing us all. Then, a stillness. A few laughs rang out. We stared at the men across from us. We all breathed in and out, not knowing what to do next. People began to back away from one another. Some gathered at the ledge to watch the man in the canal.

Fiona's hands were at her side, opening and closing, grabbing air and releasing it. She was as sturdy as the bridge she stood on, staring at the Know-Nothings, daring them to try again. Frank stood next to her, ready to fight for her. Some of the men in the mob pointed at her.

"It was her!" a man yelled from the front.

"Can't have us revealing your secrets, can you?" another sneered.

She spat in his face, and he swung at her. Frank caught the man's fist and twisted his arm until the man crumpled to the ground. The crowd started to swarm forward again, but just then, another man pushed his way through to the front.

"Stop!" he yelled as loud as he could. I recognized him. It was Reverend Edson, breathing hard. "Stop all of this!" Clearly the men recognized him, too, because they did indeed stop, though they looked at him with irritation.

"Please," he said, "go home. The church is a sacred place. Leave theirs be."

"They're hiding things in there," one of them shouted. "Plans!"

"Plans to ruin this country!" yelled another.

I stepped forward, next to Frank.

"Ruin this country?" I asked. "How? We barely have anything to call our own."

"You have enough," another said.

The man on the ground rolled to his side, still clutching his shoulder. Someone helped him up. The injured man glared at Frank.

"We came to this country for a better life," I said. "The only things you'd find in our church are Bibles."

"Catholic Bibles!" a man directly in front of me said. "Americans listen to God only, not some tyrant with a foolish hat giving commands from an ocean away. We will not be bound by Italian chains! This is a Protestant nation. If you don't like it, you should leave!"

"We've heard that before," I shot back. "We've been told we can't be Catholic. But we still are. And we will continue to be. And we're not leaving."

"Yah!" a woman behind me yelled.

The man before me stepped closer and lowered his voice.

"I'm patient," he said. "We can make things very difficult for you and your kind. And we will."

I examined his thick eyebrows and crooked teeth. He was an ugly man, and I thought about telling him so. But instead, I said, "You won't break us."

His thin lips curled into a sinister smile.

"Is that a challenge, Biddy?" he asked.

Frank lunged. I put out my arm to stop him.

"It's all right, Frank," I said. "We're done here."

Reverend Edson breathed a sigh of relief.

"Thank you, Rosaleen," he said.

"Follow the good reverend home now," I said.

The man in front of me chuckled.

"I don't take orders from you or from this old man," he said. "We told you already. We have no pope."

Then he leaned even closer and whispered in my ear, "We'll be back," before turning around to address the rest of them.

"Let's get some supper, boys!" he yelled. "We're done for tonight. They've clearly hidden or destroyed their damning documents. We'll come again when they aren't so well prepared. This isn't over!"

"Yea!" a few of them shouted.

They started to walk back to where they had come from. To the other side of Lowell. Where people had fair wages and respectable occupations and one house was for one family.

Reverend Edson came up to me and patted my shoulder.

"The Know-Nothings have gotten out of control," he said.

"It's only going to get worse now that Mayor Ward was elected," I said. "He encourages it."

People were going up to Fiona now. Rubbing her back, asking if she was all right, congratulating her on her bravery and strength.

"Thank you for your assistance tonight, Reverend," I said to Reverend Edson.

He gave me a half smile. "Good night," he said, before walking back to his church.

I watched him go, his head down, arms crossed. I thought about how much older he seemed than when I had first met him four years ago. His hair was now completely gray and he was thinner. The bones in his face at a sharper angle, yet his skin droopier.

Mairead grabbed my hand. We started back toward the Acre.

"You did good today," she said.

I sighed. "Not good enough."

"You made them leave," she said. "Those men are plain evil. You're not going to change their hearts."

"I wish I could change *someone's* heart," I said. "People are so afraid and angry. They won't listen. They won't try to change."

We walked for a moment in silence.

"Besides," I said, "I think Fiona was the one that made them leave. They were afraid of her."

We both laughed, remembering the soaking-wet man.

"I can't believe she threw a man," Mairead said.

"I can," I said. "It was probably cathartic. I say we let her toss one Know-Nothing into the canal each week."

Mairead laughed heartily now.

"It might bring everyone together. Yankee and Irish. Who wouldn't like to watch that?" she asked.

"The man being tossed," I chuckled.

When we got back, the men who had stayed at the church were listening to the others tell the story of what happened at the bridge. Emmett smiled big when he saw me.

"We did it, Rose," he said. "We saved the day."

"No," I said. "Fiona saved the day."

He nodded. "She is terrifying."

Mairead let go of my hand.

"I'm going to find Dennis," she said. "You kept him safe, didn't you?" she asked Emmett.

"Not one hair on his beautiful wee head was harmed," Emmett said.

"Ha!" Mairead said. "I knew I wasn't the only one to think Dennis's oddly shaped head is beautiful!"

I giggled. "Goodbye, Mairead!" I yelled after her.

"Frank said a man threatened your life," Emmett said as we walked.

"Don't they always?" I asked, smirking.

"I have something special planned for our evening tomorrow," he said, "so don't go biting the dust before then."

I laughed. "You sure have a way with words, Emmett Doherty," I said. "It's no wonder I've been able to keep you to myself all this time."

He made a shocked and hurt face, but I knew it wasn't sincere. I smacked him playfully. We were at the boarding-house now, and we stopped.

"I'll be dressed and ready and waiting for you at your house when you get off work tomorrow," I said.

He drew nearer.

"I'll never forget when I saw you there, waiting for me that day you came to Lowell," he said in a low, hushed voice. "Every time feels like that, you know. Fluttery stomach. Sweaty hands. Dizzy head."

I smiled and bit my lip.

"Even still? After four years?" I asked.

"Even still. Even after one hundred years," he said.

He kissed my lips softly.

"Good night," he whispered.

"Good night," I whispered back.

Inside, the parlor was empty. It was nearing curfew, and most of the girls were already settled in their rooms. Through the window, I watched Emmett walk down the street alone and longed to walk with him. To only have to say good night as I lay next to him. To watch his beautiful eyelashes close over his blue eyes. To watch his wide, strong chest move up and down in contented sleep. I wanted it so bad it hurt. I watched him cross the canal and turn down Merrimack Street where I couldn't see him anymore. Then I went upstairs.

Nessa was sitting on the edge of our bed, one hand holding a book open and the other twirling her light-brown, silky hair that fell in loose waves over her shoulders. Her left knee bobbed up and down. When she noticed me, she slammed down her book and jumped to her feet.

"What happened?" she asked, excitedly. "How did it go? Tell me everything!"

I smiled at her enthusiasm. She had asked me the same questions every night for the last four nights.

"Fiona threw a man into the canal," I said.

Nessa's mouth dropped open.

"No," she said.

"She did," I said. "And your brother probably made them all soil their pants in terror. I wouldn't be surprised if he broke that man's arm."

"Wow," she nearly whispered in amazement. "Fiona is so brave!"

"Mmmm," I replied, wanting to neither agree nor disagree with that statement.

"I wish she liked me," Nessa said. "She'll probably marry my brother someday and she barely even speaks to me."

"Have you told her how amazing you think she is?" I asked. "She likes hearing that."

Nessa cracked a smile.

"Why don't you like her?" she asked.

"It's not that I don't like her," I said. "She's . . ." I paused, thinking of a compliment. "Brave, like you said," I finally finished.

"I wish Frank would have allowed me to go," she said.

"No, he's right," I said. "Things could have been much worse. Let Frank do the defending."

"But *you* were there!"

"I'm older and bigger, and I don't have a brother." I agreed with Nessa, but I couldn't tell her that. Frank and I already had enough problems getting along.

"You have Emmett, though," she said, plopping back down on the bed.

I studied Nessa. I wished I could pull her into my cause. Any of my causes. She had a good heart and loads of energy. Every girl did at her age. I remembered having it. But I'd felt a little bit slip away every year, and in its place, I was left with more and more frustration, which I tried to keep from turning into resignation.

"Maybe there are some ways you could help," I finally said.

Nessa popped up onto her elbows. "How?"

"I'll think about it," I said. "But you can't tell your brother. Whatever it is. Do you promise?"

She nodded her head furiously. "I promise."

~

I still slept in the same bed as I always had at 17 Burn Street. Mrs. Durrand and Hattie and little Benjamin—who was not so little anymore—were still on the first floor below me, and Sarah still slept in the adjacent bed. I slept on the side of the bed where Julia used to and thought of her still every night when I put out the lamp.

Berta, who was also from Germany, had replaced Frieda. Frieda had left during the mill layoffs a few years back, and her family headed West, looking to start over one more time. This time in the new territories, where they hoped their newspaper would be a voice of freedom.

Berta was a much better roommate than Frieda. Berta and Sarah had become fast friends. They were quite opposite in most ways. They were both German, but Berta was Catholic. Berta didn't mind sticking up for her friends, even if it meant getting into a fight. She was very smart and, I think, enjoyed arguing. But they were both kind and caring, and Berta knew not to push Sarah too far. They both admitted that they wouldn't have been friends in Germany. It wouldn't have been possible. But here, it didn't matter that Sarah was Jewish. Neither of them were Protestant, so to the Know-Nothings, they were both suspicious foreigners.

I lay in bed that night staring at my most recent letter from Marie. Nessa had fallen asleep, but I kept the lamp lit, reading my letter over and over and feeling a deep guilt in the bottom of my stomach. I hadn't been to visit in nearly a year, and Marie was asking again. Miss Susan would even make a room available for me. Free of charge.

I missed them terribly, but seeing Marie always reminded me of my failures here. I wanted something to show her to prove that I was being the good abolitionist she knew I could be. But beyond the four Irish people that I was closest with, I had failed to bring about any sort of meaningful change here. If anything, many more Irish had grown resentful of Black people. And more abolitionists had grown resentful of Irish people.

Working conditions at the mill hadn't improved much, either. There had been multiple fires over the years. Another death. Various hands and fingers and arms torn off. An Irishwoman named Orla had started a women's association for better working conditions. I helped her organize strikes, but it was always the same. Some in the Acre would strike. Some would not. The strike-breaking men and women would quietly slip off to work in the mornings. I could tell which ones they were by their refusal to share a smile or a nod. They shuffled away, eyes downcast, trying their hardest to simply disappear. They were drawn to the sounds of the canal, the groan of the machines, the noise of wages. Their bodies rose from sleep before the sun, and their feet didn't know another way to go.

I finally put out the lamp when the clock read 11 p.m. and dreamt of the man at the bridge. He called me a failure and laughed in my face. Fiona was there, too.

"And she's a traitor!" she yelled, before picking me up and throwing me into the canal. I awoke just when I should have landed in the water. I gasped for breath at first and then laughed quietly at myself.

I turned one way and then the other, trying to get back to sleep. The man at the bridge still haunted me, and I finally let myself think about what he had said. He'd promised to make life difficult for us Irish. But how could it be any harder? We were already poor and sick and often out of a job. What else could they do?

Finally, I got out of bed and crept over to our desk. I quietly gathered some papers and a pen and tiptoed out of the room, careful to close the door gently behind me.

In the parlor, I started to write. Not a proper letter. My thoughts were too jumbled for that. I started to write a list of grievances. It helped spark ideas.

I started with the easy ones, the ones I had been writing about for years now. The Irish are denied jobs, housing. The Irish are paid less. Because the Irish do not have proper housing, they have no proper place to be sick. Their homes are cold, drafty, damp. The Irish are confined to the mill, the church, and the taverns, and their behavior at all of these places is scrutinized and criticized. Then I moved on to problems that had arisen as of late. The Irish are jailed more frequently, for longer periods of time. The Irish are denied public poor funds.

The moon was bright tonight, making it easy to read my list back to myself. In my head, I thought of the things a slave endured. Beaten, whipped, sold, forcibly separated from their family. If they escape, they are chased down, hunted. It didn't match up. It wasn't even comparable. But I had to make a connection somewhere. Somehow.

I sighed. I had made them all, and yet, as far as the Acre was concerned, this horror may have been happening on another planet. The colored people they knew seemed just fine. Perhaps even better off. They were paid better. Their homes were nicer. Sometimes I wondered if the Irish even believed the things I wrote.

They didn't see the fear within their Black neighbors. They refused to.

I looked at the bright moon again and thought of home. Ireland was farther from me than the slavery of the American South, but sometimes it felt just an arm's reach away. Da, Ma, our cottage, the sea. It was a different life, truly. One that I had lived a lifetime ago. And yet, it was inside of me. The smells, the sounds. When I needed strength to push through, I thought of Ma collecting those nettles. I had been wrong about Ma. She was a fighter. With time, I could see that.

I gathered my papers and walked lightly up the stairs, back to my room. I put them on the desk and fell into a deep sleep. I did not wake right away when the bell rang the next morning. My mind was slow, my thoughts moving as if stuck in molasses.

I splashed my face two extra times to wake myself. Mrs. Durrand had made egg and meat pies for breakfast with fresh strawberries. I was surprisingly hungry and ate mine quickly.

Even though summer was beginning, the mornings were still quite cool, and I hurried to the mill. Sometimes I walked with Nessa, but this morning she was eating slower than I, talking to her younger friends about the bridge incident. I thought of Nancy then and our walks together to work. I missed her and convinced myself I would visit her soon.

Work dragged on as it did on Saturdays when we were all itching to be done and have our day of rest. I stood at my weaving machines, watching over three of them for snags and jams. Sarah was to my left, and another young woman, Emily, was to my right. Mairead worked across the room. The room was scattered with men now, too. As more Yankee women left, Irishmen took their places.

As I walked out of work that sunny day, I noticed a woman sitting on a bench. That same bench I had first sat on when I came to Lowell. I'd wondered then whether I was making the right choice, coming here. But never again after. I looked again and realized I knew that woman sitting there. She shielded her eyes from the sun with her flat hand, peering into the crowd of women pouring from the mill. I ran to her and she smiled. We hugged each other tight.

"I was just thinking of you this morning!" I said to her.

"Of our walks to work?" Nancy asked. "I miss them, too."

I nodded and squeezed her hand. "How is Calvin?" I asked.

"He is well," she said. "He says this new police force needs work. He's not quite sure what to do with them. He's thinking of meeting with the Boston police officers. They just formed a department, and he thinks they could help him do the same in Lowell."

"Tell him he could start by leaving the Irish alone," I said.

She gave me a sideways smile. "You know I will," she said.

Then she grabbed my hand, and her eyes narrowed. She looked at me intently.

"I have some news for you," she said, glancing at the people around us. "It might be something . . . for your . . . you know."

My Paddy letters. I had just about exhausted every inch of the Acre, leaving my letters here or there until Irish guards—hired by the taverns and other businesses—lined the street every night. The newspapers still published my letters, though, and the *Lowell American* even gave them a prime position.

"What is it?" I asked.

"Do you know of a colored man named George Moore?" she asked.

"No," I said. "Should I?"

Nancy shook her head. "I suppose you would have no reason to. He used to live here in Lowell. He only moved a few months ago. Maybe half a year at the most. I knew him briefly. When I started teaching, he was also a teacher at the school. But he left soon after to open his own barbershop."

"What about him?" I asked.

"He was an escaped slave," she said. "He left Virginia twelve years ago. And now, with this new Fugitive Slave Law, his old master is coming back to claim him. He sent his wife and children somewhere else. I don't know where. And his community in Manchester raised money for him to go to Canada. He might be on his way there right now."

My mind started racing, going over all of the details of the Fugitive Slave Law.

"This is important," I said to her.

"That's not all," she went on. "His old master and those deputies have specifically threatened his friends in Lowell. They say they plan to bring the full weight of the law down on those who aided and abetted his escape."

"No," I said. "That's ridiculous!"

"Yes," she said. "Six months in jail or one thousand dollars! No one is going to give anyone up. And the city officials will shield the town from any consequences. But those slaveholders and Southern politicians intend to try to make an example out of us."

"Oh, Nancy," I said, the hot anger inching up my spine. "I'll be up all night with this news."

"Wait until after your date with Emmett," she said. "He told me it's a special one."

"When did you see him?" I asked.

"I bumped into him earlier this week," she said. "He seemed quite excited."

"I'm glad you reminded me," I said. "I almost forgot about our date!"

Nancy laughed. "I know how you get about writing," she said. Then she winked. "I can't have you neglecting our Emmett."

Now *I* laughed. "It's as if I share that man with all of Lowell."

"You should appoint him ambassador of the Acre," she said. "One meeting with Mayor Ward and the man would have to change his whole philosophy. They would be drinking rum together before the night was over!"

I smiled faintly. "I only wish it were that simple," I said.

I hurried back to the boardinghouse and rushed through making myself pretty. I'd promised Emmett I would be waiting for him, and I intended to keep that promise. I hated to disappoint him.

As I waited on his steps, I watched some boys playing across the street. They had scratched themselves a hopscotch board into the dirt. One boy threw a stone, and it bounced off the board. The other boy laughed, and the first shuffled over to get his stone, shoulders caved, head down. The second boy threw his stone, and it landed squarely on a section of the board. As he hopped down the board, the first boy bumped his shoulder, throwing him off-balance. The two began to push and shove one another until a woman who had been hanging clothes on the side of the house thundered over. She grabbed each boy by the collar.

"That's enough, you two!" she shouted. "I'll send you right back to your ma, Brendan."

She let them go.

"Sorry, Mrs. Kelly," the second boy said. "I'll behave."

"Yeh better," she said, before turning back to her work.

I would have guessed that the boys were about ten years old, the same age as Ronan. I hadn't seen him since last year, and it made me worry. I knew those men he lived with were no good for him, and it seemed his Aunt Maureen cared little. My guilt from last night came back, turning my stomach over. I was neglecting Ronan, too.

I was so lost in my thoughts that I hadn't realized Emmett was standing right in front of me. I stood up and hugged him.

"Should we go to the waterfall then?" I asked.

"Let me clean myself up a bit first," he said. "I'll be back in one moment. Don't go anywhere."

I nodded. Patrick went in after him, giving me a warm smile. When I turned back to the boys, they were shoving each other again. But this time they were laughing, too. It made me smile. The way children could forgive so easily. The way they trusted each other. Their comfort in closeness.

Emmett came down soon, face clean and shaved. His hair was brushed to the side. It had grown rather long lately, hovering just above his eyes, but I liked it. He grinned and took my hand, leading me toward the waterfall. We were quiet on the way, and I kept glancing at Emmett to see if anything was wrong. But his gaze darted from the sky to the road, avoiding mine purposefully.

"Are you feeling all right?" I asked him.

"I feel wonderful, Rose." He squeezed my hand.

"You seem worried," I said.

He laughed a short, funny laugh.

"I can't hide anything from you," he said, putting his arm around my shoulder, pulling me close. I could feel his heart thumping fast.

"What is it?" I asked again.

"We're nearly there," he answered.

He brought me a little farther than usual, to a secluded spot. I could only barely see the water through the trees, bubbling up from its fall. Emmett put a blanket down under a canopy of trees. The sunlight peeked through the branches, but mostly it was cool and shady. We sat.

"This is nice," I said. I leaned back between his legs, resting my head on his chest. His heart was still beating hard. He kissed the top of my head and then let his mouth rest there for a moment.

"Rose," he finally said. "I talked to Mr. Joyce. And he gave me his blessing."

"For what?" I asked.

"Will you please marry me, Rosaleen MacNamara?"

A warmth spread over my body, and *my* heart began to beat fast as well. I couldn't help but to smile big. I turned to face him. He looked a little pale. His eyebrows were squished together in anticipation.

"It's about time you asked," I whispered. "I would love nothing more."

His face relaxed, and he kissed me. It was a long, slow kiss, and I let myself enjoy it. Our lips felt like one. Our tongues knew every inch of the other's mouth like their own. Eventually, he pulled away and shifted to pull something from his pocket. It was a gray cloth with something folded inside.

"Go ahead," he said. "Open it."

I carefully unfolded it to reveal a brooch. A Celtic cross with green vines and purple flowers weaving in and out of its arms.

"This is beautiful," I gasped. "Where did you get it?"

"Mr. Joyce wanted you to have it," he said. "It was Julia's ma's. Now it's yours. And one day, you'll give it to our little girl."

My eyes welled up with tears. Emmett pulled me into his arms and I cried. Losing Julia still felt so close. Like I could turn into the past, reach out, and touch it. I knew Mr. Joyce felt the same, and yet, he was trusting me with her legacy. He knew I would honor her. Their whole family. My heart ached with joy and sadness all at once.

Emmett pulled away and wiped my tears with his thumbs.

"I thank God every day that we were together on that ship," he said. "You are life to me, Rose."

I kissed him again but more passionately this time, forcing all of my weight onto him. He grabbed my waist and moved his hands down my sides, onto my thighs, but pulled away still.

"Not yet," he whispered, breathlessly.

I groaned a little. "You're right," I said, sitting back on my heels. I gave him a sly grin.

"Let's talk to Father O'Brien right now," I said. Emmett laughed loudly.

"If you insist!" He looked up at the sky. It was turning orange. The sun was setting.

"Tomorrow," he said. "After Mass."

He stood up and offered me his hand.

"Now," he went on, "we need to get you back in time for curfew."

Chapter Three

After Mass, I stood with Emmett and Mr. Joyce as we spoke with Father John O'Brien. Father Peter Purcell now headed St. Patrick's, but Mr. Joyce had grown so close to Father O'Brien, he still went to him on all matters of faith. Mr. Joyce trusted Father O'Brien completely.

"And you give your blessing to this young couple?" Father O'Brien asked.

"Yes, Father," Mr. Joyce replied. "I believe God brought Rosaleen into Julia's life to be the sister she never had. Indeed, she feels like a daughter to me. And Emmett is a good man. Perhaps the best bachelor in all of Lowell. I could not want anything more."

I squeezed Emmett's arm and tried not to cry.

"And they will be wedded in your home?" Father O'Brien asked.

"Yes, Father," Mr. Joyce answered. "And they will live there with me after they are married."

Father O'Brien nodded in approval.

23

"You will be a steady guidance for them," Father O'Brien said. "Steering them toward the Lord in all that they do. I will be happy to perform the duty of bringing them together as one. Two weeks from today, I will come to your home after Mass to perform the service."

Mr. Joyce smiled and shook his hand.

"Thank you, Father," he said.

I walked between Emmett and Mr. Joyce as we made our way to Fenwick Street, my hands in theirs. When we sat to eat, I thought about how soon this would be our table. Our room.

"Thank you for the brooch," I said to Mr. Joyce. "I was speechless. I'm incredibly honored."

Mr. Joyce smiled and swallowed his ham.

"You remind me a little of Julia's ma," he said. "Calm and logical at times, compassionate and determined at others. She would be pleased for you to have it."

He paused to take another bite.

"Julia was all heart," he went on. "Gentle, caring. Almost to a fault. That's why I worried about her. But Brianna knew when to tell someone to mind their own."

I smiled shyly. "I wish I could have met her," I said.

"Me too," he said. "Sometimes I have to ask myself, 'What would Brianna have done?' She was special. I miss her every day, too. It's comforting to know that she's taking care of Julia now."

"I bet you felt lucky when you married her," Emmett said.

Mr. Joyce put down his fork. "I think I felt scared," he said. "I wasn't as smart as you. I didn't know yet what a good woman could do for me. But I was blessed by the Lord. And you are, too."

That night, walking back to the boardinghouse, Emmett said, "Only thirteen more nights until I get to fall asleep next to you."

"So you've been thinking about that, too," I said.

"Only every day for the last five years," he said.

"I'm the lucky one," I whispered, before kissing him good night.

I ran up the stairs as soon as I got in to tell the girls the news. Sarah was at her desk and Berta on the bed.

"Where is Nessa?" I asked. "It's almost curfew."

Berta shrugged. "I haven't seen her," she said.

"She better get here soon," I said. "Sarah, hurry up with whatever you're writing. I have news, and it's about to burst right out of me!"

"Just one more minute," she said, scribbling a little quicker. Berta put her book down.

"All right," Sarah said, setting down her pen. "Tell us!"

"Emmett and I are getting married in two weeks!" I practically shouted, unable to contain my excitement.

Sarah stood up and hugged me. "Oh, I am so happy for you, Rosaleen!" she cried.

Berta stood up and came over to hug me, too.

"Congratulations," she said. "You two were meant for each other."

I beamed. My cheeks were starting to hurt from smiling so much. Then, Nessa burst in.

"Just made it!" she said. "What's going on here?"

"Emmett and Rosaleen are getting married in two weeks!" Sarah said.

"Finally!" Nessa shouted as she threw her arms around me.

"Oh." Nessa's face dropped. "But that means you'll move out."

I brushed her hair out of her face.

"I know," I said. "I'm going to miss you all. But I'll still see you at work, and I promise I'll still come around all the time."

I looked at Sarah and smiled. "What an amazing four years," I said.

Sarah stepped closer to me. "Julia would have been so happy for you," she said. "She loved Emmett."

"She did," I said.

"You and Julia were my first true friends here," she said. "We were so young. And Nancy was like our older sister. Trying to help us navigate this town but mostly getting us into trouble."

I laughed. Nancy! Had she known Emmett intended to propose? I had to tell her. Then I remembered what she had told me on Saturday. About George Moore.

"Berta," I said. "Have you heard about George Moore?"

Her eyes got big and her face animated. Berta was an abolitionist, too. And like me, not exactly accepted as one.

"Yes!" she said. "I heard he made it safely to Canada, thank the Lord."

"Who?" Nessa asked.

"George Moore," I said. "One of your brothers might have had him as a teacher at the school. He's an escaped slave. But he had been here a long time. With this new Fugitive Slave Act, his old masters thought they would come take him. But he made it to Canada."

"Oh," Nessa said.

"Have you read that book yet?" I asked Nessa. I had let her borrow my copy of *Uncle Tom's Cabin.* She shook her head but said nothing else. She always got quiet when I talked about slavery. I knew she heard all sorts of things from all sides. It was no secret what Frank thought about it and no secret that I felt the exact opposite. I didn't know how Nessa felt. Or if she even knew how she felt. But I was trying to help her figure it out. If only she would let me.

"This Fugitive Slave Act is so absurd," Berta said. "I am horrified that Congress passed it."

I nodded. "Hypocrites," I said. "The South only wants states' rights when it's their state having the right to own people. But now, what about the rights of Massachusetts or New Hampshire? Now, they want to trample on our states' rights!"

"Precisely!" Berta agreed. "I heard that Massachusetts is going to pass its own law in response."

"Truly?" I asked. "That says what?"

"I'm not sure," Berta admitted. "I was going to try to read about it."

"Should we go to the library together?" I asked. "After work tomorrow?"

"Yes!" she said, eagerly. "Let's!"

Berta and I were finishing our supper, getting ready to go to the library, when Mrs. Durrand approached me.

"You have a letter, Rosaleen," she said, handing it to me.

"Thank you, Mrs. Durrand," I said. I opened it right away.

To my dear friend, Rosaleen,

Something terrible has happened in Boston with this new kidnapping law. I'm not sure if you've read about it. A young man, Anthony Burns, arrived in the city earlier this year. He escaped from his master in Virginia.

Well, his master came to get him, and although we tried, we could not save this young man. We went to the courthouse. Some of the men were armed. Miss Martha was, too. We demanded he be released, but that evil man who occupies the White House and loves the South sent United States Marines and Massachusetts militia to hold us back. They took him to a ship waiting to bring him back to Virginia. Marched him right down these streets that I walk on every day.

I tell you, Rosaleen. I am shaken. Please pray for me. I walk around with such anger. I can't get away from it. You might think that I am afraid, and maybe I am. But I can't feel it. The anger is too strong.

Write to me with good news. Any good news. I cannot bear to read anything else. I see nothing good in this world. What am I supposed to tell Angel?

All my love,
Marie

I read it twice before saying to Berta, "I'll be ready in a few minutes. I just need to write a quick letter. I'll meet you back down here as soon as I am finished."

She nodded, still chewing and swallowing the last bites of her supper. I hurried upstairs to our desk.

To my Marie,

This is terrible news. I am so sorry for Mr. Burns. I, too, am angry, although I know your anger runs deeper. You have every right to feel as you do.

Tell Angel that evil men are real but tell her how hard we are fighting to rid this world of them. She is watching and learning. God willing, this world will be very different when she is grown.

A man that used to live in Lowell was pursued as well. He made it to Canada, though, and is safe for now. What do you know of the counter law Massachusetts is writing? I'm on my way to read about it right now, as soon as I finish this letter. Don't give up hope, Marie. We will beat them.

Emmett and I are to be married in two weeks! And then we will visit. I promise you. That is, I hope, some good news. I miss you all dearly. Please stay safe. I will be praying.

Your dearest friend,
Rosaleen

I folded it, addressed it, and brought it with us. We stopped at the post office first, where I paid for my letter to be sent right away. The clock at the library read eight o'clock, and I silently cursed our curfew. As Berta flipped through months of Massachusetts legislative records, I reread the Fugitive Slave Act and made notes:

1. US Marshals issue arrest warrants to slave owners.
2. State and local police, as well as other persons, must assist in capture of slave. Punishment for refusal is $1,000 or six months in jail.
3. Federal commissioners decide if person in custody is escaped slave.
4. Person in question cannot have representation and cannot argue their case.
5. Slave owner presents "evidence," although it is often simply their own testimony.
6. For every judgment that rules against the slave owner, commissioners are paid $5. For every judgment that rules for the slave owner, commissioners are paid $10.

I could see why Marie called it the kidnapping law. There was no motivation to uncover truth. Not only were escaped slaves in danger, so were all Black people. I had read a few months earlier about free Blacks being captured and then sold once they arrived back in Virginia.

"Rosaleen," Berta said. "Look at this."

She had a record in her hand that referenced a "personal liberty law." The law proposed to ban state and local police, lawyers, and judges from assisting slave owners. It would also refuse to allow federal agents to use state and local jails and courthouses.

"This is it!" I said.

I kept reading. It also allowed legal representation for the accused and required a jury trial to decide if the slave owner's affidavit was legitimate. It opposed the Fugitive Slave Act on every point.

"Do you think this will work?" Berta asked.

"I haven't a clue," I said. "But it has to pass. It has to."

I lay awake in bed that night, unable to sleep once again. My brain was doing flips thinking about George Moore and Anthony Burns and the Fugitive Slave Act and the personal liberty law. It needed to pass. Could the Irish help? Some of them were citizens by now. They could vote. Did the lawmakers care?

I wasn't sure the Irish wanted to help. I thought of Fiona. How could I convince her to agree with a man who she'd thrown into the canal only a few days ago. To agree with a Know-Nothing who resented her very existence. How could I convince her to agree with him on some things and still fight him on others?

I wanted badly to write a Paddy letter, but I hadn't connected anything yet. A bunch of loose thoughts drifted in and out in an unsatisfying web of irritation. Finally, I drifted off into a fitful sleep.

The next day was hot. I sweated on my way home for dinner, and I sweated at work. Strands of my hair clung to the back of my neck, and I had to stop and wipe my forehead frequently. My palms were slippery, too. I thought constantly about a cold ale and longed for the day, in less than two weeks, when I would have no curfew and plenty of time to enjoy a drink.

At supper, Mrs. Durrand had dropped a few ice cubes

in our tea to cool it off, and I gulped it down quickly. As I started on my food, Nessa burst into the room once again. I was about to tease her for her new dramatic habit when I saw her red and puffy eyes. She looked afraid and ran straight to me.

"Frank has been arrested!" she cried.

"What?" I asked. "What for?"

She started sobbing, and I sat her down.

"I don't know, Rosaleen," she said. "I don't know!"

"All right," I said, rubbing her back, trying to calm her a bit. Then I took one bite of my supper and stood up. "Let's go figure it out. Come on."

She jumped up and followed me out the door.

"Where are we going?" she asked.

"To the jail," I said.

The jail was near the end of Dutton Street, nearly at the bridge crossing the main canal, Pawtucket, where the train station was. We walked along the Western Canal, which was quiet now that the mills slept. The sun was setting as we passed the Acre. A few stores dotted the outskirts of the Acre, and I saw store owners helping customers, opening doors and tipping their hats.

I walked quickly, knowing we didn't have much time until curfew. With her long legs, Nessa had no trouble keeping up. Every few strides, she did a nervous sort of hop. She fiddled with her apron and kept sniffling.

"What will you say?" she finally asked.

"I'll ask them why he's in there and when they intend to let him out," I said. "Does Fiona know?"

"I don't know," Nessa said. "I couldn't find her."

Suffolk Street turned the corner to become Cushing

Street, and we found ourselves looking at the back of the jail. It was ugly, made mostly of concrete. The windows were yellow and brown so that you could not see into them. We walked down an alley to the front. A rat scurried next to us. Nessa grabbed my hand and gripped it tightly, her nails digging into my skin.

"Don't be afraid," I said. "We have a right to know what's going on."

She nodded quickly. We climbed the four steps leading to the main door and walked into the jail. A man sat at a desk in front of us, scribbling away. A lamp was next to him, but everything else was very dark. Behind him, I could barely make out a hallway leading to the rest of the building.

"Yes?" the man asked, without looking up.

"We're here to see about a prisoner," I said.

Nessa's grip tightened. Then, the man looked up. I recognized him. My stomach tumbled. It was the man from the bridge. His thin lips formed into that awful smile again.

"Rosaleen, isn't it?" he asked. My mouth was suddenly very dry. I lifted my chin higher and willed myself to be steady.

"We want to know about Frank McHugh," I said.

"I don't know which one that is," he said, still smiling. "We get an awful lot of your kind."

"He was arrested today," I went on. "We don't know what for."

"Ah, yes." He sat back in his chair and rested one foot on his opposite knee. "That Mick of yours sure is a big fella. I remembered him from *our* little encounter, too."

"Why is he here?" I asked.

The man sat forward again and flipped through his papers, scanning them for information.

"Let's see, what was it this time?" he said. "That's right!" He stopped flipping and pointed his pen at the paper. "Public brawling. Can't have a man like that on the streets. Could be quite dangerous."

"What do you mean 'this time'?" I asked. "Frank's never been arrested before."

"He has," the man said. "This here says this is his third arrest."

Before I could warn Nessa to keep quiet, to tell her just how dangerous I could feel this man to be and how little he needed to know about her, she interjected.

"I think I would know if he had been arrested twice before," she burst out. "He *is* my brother."

The man twisted his face into a pleased half smile.

"Well, young lady," he said. "Miss McHugh is it? Perhaps big brother had the means to bail himself out before. He wouldn't want to worry his little sister's head, I imagine."

"No," I said. "I'm certain Frank would have told us. Maybe, since we are all the same to you, you've confused him for someone else."

Now the man stood up and walked toward us. He wore a long coat with copper buttons down the center and a badge. A belt wrapped around his waist. His uniform was a bit small for his belly, the buttons straining to stay closed. Nessa shuffled back a half step, but I stayed rooted in place. He stopped about a foot away. I could read the name on his badge: Keyes. His thick eyebrows were furrowed, and he was no longer smiling.

"I am a damn good police officer," he practically growled at me. "*I* don't make mistakes, and *you* don't question me."

My heart thumped loudly, but I refused to let this man scare us away without seeing Frank.

"It's nothing to be ashamed of," I said. "You've only been on the job for a short time now. All of you."

"I have been doing the work of rounding up this city's vermin for much longer than that," he replied, his voice still low and deep. "The uniform is new, but I am not. You're lucky that this Mick of yours isn't at the Middlesex County House of Correction. For the violent criminals. I've heard simply horrific stories. Perhaps I could arrange a transfer."

Just then, the loud sound of large, clomping boots echoed off the walls. I peered around the man.

"Abner!" someone called from the hallway. "Shift is up. Time to go home."

Chapter Four

Officer Keyes spun around, and we both looked at the other officer. He was tall and thin and had hair so blond it was almost white.

Officer Keyes cleared his throat. "Yes, sir," he said.

He turned back toward me, and as he walked by, I willed my voice not to quaver or crack as I said, "Thank you for your help, Abner."

He smiled sweetly at me. "I'm sure we will meet again," he said, before walking out the door.

I let myself take a deep breath and looked at the clock on the wall: 8:30 p.m. We didn't have much time. I focused my attention on the new officer.

"Sir," I said. "We would like to see prisoner Frank McHugh. He was arrested earlier today."

The man looked down at the papers Abner had left on the desk.

"Hmmm," he said, thinking to himself. "Cell four. All right, come with me."

Nessa and I followed him down a long hallway, passing

cells filled with men, the sound of their brogue bouncing off the walls and filling the jailhouse. The smell was strong and terrible. As if the chamber pots hadn't been emptied for days. Cell number four, the one Frank was in, contained seven other men. The next cell, cell number five, was filled with women.

"Sir, where are the Yankee prisoners?" I asked the officer.

"At the end of the hall," he said. "We like to keep them separated. Fewer fights. We only need one cell for them. Nearly everyone we bring in here is Irish."

"Why is that?" I asked him.

He shrugged. "I suppose because your kind are the ones gettin' drunk, fightin' each other, beggin' for coin, and just bein' an all-around nuisance," he said.

My face grew hot with anger, but I forced myself to ignore the slur. Nessa and I had to leave soon. When Frank saw Nessa, he stood up and approached.

"What are you doing here?" he asked, clearly distressed by her presence. He looked through the bars down the hall in both directions.

"I needed to see what happened," she said. "I want to help."

He glanced at the officer and lowered his voice.

"I got in a fight," he said.

"They said you've been arrested before," Nessa said. "That's not true, is it?"

He shook his head, confused.

"What?" he asked. "No, I haven't been arrested before."

Nessa started to cry again, and I rubbed her back.

"We'll figure this out, Frank," I said.

He nodded but looked down at his feet.

"They want twenty dollars to let me out," he said.

My eyes widened. "Twenty dollars?" I asked, unsure I'd heard correctly.

He nodded again. "I don't have that," he said.

"Oh, Frank," Nessa sobbed. "Why did you have to go and do that?"

His scowled. "I didn't want to, but he kept provokin' me," he said.

"Who did?" I asked.

"I don't know the man. He works with Patrick."

"We have to go," I said to them both.

Nessa grabbed Frank's hands through the bars.

"We'll get you out," she said. "We'll find a way."

Frank nodded for a third time. "I love you, little sister," he said.

She smiled. "I love you, big brother."

Before we left, I stopped to ask the officer one last thing.

"Do you do the arresting, too?" I asked him.

"Not always me." He chuckled. "Sometimes it's Abner or Chester or Nathan. Any one of us police officers or watchmen."

I nodded. "And what's your name?" I asked him.

He stood up straighter and puffed out his chest to show off his name badge.

"Officer Yates," he said.

"Thank you for your time, Officer Yates," I said.

He nodded once and we left.

Nessa couldn't stop asking questions while we practically ran back to the boardinghouse. It was dark now, and the streetlamps lit the walkway and shone into the canal.

"They can't do that, can they? How will I get twenty dollars? Why do they think Frank's been arrested before?" she asked.

I was deep in thought and could only shake my head at most of her questions.

"There are so many in there," I muttered. "Why?"

Chapter Five

I reread what I had written and decided I was as satisfied with the letter as I ever would be. Then, I copied it two more times, folded them, and addressed them. But I frowned, knowing that I would be leaving readers with no clear instruction on what to do next. I was asking them to write letters, but that took time. Time that most families didn't have. But it wasn't just that. This letter was one of the worst I had written. I was reaching for strands of yarn to tie together, but they kept disintegrating in my hands. I was tired. In my heart and in my soul. I didn't know what else I could say. How else I could convince them to help.

I took the letters to the post office anyway, on my way to see Nancy. It was Saturday, and even though I didn't have to rush as much, I hurried along. I wanted to spend as much time with her as I could.

After I sent the letters to the papers, I walked farther and farther away from the Acre. With each step, I breathed deeper. It smelled better over here. It looked better, too.

There were carriages and large homes. Parks for children to run in. Young ladies with fashionable hats and jewelry and gloves. Men with top hats and long suit coats. I thought of how uncomfortable Mairead would be here. Every time we left the Acre, I watched her try and make her body smaller. She would cast her eyes down, fold her arms across her chest.

"They'll never know you're Irish if you don't act like that," I'd whispered to her once.

She glared at me. "Until I have to speak," she said. "Besides, look at this dress. Even when it's clean, it's dirty."

I bumped her gently. "They aren't going to tar and feather you just for walking on the street."

She gave me a half smile. Her shoulders lifted just a bit then.

But today it was just me, and I didn't care if they saw me enjoying myself. I stared at their fancy clothes and flashed them big smiles. I picked a flower next to their big houses and gave it to a little girl. By the time I got to Nancy's, a small dog was following me and I was giving him pieces of the biscuit Mrs. Durrand had made.

I walked up the steps of Nancy's house and knocked on the door. The house was perfect. It was painted yellow and had a beautiful garden that snaked around the back, climbing over the white gate that separated the backyard from the front. It was smaller than the neighboring houses, but to Nancy and I, it was perfect. Calvin said that as long as it had walls and a roof, he didn't care much about how it looked.

Calvin was not Nancy's first love. Peter was. Nancy had been right, though, about her family. They didn't like Peter much. He was loud and passionate, just as she had told me before their first date. And funny and lively. But Peter was restless. I think Nancy knew from the beginning that she wouldn't be able to hold on to him. She tried to make him love her enough to stay. They'd had more fun than they should have.

But then, a prospector found gold again. This time in the northern part of the California territory. Peter kissed Nancy passionately and told her he would send for her once he struck gold. But Nancy knew he wouldn't and cried for days. On some nights, I would sit in the parlor with her as she sobbed, her head in my lap. I would run my fingers through her hair and say nothing.

A few months later, one of Nancy's brothers introduced her to Calvin. Calvin was tall and handsome. He had a strong jawline and blond hair, perfectly brushed to the side. He was more solemn than Peter, but most men were. Calvin was a logical man and kind. He loved Nancy wholly. His loyalty to her never wavered.

Nancy came to the door to let me in. Her dress and face and hair were covered in flour.

"What happened to you?" I asked.

She burst out laughing. "Oh, help me, Rosaleen," she said. "I am the absolute worst baker. Why do my cookies taste like chalk?"

"Did you remember the sugar?" I asked, smiling.

She smacked my arm gently. "Of course I remembered the sugar! Come in and help me."

I shuffled my boots on the rug before following her to the kitchen. Everything in the house was the newest and best a person could find. Calvin made sure of it. His Nancy was not about to cook in a primitive kitchen. Even though she didn't know what to do in it anyway. She had never been one for cooking or baking or mending or sewing. Her mother tried for years, she told me. Tried to teach her how to make Portuguese egg tarts, her father's childhood favorite. But Nancy never showed any skill or interest. Her brother Joseph enjoyed it, though, so Nancy's mother taught him. It was a little secret in the Gomes family that Joseph was the best cook of them all.

Their brand-new oven was smoking, and burnt cookies sat on the stove. She had opened the windows, but the smoky air still lingered. I laughed at the sight.

"What are you making cookies for?" I asked her. "Just buy some at the bakery."

Nancy shook her head. "They'll all know," she said. "The Society for the Betterment of Lowell Education is having a picnic tomorrow. The teachers are supposed to bake something to sell and raise money for the school. Bake something! Not buy something! Everyone knows what the cookies at Newman's Bakery look and taste like."

"Go to Bradt's," I said.

"Where?" she asked.

"It's a little ways past the Acre," I said. "Amanda Bradt and her parents run it. It's quite delicious. And I doubt anyone over here goes over there for their baked goods."

Nancy's eyes lit up, and a big grin spread across her face.

"You are a genius!" she exclaimed. "I would hug you, but I don't want to get flour all over you. Stay here while I change and then we'll walk over."

Calvin was coming down the stairs while she was going

up. They stopped and kissed each other. My heart started to beat quicker at the sight of him. Nancy didn't know what I was about to ask.

"Rosaleen," Calvin said when he saw me. "Come have a seat. It's so nice to see you."

"Likewise, Calvin," I said, following him into the parlor.

"Would you like some tea or coffee?" he asked.

"No, thank you," I said. "Nancy and I are about to take a walk." I cleared my throat a little nervously and then said, "I was hoping to ask you something, actually."

His eyebrows went up. "What's that?" he asked.

"There's a man I know," I started to say. I paused to think of how to describe Frank. "My roommate's brother. He was arrested last week. The officer at the jail said he had been arrested twice before, but Frank insists this is the first time. I was hoping you could help me to sort it out."

I realized I had been looking down at my hands and quickly glanced up. He was looking at me intently. And thinking.

"And you believe this Frank?" he asked me. "Is he a friend of yours?"

"He's not a friend exactly," I said. "But still. I know him well and believe him. He's not much of a liar. He's usually proud of his decisions. Even when they're bad ones. I think he would tell his little sister. He loves her a lot."

Calvin nodded. "I can look into it," he said. "With a new set of recruits and a new way of doing things, people are bound to make mistakes."

"Thank you," I said. "His name is Frank McHugh." I ran my thumb along the broken nail of my middle finger, feeling the sharpness of it. "There's one more thing," I said.

Just then, Nancy ran down the stairs in a clean purple dress, hair fixed and face free of flour.

"Come join us, honey," Calvin said. "Rosaleen was just talking to me about my new police force."

Nancy shot me a sideways glance. "Was she?" she asked, knowing how bold I could be and how much distaste I had already shown for the force.

"It seems a friend of hers has been arrested and there may have been a mix-up about his past." Then Calvin looked back at me. "Well, not a friend," he corrected himself.

Nancy sat on the arm of Calvin's upholstered chair, and he looped his left arm around her waist.

"I was just wondering," I began. "Hoping really. That you've been thinking of measures to put in place to make sure your officers aren't making mistakes . . . on purpose."

Calvin cocked his head to the side. "What do you mean?" he asked.

I looked away and thought for a moment.

"I saw two boys the other day," I said. "In the street, shoving each other. They were perhaps ten or eleven or twelve years old. What if one had hit the other? Could they have been arrested for brawling? Or are there rules in place to prevent that? How young is too young?"

"I wouldn't arrest anyone under the age of fourteen for a fight," he said.

"What about the other officers?" I asked.

Calvin frowned a little. "Until we have a true handbook, you'll just have to trust that I hired good men with discretion," he said.

But I already know you haven't, I thought.

"The laws are clear on some things, but not others," he went on. "There's going to be some ambiguity at first with these new police units. But not all of them are new. Some have been watchmen and constables for some time now."

I nodded. "But that doesn't make them good men."

"No, it doesn't," Calvin agreed. "Is there someone you're concerned about?"

I looked at Nancy. She was watching me in anticipation, too.

"Officer Keyes," I said. "He was part of that mob that tried to raid the church."

"Inspect the church," he corrected me.

I brushed his ignorance aside.

"He's a Know-Nothing," I tried again.

"Many people are," Calvin said. "He's allowed to be. Just because he puts on a uniform doesn't prevent him from participating in politics."

I knew our conversation wouldn't go anywhere good from here, and I didn't want to jeopardize his help with Frank. I didn't know if he would believe that Officer Keyes had threatened me. I had no proof.

"I know you'll smooth out the rough parts," I said, smiling. "And I appreciate your help with Frank. Please let me know what I can do."

His face relaxed, but his smile remained a little strained. Nancy grabbed the hand that was wrapped around her waist and kissed it.

"Rosaleen and I are going to a bakery on the other side of town," she said.

He looked at her and smiled bigger now.

"You've given up on yours?" he asked.

Nancy shrugged. "Maybe next year."

He chuckled and patted her thigh.

"I'm confident in you," he said. "You'll get it eventually."

She kissed him and stood up.

"Until then," she said. "I actually want to sell these cookies. We desperately need new chalkboards. And Mr. Clark is talking of dissecting frogs next year! I don't even know what kind of equipment he'll need for that, but I'm certain we don't have it."

Calvin got up too. "Good luck," he said. "I'll see you soon, love."

The next day was Sunday, and while Nancy sold Bradt's Bakery cookies as her own, I helped the nuns clean the girls' school after Mass. Once a week, I helped tutor the girls on their letters—usually on Wednesday evenings. And whenever I could, I helped the nuns clean. The Notre Dame Academy grew in popularity every year. It was what worried the Know-Nothings the most. It had been built as a safe haven for the Irish girls and their families. It satisfied the city's education requirement and was a place to grow as a good Catholic girl. The sisters of Notre Dame came from Boston, and before that, a city called Cincinnati. The nuns had even created a nursery for the youngest children while their mas worked at the mills. The Know-Nothings hated the nuns. The Irish loved them as their own.

I sat next to Sister Celeste and Sister Hunna in the kitchen. We had just finished our dinners. Sister Edith washed dishes behind us. Sister Hunna was reading the newspaper with wide eyes. Her right hand delicately touched the place where her neck met her collarbone. She shook her head.

"This Paddy is such a menace!" she said in disbelief. I bit my lip to keep from laughing.

"What is it now?" Sister Edith asked.

"This latest letter," Sister Hunna said, "nearly forgives criminal activity!"

Sister Celeste sat forward in her chair wearing an excited grin. "Read it to us," she said.

Sister Hunna cleared her throat and read:

Dear friends and neighbors,

One of Lowell's own has just evaded capture! Twelve years ago, George Moore escaped slavery and came to Lowell. He was a teacher of our boys. A neighbor. A friend. This Kidnapping Law allowed his old masters to hunt him down anyway.

The Fugitive Slave Law is its official name. But it allows them to kidnap free people. It allows police and constables to hunt free people down in the streets. It FORCES them to do so. It fines and jails those who will not. Even everyday citizens must assist! It forces us all to violate the rights of free people!

WE know how that feels. We, too, are hunted down in the streets. We, too, are assumed guilty first. We, too, are shackled. For being too drunk. Too loud. Too poor. Too Irish. This law is yet another excuse to punish us, too.

We came to this country for freedom. Now, they are taking it away. Free Black people are being unlawfully captured and sent away in chains. Fight for the freedom of all men and women! If you can write, write to your representative! If you cannot, ask your children to do it for you. The Massachusetts legislature is debating a bill now that would give TRUE freedom to all. Tell them to pass the personal liberty laws now!

District 3 Representative

24 Beacon Street

Boston, MA

Signed,

A Paddy

The room was quiet. Then, a few moments later, Sister Hunna spoke up again.

"Does Paddy mean to say that these ornery men do not deserve their fates?" she asked. "They are drunk at noon!"

"We all sin, sister," I said.

"She's right," Sister Celeste said, quickly coming to my defense. "God is our judge, and yet, these police officers will arrest an Irishman for much less than a Yankee."

Sister Hunna looked at us with scolding eyes.

"Then they are too lenient with the Yankees," she said. "Not too harsh on the Irish."

I looked sideways at Sister Celeste but kept quiet.

"This is for the men to debate," Sister Edith finally said in a quiet voice. "It is not our place. We are to care for the children. Feed the poor. That is what God calls us to do."

Sister Hunna put the newspaper down. She stood with pursed lips.

"Sister Edith is right," Sister Hunna said, before leaving the room.

"And who will care for the men in prison?" Sister

Celeste said so quietly that I wasn't sure if I was meant to hear her. "Jesus did that, didn't he?"

I squeezed her hand before we went back to sweeping.

The week passed with little fanfare. Men grumbled about the letter as I knew they would. Fiona called it "garbage."

"It's true enough that they would throw us all in jail if they could," she said. "But who would believe that the Irish would help a nigger?"

"Don't use that word, Fiona," I said.

"Oh, yes, you have a friend." She rolled her eyes.

Then she smiled at me, and I got nervous. We were having a pint in the tavern after work that Thursday. Fiona was more agitated than usual with Frank in jail. Mairead and Dennis weren't paying much attention to us.

"Maybe *you're* the Paddy," Fiona said, eyes gleaming.

Emmett nearly choked on his beer, and I forced out a loud laugh.

"Don't be silly, Fiona," I said. "It's clearly a man. It's not signed, 'A Biddy.'"

"I don't know any Irishmen who love . . . Negroes." She smirked.

"Emmett does," I said.

"Maybe it's me," he said.

Fiona rolled her eyes again.

"He only says he does because he's your little puppy dog," she said.

I was getting agitated. And now Mairead and Dennis *were* paying attention. I felt a bit of Dutch courage rising inside of me. I sat forward so that my face was only inches from Fiona's.

"Why would any respectable, kind man want to spend any time around you?" I asked her.

I watched her run her tongue across her teeth behind closed lips. Then she cracked her knuckles.

"Watch yourself," she hissed.

"I'm not afraid of you."

"Maybe you should be."

The others were quiet, waiting to see what we would say or do next. I decided to leave. I turned to Emmett.

"Are you ready then?" I asked.

He looked at his half-full beer.

"Just a minute." He tipped it back, finishing in just a few gulps.

I smiled at Mairead. She raised her eyebrows and smiled back.

"I'll see you on Sunday," I said to her. She hugged me.

"I can't wait," she said in my ear.

It had been decided that Nancy and Mairead, Dennis and Patrick, would be witnesses to the wedding ceremony at Mr. Joyce's. Nancy had said she would sew me a dress, and I hoped dearly that she'd bought one instead. Mairead claimed she was in charge of my hair, although I wasn't sure what that entailed.

It was nearly curfew and Emmett walked me straight home to the boardinghouse.

"It's hard to believe that I only have three more nights here," I said.

"Are you going to miss it?" Emmett asked.

"No." I laughed. "At least not the curfew. But I will miss

the girls and Mrs. Durrand. I apologize now if you find me here too many nights, having tea with everyone."

"Nessa will need you still," he said. "She looks up to you. Not having a sister herself and all."

"I know," I said. "I worry about her like a sister. I'm not sure why. She has the potential to be a leader, a changer. But she can be rash."

Emmett stopped walking, brushed my hair away from my face, and kissed my forehead. We were at the boardinghouse.

"You worry because you have a big heart," he said. "One of the many reasons I love you so much. You're going to make a wonderful ma one day."

I felt my face get red. "One day," I said.

He grinned. "Enjoy these last nights," he said.

I kissed him. As always, it was so hard to pull myself away.

"Saturday," I reminded him.

"Saturday," he said, right before I walked into the boardinghouse.

Benjamin greeted me with a big smile.

"What did you just do?" I asked, skeptically.

"Come see!" he said.

I followed him down the back hallway, where he lived with his ma and sister. I wondered how long he could stay here in this house full of women. He was only eight now and had nowhere else to go, even when he did get older. He turned back and motioned for me to follow him to the washroom.

"Look out the window here," he said.

I stepped onto the stool he had pushed against the wall.

"What am I looking for?" I asked. "It's dark."

"I know," he said. "Look all the way to the left, on the ground, next to the bush."

I looked and saw a pair of eyes blinking in the shine of the streetlamp. I squinted. It was a dog. Then I saw more eyes.

"She has puppies!" I exclaimed.

He nodded. "Yes, she does," he said.

"Do you like animals?" I asked him.

He shrugged. "They're all right," he said. "But Hattie loves puppies! It's her birthday next week. Maybe I can give her one."

I looked at them again.

"They aren't ready to leave their ma," I told him. "But you can show her. And then she can have her pick when they are ready."

He smiled big. "She is going to be thrilled."

It was Saturday, the day before our wedding, and Emmett had promised to bring me to the North Common for a picnic and to watch the Independence Day fireworks. It seemed that all of the Acre was out on this hot summer night. We hadn't been in America for long, but we loved a celebration.

Emmett found a spot under a tree and put a blanket down. We sat and watched little kids chase each other with chocolate-covered faces. Mrs. Bradley, the ma of some of them, passed around some soda bread she had made for the occasion.

"Thank you, Mrs. Bradley," Emmett said. "Your soda bread is the best on this side of the ocean!"

She beamed.

"Oh, Emmett," she said. "You're too kind."

Then she turned to me. "You better watch him!"

I laughed as Emmett pulled me close.

"Rose knows she has my whole heart," he said.

Mrs. Bradley smiled and shook her head. "Young love," she said. "It's the greatest thing in the world!"

Then she walked off to give away more bread. I rested my head on Emmett's shoulder.

"I really loved that column this week," Emmett said. I knew he was talking about mine. He didn't talk much about other news in the papers.

I sighed. "It wasn't my favorite," I said. "What did you like about it?"

"I liked reading that there might be a way to protect ourselves," he said. "At least from one law. This new police force is making us all a little ill at ease. I feel it. Whenever I leave the tavern. Or pass one of them on the street. I try not to look at them."

I hadn't thought much about Emmett getting arrested. He wasn't a fighter or a drunk, but now, I felt a little fear creep into my heart, causing it to beat faster.

"Do you think they would try to arrest you?" I asked.

"I don't know," he said. "I am an Irishman. What if I'm having a bad day? I don't want them to see it. If I'm a little galled. Who knows if they'll think I look dangerous?"

"They can't arrest you for just looking a certain way," I protested, more to my own self than to him.

He shrugged. "I don't know what they can arrest me

for. Sometimes it feels like anything at all. Like the letter said."

I'd almost never seen fear in Emmett. Not on the ship. Not since we came to Lowell. But now I felt it, and it hurt me, too. I hugged him tight. He hugged me back and sat a little straighter.

"Don't you worry now," he said. "I'll be all right. I'm just thinking about it too much is all."

"Sister Hunna thinks Paddy is giving a pass to criminals," I said.

"Ha!" Emmett said. "I'm sure she does. I reckon a lot of people do. I wonder if Mr. Joyce does."

I sat up and looked at him. "Do you think so?" I asked.

Emmett shrugged again. "He has said things about being glad that they're cleanin' up the neighborhood. I don't know if he sees that he could be a target, too. He seems to trust that they're doing their jobs properly. Without hate in their hearts. But I don't."

We sat quietly, thinking. It was getting darker. The fireworks would start soon. Emmett cleared his throat.

"So," he said. "Are you nervous about tomorrow?"

I blushed. "A little," I said. "Are you?"

"Yes," he said. "Only because we've been waiting for so long. I want it to be perfect."

I smiled a little and thought if I wanted to tell him the truth. Of course I did. It was Emmett.

"I'm worried because Nancy said it hurt the first time she and Calvin tried," I said.

He looked at me with surprise. "I wasn't talking about *that*. But we can if you want to." He smiled mischievously, and I felt my face turn even redder.

"Oh," I said, quietly.

"No, no," Emmett went on. "Don't get quiet on me. We're talking about it now. Nancy said it hurt?"

"Well, yes," I said. "Her body had never done that before."

"I hadn't thought of it like that," he said. "The lads never talk about that part."

"I guess they wouldn't," I said.

He grabbed my hand and rubbed the back of it with his thumb.

"Look at me, Rose," he said. "I'm serious now." I looked at him.

"I promise to be gentle," he said. "You'll tell me if it's too much, won't you?"

I nodded.

"Good," he said. "I would never want to hurt you."

I breathed a deep breath and let out the worry. I was still a little embarrassed, but I trusted Emmett in everything. I looked out at the crowded park and marveled again that of all these men, I had found the perfect one.

Chapter Six

The next day, I arrived at Mairead's house during Mass.

"Are you nervous?" she asked me, excitedly.

"Not at all," I said.

"You're lyin'," she said.

"I'm not!" I insisted.

"What about after?" she said, lowering her voice, even though we were the only ones there. "Tonight?"

"I talked to him about it already," I said.

Her eyes got big. "You did?"

I nodded. "We talk about everything."

She shook her head as if she had never heard anything so outrageous. "Unbelievable."

"What was it like with Dennis the first time?" I asked.

"It was over before I had the chance to think much of anything," she said.

I giggled. "Poor Dennis."

"Don't you say a word to anyone about that!" she said, jabbing a finger at me. "That was said in confidence!"

"I wouldn't!" I said. "Dennis is a good man. His secret is safe with me."

"Now," she went on, smiling to herself, "it's wonderful. Like nothing I can describe. You'll love it, too —eventually."

She opened a drawer in her dresser.

"I got you this face cream from the drug store," she said. "It's supposed to make your skin smooth and hide pimples and whatnot."

I looked at the bottle skeptically. She rolled her eyes.

"You won't turn into a toad," she said. "Put some on your hand first."

I did as she said. "Looks the same," I said.

"Well, you haven't got pimples on your hand, now do you?" she asked, crossing her arms over her chest.

I furrowed my eyebrows. "Do I have them on my face?" I asked.

Mairead leaned closer and squinted.

"Two," she said.

"Fine," I said.

I sat still as she rubbed it all over my face. Just then, there was a knock at her door. It was Nancy. She swept into the room holding a dress of the most beautiful blue, like a robin's egg. It had white-and-gold trim across the swooping neckline and around the wrists and lining the bottom. It made me gasp. I had never worn anything so fine.

"Nancy," I said. "That's beautiful. It must have cost a fortune."

"I have no idea what you're talking about," she said, smiling. "I sewed it by hand."

I smiled and hugged her. "Thank you," I said. "Both of you. Really, this all means so much to me."

After I stepped into the dress and Nancy laced it up, Mairead braided my hair and wrapped it over my head like a crown. Then, she pinned Mrs. Joyce's brooch onto my dress.

Mairead teared up. "You look breathtaking," she said, dabbing her eyes with a handkerchief.

Nancy nodded. "You truly do," she said.

Then Nancy turned and retrieved something else from her bag.

"I'm not sure if you want it, but long veils are quite fashionable right now," she said. "I brought mine, if you'd like to borrow it."

"I would love to," I said.

She pinned it on both sides of my head, and it cascaded down my back.

We walked to Mr. Joyce's house just as Mass was ending. Passersby clapped and cheered.

"Happy wedding day!" a few shouted. I felt myself blush.

We found Mr. Joyce waiting in the parlor for me. He stood up when we came in and took both of my hands in his. His eyes turned red. He sniffed.

"I couldn't be more proud if you were my own daughter," he said.

I hugged him, and he carefully rested his head atop my braid.

"I miss her, too," I whispered. I heard him sniff again and felt him gently nod.

"Ladies," he said to Nancy and Mairead as he let go and

pulled himself together. "Please come sit. I made some tea. Father O'Brien will be here soon."

"Thank you, Mr. Joyce," Nancy said.

Mairead gave him a kiss on each cheek. We heard someone tiptoeing down the hallway. It was Patrick. He smiled at me when he saw me.

"Rosaleen," he said. "You look lovely. Emmett is one lucky man."

I felt myself blush again. "Thank you, Patrick," I said.

"I'm coming down here to see if Father O'Brien has arrived," he said. "But I don't see him."

Mr. Joyce shook his head. "Not yet," he said. "Soon."

Patrick nodded and bounded back up the stairs, taking two at a time easily with his long legs. The ladies sipped their tea.

"I want to show you something, Rosaleen," Mr. Joyce said. He opened a drawer in the side table next to the couch and pulled out a rope.

"Since it was a surprise, I had to speculate for the colors," he said. "I chose black for your hair. Green for your eyes. And blue for Ireland."

Of course, I thought. *For the handfasting ceremony.* Now, I couldn't stop the tears.

"I love it," I said, carefully wiping the tears from my cheeks. "It's beautiful. Did you do this yourself?"

He grinned shyly. "No," he said. "I had Mrs. Gallagher next door help me with the dye. Never done one before."

I smiled back at him. "It's perfect," I said.

Just then, Father O'Brien knocked, and Mr. Joyce let him in.

"Weddings are such cheerful occasions," Father O'Brien said. "And it brings me great joy to perform one today."

He turned to me. "Are you ready, my child?" he asked.

"Yes, Father," I said.

"And where is the groom?" Father O'Brien asked.

"Upstairs," Mr. Joyce said.

"I'm here," a voice said from the stairs.

I turned to see Emmett there, dressed in a suit with a vest and a blue bowtie. His pants were a bright blue, too, and his vest was striped blue and green. His blue eyes shone even brighter than usual. He smiled at me. I was content. I felt my hands tingle.

"Come then," Father O'Brien said. Patrick and Dennis followed behind Emmett. The ladies stood and joined us, too.

"Father, if I may," Mr. Joyce said, "I'd like to perform the handfasting before we begin."

Father O'Brien nodded and stepped back toward the large armchair in the corner of the room.

Mr. Joyce stepped toward us with the rope. Emmett put his right hand out, palm up. I placed mine on top of his and my left hand underneath.

"To support," I said.

He put his left hand on top of my right. "To protect," he said. Mr. Joyce then looped the rope overtop of our hands and tied it three times underneath.

"The first knot it for Rosaleen's love for Emmett," Mr. Joyce said, while tying. "The second knot is for Emmett's love for Rosaleen. The third knot is for the couple's love for all who are here today and all who did not make it but are here in our hearts."

Mr. Joyce stepped back and Father John stepped forward. My heartbeat quickened as I stared into Emmett's eyes and felt our fingers and palms holding one another. I felt the strength of our love then and knew it would last. I wasn't naïve. I knew there would be times when I would be frustrated at this face before me. Angry too. I knew we would feel pain and sorrow. But we would feel it together. Side by side. It might shake us, but we wouldn't fall. We were steady together. Strong.

"Emmett and Rosaleen," Father O'Brien began. "Have you come here to enter into marriage without coercion, freely and wholeheartedly?"

"I have," Emmett and I said together.

"Are you prepared, as you follow the path of marriage, to love and honor each other for as long as you both shall live?" he asked.

"I am," we said.

"Are you prepared to accept children lovingly from God and to bring them up according to the law of Christ and his church?"

"I am," we said. The corners of Emmett's mouth curled into a smile and his dimples started to form.

"Since it is your intention to enter into the covenant of holy matrimony, declare your consent before God," Father O'Brien said.

Emmett cleared his throat a little and then said, "I, Emmett, take you, Rosaleen, to be my wife. I promise to be true to you in good times and in bad, in sickness and in health. I will love you and honor you all the days of my life."

I smiled now, too. Even though these were words that

were memorized and repeated with each couple, with each season, throughout the years, I believed them.

Then I said, "I, Rosaleen, take you, Emmett, to be my husband. I promise to be faithful to you in good times and in bad, in sickness, and in health, to love you and to honor you all the days of my life." And I meant those words, too. With every ounce of my being.

"This couple declares their consent to be married," Father O'Brien said. "I pray that God bless them in all that they do. What God joins together, let no one put asunder."

We all bowed our heads as Father O'Brien recited the Universal Prayer. When he looked up, he was smiling at us both.

"Congratulations, Mr. and Mrs. Doherty," Father O'Brien said.

We slipped our hands from the rope as Mr. Joyce gingerly took it from us and handed it to me, still tied.

"Keep this safe," he said to me. I kissed his cheek, and then I kissed my husband. Emmett wrapped his hands around my waist, and Dennis and Patrick whooped. Then Dennis threw a shoe over our heads for luck. He looked at Father O'Brien sheepishly.

"Sorry, Father," he said.

Father O'Brien shook his head but smiled. "Don't need luck with God on your side," he said to Dennis.

"Will you join us at Doyle's Tavern for dinner?" Mr. Joyce asked Father O'Brien.

"I think I will, yes," Father O'Brien said, gently slapping Mr. Joyce's shoulder. Emmett and I let our guests go first.

"Shall we make them wait a bit for us?" Emmett whispered into my ear.

I spun around to look at him. He had that same mischievous grin as yesterday. I raised my eyebrows and nodded vigorously. He grabbed my hand, and we raced upstairs to our new room.

Mr. Joyce had made up our bed and left a note that said: *We'll see you at the tavern.* I laughed.

Emmett and I stood, staring at each other for a moment. I was nervous but ached to hold him in my arms. Emmett came to me first. He grabbed my hands and kissed my lips softly, and I started to relax. He ran his hands up my arms and neck, holding my face in his hands. I grabbed him by his waist and pulled him closer to me. I pressed my body against his.

Then he bent his knees, grabbed the outsides of my thighs, and lifted me up. I wrapped my legs around him, and he carefully carried me to the bed, laying me down with care. He started with my boots and then took off my dress and undergarments.

"You next," I whispered, playfully. He grinned.

"All right, all right," he said. "You don't have to beg."

He took off his jacket. Then his vest, his boots, his shirt, his pants. He lay on top of me, his elbows propped up on each side of me. Then he kissed me all over. His lips took their time exploring every inch of my body. When he was ready, he was gentle, like he promised. It still hurt a bit, but not too bad. And in a good way.

Afterward, he lay, cheek down, head resting on his arms, face toward me. He was still breathing heavily. I scratched his back softly and admired his body. The ripple of his muscles.

"Can we do that again tomorrow?" he asked. "And the day after that?"

I giggled. "Yes," I said.

"Good," he said, propping himself up onto one arm so that his body faced mine.

"I can't wait to have little Rosaleens running around," he said.

My heart fluttered. "I guess that might happen now," I said.

He chuckled. "That's the only way I've heard of to make babies," he said.

I smacked him gently. "And little Emmetts?" I asked.

"Little Emmetts," he repeated, as if thinking of the idea for the first time. "They better behave themselves!"

"The little Emmetts will be the best behaved," I said. "They'll learn it from their da."

He leaned forward and kissed me gently.

"Rose," he said, "have you ever kissed another man?"

"No," I said, immediately. "Have you ever kissed another woman?"

He nodded. "She was still a girl, really," he said.

I sat up. "Who?" I asked, incredulously. "You told me you only had eyes for me."

"I do," he insisted. "I always have. But I hadn't met you yet. This was back in Ireland."

I lay back down and waited to hear the story.

"She was one of maybe three or four girls in my town near my age," he said. "Her name was Aisling. She grew up with us. She had wild hair and big teeth and used to boss us around. Me and my brothers. We liked to play tricks on her to see her get mad. And then we'd try to run away from her. One day, when I was maybe thirteen, we went to her barn. Her family owned their own plot of land and built a barn there."

He flipped onto his back now and stared straight up at the ceiling.

"We thought we'd play a trick on her. So we waited in the hay for her to come and give the pigs their supper. We thought to scare her, perhaps. Well, she took so long I must have fallen asleep. I woke up to a kiss. She stood there looking so smug and said, 'Who's the fool now?' I looked around, but my brothers were already gone."

I laughed. "She sure showed you, huh?" I asked.

Emmett laughed, too. "I suppose," he said. "I didn't know what to think of it all. I was so confused all I could do was sputter, 'Thank you,' and then run away. I kept my distance for a while, too. I had to give that round to Aisling."

I laughed again and thought of that Emmett. Not quite a boy, not quite a man. I lay my head on his chest.

"Are you tellin' me the truth?" he asked. "I'm really the only one you've ever kissed?"

"Yes," I insisted. "Although I did hold another man's hand."

I listened to his heart beat harder.

"In Boston," was all he said. It wasn't a question.

"His name was Henry," I said. "He was from Germany. He was nice."

"Did he want to marry you?" he asked.

"I don't know," I said. "Perhaps."

I listened to Emmett's breath for a few minutes. He was trying to keep it steady.

"I'm glad you picked me," he finally said.

I rolled over to look at him. "It was never a competition."

He looked in my eyes, searching for the truth. Then he looked back at the ceiling.

"It wasn't between you and Aisling either," he said.

I laughed and he smiled at me. And I knew he believed me.

Chapter Seven

"How does my hair look?" I asked Emmett after we were dressed.

He started to laugh. "I think you ought to take that braid out now. You have pieces stickin' out all over."

I clicked my tongue. "After all Mairead's hard work," I said, unpinning it and unraveling the strands through my fingers. I shook my head from side to side, smoothed out the top, and tucked my hair behind my ears.

"Better?" I asked.

"Better," he said, kissing my forehead.

Then he grabbed my hand. "Let's go celebrate us, Mrs. Doherty!" he said.

The tavern was full when we arrived. I looked around. Mairead and Dennis and Patrick were at a table with Patrick's new girlfriend, Shona. Shona was tall like Patrick and thin. She was shy and had a pretty smile. Mr. Joyce sat at the bar next to Father O'Brien. On the opposite side of the bar, Nancy sipped a beer and talked to Nessa. I was happy. If only Julia could have been there.

Someone tapped my shoulder. I turned around to see Sarah and Berta.

"You came!" I cried, hugging Sarah first and then Berta.

"Of course we did," Berta said.

"You're glowing," Sarah said.

"Thank you," I said. "Please stay for a bit! Have a drink and some food."

Berta smiled and nodded while Sarah looked around with trepidation. Berta grabbed her hand, and they headed over to Nancy and Nessa. Just then, I heard some music. In the far corner, a group of musicians had set up and were playing an old tune. One man had a flute, another a fiddle, and the last, a tambourine.

Emmett grinned at me and grabbed my hand, pulling me toward the music. We danced a dance Aileen had taught us on the ship, him spinning me around and around. I laughed as I tried to keep up. The next thing I knew, he spun me toward Dennis waiting a few feet away. Then to Patrick and then to Mr. Joyce. People were clapping, and I saw Nancy and Shona and Mairead had joined us. Emmett caught me again and kissed me.

"Whooowheee!" someone whistled. I pulled away and stared into Emmett's blue eyes. I couldn't remember being so happy.

After many more hours of dancing and drinking and eating and talking and laughing, people began to leave for home. The tavern maids were walking around seeing who might want to stay the night. Mr. Joyce was back at the bar talking to a friend, and Mairead and Dennis were giggling to themselves at a far table. Nancy left to make Calvin supper and Nessa to make curfew. She teared up saying good night. It was our first night apart in two years.

"I'll come have tea after work tomorrow," I said to her. "I promise."

I watched her stumble down the sidewalk and then stop to talk to someone. It was a man. He put his arm around her. She leaned into his shoulder, and they walked toward the boardinghouse. He looked a little like Quinn, and I worried for a moment. I would talk to her about it tomorrow. I didn't wholly trust Quinn. I wasn't sure why, but I never had. And he was entirely too old for her.

Then I saw something else. A police officer. What was a police officer doing here on a Sunday? The officer was talking to two men who had just left the tavern. The officer was getting closer to them. His hand was on his pistol, which was still secured in his holster. One of the men took a step toward him.

I turned to Emmett, who was talking to Patrick.

"I need to go see what's happening," I said to him, before running out the door. But by the time I got outside, the officer and one of the men were yelling at each other, faces only inches apart. I ran toward them. The man suddenly hunched over, and I realized the officer had hit him. His friend swung at the officer but missed. The officer was smaller than both men and clearly agile.

"Stop!" I yelled. But it was too late. The officer turned and elbowed the second man in the face. Blood started to pour from his nose. He cupped it with his hands. I was right next to them now.

"Stop this!" I yelled. Emmett came running up behind

me. He grabbed the two men, one in each hand, and pulled them away from the officer. The officer put his thumb and forefinger into his mouth and whistled loudly. Once, twice, three times. Suddenly, another officer came running around the corner.

"What is this about?" I asked the officer and the men. The officer glared at me. He breathed through his wide nostrils heavily, like a bull.

"These men—these very drunk men—just threatened an officer of the law," he said. My eyes darted to the men and Emmett.

"We're not drunk," the first one yelled. He looked at Emmett and indicated the police officer. "This officer here was harrassin' us for no reason."

The officer was still huffing, and his face reddened. Then, the other officer caught up, truncheon in hand, ready to fight. It was Abner Keyes.

"They were just going home," I said, loudly. "We all are."

"Is that so?" the first officer asked. "Well, it's too late for these men. They've assaulted a police officer." He pulled out handcuffs. Two pairs.

"Turn around!" he yelled. "I'm taking you in. Both of you."

I stared at Emmett. I couldn't help them and neither could he. The man *had* swung at the officer. A crowd had started to form behind us. More people from the tavern. They watched silently as the officer slapped the handcuffs on the men. Abner Keyes stared at us coldly, a smile forming at the corners of his mouth. He turned to the tavern crowd.

"Who is the owner of this wretched establishment?" he shouted. People looked quietly at one another but said nothing.

"I asked a question!" he shouted at a woman in the front. Her eyes were open wide. Her mouth tried to form words.

"Enough of that now," a man said, pushing through the crowd. "I tend the bar here. Leave my patrons alone. What is it you need?"

"What is it that I need?" Abner asked. He laughed. I could see his crooked, rotting teeth. "What is it that I need?" This time he shouted it.

"I need you to shut this tavern down right now!" he screamed in the barkeep's face. The man breathed deeply and steadily and then wiped a bit of spit off his cheek.

"Yeh can't do that!" a woman shouted.

"We can do whatever we like," Abner said, turning his head to see where the voice had come from. "In fact, anyone who is still on the streets when the rest of my men get here will be arrested for drunkenness," he yelled, addressing the crowd.

"But what if they aren't drunk?" I asked. "You can't order a curfew."

Abner spun on his heels to face me. He knew me by now, of course. "Oh, Rosaleen," he said. "Of course I can." He walked closer. "And when are you Irish ever not drunk?"

I looked at Emmett. He was staring at Abner. Angrier than I had seen him in a long time. His chest was rising and falling with short breaths. His hands clenched into fists. I went to him and gently put a hand on his shoulder.

"Come on," I whispered to him, "we need to go home."

But Emmett didn't move.

"I wasn't aware the city had a curfew," he said to Abner.

Now Abner smirked. "Don't get smart with me, boy," he said. "If I say there's a curfew, then you take your filthy, drunk, diseased friends home and you all stay there."

"And if I don't? You can't arrest us all," Emmett said.

"No, I can only arrest you," Abner said. "But the other officers will get your friends. I'll make sure of it. I'll get every damned police officer and watchman in Lowell. And we'll arrest every last man in the Acre."

Emmett opened his mouth to say something else, but I stepped in front of him. I looked into his eyes, pleading.

"Please," I said. "Let's go home."

The first officer put a hand on each of the men's shoulders and pushed them away from the crowd toward the jail, none of them looking back.

Mr. Joyce walked up behind me.

"What's happened here?" he asked me.

"We all need to leave," I said in a hushed voice. "Or else the police will arrest us."

"What for?" he asked.

"Drunkenness," I said, glancing around to my still lingering friends.

Mairead and Dennis scurried past the crowd toward me. "Congratulations, love," she said, kissing my cheek quickly.

Mr. Joyce nodded. "All right, come on," he said, grabbing my arm.

~

There was one window in our apartment, and I sat in front of it, face pressed to it, watching. Abner had left. I assumed he was doing just what he'd said he would. Getting more officers. Behind me, I could hear Emmett's footsteps pacing back and forth across the room. I knew Mr. Joyce was sitting at the table in the corner with his Bible open. But from the sound of his fingernails tapping the table, I doubted he was doing much reading.

A man across the street opened his front door and stepped outside. I rushed to open the window.

"Go back inside!" I yelled at him, glancing nervously up the street.

"What?" he yelled back, squinting up at me.

"The police will arrest you!" I said.

"Why?" he asked.

"A curfew has been declared," I said.

He swatted the air with his hand. "Yeh daft," he said.

"Please," I said.

He crossed his arms and shifted his weight.

"Yeh tellin' the truth?"

"Yes, sir," I said. "It's my wedding day. An officer broke up my party. Hit two men. Made one of them bleed from his nose."

He nodded now. "All right," he said. "It's not lucky to lie on your wedding day."

"Thank you," I said.

He went back inside.

"This is bloody absurd," Emmett muttered.

Mr. Joyce was still quiet. I wondered what he was thinking, but the room was far too tense to ask

And then I saw them. Abner Keyes had indeed brought at least ten more officers with him. They walked down the street, looking down alleys, swinging their truncheons, laughing.

"There they are," I whispered. Emmett and Mr. Joyce both came to look.

"Bastards," Emmett said. We watched them walk down the street. When they had almost reached the end, an older woman stepped out of her house with a full chamber pot. One of the officers ran up to her and pushed her down. The full chamber pot fell, emptying most of its contents onto her. I couldn't see her face very well, but I imagined her fear.

"What does he think he's doing?" Emmett shouted in my ear. I could only shake my head. The woman struggled to get up while the officer shouted in her face. She left the chamber pot where it lay and scurried back into her home. The other officers slapped one another's backs and threw their heads back with laughter.

Emmett stalked to the corner, picked up a chair, and threw it against the wall. One of its legs snapped off, and the chair fell to the ground. Then Emmett yelled. A deep, guttural yell that frightened me. Mr. Joyce said nothing, and I could see he was struggling to keep his own anger at bay. We all felt desperate. And helpless.

"You need to speak to Calvin about this," Emmett finally said, looking at me with fury. "Tell him exactly what those officers did. Make him see it. Tell him again and again until he understands what terrible men he has working for him."

I nodded. He was right. Calvin wouldn't allow this. Not if he knew what was happening. He didn't know. He couldn't know. But I would tell him.

Chapter Eight

I was tired at work the next day. Tired in every way a
person could be tired. Tired in my mind and my body
and my spirit. But I remembered my promise to Nessa and
went to the boardinghouse after work.

"I'll make you a plate, too, Rosaleen," Mrs. Durrand said
when she saw me walk through the door.

"You don't have to bother," I told her.

"Nonsense," she said. "We have plenty. And we haven't
replaced you yet."

I smiled faintly. "Thank you."

"Remind me after supper," she went on. "I have a letter
for you."

I nodded. We were quiet while we ate. Everyone else
seemed tired, too.

The letter was from Marie. I'd known it would be. I
reminded myself to give her my new address when I
replied.

. . .

Dearest Rosaleen,

I am sure you've read it by now, but the personal liberty law will try to push back against the Fugitive Slave Act in every way it can. I'm not sure it will be enough. I try to distract myself. To not spend every minute of every day thinking of it. But it's hard.

I am so happy that you and Emmett are married. Please tell me that you are bringing him with you so I can finally meet him. Miss Susan says you both can have the honeymoon room, which, as you know, is not a real thing.

Angel is starting to read already. The child is smarter than any I've ever met. I suppose we have Miss Martha to thank for that. She arranged a tutor for Angel as soon as she noticed her natural abilities. Sometimes Angel will point to signs and read the letters. Say the sound they make. Write her a response too. She will love it.

All my love,
Marie

I smiled as I read her letter and thought of all the joy that Angel brought. That most children bring. To parents and aunts and uncles and grandparents and friends and neighbors. I thought of Ronan and how much joy he'd brought to me.

I tucked the letter into my apron and walked over to Nessa. She smiled at me.

"No one kicked me or stole my covers last night," she said. I laughed.

"See?" I said. "Me being gone isn't all bad. The whole bed to yourself!"

"Until Mrs. Durrand finds another boarder," she said.

"Let's have our tea in the parlor," I said.

"Sure." She picked up her cup. We sat on the sofa and sipped our tea. Nessa stared out the window.

"What are we going to do about Frank?" she asked me.

"I talked to Calvin," I said.

"Nancy's Calvin?" she asked.

"Yes," I said. "Didn't you know? He's the new city marshal."

Nessa's eyes narrowed. "No," she said. "I didn't. Nancy didn't mention that."

I realized Nessa was hurt by this information. I didn't want to hurt her relationship with Nancy. No matter how distant or close it was, I didn't know.

"He's been tasked with turning these old constables and new recruits into a real department," I said. "I don't think he knows most of them very well. And these police departments. They're all new. It's a new idea. He's trying to learn from Boston's force. Whatever he does here will be important for how all police departments are run."

Nessa nodded but said nothing.

"He's going to see why Frank has a record of being arrested before," I said. "I think he'll help if he can."

Nessa pursed her lips. I saw anger behind her eyes. She looked at her tea.

"Of course he can help," she practically spat. "He's in charge, isn't he?"

"Yes," I said. "But there are people above him, too. The mayor."

She looked back up at me. "The one that hates us," she said.

I nodded and sighed. She had been so optimistic only a

few weeks ago. She'd been convinced that Fiona had put a stop to it all by throwing a man into the canal. Now, she was seeing the enormity of it. Of all the people who hated us. Or were disgusted by us. Or who would push an old lady to the ground and laugh as she was covered in waste. Who would like to see us all gone. To have us all disappear. And all of them, together, against us. I wished I could tell her how it felt to write as Paddy. The small amount of pride and hope I felt after putting my pen down. I wished I could find that for her, too.

"Quinn says to be patient," she said. "He still thinks if we're quiet and well-behaved they'll leave us alone."

She stirred her tea. So it *was* Quinn that I'd seen.

"I know what Frank did was wrong," she went on. "He shouldn't be fightin'. But you saw all those men in there. And the women. Do you think they all did somethin' so wrong that they need to be locked up in that filthy place? Do you think we're all just bad people? The lot of us?"

I put my tea down and hugged her. She rested her head on my shoulder, and I felt her sobbing softly.

"I think we're people," I said. "Just like the Yankees. Sometimes we do good things, and sometimes we do bad things. Most times, it depends on the hand we've been dealt."

I rubbed her back gently.

"But the laws are written for a reason," I went on. "Those police officers. They don't get to decide if what we're doing is good or bad. If we can't have a drink or two at the tavern and walk home to our houses on a Sunday, then the Yankees shouldn't be able to, either. But the Yankees can, because there's no such law. So we have to make sure they're bein' fair to us. No one else is going to protect us except for us. I know it's hard. But we're in this together."

Nessa pulled away. "All right," she said. I wiped the tears from her eyes.

"And do me a favor," I said.

"What?" she asked.

"Be careful with Quinn," I said.

She looked down at her lap, and her cheeks turned red. "I know," she said. "He's much older than me."

I nodded. "But more than that," I said. "I'm not sure I trust him. I can't say why. Just be careful."

She looked at me strangely. I grabbed her hand and squeezed it.

"I know you're smart," I said. "Just look out for yourself, all right?"

Chapter Nine

C alvin's office was on the second floor of city hall. He wore a crisp, pressed uniform coat down to his knees, much like the ones the other police officers wore. He smiled when I walked in but not big enough to show his teeth. He adjusted his tie and cleared his throat. He had been expecting me. In fact, he had asked me to come. Nancy had relayed the message a few days prior.

"Rosaleen," he said. "I'm glad you came. Please sit."

I sat in the chair across from him, on the other side of his desk, which was cluttered with papers and books. I could see his feet underneath, crossed at his ankles. His black shoes were very shiny. He hadn't left this desk today. Behind him was a large window, facing his neighborhood and away from mine.

"Have you found anything about Frank?" I asked him.

He opened a notebook and nodded.

"I was able to have the first arrest taken off his record," he said. "Other than the jail's logbook, I could find no proof he was arrested that day. No officers could recall it, and there were no witnesses."

I nodded.

"The second arrest, however," he went on, "was for brawling. Like the third. And there were witnesses. Two police officers remember the incident, as well as another prisoner. A lot of these men are in and out on charges. Or can't make bail and spend some time waiting for a delayed trial for whatever reason. One of them remembers Frank. He is a memorable-looking man."

Calvin studied me for a reaction. I nodded again.

"That's . . ." I paused to think of the word. "Disappointing," I finally said. "But I understand the position you're in."

Calvin sighed. "I know you think our officers are unfair toward the Irish," he said. "I understand your concern. I do."

"Did you hear about my wedding day?" I asked.

"Yes," he said. "That was regrettable. And that officer has been reprimanded."

"Which officer?" I asked.

He looked at me, slightly confused.

"The one who declared the curfew," he said. "That's unlawful for him to do."

"And how about the officer who pushed down an old lady carrying a chamber pot?" I asked. "She could have been hurt. And she was covered in waste. It was grossly indecent."

He raised his eyebrows. "Of that, I wasn't aware."

"Ask your officers about it," I said. Calvin sat back and sighed. I fiddled with the hem of my apron.

"You've met Emmett before," I said.

"I have," Calvin said. "I like Emmett."

"He walks around with this fear and anger like I've never seen in him before," I said. "It isn't just me who thinks the officers treat the Irish unfairly. We're all on edge. You might have a beer or two after a long day. Maybe even a whiskey. Why can't we?"

"You can," Calvin said. "There is no law that says you can't. Not anymore. It was overturned last year. But if someone is drunk and causing a disturbance, my officers need to be involved. It's better for your neighborhood, too. I believe you'll be more concerned when you and Emmett are blessed with children. Drunks are a serious nuisance."

I stared at Calvin now. "I know you are a friend," I said. "And I know you have the ability to hire and fire these officers. Please. Make sure your men are good men. Watch them on patrol. Listen to how they speak to us."

He rubbed his forehead with his thumb and index finger. He stared at his notebook. Then he looked up at me again.

"I will," he said. "I've been busy lately. Coming and going to Boston. Writing this handbook. But I should be on the streets with them. Not that they'll act natural around me. I am their superior."

"I know," I said, quickly, eager to see more of this side of Calvin. The man, Calvin. Not the representative of the city of Lowell. "They will be on better behavior. But they don't know you well. They might assume things about you. They don't know yet that you are a true professional. A fair man."

He studied me with a relaxed face and then chuckled a little.

"You have quite a bit of vigor," he said. "I should have known, being such a close friend of Nancy's. You ladies wake up every day, ready to change the world. I wish I could hire you both."

I smiled a true smile for the first time that day.

"I wish you could, too," I said. "We would make excellent officers."

Calvin's eyes and mind wandered to a distant place, and I wondered what he was thinking. Of a world that didn't exist, where his wife's true potential could be seen? Hers, and that of women like her? Her skills and talents utilized? Was he brave enough to even think such a thing? He returned to his notes. The corners of his mouth dropped into a frown, and his eyebrows scrunched together.

"Regardless," he said. "Frank's trial is next Saturday, August the fifth. There will only be a judge, no jury. I can't tell you what the outcome will be, but usually in these cases, when the accused has multiple arrests, the judge will sentence them to some time at the city's poor farm."

"I've heard of it," I said. "I thought it was only for the poor."

"And petty criminals and the insane," he said. "He'll probably only be there a few months. But again, I can't say for certain."

"Can we attend the trial?" I asked.

"You can," he said. "But it won't affect the outcome."

I nodded and stood. "Thank you, Calvin," I said.

He walked me to the door.

"Emmett will be fine," he said as I started to leave. "Tell him that for me."

I sat at the back door of 17 Burn Street with Benjamin.

"Which one did Hattie pick?" I asked him.

"The one with the white spots," he said.

We watched all the puppies drinking milk from their ma.

"Do you think I could have one?" I asked him.

He looked at me with wide eyes and nodded quickly.

"You're a grown-up," he said. "You can do whatever you please."

I laughed. "Not whatever I please," I said. "I think she trusts you. The ma. I saw her take that piece of ham from you. That's why I asked you for permission."

"Which one do you want?" he asked.

"I like the little one," I said. "With the black streak down her nose."

"She's cute," he said.

The door behind us slowly brushed open, and Hattie tiptoed out. I smiled at her.

"Your puppy looks healthy," I said.

She smiled big. "I think I'll name her Sugar," she said. "Because she looks like she has little specks of sugar all over."

"How do you know she's a girl?" I asked.

Hattie frowned and squinted at the pile of puppies.

"I suppose I don't," she said.

"Rosaleen is going to have one, too," Benjamin said.

Hattie giggled and quietly clapped her hands.

"Which one?" she asked.

"The little one," I said.

"The one that looks like it has ashes on its nose?" she asked.

"Maybe that's what I'll name it," I said. "Ashes."

"That's a sad name," Benjamin said.

"You're right," I said. "I'll keep thinking."

I looked at the setting sun dipping behind the buildings.

"Isn't it your bedtime?" I asked them.

"Yes," Hattie said. "Sorry, Benny, but we've got to get ready for bed."

Benjamin rolled his eyes but stood up.

"Good night, Rosaleen," they both said.

"Good night."

I sat there a few minutes more, watching the puppies nurse. Their ma looked relaxed, but to me, it looked painful. A few minutes before, the puppies had pushed and squeezed their way in, squeaking and wagging their tails in excitement. Now, they were starting to fall asleep.

I stood up and tiptoed away, toward the gate in the back fence. When I got home, Emmett was in a good mood. I decided to wait to ask him the question that had been on my mind. Mr. Joyce wasn't home yet, and we hungrily tore at each other's clothes.

"Have you missed your cycle yet?" Emmett asked me after, while we lay in each other's arms.

"No," I said. "It's only been a few weeks. It would be too soon for that."

He nodded. "You'll tell me if you do, right?" he asked.

I smiled with the corner of my mouth. "So eager to be a da," I said.

He pulled me closer and smiled big. "I am."

Then we heard Mr. Joyce coming up the stairs. He

always made a point to do it loudly, and I was grateful for that. I scrambled to put my clothes back on and pressed my hair to my head. He even took a long time to open the door. Like he had forgotten how a doorknob worked.

"Good evening, kids," Mr. Joyce said.

"Good evening, Mr. Joyce," Emmett said, still shirtless.

I got up to make some tea.

"I talked to Calvin today," I said. "He wasn't aware that an old lady was accosted. But I told him. He was able to get rid of the record of one of Frank's arrests but not the other. His trial is next Saturday. Calvin thinks they'll send him to the poor farm for a few months."

"The poor farm?" Emmett asked.

"Yes," I said. "Apparently, they also send . . ." I stopped myself from saying "criminals." As much as I didn't like Frank, it was hard to call him that. "People convicted of crimes there," I finished.

"Well, it's certainly better than a jail cell," Mr. Joyce said. "At least he'll be contributing to something."

"I also asked Calvin to patrol with the men," I said. "Maybe they'll act proper when he does. Or maybe he'll see for himself if they don't. He said he would do it."

Mr. Joyce sat at the table, and I took him a cup of tea. He nodded. Then I took Emmett his tea, where he was still sitting on the edge of our bed.

"He wanted me to tell you that you'll be all right," I said to Emmett. "He'll make sure of it."

Emmett sighed. "I supposed that's nice," he said. "But what about Dennis? Patrick? The rest of our friends and neighbors? What about Mr. Joyce here? And the old ladies and the young ladies?"

I didn't say anything. I knew I couldn't guarantee their safety.

"Maybe we patrol ourselves," Mr. Joyce said. "Stop bad behavior before the police can make arrests. We already have guards at night, watching for that writer. Why can't we warn our own people? Help them home when they've had too much to drink?"

I kept my eyes down when he mentioned "that writer." I wondered how long it would take, living together in the same house, before he knew that *I* was that writer. I had kept it from Nessa. But Mr. Joyce was more observant.

Mr. Joyce had been full of ideas lately. All kinds of ideas —except for ones that involved holding these police officers accountable for their unfair behavior.

Emmett let out a half laugh. "They're the ones doing the brawling. The guards. They switch out every few weeks when one of them gets thrown in jail."

I thought about what Calvin had said earlier.

"Maybe we can find some women to help," I said.

They both raised their eyebrows in surprise.

"The women have enough responsibilities with the children," Mr. Joyce said. "You'll know soon enough."

But I pushed back. "There are plenty like me, too," I said. "And a little younger or much older. With no children."

Emmett shook his head. "It's too dangerous," he said. "I wouldn't trust those drunkards on the street to treat you with any sort of respect."

I crossed my arms and looked at him, somewhat annoyed.

"Not alone," I said. "A group of us."

"I don't like how it would look," Mr. Joyce said. "Walking the streets is not what respectable young ladies do."

I knew Mr. Joyce's word was final, so I scooped extra sugar into my tea and stirred.

Chapter Ten

It was impossibly hot on the day of Frank's trial. It hadn't rained in nearly a week, and the heat suffocated us wherever we went. Even when the sun was gone, sleep only came in the middle of the night, and it was sweaty and fitful. In the courtroom, we all sat as still as possible, moving only to fan ourselves when the air was stagnant.

The courtroom windows were all open. The bees and flies flew in and out, pestering us with their buzzing. I had prepared Nessa as best I could for the likely outcome, and she'd nodded silently as a few tears rolled down her face. She sat now with her parents and her other two brothers, Art and Brian. I sat with Emmett, Mairead, Dennis, Patrick, and Shona. Fiona sat alone, in the row behind Frank's family. No one spoke.

The prosecutor sat alone, head down, scratching away at his notebook. I watched a bead of sweat crawl down the back of his neck. Windows lined the room and even the setting sun was too much light. I sat forward, at the edge of the bench, while Emmett softly scratched my back, careful not to touch me too heavily and make me sweat even more.

Then, the large doors at the back of the courthouse opened, and two officers led Frank down the aisle to the table in the front. He looked down at his feet and only briefly glanced at his family when he passed. His wrists were shackled together. He was filthy. Fiona teared up and looked away.

After Frank was seated, someone announced the judge. We all stood. It felt like church but much more frightening.

The judge wore large glasses perched at the end of his very long nose. Tufts of gray hair stuck out on each side of his head. He looked uninterested.

"Please sit," the judge said. Everyone sat. Then, the prosecutor stood up and spoke.

"Your honor." His voice was surprisingly deep for his rather small body. "You will not be hearing any testimony today, and we will not be putting forth any evidence. Mr. McHugh has admitted his guilt regarding the brawling incident on the thirteenth of June."

"Very well," the judge said. He stared at Frank for a moment, taking in the man before him. His size. His unwashed state. "Frank McHugh, is there anything you would like to say to the court?"

Frank nodded. "S-s-sir," he stuttered. He sounded afraid. And tired. I had never known him to have trouble speaking. I had never seen him so unsure. "I did hit a man a couple of months ago. For that I am sorry. I shouldn't have done it. But it was my first time getting arrested. They're trying to say I was arrested twice before. But the other times . . . they didn't happen. It's a mistake."

The judge looked down at his notes.

"It says here that Chief Parker struck a prior arrest from your record on grounds that there was no evidence," he went on. "But this other, let's see, brawling arrest on March 11. He has two officers and one prisoner who can attest to it."

He looked at Frank, eyebrows raised. He tapped his pen as he waited for a response.

"Perhaps they confused me with someone else," Frank suggested.

"Hmmmm," the judge grunted. "Normally, this would be a three-month sentence. But since I see no penitence and, in fact, a complete denial of your actions, I'm going to raise it to five months."

I heard Nessa sobbing, even from a few rows back.

"Five months at the city's poor farm," the judge went on. "If you can behave, perhaps you'll be out sooner. If you continue this rash behavior of yours, certainly longer."

Then the judge hit his gavel on the table and stood. We were told to do the same, and the judge left. The officers each took Frank by one arm and led him from the courtroom. Now he looked at us all with pleading eyes. Nessa cried into her ma's chest.

"Visit me," he said to Fiona as he passed.

"I will," she said. She looked at her hands, squeezing them together. When she raised her eyes again, they frightened me. There was no fear there. Only anger. Emmett's hand had found mine and squeezed. I looked at him and sighed. I thought I believed Frank, but I didn't know for certain. I knew he would be home again when his time was done, and for me, it would feel like no time at all. But for

Fiona, Nessa, and the rest of his family, it would be difficult. And what would Frank be like when he came back?
Better? Or worse?

We were all quiet on the walk home. I kissed Mairead
goodbye at their apartment on Adams and walked with
Shona to her parents' house on Suffolk.

"Normally, I would say Frank deserves it," Emmett said
once we were alone. "We all can be sure that Frank has
gotten into more than one fight and pummeled more than
one man. But I've never known him to lie. Not once. I wish
I could remember if I was with him on March 11. Not that
it would matter."

I pulled our entwined arms even closer.

"It's frightening," I said. "If Frank *is* telling the truth,
that means they can make up anything, and it's our word
against theirs."

Emmett looked down at the sidewalk but said nothing.

"We should be looking forward to our Boston visit," I
said. "It'll be a nice break."

Now Emmett looked at me and smiled.

"I'm eager to meet your friends," he said. "And have a
bedroom all to ourselves," he added in a whisper.

I laughed and smacked his arm gently, although I was
eager, too.

It rained the next day, and people were so happy that after
Mass, they danced in the streets. Children, parents, grand-
parents. No one rushed home. Everyone took their time.
We were wet, but we could breathe again. I watched the

brown sludge that normally lined the streets get picked up and washed away. I wondered what color was the water that ran in front of Nancy's house. I would see her tomorrow after work. When we were apart, it felt like the gulf between my life and hers grew and grew. But when we were together, it disappeared entirely.

That night, while I was hanging our clothes to dry and Mr. Joyce was making dinner, I decided to finally ask them the thing I had been thinking about for weeks. Ever since I had made our trip to Boston official.

"I need to ask you both something," I said.

Emmett looked up from the book he was reading. Now that we lived together, we shared my little collection, and watching him read my books made my heart feel full.

"What's that, love?" Mr. Joyce asked, stirring the pan of onions and garlic.

"There's a boy," I began. "He was on the ship with me and Emmett coming here. His name is Ronan."

Emmett's eyebrows went up, and I could tell he knew what I was thinking.

"He lives with family in Boston," I went on. "But they've never been very good to him. He'll be about ten now, and I'm afraid those men he lives with will lead him down the wrong path. That place is no good for him. And, well," I paused, thinking of his rueful eyes the last time we'd seen each other. "I think he should come live with us. If that's all right with you both. We have an extra bed. And I can have him enrolled in school with Nancy."

Mr. Joyce turned to look at us. And then, he surprised me.

"I would love that," he said. "I think it's a brilliant idea."

From Emmett's expression, it was clear that neither of us had expected that.

"Are you sure you wouldn't mind feeding another mouth?" Emmett asked him.

"I only cook the food," he said. "You and Rosaleen earn your own wages. This would only be one mouth for me to feed. Feeding and sheltering God's children in need is no burden to me. Ten-year-old boys need guidance. Support. Rosaleen is right to be concerned."

Mr. Joyce turned back to dinner, and Emmett looked at me, shocked. I shrugged and smiled. Emmett might not have understood, but I was beginning to. Mr. Joyce missed being a da. It was that simple.

That night, as I lay in bed listening to Emmett's steady breathing, I thought, for the first time since getting married, of being a ma. Although I would never say it to Emmett, I didn't feel ready. I liked to work and be with my friends and write and read and learn. Motherhood would change everything. But suddenly, I knew I wouldn't feel so afraid of it forever. One day, I would feel that ache. I would crave that bond like Emmett already did and like Mr. Joyce had never stopped craving. I only hoped God, and my body, would wait until then.

Nancy was glowing when I saw her after work the next day. We sat on a bench in the little park behind her house, overlooking the river. Her smile hadn't wavered since I first knocked on her door twenty minutes earlier.

"You're obviously giddy to tell me something," I said. "What is it?"

"Calvin and I are going to have a baby!" she blurted.

I beamed and hugged her.

"Oh, Nancy," I said. "That's splendid. I'm happy for you both."

She pulled away. "Will you help me with everything?" she asked. "Names and nappies and paint colors for the room?"

"Of course," I said. Nancy's ma had died the year before, after suffering a bad case of pneumonia. I knew all of this would be hard for Nancy without her. I saw her tear up a little, even though she was still smiling, and I knew she was thinking of her ma. I hugged her again.

"Blue would be a nice color for the room," I said.

She wiped her eyes with her handkerchief.

"Do you think so?" she asked. "I was thinking maybe pink. Or green."

"I like green," I said. She squeezed my hand.

"How are you doing?" she asked. "Calvin told me about Frank's trial. That judge is always so foul and impressed with himself."

I squinted at the sun reflecting off the river.

"It's not that Frank shouldn't do time at the poor farm," I said. "I'm just worried that he's telling the truth. I'm worried about what that would mean for all of us in the Acre."

"Calvin has to play by the rules, you know," she said. "Even as he tries to make them. I think he'll find a way to get rid of the bad ones. Keep pushing him. You know I will, too."

I smiled a small, close-lipped smile. I wanted to put my faith in them both. But I knew, as I had told Nessa, that this was bigger than Calvin. I only hoped he had enough courage to take it on.

Chapter Eleven

Emmett and I stood on the platform, waiting for the train to come. I was wiggling with excitement.

"I hope Ronan says yes," I said. "That he'll come back with us."

"I hope his aunt and uncle do, too," Emmett said.

"They don't seem to care too much about him," I said.

"Perhaps not," Emmett said. "But they get his wages. They might be displeased if we take that away from them."

I bit my bottom lip. I didn't know why I hadn't thought of that.

"Can we just take him anyway?" I asked.

Emmett laughed. "We may have to."

"I always knew it would come to this," I said. "Me versus Beth and Maureen."

"Maureen looked rather quarrelsome to me," he said. "But you are fearless. That's a tough bout."

I giggled. I looked up and down the tracks and back at the clock tower. The train was two minutes late. The idea of a whole week with no chiming clock tower telling me where to be and when was thrilling. It had been so long. I'd told the mill, and Emmett told the machine shop where he now worked, that we had pressing family issues to attend to. That was a wonderful thing about being an orphan: We decided who was family. We chose each other. And now we could choose whomever else we wanted. To me, Ronan and Marie were as much family as anyone could be.

The train arrived six minutes after it was scheduled. I picked a seat next to the window, and Emmett sat in the aisle. Every year, the trains grew larger and prettier and more comfortable. This train was even longer than the last I had been on, with nearly twice as many seats. It was a short ride, but I marveled at the passing scenery as if it were my first time again.

Once we reached Boston, I practically dragged Emmett to the inn. He laughed trying to keep up.

"Do you remember it?" I asked him, excitedly.

"I do," he said. "The look of it ties my stomach in knots. I was so worried I would never see you again. I almost ran back. That walk to the train station nearly killed me."

I smiled at him. "This time you can be sure that you'll get to see me tomorrow," I said. "And the next day and the next day until forever."

He pulled me close and kissed me before we walked in. The dining room was empty. It was that time between breakfast and dinner when everyone was busy with the business of running an inn. Emmett looked around at the dark wooden structures. The tables, the chairs, the beams, the stairs leading to the rooms. All the same color. All simple yet pleasing. Then I heard some movement behind the kegs.

"I'll be right with you," a voice said.

I poked my head above the kegs, trying to catch a glimpse of her.

"It's all right, Miss Susan," I said. "It's only me."

She popped up quickly and beamed. "Rosaleen! Let me come greet you properly."

She wiped her hands on a rag tucked into her apron before hurrying around to see us. There were a few more wrinkles around her eyes, and her hair was almost all gray now, with brown streaks throughout. Her hair was tied up tightly in a bun, and a few strands hung in her face and down her neck. She hugged me tight and then turned to Emmett.

"I believe we met once before, briefly," she said. "Some time ago."

Emmett smiled and shook her hand.

"You treated Rosaleen so kindly," he said. "I am forever grateful to you."

Miss Susan blushed a little but said, "It was what any sensible person would have done for a hard worker like Rosaleen."

She motioned for us to follow her. "I'll show you both to your room so you can settle. Marie and Eileen are at the market now, but they'll be back soon."

We went up the stairs and down the hall, Emmett carrying a bag for both of us. She had saved the largest, nicest room for us. I stopped her before she left and took her hands in mine so I could look at her straight on.

"Are you sure I can't pay for this?" I asked. "It's your best room."

She shook her head. "It's a wedding gift," she said, smiling. I smiled back and let her go. After she left, I looked around the room, remembering it. I was grateful that it was not the room Oliver had stayed in. There were no ill memories here. Only ones of sweeping, dusting, and wrestling with the sheets. This time, I noticed how high the ceilings were and how beautifully intricate the fireplace was. There was a writing desk by the window, and in the corner, a couch, a table, and two chairs. The dark-blue velvet curtains were pulled back partway to reveal the busy streets outside. Above the bed was a painting of a waterfall.

Emmett took my hands and pulled me onto the bed, where he made quick work of my dress.

"Until your friends are back," he said, kissing my neck, "you are mine."

I snuck into the kitchen before dinner while Marie and Eileen were cutting onions. Marie was talking about the differences between yellow and red onions and what dishes to serve with each. I tiptoed behind her. Eileen saw me out of the corner of her eye and started to turn and smile, but I put my finger to my lips to keep her quiet. She turned back to her chopping, still smiling, and I waited for Marie to put down her knife before I put my hands over her eyes.

"What in the world—" she said as she spun around.

"Rosaleen!" she yelled. "You weren't supposed to be here until tomorrow!"

I laughed, and we hugged each other tight.

"Oh, Marie," I said. "I'm so happy to see you. I have to

confess, I wrote a secret letter to Miss Susan telling her I was coming today. I wanted to surprise you."

She pulled away and looked me over. "Marriage looks good on you," she said. "We have so much to talk about! Come help with dinner. You can shuck that corn in the corner."

"Yes, ma'am," I said, rolling up my sleeves.

"Where is that husband of yours?" Marie asked.

"I left him upstairs, asleep," I said. "Why is it that men can fall asleep anytime, anywhere? Have they no worries at all?"

"None," Marie said. "Did you know Eileen has got herself a beau?"

I looked at Eileen and smiled. "Congratulations," I said. "Tell me about him."

She blushed. "His name is Edward," she said. "He's real kind to me and my ma. He's working the docks right now. Brings us baked treats or flowers all the time after his shift. His hair is even redder than mine."

I laughed. "He sounds lovely," I said.

"Did you know *Marie's* got herself a beau?" Eileen asked, grinning.

I gasped. "Marie! You didn't tell me!"

She looked at Eileen with a wide-open mouth.

"I was about to!" she said. "But I guess this one got to it first."

Eileen looked at her sheepishly. "Sorry, Marie," she said. "Only, I'm so excited for you!"

Marie rolled her eyes but couldn't help smiling.

"Did Gil show up with flowers, like you prayed for?" I asked.

"Not quite," she said. "But God did bring me my Gil back."

I squealed with excitement. "Please tell me what happened," I said.

"I can't," Marie said, laughing. "Not now. I've got to finish this dinner."

"After?" I asked. "Emmett will clean the dishes."

"Nonsense," Eileen said. "I'll clean the dishes. I already know the story."

I felt a pang of jealousy, then, right in my chest. I loved Eileen, but I missed being close with Marie.

"All right," Marie said. "After I finish making dinner. Now give me those cobs and shoo!"

I giggled and did as she said. When I got back to our room, Emmett was already ready.

"Don't you look handsome," I said.

He grinned. "I need to impress your friends," he said. "Do you think they'll think I'm more handsome than Henry?" he asked, dragging out Henry's name in a high-pitched voice.

"Oh, stop it," I said. "It's not even worth bringing him up."

"But I will," Emmett said. "Until I'm done being bitter about it."

"And when will that be?" I asked.

"Maybe today," he said, still smiling. "If your friends think I'm better-looking."

I laughed. "So petty," I said, sitting on his lap.

"I know I'm better than this *Henry*," he said. "But please, tell me why."

I rolled my eyes but indulged him. "Because you know

me better than anyone has ever known me. You make me laugh like no one else ever has. You care for everyone as if they are your own kin. Your mere presence makes people smile. You're honest, even when it doesn't help you to be. And you're brave. You pulled me through the darkest time of my life. When I look at you, I feel at home," I said. Then I turned my head to look at him. "Is that enough, or shall I go on?"

He didn't answer. He only kissed me passionately.

~

I already knew that Emmett had nothing to fret about when it came to impressing my friends. But still, he exceeded my expectations. Marie joined us for dinner, and by the end of it, the two were laughing and joking like old friends.

"Won't you tell me about Gil now?" I asked while we were having our after-dinner tea.

Marie looked into her cup and blushed.

"Ummm," Emmett said, sensing he was intruding. "I'll go help with the dishes. Her name is Eileen, isn't it?"

I smiled and touched his arm. "Yes, it's Eileen. The kitchen is through that door." I pointed to the corner of the dining room. "Thank you."

He scurried off, probably to give Eileen a proper surprise. Marie stirred her tea.

"I have this friend, Frances," she started. "An old friend. We went to school together as girls, but I hadn't talked to her in some time. She's well-known now, an organizer and a lecturer. An abolitionist, of course. But she's also a leader of the temperance movement. Like a lot of other Black folks, she recognizes the obstacle that is alcohol."

"What do you mean?" I asked.

"Well, it started on the plantation, really," she said. "Slave owners making sure slaves had just enough of it. Alcohol makes you feel happy, doesn't it?"

"Yes," I said. "Usually."

"Numbs the pain, at least," she said. "If the slaves got too melancholy or restless or angered with their lot, their masters knew that just the right amount of drink would help. Rather than getting any funny ideas about escape, they could drink."

I nodded. "It's another way to escape. But only in your mind."

Marie nodded. "Exactly. There's a growing number of us that feels that applies to Black folks everywhere. Free ones too. Drinking makes people more complacent, more content with what they have."

She looked at me and bit her lip, thinking of how else to put it.

"We won't be great if we spend our time drinking our problems away rather than facing them head-on. Fighting for equality with a clear and sober mind," she said.

"Hmmm," I said. "I've never thought of it like that."

"Maybe you ought to," she said. "Think about all of the time men—and some women—waste being drunk and sick the next day, too."

"And in jail," I added. "If you're Irish in Lowell."

She nodded again. "Alcohol leads to all sorts of bad outcomes," she said. "Frances talks a lot about that when she lectures. When I heard she was coming to Boston, I decided to go and listen. It would be nice to see an old friend again, I thought."

"Was it?" I asked. "Nice to see her? What did you think of what she had to say?"

"Oh, I agreed with her wholeheartedly," she said. "I've only drank a few times, and I've never liked it much. I spoke to her after she finished, and she urged me to start a group here. To organize Black folks in Boston who feel like us. So I did."

"Wow, Marie," I said. "How do you do it? You're awfully busy here at the inn."

"Plenty of late nights and early mornings," she said. "It was exhausting getting that first meeting together. Finding a place to hold it, getting the word out, deciding what to talk about and what to do. But it was worth it. Fifty people came to that first meeting!"

I smiled and shook my head. "So that's what you were doing when you weren't answering my letters."

She laughed. "That's what I was doing," she said. "And guess who one of those fifty people was."

I sat forward in my chair. "Gil?" I asked, excitedly.

She smiled wide and nodded.

"So that must mean he quit drinking," I said.

"Yes, he did," she said. "I'm so proud of him. And let me tell you, it's better than it ever was before."

I squeezed Marie's hands in mine.

"All that praying," I said. "God really did bring him back to you."

"Trust and patience," Marie said.

"Do I get to meet him?" I asked.

"Of course," she said. "You and Emmett can come to

church with me on Sunday if you'd like. He attends too now."

"We would love to," I said.

"I can see why you were so eager to get to Lowell," she said. "Emmett is a good one. I like him."

"I haven't met anyone who doesn't," I said. "Except for those police officers. But they hate us all."

"That's the second time you've mentioned them," Marie said. "And in the letter. You mentioned being arrested."

I had sent Marie clippings of every one of my letters as Paddy. I never said who wrote them. I didn't have to. She knew. She told me as much the first time I came back to visit. She hugged me and said, "If it isn't 'a Paddy,' back to visit me."

I sighed now. "I can't know how frightening it must be to be a Black person with this kidnapping law in place," I said. "Jail is jail. Your family and friends are still there, waiting for you. They know where you are. But slavery. It's as good as a death sentence as far as your family is concerned. They might never see you again. Never know where you end up. Never know if you do indeed die."

She sipped her tea, listening to what I was trying to say.

"But I *am* starting to know how it feels to be hunted down," I said. "These police officers. They come into the Acre and they study our every move. They watch us leave the tavern. They watch the poor ask for coins on the street. They scrutinize a woman's face to see if it's painted. And if we have one word to say about it, they threaten us, they arrest us, and sometimes they beat us."

Marie's eyes narrowed. "And you know they're specifically going after you all? Or are they treating everyone in Lowell this way?"

"It's only us," I said. "I suppose I wouldn't have known if it weren't for two things. The Know-Nothings tried to raid the girls' Catholic school at our church. We met them in the streets and stopped them. I saw their leaders. I talked to them. One of them is a police officer. And they talk to us with such hate in their voices."

Marie nodded. "I certainly know how that sounds," she said.

"And the second thing," I went on. "My friend's older brother was arrested. So I went to the jail with her. Jail cell after jail cell echoed with Irish voices. The officer said they only keep one cell for the Yankees. That's all. The rest are for us."

Marie frowned and touched my hand.

"These people," I said. "Their families miss them. And they miss their wages. They can't pay for bail most of the time. These children miss their parents."

I looked past Marie to the street. To the people walking by. "Most people would say it's because we're all criminals," I said. "We can't control ourselves. We're a different class of people. But I don't believe that."

"I don't, either," Marie said.

Chapter Twelve

I sat outside of Ronan's house, waiting for him to come home from work. The parlor still stank of the unemployed drunk men who did not welcome my presence. I knew how hard work was to come by, and yet, I was still bitter that Ronan had to work because they couldn't. I wished they would demand work. Leave the city if they had to. Their inactivity infuriated me, and I knew that was not fair to them. Their demands would fall on deaf ears. Moving their families again, unfeasible.

I watched a boy chase a chicken in the street. A girl emptied a chamber pot. She was too close to me, and it smelled awful. I thought again of the old lady who that officer had pushed, and my heart ached. Then I thought of Miss Martha. She wasn't all that much younger. She only had better health. And now, she had a flushing toilet in her house. Ruth had told me so in her most recent letter. I couldn't imagine what that meant, but Ruth said they would never have to empty a chamber pot again. And neither would their maid. It simply flushed away, out of the house.

The girl looked a few years older than Ronan. Some of the waste had gotten on her shoe, and she rubbed it against the brick wall. She saw me watching and stared back for a few seconds before retreating into her house to clean clothes or cook food or rock a screaming baby back to sleep. She must have wondered who I was to just be sitting on the steps in the middle of the evening. Men did that, but women did not.

To my left, I saw Ronan approaching, kicking a rock as he walked. His dark-brown, bone-straight hair hung into his eyes and over his ears, too. He needed a cut. When he looked up and saw me, he smiled a small smile.

"Didn't know you were comin'," he said, sitting down on the steps next to me.

"Well, when I surprise you, I get to see that smile I love," I said.

He smiled a little bigger.

"What did you do at work today?" I asked, knowing it was a silly question as soon as it left my mouth.

"Hauled wood," he said. "Like always."

"I don't like that job," I said, looking down at his feet. "I never wanted this for you."

"We all had big plans, didn't we?" he asked. "But it was nothing like we hoped."

"What if I could make it better?" I asked. "What if you could go to school?"

"I can't," he said, the frustration rising in his voice. "I have to work. Stop trying to be my ma, Rosaleen."

"No one will ever be your ma except your ma," I said.

"I wish I could have seen her one more time," he said. "I still have dreams of her dead face. It's like I just come up with it while I'm asleep. What she might have looked like."

I put my arm around him and pulled him close. He let me.

"I know," I said. "I still have dreams about my ma's dead face, too. And I *do* know what she looked like, because I was there. Nothing makes it easier. Seeing them. Not seeing them. Knowing it will happen. Not knowing it will happen. There's a big ma-sized hole left in all of us."

Ronan sighed.

"Emmett and I got married," I said. "And we want you to live with us in Lowell."

He pulled away and studied my face.

"You're serious?" he asked.

I nodded. "We live with our friend Mr. Joyce," I said. "He doesn't have family left, either. It's a nice home. We want you to be a part of it. You can go to school there. We won't ask you to work."

I saw the hope in his eyes go out as quick as it had come.

"Aunt Maureen and Uncle Will would never let me," he said.

We sat in silence for a moment.

"What if we did it anyway?" I asked. "What if you left for work in the morning but got on a train to Lowell with us instead?"

He looked confused. "Then they would lose all of my wages," he said.

"They would figure it out," I said. "They did before you came."

I saw his brain working hard now as his eyes narrowed, weighing whether he could forgive himself for such a selfish act.

"Yes, your uncle *was* your ma's brother," I said. "But that doesn't make him a good man or a good uncle. My da was the best man this world has ever seen. And his sister was mean and nasty. Sometimes family isn't about blood relation. It's about who is going to look after you. Emmett and you and me. We were all on that ship together looking after each other. We can do it again."

"I'd be a burden," he said.

"You wouldn't," I said. "Mr. Joyce lost a son who was younger than you. He is a good man. He's eager for you to come."

"I don't know," he said. "I want to, but it seems wrong."

"I won't drag you," I said. "But I think you should. It's a choice only you can make. We're leaving on Monday. Our train departs at 8 a.m. I would love to see you there. You don't need to bring anything. Just meet us there."

He nodded. "I'll think about it," he said.

Then I hugged him, and slowly, arm by arm, he hugged me back.

"What sort of church is this again?" Emmett asked, adjusting his collar.

"A fun one," I said. "You'll like it."

Emmett scowled, afraid, like I had been, of attending a church that was not Catholic.

"You know Marie now," I said. "Would she lead us astray?"

His face relaxed. "I guess I am a bit intrigued," he said.

"That's the spirit," I said, tying my hair back. "We'll get to meet Gil, and you'll get to meet Ruth and Miss Martha. Ruth promised me they would come."

"I thought they were Irish," Emmett said.

"Miss Martha is," I said. "Her parents were born in Ireland. Ruth is some mix of Irish and whatever Ruth's da is."

"And they aren't Catholic?" he asked.

"They're rebels like us," I giggled. "I believe Ruth called them Presbyterians, actually."

"Isn't that what the Scots are?"

"Perhaps," I said, shrugging. "This is America. We get to forget the rules sometimes."

"Don't tell on me to Mr. Joyce," Emmett said, smiling now.

"It's our little secret." I kissed him.

The walk to church was pleasant, the morning air still cool. Emmett had helped with the dishes again after breakfast while Marie fixed her hair. Two braids parted from the middle of her head, meeting at the nape of her neck, where they were tied together into a bun.

"Gil can be a little quiet at first," Marie said while we walked. "Especially toward white folks. Although I'm not sure he's ever met any Irish before."

"It's his lucky day then," Emmett said. "We're the best kind of white folks."

"Ha!" Marie said, smiling, but neither agreeing nor disagreeing.

When we got to the church, Marie went in first, sweeping through the doors, her eyes eagerly taking it all in, searching each face. Then she stopped. She turned around and motioned for us to join her. She must have seen him. We followed as she approached a tall man standing in the middle of the aisle. He was broad-shouldered with a round belly, a gentle, soft face, and a nearly shaved head. He smiled contentedly when he saw her. They joined hands, and he kissed the top of her head. We came up behind her.

"Gil," she said, turning her body half toward us. "These are my friends Rosaleen and Emmett."

He shook our hands.

"It's a pleasure to meet you," I said.

"Yes," he said. "Marie talks about you a lot. Will you sit with us?"

"Of course," I said, quickly glancing around for any sign of the Collins women.

We scooted into the pew, and people began to fill in all around us.

"You're part of Marie's temperance society," I said to Gil. "Is that right?"

Gil nodded. "I wasn't raised free like Marie," he said. "I didn't get to Boston until I was sixteen. Escaped from my master's home in Maryland. But already I was addicted. Rum, whiskey, anything. Spent my first wages as a free man on it. Only thanks to the good Lord was I able to finally stop for good. And get my Marie back."

He squeezed her hand and she smiled at him. I looked

at Marie, my eyes wide, but she didn't see me. I hadn't realized Gil had escaped.

I lowered my voice and said, "I hope you're safe here."

His eyes darkened. "None of us are safe here," he said. "But this is my home. I'm not leaving."

I nodded but said nothing. I desperately wanted to urge him to leave. Go to Canada. Take Marie. Even though I would miss her dearly. But I knew it wasn't for me to say, and so I kept it to myself.

Before any of us could say another thing, a man approached the pulpit. This was a different man from years before. A younger man. He was taller and thinner, too. He wore glasses and had a mustache. His skin was very dark. When he smiled, his face exuded joy, and his poise was calming. He seemed immediately in command of the whole room.

"Good morning," he bellowed.

"Good morning!" people shouted back.

"I hope you've all come in good health and high spirits today. We've talked a lot lately about hope," he began. "And perseverance. And strength. And love. These are all good things from God."

"Praise be!" shouted a man a few rows back. I glanced behind me and saw Lydia and Zeke and Angel, who must have just arrived. As Lydia and Marie aged, their likeness grew more and more. Marie's face had grown a bit fatter and softer like Lydia's, and Lydia had creases at the corners of her eyes now when she smiled, just like Marie. It was easy to tell they were sisters. Angel, however, looked most like her da. Curious, eager eyes. A mouth always slightly curved, as if she were in on a secret.

Zeke smiled wide at me and waved, and Lydia whispered in Angel's ear while pointing at us. I blew Angel a kiss, and she smiled shyly, melting even further into her ma's arms.

"Today, I'm going to be talkin' about a different feeling," the reverend went on. "One that I've been avoiding, but one that plagues us all, especially of late."

He looked down at his notes and his smile faded into seriousness.

"Today, I'm going to be talkin' about fear," he said.

The room fell quiet. He let it remain that way while he looked out among his congregation, his chest rising and falling steadily.

"Fear is powerful," he went on. "It's contagious. Fear will drive men and women to do things they never imagined. To act in ways they wouldn't normally."

He bit his bottom lip and looked down again.

"Sometimes fear can be useful," he said. "A child touches a hot pot and gets burned. They're afraid of fire now. That's good. Other times, fear seems irrational. Fear of the dark. A child's dark room is the same as it was when the lamp was lit a minute before."

He looked up at us all again. People waited in anticipation to find out why their favorite reverend would bring up such a topic. One that haunted them. One that they came to church to forget.

"Fear is a big part of our lives, whether we want it to be or not," he said. "And yet, the Bible tells us over and over again not to be afraid. Paul even goes so far in his second letter to Timothy to say, 'For God hath *not* given us the spirit of fear; but of power, and of love, and of a sound mind.' And yet, I feel fear."

Now, a few heads nodded in agreement.

"If God did not give us this spirit of fear, where does it come from? Are we afraid of other men? Again, Jesus tells us not to be. In Matthew, chapter ten, verse twenty-eight, Jesus says, 'And fear not them which kill the body, but are not able to kill the soul: but rather fear him which is able to destroy both soul and body in hell.' Of whom is he speaking?!"

"The devil!" a woman shouted in the first row just as Marie muttered the same thing to herself.

"The devil," the preacher confirmed, nodding. "The devil puts that fear in us. And how do we beat the devil? The same way that we conquer these fears. By speaking the truth of Christ our Lord!"

"Amen!" someone yelled from the second level.

"In Galatians, chapter three, we are told, 'For ye are all the children of God by faith in Christ Jesus. For as many of you as have been baptized into Christ have put on Christ! There is neither Jew nor Greek, there is neither bond nor free, there is neither male nor female: for ye are all one in Christ Jesus.' *That* is the truth we must continue to speak! We are not property. We are not for the taking, and we never will be. We are children of God. He has saved us all, and his truth will free us from fear!"

"We are all saved!" a voice from the back thundered.

"Let us pray," the reverend said. "You all know this one, so please join me."

All together, many voices in the church joined in prayer:

"The Lord is my shepherd; I shall not want. He maketh me to lie down in green pastures: he leadeth me beside the still waters. He restoreth my soul: he leadeth me in the paths of righteousness for his name's sake. Yea, though I walk through the valley of the shadow of death, I will fear no evil: for thou art with me: thy rod and thy staff they comfort me."

Chapter Thirteen

W e all walked back to the inn together—Emmett and I, Gil and Marie, Lydia and Zeke and Angel, Miss Martha and Ruth. Miss Martha bought Angel an ice cream on the way, and sticky chocolate lined the child's mouth.

We hadn't spoke of the sermon yet. Fear was personal to us all, and only Miss Martha seemed to lack it. Although I suspected that even she was afraid of *something*. Emptying chamber pots, perhaps.

We all sat in the dining room, except for Marie, who had to start preparing dinner.

"It's simply infuriating that they have to split the party and distract us from our true purpose," Miss Martha was saying. "There is no reason for it."

"Other than fear," Lydia said, finally bringing up the topic as she wiped Angel's sticky face with her handkerchief.

"I suppose the reverend is right about that," Ruth said. "Even these men in positions of power are fearful. It's

119

certainly the devil's work, what they're doing. Trying to turn us against the Irish or the Germans. The Southern aristocracy is the true enemy."

I could see that Emmett was listening intently. Intrigued by these people who were unlike any he had ever met before.

"The new mayor of Lowell is one," Emmett said. "They tried to raid our girls' school. Thought we were hiding something in there."

"Their behavior is absurd," Miss Martha said. "And frankly, it's embarrassing that the Know-Nothings call themselves abolitionists. I don't believe they care about the cause one bit. They've only attached themselves to it for more votes."

"I'm not sure about that, Miss Martha," I said. "Those antislavery society meetings in Lowell are full of Know-Nothings."

She sighed and shook her head. Zeke and Angel were playing a hand-clapping game. Angel couldn't keep up and giggled when her da tapped her head instead of her hand.

"I didn't know there were any like you," Gil said to me, "until Marie told me."

"Any what?" I asked.

"Irish abolitionists," Gil said.

"Emmett's another," I said. "And I have a friend named Mairead. That might be all for now. I'm trying to recruit more, but that fear is so tangible. The Irish are afraid, too. Of losing the few jobs they're allowed to have now. They only know what they've been told. Which is mostly lies."

Gil nodded. "So many lies in this world," he said. "We've got to speak the truth, like the reverend said."

"Amen," Lydia said.

As they were leaving, Miss Martha took me aside.

"If you need anything at all, write me," she said.

I nodded. "Thank you, Miss Martha."

She smiled and squeezed my hand.

Emmett and I packed our things and enjoyed our last night at the inn, taking our tea and supper with Miss Susan, Marie, and Eileen.

"Do you think Ronan will come?" Emmett asked as we lay in bed later.

I traced the contours of his chest with my finger.

"I hope so," I said. "He'll never be happy if he stays."

"Do you think they're all unhappy?" he asked. "All the young boys who live like him?"

"Maybe not," I said. "If they still have mas or das or brothers or sisters who love them."

The question made me toss and turn for too long that night, and I woke Emmett more than once. We were up early for breakfast before our train. We ate quickly, and Marie and I cried openly while we held each other.

"Come back soon," she said to us both.

I nodded. "If you and Gil ever want to come to Lowell, you can," I said. "It isn't as lovely there, but you're welcome."

She smiled. "Maybe once we're married," she said.

I smiled back. "I hope it's soon," I said.

She kissed my cheeks and hugged Emmett. I practically ran to the train station, even though we were early. The clock read 7:40 a.m. I paced up and down the platform while Emmett sat on the bench. He pretended to read a newspaper, but I saw his eyes stray every few minutes, too.

7:50.

7:53.

7:56.

7:58.

The train pulled into the station and people started to climb aboard. We were last and got the last seat in the back. I stared out the window, holding my breath. The clock struck eight. No Ronan. The train pulled away.

Chapter Fourteen

The disappointment sat heavy in my heart. A few days after we returned to Lowell, I visited the puppy I had picked out for Ronan. The puppies weren't afraid to stray from their ma now, at least in the yard, where they could still see her. Girls waiting outside for the privy threw sticks for them or petted their heads or brought them scraps from their breakfast or supper. The puppies pranced about, very proud of themselves. They would wag their tails and jump up on the girls' legs and lick their fingers. I decided to call Ronan's puppy Cocoa. Cocoa was a clumsy girl, whose big paws often got in the way of her small body. But she still followed everyone from door to gate to door to gate until she collapsed from exhaustion, tail still wagging at every passerby.

I sat on the ground, cross-legged, feeding her bacon bits.

"I should have told him about you," I said to her. "Maybe then he would have come."

She rested her small tan head on my leg. I stroked her back as she closed her eyes.

"Maybe I'll write him a letter," I went on. "He won't be able to respond. At least not on his own. But he can read well enough now."

A man Ronan worked with had taught him to read, and for that I was grateful. It made him more valuable at work. He could read signs and instructions now. It would help him keep his position in the future. Maybe even be paid higher wages.

I gave Cocoa a kiss on the nose before getting up. She stood up too and lazily wagged her tail, looking to me for guidance.

"Go back to your ma," I said. "You can come home with me soon enough."

She cocked her head to one side but stayed put, watching me leave with curious eyes. I arrived home with not quite enough sunlight to write, and so I lit the lamp on the writing table.

Dear Ronan,

While I am disappointed you weren't at the train station, I understand that you feel a duty to your family. Your intentions are good, as they always have been. I'm not sure your aunt and uncle deserve such things. If you change your mind, we will be here waiting at 8 Fenwick Street. This will always be a home for you.

I also have a puppy. Her name is Cocoa, and she is very cute.

All my best,

Rosaleen

I read it twice, debating whether I'd set the correct tone. Was it too forceful? Too forgiving? Finally, I folded it and addressed it. I hoped it would make it to him and that his prying aunt and uncle wouldn't read it first and keep it from him. I prayed that they couldn't read.

Emmett got home late that night, and in between dreams, I felt him climb into bed, nuzzle my neck, and wrap his arms around me.

The next day was Wednesday, and after work, I trudged over to the girls' school for tutoring. Alice and Ina would be waiting for me. They were the latest twelve-year-old girls to be deemed in need of additional help. This did not mean they were unintelligent. It was usually the opposite. Their minds were sharp but restless. The structure of a school run by nuns and ultimately overseen by priests did not lend itself to the type of knowledge they craved. The girls I tutored were curious about other things. They itched to become something they could not. Travelers, discoverers. They had dreams and hopes that the church could and would correct over time.

But *I* would not. When the nuns left us alone, I indulged in their wishes, and we learned about anything we wanted. I smuggled books from the public library—a prohibited place. They practiced their letters and numbers first, and then we found out what the structural plans were for the new city hall. Or how much the newest rail line cost and the places where it would lead. We gaped at drawings of animals they had discovered out West. We studied how rain clouds formed and the dangers of winds colliding in the air. The nuns didn't know why I was their favorite tutor, but they saw progress and left us alone.

Today, I had brought books about carnivorous plants. Alice loved violence, I had learned, no matter how large or small the scale. And Ina hated insects. I knew they would be fascinated.

Thinking of their excitement lightened my mood, and when I got to the school, I greeted the nuns with a genuine smile.

"Sister Edith," I began, going down the row of nuns who were ensuring that departing students left with an older sibling or neighbor.

"Sister Hunna," I went on. "Sister Celeste."

Sister Hunna nodded in acknowledgement. She was the tallest and most imposing of the nuns. Her gaze always sharp. Sister Celeste smiled her familiar, warm smile. Sister Edith was busy with the smallest children. Tying their boots and buttoning their bags.

"Alice and Ina are waiting in the meeting room," Sister Celeste said. I smiled back and nodded.

"Thank you, Sister," I said.

I walked to the last room in the east wing and opened the door to two smiling faces eagerly awaiting the forbidden knowledge I carried with me. I welcomed this escape into our secret world and allowed it to fill my heart again.

After the girls left, I joined the nuns for a light supper. Sister Hunna was reading the newspaper again, but this time she looked quite pleased. It was the *Catholic Weekly*. It wasn't published out of Lowell.

"Now here is a writer with whom I agree," she said. And then she read:

Red Republicanism is not only a threat to a civilized society. It is also an affront to God himself.

These lawless, free-soil fanatics encourage a state education system that will poison our children's minds. They favor abolitionism and women's rights, which will disrupt the natural order that God has created. They call for workers' rights and socialism, which will lead to atheism—just as it has throughout Europe. From Italy to France and Germany, socialists everywhere have turned away from God!

These extremists advance prohibition, which unfairly affects Catholic immigrants, our traditions, our customs, and our businesses. They wish to keep us dependent upon this loathsome system. They wish to lead us astray! We will not remain dependent. We will keep doing what we know to be right in the eyes of God!

She put down her paper and looked at us with satisfaction. I could tell she expected approval from the rest of us.

"Sister," I said, "if you're against prohibition, why are you in support of our young men being arrested?"

Her eyes narrowed. "Drinking alcohol in moderation is acceptable, even expected," she said. "And it is our right to do so. But this lawlessness in the Acre is quite something else."

Lawlessness, I thought. The lawless abolitionists and the lawless drunk Irish. Sister Hunna was certain that she knew lawlessness when she saw it. But I didn't want to be disrespectful to a nun.

"What if . . ." I tried again, "what if this is their way of enacting prohibition without having to pass a law? They can arrest whomever they like for drinking and then lie and say they were drunk. Perhaps they could eventually close down the taverns."

Sister Hunna still stared at me. She did not want her rock-hard beliefs chipped away at.

"I haven't seen anything of the sort," she said.

I thought of how far the church had come since the temperance pledge Mairead joked about at our first meeting. The sort of mental twists that people had to perform to hold their views in opposition to their enemy's.

Then Sister Celeste spoke up.

"What problem have you with the abolitionists?" she asked.

Sister Hunna raised her eyebrows, surprised.

"Perhaps you were not paying attention," Sister Hunna said. "It disrupts the natural order of things. Would you want our girls mingling with Negro boys? Do you want our men jobless and penniless after losing their jobs to Negro men? These are an uncivilized and savage race. They may very well be descendants of Cain."

"Sister Hunna, do you truly believe that?" Sister Celeste asked. "Have you not met or spoke with a Negro before? We are all God's children, and if you are to serve Him, I suggest you make yourself familiar with us all."

"You sound like a Protestant," Sister Hunna replied.

"God created us all, this is true. But with noticeable and purposeful differences. Men are different from women. Black different from white. Are you questioning this truth?"

I thought about the church in Boston. What the reverend there had said. I combed my brain for the chapter and verse.

"What about Galatians?" I asked, finally remembering. "We are all one in Jesus. Neither bond nor free, male nor female."

"Perhaps if the Negroes started showing up for Mass on Sunday and repenting for their sins, I would believe differently," Sister Hunna said, before standing up, washing her dishes, loudly clinking the silverware and plates together, and storming off without another word.

Sister Edith looked distraught. "I wish you wouldn't pester her in that way," she said, perhaps to Sister Celeste and perhaps to us both.

"And if I didn't," Sister Celeste said, "she would never be defied, and she would walk around here as if she were the Mother Mary herself."

Sister Edith gasped and shook her head at such a bold statement. I smiled at Sister Celeste and hoped that, even with only myself for support, she would never stop.

It rained for two days straight, delaying Nancy's and my trip to the furniture store. We went as soon as I left work on Saturday.

Calvin had one younger sibling, his sister Rebecca, and

she already had four children. Their family had used up all of the cradles they had once stashed away. Nancy's family had only two that they'd used for all six children and they were in poor shape, so today, we shopped for a cradle. It was the first thing Nancy was allowing herself to buy now that her belly had a small bump.

"What if it's a girl?" Nancy asked as we walked. "I won't be able to teach her anything useful."

"Except how to stand up for herself," I said. "And how to be a good leader and a friend. Things you've taught me and all the other young women you've known in Lowell."

"Thank you for saying so, Rosaleen," she said. "But have any of those things been truly useful to any of us?"

"I think so," I said. "And we can hope they will be even more useful to our daughters."

"Our daughters?" Nancy asked. "Do you have something to tell me?"

"No," I said. "Not yet. But one day I might have a daughter."

"From what you have been telling me, you and Emmett are certainly trying," she said.

I giggled and smacked her gently.

"That is inappropriate talk for public places, Mrs. Parker," I said.

"Will you be happy?" Nancy asked. "If you become a mother?"

I looked down at my feet. "I don't know," I said. "Being a ma is so onerous. You can't go about on your own anymore. You must do everything for the baby."

Nancy laughed. "Well, yes. They aren't elephants."

"Can baby elephants do things on their own?" I asked.

"They can walk, at least," she said. "And drink and eat."

"Perhaps I'm ready to be an elephant ma, then," I said. "That seems less intrusive."

Nancy smiled. "They're pregnant for nearly two years, though. So I'm not sure that's a fair trade." She stopped to sigh. "It is certainly going to be a big change," she said. "But I think I'm ready. You'll need to come read to me and debate with me still. I don't want my brains to turn to mother mush."

"How is school?" I asked. "How are the kids in your class?"

"They're great," she said. "I have Hattie this year, you know."

I nodded and thought of how she ought to have Ronan, too.

"We've only just started," she went on. "So everyone is still on their best behavior. In a few weeks I'll be able to tell you who likes to pull the girls' braids and leave naughty messages on the chalkboard."

"Speaking of wayward children," I said, "Alice and Ina loved learning about carnivorous plants. Thank you for the suggestion. They want to find one and feed it bugs now. I told them they'd have to leave the Acre first. They think that's a marvelous idea."

Nancy grinned. "We're dreadful influences," she said. "I can't believe this town allowed me to be a teacher after all the trouble I caused the mills. My name is on just about every petition they have filed away."

"They keep underestimating us," I said. "It's a good thing the church doesn't know the half of it with me. Sister Hunna would faint."

We both laughed. We reached the furniture store and went to the salesman and told him what we needed. They had a number of cradles available. They were in high demand, so the carpenters kept making more and more. Babies were a sure thing no matter which side of town you came from.

We decided on a white one with a tree engraved at the top, where the baby's head would rest. The man at the store put it aside for Calvin to pick up later with the horse and cart. Then Nancy and I parted, and I told her I would come by after work during the week. I started to walk toward the Acre, but instead turned toward 17 Burn Street. I wanted to see Nessa.

I arrived just as Mrs. Durrand was finishing supper, and I helped her serve it to the girls without asking for permission. I had never known Mrs. Durrand to willingly accept help, so I'd learned not to ask. Nessa sat with Sarah, Berta, and their new roommate, I assumed, whom I had not yet met. Nessa smiled faintly at me as she introduced her.

"Rosaleen," she said, "this is Helen. Helen, Rosaleen used to sleep where you do now." Helen nodded while she swallowed a mouthful of bread.

"Pleased to meet you," Helen said. "Everyone's told me about you."

Helen was Irish, too. Her hair was very dark, but not quite black, and she was short like Sarah. She had a button nose that widened at the end, and when she smiled, her eyes nearly closed shut.

"It's nice to meet you, too, Helen," I said. "You lucked

out with roommates. These three ladies are simply the best."

She nodded again. "Better than at home on Adams," she said. "Nine of us lived in that room."

She took a sip of her tea. "It's lovely that Mrs. Durrand takes in the Irish," she went on. "So many boardinghouses won't."

"I know," I said, looking up at Mrs. Durrand, who was serving more tea to the girls across the room. I thought of how long it had been since Mrs. Durrand had taken in a Yankee girl. In that regard, she had paid dearly for her decision to house Irish girls. These new Yankee girls—no matter how few there were now—insisted on boardinghouses with no Irish.

I looked back at the table. Nessa only had a few more bites left.

"When you're finished," I said to her, "let's go for a walk."

Chapter Fifteen

I took her away from the Acre, along the canals and then
the river, as if I were walking to Nancy's house.

"How is Quinn?" I asked her. She shrugged.

"We got in a row the other day," she said.

"What about?" I asked.

"He wants to be a police officer," she said. "I got so
angry. After what they did to Frank?"

She looked at me with fire behind her eyes.

"Frank isn't lying," she said. "But *they* lied so they could
send him to the poor farm. How much must they hate us to
do that? And Quinn wants to be one of them? Work with
those monsters every day?"

"Perhaps he could make them see the Irish differently," I
said, surprised to be defending Quinn. "At the very least, he
wouldn't go around arresting his own for no good reason."

"I would hope not," she said. "Sometimes he feels just as
Irish as you or me. But other times, I feel like he's ashamed
of it. He tries to talk like them and walk like them. I know
his parents taught him to be agreeable. Things were

different for them. They tiptoed around here quietly, building this whole town without asking for anything in return. They thought with time and patience the Yankees would respect the Irish. But then we all showed up and ruined it for them."

I stayed quiet, listening.

"I'm only worried that he would still let them get away with too much," she went on. "That he would be afraid to stand up to them. He's been taught not to for so long."

"Maybe," I agreed. "But he also might show them that we are smart, reasonable, hardworking people. Quinn is all of those things, isn't he?"

Nessa sighed heavily. "Yes," she said. "I'm not only with him because he is shockingly handsome." She finally cracked a smile, and I laughed.

"Has he told you why he wants to be a police officer?" I asked.

"For all the reasons you said."

"So, trust him," I said. "Calvin is likely to hire him. He has good standing in the community. Calvin would be hard-pressed to find an Irishman more liked by the Yankees."

"I guess I'll have to try," she said.

"Have you visited Frank yet?" I asked.

She shook her head. "Ma and Da don't want to. I think seeing him in there, as a prisoner, would be too hard. And you know Fiona isn't going to bring me along. She only talks to me if she absolutely has to. And my brothers . . ."

"I'll go," I said, interrupting her.

She looked at me, surprised. "Truly?" she asked.

"Yes," I said. "I'll come with you. You aren't going to go alone."

"All right," she said, still sounding hesitant. We walked in silence for a few minutes.

"What if it's awful?" she finally said, almost in a whisper.

I stopped walking and tugged her arm to stop her. I looked into her eyes.

"Frank will be all right," I said to her. "He can manage whatever this poor farm gives to him. And if he can live it, you can see it. I'm sure it would mean the world to him."

She stood up a little straighter and nodded. I knew I was asking her to do a lot of growing up. I had been for these past few months. But it wasn't just me. Events out of our control were forcing it. I was only asking her to face them rather than run from them. I knew she could. I knew she wasn't fragile.

"When should we go?" she asked.

"We can go tomorrow if you would like," I said. "After Mass?"

"That will be fine," she said, her voice wavering a bit. "Do you know where it is? How will we get there?"

"It's a bit of a ways," I said. "It would take us nearly an hour to walk there. I'll bet we could take Mr. O'Neal's horse. Mr. Joyce borrows it sometimes. Neither of them will be needing it on a Sunday."

"It's settled, then," she said. "We'll go no matter. I'll walk if he won't lend us his horse."

"I'll ask tonight," I said.

〜

I did ask that night. After knocking on Mr. O'Neal's door and having tea with Mr. O'Neal, Mrs. O'Neal, their six children, and two stray cats that came in for company. Mrs. O'Neal asked after Mr. Joyce, Emmett, Emmett's and my future children, and my work at the mill. I asked about their jobs, school, and their family back in Ireland. By the time I asked about the horse, I was half-asleep in their parlor.

"Of course, Rosaleen," Mr. O'Neal said. "Billy is available anytime I'm not usin' him. Sort of a neighborhood horse."

"Billy?" I asked.

"The horse's name is William, but you can call him Billy," Mr. O'Neal said.

I laughed. "Well, all right," I said. "I'll come get Billy after Mass tomorrow. Many thanks to you all."

When I finally got home, Emmett was already asleep. I itched to cuddle up next to him, but first I wanted to write to Angel. I winced as I lit the lamp, worried I would wake one of the men. Mr. Joyce turned over but kept snoring. Emmett didn't move. I sat at the table and wrote quickly.

Dear Angel,

Did you know that plants make their own food? They use the sunlight and water to make their own sugar. Can you imagine eating sugar all day? But some plants eat other things, too. They are called carnivorous plants, and they eat bugs! They snatch them right up, or catch them using sly tricks.

I'll write you again soon. Listen to your ma and your da and your aunt Marie.

All my love,
Rosaleen

~

The ride to the poor farm was long and quiet. Nessa tried to cover up her nerves when she spoke, but her all-around quietness gave her away.

"It's a beautiful day," she said. And it was. I always loved September in Lowell. The days were still quite warm, but the nights and mornings were cool. We rode at the part of the morning where the warmth was creeping in. It wasn't cool anymore, but it wasn't particularly hot, like it would be after dinner. A few leaves had even started to change colors, just a little early. As we reached the outskirts of the city, I breathed a long, deep breath that smelled of flowers and soil.

We arrived at a large, unassuming house at the corner of two streets. The lot was elevated from the street and surrounded by a short stone wall. We hopped off Billy and tied him up along the side of the main house. In the distance, scattered among the field, other smaller houses sat. Behind a medium-sized house, long rows of cornstalks stretched southward, away from the city. Two long barns butted up against the edge of the farm. It felt almost peaceful. I looked at Nessa. Her shoulders seemed to relax, just a bit.

We knocked on the door of the large house. A woman nearing sixty answered. She was plump and had a full head of gray hair tied in a bun atop her head.

"May I help you?" she asked.

"Yes," I answered. "We were hoping to visit one of the prisoners staying here."

She raised one eyebrow and then the corner of her mouth. "A man or a woman?"

"A man," I said.

"The last house in the back," she said. "Black doors. Red shutters on the windows. There is an officer on guard. It's entirely up to him whether he'll let you in."

I nodded. "We understand," I said. "Thank you, ma'am."

She looked us over one more time before nodding and shutting the door. Nessa gripped my hand so tight, I thought she might crack my bones.

"Come on," I said, leading her to the back.

The field was still soft from the days of rain we'd had the week before. It wasn't muddy, but the earth still felt springy and not at all hard, propelling us forward with each step.

We passed a sky-blue house with white shutters. It was plain, but clean. Then, a yellow house with flowers growing all around and over it. The last house was white with black doors and red window shutters. It was cracked in some places, and outside the door sat a man in a uniform, similar to the ones worn by the police officers in Lowell, but a little shorter with no belt. His hat was low, and he slouched in his chair, fiddling with a few blades of grass. He looked up as we approached, squinting in the sunlight. He sat up straighter when he realized he didn't recognize us.

"This here is the house for men," he said. "Maybe you're looking for the women's quarters. That was the yellow one. You passed it." He lifted his arm and pointed.

"Visiting Granny?" he asked as we kept walking toward him.

"No, sir," I said. "We're here to see a male prisoner. Frank McHugh."

He broke into a slow smile. He had the face of a boy, even though by the look of his frame, he was clearly a man. "Truly?" he asked.

"Yes," I said. "Truly."

"Well, you're his second visitor today," he said. "The other was a mighty pretty young lady, too," he went on, suddenly animated.

Nessa was quiet. I smiled.

"What a happy coincidence," I said. "So, can we go in?"

"Oh yes," he said, standing up quickly, dropping his blades of grass. "But I will need to accompany you."

"Yes, sir," I said.

He went into his pocket and pulled out a key. The house inside was, surprisingly, very much like a house. We stepped into a long hallway where two open dining rooms greeted us on each side. I could hear and smell the kitchen, probably in the back of the house. Dinner was being prepared, and I smelled a broth of some sort. It was salty. The stairs in front of us led to the second floor, and the officer guided us there.

"What's your name, sir?" I asked.

"Josiah," he answered. "Well, Officer Sallow, actually. Keep forgettin' I'm a real officer. Only been doin' this job a few months now." He took us up a second set of stairs.

"We're from Ohio," he went on. "My folks and I. Moved to Lowell because my father is real good at buildin' the machines they use in those mills."

I smiled to myself. I had yet to meet a talkative officer of the law until now. He seemed congenial. And not at all spiteful or angry or mean.

"Hopefully after another few months here, they'll make me a city police officer," he said, stopping at a room that had the number 332 on the door.

"I remembered the room number, because, like I said, that other young lady," he reminded us, smiling, quite proud of himself. Nessa looked at me with wide, frightened eyes.

"Go on," I said to her, quietly. "I'll wait out here for you. Let you and Frank have some time. It's all right."

She nodded and went in. Josiah stepped a little closer to me and lowered his voice.

"Are they sweethearts?" he asked. I shook my head.

"Frank is her brother," I said. He nodded deep.

"That girl from earlier was most certainly his sweetheart," he said. "And I thought maybe he had two of them."

"What makes you say she was his sweetheart?" I asked.

His face turned red. "I had to wait for her outside the door," he said. "I didn't mean to eavesdrop." I laughed, and he looked alarmed at first, but then his face softened.

"Tell me more about your position here, Officer Sallow," I said.

Chapter Sixteen

Josiah Sallow was so eager to do good in the world that it made my chest ache. He wanted to help everyone. He wanted to help the prisoners get through their time there. He wanted to help protect his community from violence and thievery. He wanted to make sure the evil were punished, and yet, he also understood the imperfection of mankind and was willing to forgive anyone who showed remorse.

"We all make mistakes, right?" he said. "The good Lord tells me to be humble, so I am. Everyone makes mistakes. Some people just get caught makin' them, is all."

I nodded along, wondering how long he would last patrolling the streets with those other officers. Would his optimism be strong enough to keep his morals intact? Could his cheery outlook possibly spread to the other officers? Or would he become hardened and cynical?

"I'm a real strong believer in second chances," he was saying. "That's why I'm always glad when a man gets to leave early on good behavior. The strange thing is, though, they haven't been askin' me even. They just come and take 'em before their time is up. No questions about behavior or nothin'."

"That's strange," I said, listening more intently now. "Who comes and gets them?"

"The city," he said. "The mayor's people. People much more important than me. And they usually have a couple officers with 'em."

My eyebrows furrowed. "*Irishmen* are being let out early?" I asked.

He nodded. "Most of our prisoners are," he said. "Are Irish, I mean."

Why would the mayor's men release Irish prisoners early? That was indeed suspicious.

"Where do they take them?" I asked.

"Back to their homes, I imagine," Josiah said.

But why would they need officers and city officials to do that? Couldn't they just have Josiah open the door for them? Let them walk home? Why would they be escorted?

Just then, the door opened and Nessa emerged. Her eyes were red and a little puffy, but she was smiling. I squeezed her hand, glad that I'd come with her. I could see her relief. Her face wasn't so weighed down.

"Ready to go?" I asked. She nodded.

"I'll walk you two out," Josiah said. He kept talking as he did. "Now, usually at this time of day, the prisoners are workin' in the fields. But seein' how today is Sunday, we give them a day of rest like Jesus tells us to do. Bible readin' and reflection on Sundays. Usually, a reverend even comes by to say a little sermon. Nice man."

"What's his name?" I asked as we descended the second set of stairs.

"Reverend Edson," Josiah said.

"He is a good man," I said.

"Do you know him?" Josiah asked. "I thought all you Irish were Catholics."

"Most of us are," I said. "I am. Reverend Edson's only a friend."

We had reached the front door. Josiah held it open for us.

"It sure was a pleasure talkin' to you ladies," he said. "Come back and visit anytime now."

"Thank you, Officer Sallow," I said. "We just might do that."

He smiled and squinted in the sun again. He stood there for a few moments, watching us walk away. I could feel his gaze, and it felt purely protective.

"How is Frank?" I asked Nessa.

"He misses us, but he's all right," she said. "He says they're treated well. It's hard work, but they get fed enough. He says he's sleeping better than he has in a long time."

"That's wonderful news," I said.

"The best we could hope for," Nessa said. "Thank you, Rosaleen. For coming along with me."

I put my arm around her waist and gave her a quick squeeze. She rested her head on my shoulder as we walked toward Billy.

The ride back to the city was much hotter. It was the heat of the day now, the sun beating down on our bonnets with full force. My stomach groaned. I guessed that

Emmett and Mr. Joyce were having dinner now and was grateful to know that my portion would be waiting for me.

"That officer was quite chatty," Nessa said. "Did he take even one breath while I was talking with Frank?"

"Barely," I said. "But he's a nice boy. Or man, I suppose. It was hard to tell his age."

Nessa laughed a little. "Yes, his face and body did look a little mismatched."

"He seems like a good one, though," I said. "He wants to be a police officer, but I fear the rest of them would turn him."

She said, quietly, "They will." I knew then that she was thinking of Quinn.

The following Sunday, Mairead made boiled ham with mashed potatoes and peas for dinner. Patrick and Shona were invited, but busy, so it was the four of us. Mairead and Dennis lived with Mairead's family—her parents, her three younger sisters, her two cousins, and her aunt and uncle. They went to the tavern after Mass for dinner, and often Mairead and Dennis did not join them. Quiet and privacy was hard to come by in the Acre. Mr. Joyce was having dinner at the church today. Once every month, he helped to cook for the town's poor and spent the afternoon spooning out stew and comforting the most destitute.

"Emmett tells me that you visited Frank at the poor farm," Dennis said to me.

"Yes," I said. "I went with Nessa."

"Is he doin' all right?" Dennis asked.

"I suppose so," I said. "I let Nessa see him alone. But she said that he looked healthy and he told her he was being treated well."

Dennis nodded. "Probably lives better there than he does at home."

I took a bite of my ham and thought about that.

"He does have his own room," I said when I finished chewing.

Dennis raised his eyebrows. "His own room?"

I nodded. "Nessa said there were two beds in there but that Frank was alone," I said. "Apparently, they're shortening many of their sentences. Which seems rather strange to me."

Mairead poured us all another round of tea.

"Why would they do that?" she asked.

"I don't know," I said. "The guard told me they don't even ask him about the prisoners' behavior. And he would have been happy to tell them about it. He's real sympathetic to the prisoners. Wants to help everyone."

"Do we know anyone else who has been to the poor farm as a prisoner?" Mairead asked.

"A man I work with," Dennis said. "Mr. Kelly's brother. I haven't seen him back at work, come to think of it. I could've sworn his sentence was over by now. If he comes back, I'll ask him what he knows."

"How have the police officers been around here?" I asked the men. I looked at Emmett. "Have you seen Calvin?"

"No," Emmett said. "I wish I had."

"I haven't been to the tavern in weeks," Dennis said. "Mairead and I and the rest of the tenants here drink and talk downstairs. I miss the tavern, but I'd rather not run into one of those police officers. They just stand across from the taverns, waiting. Mr. Doyle must be worried about losing customers."

"First they want into our schools and our church," Mairead said. "And now it's the taverns. They'll be comin' into our parlors next. They don't trust us to be gatherin' anywhere."

"No," I agreed. "They don't."

Dennis had said that Mr. Kelly's brother ought to have been released by now. If he had been, perhaps he knew what was going on with these early releases. I needed to find him. I needed to ask.

After work the next day, I walked up to Mr. and Mrs. Kelly's door and knocked. I knew this was all very strange, and I prepared for the sideways looks and prying questions.

Mrs. Kelly came to the door, a small child toddling behind her, squealing with delight.

"Hello there, Rosaleen," Mrs. Kelly said. "What can I do for you this fine evening?"

Her hair was falling out of her crooked bun and dark circles shadowed her eyes, but still she looked happy. Her eyes were relaxed, her mouth content.

"I'm actually looking for Mr. Kelly's brother," I said. "He works with Dennis at the canal. Where does he live?"

Mrs. Kelly's eyebrows went up. The child grabbed at her waist, trying to command her attention.

"We haven't seen John in months," Mrs. Kelly said. "He lived with us before going to the poor farm to serve his sentence. He was supposed to be released three weeks ago, but he hasn't come home."

"Have you looked for him?" I asked.

She shook her head and finally looked down at the child. She brushed a curl out of the little boy's face but did not scoop him up into her arms, which was what he was clearly begging her to do.

"It's not unlike John to move about," she said. "It's likely he was tired of Lowell. He might have gone somewhere else for a bit. He's a restless soul. Always has been. We keep a space in his bed for him, but we never know when to expect him."

"Would he have had money for a train ticket?" I asked.

She looked back up at me, still smiling faintly.

"Perhaps," she said. "He had some coin when he left for the poor farm. Didn't have much to spend it on in there, did he?"

I shook my head. "I suppose not," I said. "Thank you for your time, Mrs. Kelly, and if he does come home, will you please send him to 8 Fenwick Street? I'd like to ask him a few questions about his time at the farm."

She finally picked up the boy and grabbed the door with her other hand. She was ready to close it. "Of course," she said. "Have a lovely night."

"Good night," I said. I gave the little boy a small wave, and he grinned and waved his whole arm up and down before the door shut.

I walked home with a gnawing in my brain. John Kelly's family knew him best and they weren't concerned with his whereabouts. But I was frustrated. John Kelly might have had answers for me. What was going on at the poor farm?

∿

Cocoa followed me everywhere those days. And that Friday was no different. I gave her little bits of my supper every night and wondered how I would soon feed her whole meals. But she happily bounced along by my side with no worries at all. We walked down Fenwick toward Lowell Street to cross the canal. The sun was setting earlier than it had just a week ago, and already, the town was clouded with the serene veil of dusk. We walked toward the church, but not St. Patrick's. We were headed further north. Toward the heart of the city.

The large, stone church also sat behind an iron gate, much like St. Patrick's. The windows and doors were all the same shape, rectangular until you came to the tip, where the sides met in a sloping, triangular, teardrop shape. The windows were stained blue and red, with simple designs etched into them. The front door was red, but I did not enter it. Cocoa and I looped around to the side of the building, where we knocked on a small brown door. At first, there was no answer. I knocked again. I wasn't sure if he would be there at this hour. Perhaps he had gone home.

"Coming," a voice said from inside.

Reverend Edson opened the door. His face lifted a bit when he saw me.

"Rosaleen," he said. "I wasn't expecting you. Please come in."

Cocoa assumed the invitation extended to her, too, and pranced on in.

"This is Cocoa, Reverend Edson," I said, introducing him to the puppy. "She's become quite attached to me."

Revered Edson smiled warmly at her. "Of all of God's creatures," he said, "puppies are wonderfully special. Who doesn't smile when confronted with a puppy?"

I bent over and picked her up. I scratched her ear for a moment.

"I've never met such a person," I said.

"Please come sit," he said, gesturing toward the couch and chairs in front of a glowing fireplace. I did as he said, and Cocoa snuggled into my lap.

"What can I do for you this evening?" he asked.

"I was at the poor farm last week," I said. "With a friend. Visiting her brother. He's a prisoner there. Accused of brawling. The guard told me that you are often there on Sundays giving a sermon."

"That is true," Reverend Edson said. "I enjoy helping the men there repent for their sins and redirect their lives toward one of service. The women, too. Did you know they even house children along with their mothers?"

"I did not know that," I said. "The woman who answered the door was quick to send us on our way."

"Mrs. Patterson," he said. "She is the landowner's wife and keeper of the grounds. She runs a tight ship, as they say, but she's a woman of good character."

I nodded but wasn't interested in Mrs. Patterson.

"The guard said they've been letting some of the Irish prisoners out before their sentence is over," I said.

"I imagine you are happy for that?" he asked.

I stared into the crackling fire. On the mantel, urns lined up from end to end. I wondered whose they were.

"The guard said no one ever asks him about their behavior," I said. "For what reason should they be shortening their sentences? It's not for lack of space. Nessa said that while there were two beds in her brother's room, he was alone."

"Perhaps it is as simple as a blessing from God," he said.

"I don't believe the Know-Nothings are working for God," I said. The reverend raised his eyebrows.

"I can see why this would weigh heavily upon you," he said. "You see nefarious acts in every imaginable place."

"Wouldn't you?" I asked. "Don't you remember where we met? The things that man said? Those are the people who are in positions of power now. They don't want to help us with anything. Especially getting released from prison. It doesn't make sense."

"Have you been to an antislavery society meeting recently?" he asked.

"Not in several months," I admitted.

"But you are still doing the work of an abolitionist," he said. It was a statement, not a question. I had never spoken to Revered Edson about the Paddy letters, but I suspected that he had an idea of who the author might be. After all, *he* had put the idea into my head. He and Julia.

"I have been a bit distracted lately," I said. "Ever since Mayor Ward was elected. These Know-Nothings seem so emboldened. Many of them are police officers, and it frightens us. Did you know one of those men on the bridge is an officer?"

Reverend Edson's eyes shot up. "Which one?" he asked.

"The one who threatened me," I said. "Abner Keyes is his name."

The reverend pursed his lips and shook his head in disappointment. He stood up.

"I'm going to pour myself some tea. Would you like some?" he asked.

"Yes, please," I said.

Reverend Edson walked away from the fire, through a door to the kitchen. Cocoa lay with her head rested on her front paws and was struggling to keep her eyes open. Reverend Edson returned with two cups of tea.

"You want me to gather information for you, is that right?" he asked me.

"I need to know what's happening," I said. "Are they taking them back home when they're released? Are they threatening them in some way? Are the Irish prisoners making some sort of deal with these men? Do they owe them now? I can't find this information on my own."

Revered Edson sipped his tea.

"They don't see *me* as a friend, either," he said. "Not after the incident on the bridge. They thought I would be like John Orr. They call him the Angel Gabriel. He whips them up into a frenzy, spouting off lies. Feeding them what they want to hear. When, in fact, *I* listen to the word of God."

I stared at him, hoping the word of God would come to him now. Would move him to help me. To help my people.

"I can make some inquiries," he said. "I will see what I can learn."

Chapter Seventeen

I took Reverend Edson's subtle suggestion and attended the antislavery society meeting the following week. I knew my attendance and participation was less than welcome, but I also knew that wasn't why I was going. I needed to know what was happening in the abolitionist community. If I saw myself as the converter of the Irish, I needed to know how to convert them. I would never get ideas by isolating myself. I needed to be around them, as awful as it was. The harder they fought my presence, the harder I would insist that I belonged there, too.

I had asked Berta to come along, but her patience was wearing thin with the Know-Nothings.

"Perhaps next time," she said. "I have a headache and am already in no mood to put up with their antics tomorrow. I'm sorry, Rosaleen."

"It's all right," I said. "I'm already in no mood, either."

Next, I tried Mairead, who had no good excuse.

"I hate the way they look at us," she said.

"They won't know who we are," I said. "We'll blend right in. Those meetings are packed these days."

"Fine," she said. "If we must. Where is this Paddy? Doesn't he ever go to these meetings? Where are his people? I would rather go in a mob like we did on the bridge."

I didn't say anything at first. Even though I considered Mairead one of my closest friends, I hadn't told her my secret. I loved her dearly, but she rarely thought about the words that were about to come out of her mouth. I knew she would *want* to keep it secret, but I didn't know if she could. It felt too risky.

"Maybe he does go," I said. "We should try to spot him this time."

She glanced at me slyly and smiled. "All right," she said. "I'll play that game. I'm certain I can pick an Irishman out of a crowd of Yankees."

"If you say so," I said. "But you can't tell anyone who he is if we find him out."

"I would never do that," she said. "It's only speculation."

So Mairead and I went off to the meeting to try to catch Paddy in the act of abolitionism. I buried the wave of guilt I felt rising up in my stomach. Mairead had a good heart, and I had heard her on many occasions speaking against slavery to our neighbors and friends. I knew if she weren't so intimidated by the Know-Nothings, she would be here on her own, every time.

The meetings had gotten too large for the first floor of city hall and were now being held in a larger venue. I found myself at St. Anne's church yet again, this time following a crowd of people—some of whom hated me and some who simply wished I would go away—into the anti-slavery society meeting. I looked at Mairead and saw her scanning the faces of all of the men, trying to focus on her new mission.

We sat in the third row, at the very end near the outer aisle.

"That man we passed two rows ago," Mairead whispered. "He looked a little Irish."

"How so?" I asked.

She turned back around for a quick glance and then snapped her head forward again.

"His ears," she said.

I stifled a laugh just as the room started to get quiet. "He has Irish ears?" I whispered.

"Yes!" she exclaimed, very softly.

At the front of the church, a woman stood tall, waiting for the last soft conversations to die down. It was Caroline Hopwell. I knew her face well now, although I never had introduced myself to her like Miss Martha said I should. Mrs. Hopwell was most likely just being cordial when she'd told Anne Weston she would welcome me. I had not heard Mrs. Hopwell say disparaging things about the Irish, but she certainly allowed others to do so, and that told me enough about how much to trust her. Her green hats had changed over the years, and today's was a light green with a short rim and a tidy brown ribbon. The rest of her outfit matched. The overwhelming amount of green certainly commanded attention. Her blond hair was graying, and she kept it hidden away as much as possible. Not one strand fell into her face or peeked out from under her hat that day.

"Good evening," her voice bellowed across the church. The whispers stopped.

"We are going to spend the majority of this meeting talking about the personal liberty laws that will be put up for a vote in just a few weeks."

She scanned the room. "It will most certainly become law," she said. "Barring a handful of Democrats and Catholics, the support is overwhelming."

The room began to clap. "Yea!" shouted a very deep voice from the back of the room.

"While we hope this law will go some ways in protecting our community and our colored friends, it does not erase the existence of the Fugitive Slave Act. It is meant to be a deterrence, but we do not know which will prevail when these slave catchers do show up at our doors."

Now there was some murmuring among the attendees.

"This must be a coordinated effort," she continued. "The whole community must understand what is expected of us. Mr. Wilcox has agreed to organize and inform all practicing lawyers in the city, but we are still looking for a liaison between us and the new police department. Are there any volunteers attending tonight who would be willing?"

My hand shot up. I felt Mairead's eyes piercing into the side of my head like daggers. Mrs. Hopwell saw me immediately. Her eyebrows went up.

"And you are?" she asked.

"Rosaleen Doherty," I said, standing. I felt every head turn in my direction and heard bodies shuffling to see me better. My face got hot, but I went on, "The new city marshal is a friend. I'm glad to do it."

The church was silent. I realized what I had done just a few seconds too late. I had never spoken in these meetings. Now, not only had I identified myself as Irish, I had also identified myself as an abolitionist and a person with an interest in the police force. I could only be grateful that I had spoken of Calvin as a friend.

Finally, Mrs. Hopwell cleared her throat.

"Very well, Rosaleen," she said. "Please see me when the meeting is over."

I nodded and sat back down. I could hear Mairead trying to steady her breath and felt guilty again for my poor behavior as a friend. The meeting went on, but the stares continued. I could feel the disbelief. The indignation. I could hear the low mutterings. When the meeting was adjourned and people began to move about, I stayed seated.

"What were you thinking?" Mairead hissed.

"I'm sorry," I said. "I probably shouldn't have volunteered, but I knew I could help."

"Next time, please be quieter about it," she said. "And more discreet."

I looked at her with regret. "You don't have to wait with me if you don't want to," I said.

"Have you lost your mind, Rosaleen?" she asked. "Do you think I'm going to get up and walk home by myself now that all of these people know I'm Irish? No, thank you. Whatever this moss-colored lady has to say to you, she can say it to me, too."

I smiled. "It's too much green, isn't it?"

"It's the shade," Mairead said. "She shouldn't have."

I laughed. After the church cleared out, the click-clack

of Mrs. Hopwell's boots echoed off the church walls as she approached. I stood.

"Please," she said. "Sit." I did.

"Can you tell me why you're here?" she asked.

"At this meeting?" I asked.

She just stared.

"Because I'm an abolitionist," I said.

"Why?" she asked.

"Because slavery is evil," I said. "And it must end."

Her eyes narrowed as if she were trying to see past my exterior, straight into my soul.

"Who told you this?" she asked.

"Friends of mine told me about slavery, and I decided it on my own," I said. "You might know of Martha Collins. She's a friend of Anne Weston's. And of mine."

Mrs. Hopwell's demeanor changed at once. She sat a little straighter. Her face relaxed a bit.

"You know Anne?" she asked.

"I met her once," I said.

Mrs. Hopwell nodded.

"Well then," she said. "You know this new city marshal, you said?"

"Yes," I said. "He's a friend."

"You seem to have quite a number of . . ." she paused, looking me up and down again, "unusual friends."

I smiled. "I'm of the belief that all people deserve the same chance of being allowed to be decent," I said.

She smirked a little. "I suppose you *are* an abolitionist," she said.

She briefed me on the law, then, and although I already knew it well, I let her. I nodded patiently as she explained point by point how it counteracted the Fugitive Slave Act.

"What I want you to do," she continued, "is make it clear to this city marshal that his officers are, under no circumstance, to assist in the capture of an escaped slave. They are not to speak to a slave catcher, a slave owner, or US marshal about an escaped slave at all. They are to reference the personal liberty law, but they are to do and say nothing else."

I nodded. "Mr. Parker will certainly understand what is expected of him," I said.

"Good," she said. "And if there is anything else he should need on the subject, he should go to you, and you will come to me."

I nodded again. "Yes, Mrs. Hopwell."

She sat a little further back now, crossed her arms, and looked me over again. It seemed she couldn't stop examining me.

"Well, I guess that's all, then," she said.

"Where am I to find you if I need you?" I asked.

Her eyes darted from Mairead's to mine, as it occurred to her that she would have to give an Irishwoman her home address.

"Tyler Street," she finally replied. "Two hundred and twelve." Her lips pursed, like she had tasted something sour.

I stood up and Mairead followed. "I'll be seeing you, Mrs. Hopwell," I said. Then, we left the church. Mairead started laughing as soon as the door closed behind us.

"Miss Hummingbird truly did not want us to know where she lives," she said.

"And that is why," I said. "I have a little fun around these people sometimes."

"Who is Anne Weston?" Mairead asked. "She sure did straighten up when you mentioned her."

"A lady I met in Boston once," I said. "All the abolitionists know of her family. They're quite important and influential."

Just then, a man came into view. It was Reverend Edson walking back to his church from wherever the evening had taken him.

"Good evening, Reverend," I said.

His eyes met mine, and he looked very grave.

"Rosaleen," he said. "I need to speak with you. Alone."

Chapter Eighteen

I walked Mairead home that night and told Reverend
Edson I would meet him at the parish house after work
the next day. Mairead looked concerned but said nothing.
She did not pry, but I could see her thirst for knowledge.

When I arrived at St. Anne's, I found Reverend Edson
pacing outside his door.

"Rosaleen," he said when he saw me. "Please come in."

His demeanor was troubled and urgent, and he hurried
me inside. He had supper set up for the two of us at the
long, wooden, and slightly worn, table that stretched
across the back of the room, behind the couch and chairs
at the fireplace. Two settings at such a long table looked
lonely, and I thought of how much lonelier one setting
must be. Reverend Edson had a wife and a daughter near
my age, but I couldn't imagine that he saw them often. He
was so busy in his community that I imagined he often
took meals alone.

On the plates were two blocks of cheese—one white in
color, the other a darker, almost yellow shade—along with

some sliced meat. A bunch of grapes, apples, and a loaf of bread with butter sat in the middle of the table.

Cocoa had followed me again, and as we entered, she lifted her nose into the air to sniff the scent of food. Her tail wagged a low wag as she looked to me for help obtaining those delicious smells. I patted her head and sat at the table.

"Thank you for feeding me, Reverend," I said.

"I'm afraid I've learned some news that you won't be happy to hear," he said. "Let's enjoy our supper before I must tell it to you."

I cut myself a slice of bread and spread butter on it. I fed Cocoa a piece. She sat patiently next to my feet, waiting for the part that she really wanted: the meat.

"When I opened the school here in Lowell, Kirk Boott decided to wage a war against me and it," Reverend Edson said. "Truth be told, Hugh Cummiskey didn't much like it, either. It took children from the mills. And worse, I taught those girls that they should be treated better than they are. We both know *that* attitude is very much looked down upon in both our communities."

"I didn't know you opened the school," I said.

Reverend Edson nodded. "The more I pushed for public education, the angrier Boott got. He wanted to keep those girls—those children—in the dark. The more people know, the more powerful they become. He wanted power only for himself."

"Were you ever frightened?" I asked. "Standing up to those powerful men in that way?"

"Yes," he said. "I was. But I knew God was behind me. I believed he would guide me."

"And did he?" I asked.

"He did," Reverend Edson said.

We finished eating in silence. After we were done, Revered Edson poured me some tea.

"I stumbled upon this information without having to ask," he said. "I was visiting the paupers. I saw old Mrs. McDonough. I hadn't seen her in weeks. She looked very distraught, so I sat and spoke with her."

He sipped his tea.

"The poor of the poor farm come and go, you must understand," he went on. "Those who are old may stay all year, but younger paupers come and go as the seasons change. The poorhouse is fullest in the winter."

I nodded.

"Mrs. McDonough's son had gone missing," he said. "The last time I saw her, I assured her that he had probably left in the warmer weather to find work. But yesterday, she told me she received a letter. From her son."

He stopped and looked at me with tired eyes. The corners of his mouth drooped. He took a deep breath and set his teacup down on the table.

"He has been deported," he continued. "Sent on a ship to Liverpool. He, and others at the poor farm—including prisoners and insane patients—were taken from the farm and forced onto a ship. They arrived in Liverpool but were quickly deported again. This time, back to Ireland."

My breath quickened, and the room seemed to tilt. I struggled to understand what he was telling me.

"He was sent back?" I said in a voice I barely recognized as my own.

"Yes," he said. "At first I wasn't sure whether to believe

it. Mrs. McDonough is awfully old, and I thought perhaps her mind was beginning to fail her. So I asked a few more inmates. They've heard the rumors, too. I suppose it makes sense. The poor farm is funded by tax money. I can imagine that people wouldn't be so happy to pay taxes to support the poor and the insane and the criminals. At least not the Irish ones, which most in this town are."

I felt blood rush to my face, and I knocked my chair over as I leaped up.

"They wouldn't have to if they would give us jobs! Pay us fair wages!" I was shouting now and couldn't help myself.

Revered Edson put his arms out.

"I know, Rosaleen," he said. "I know it's unjust."

I walked away from him before I clawed his eyes out. It was not his fault, and yet, my anger felt uncontrollable.

"They have nothing in Ireland," I went on, the rage still rising in me much as I tried to suppress it for the reverend's sake. "That's why we left. No family, no homes. Most people sold everything they had to get here. Or saved scraps that might have fed their family for one more day. And then the ship! We were packed from end to end. Shitting and vomiting on each other. All of that to be sent back?"

Reverend Edson said nothing. I could see the sorrow in his eyes. He closed them and shook his head.

"What will they do?" I yelled.

He didn't know. He had nothing to say to me. I glared across the room in defiance.

"No," I said. "No. We won't go back there."

Cocoa had scurried over to the door and sat with her

head slightly dipped down, unsure if she should fear me or fight for me. Her eyes were focused on the reverend, trying to determine if he was the enemy. I felt the same.

"I need to leave, Reverend," I said.

I opened the door, and Cocoa ran out, happy for some direction and an escape.

"Wait!" Reverend Edson yelled after me. I paused and looked back. He walked to where the floor met the dirt. "Before you tell everyone, think about what's keeping them going. Is it hope? You'll crush that."

"We're running quite low on hope, Reverend," I said. "Anger will have to do."

Chapter Nineteen

I took the long way home, trying to walk off my fury, but it only grew. Cocoa trotted a little ahead of me but kept glancing back to make sure I hadn't abandoned her. When we got home, she ran up the stairs and settled into a bed I had made for her from old clothes and blankets.

Mr. Joyce was in bed, but Emmett was still up, reading. I tore off my jacket and started to pace. Thoughts bounced around my head, and I was so frustrated that I couldn't answer any of the questions that were irritating me. Emmett put his book down and came to me.

"What is it, Rose?" he asked.

"Nothing," I muttered, pacing away from him. When I got near him again, he caught my arm.

"Tell me," he said.

"I'm not sure I should," I said. Even though I had made Reverend Edson believe I would tell everyone, the consequences of doing so started to weigh on me during my walk home.

He took both of his hands in mine.

"We aren't separate, Rose," he said. "I'm not just Emmett anymore. I meant those vows. We are Emmett and Rosaleen now. Forever. Your burdens and your fears are no longer only yours to keep for yourself. We share them. Tell me what bothers you."

I looked in his eyes and saw the love and concern, but also the stubbornness. When Emmett wanted something badly enough, he made it happen. Usually with his charm. His support for me was relentless. He wouldn't let this go. He was telling me, with that look, that no matter what my intentions were, this secret would not be kept from him.

I looked at Mr. Joyce. He couldn't know yet. We had to talk privately.

"Not here," I said.

"We'll walk then," Emmett said, already grabbing both of our jackets.

Cocoa lifted her head curiously but stayed put in her safe corner, certain that she had experienced enough conflict for one evening.

We walked through the Acre. Past the guards who were on the lookout for Paddy. Past the taverns and the prostitutes and the drunks. Past the watchmen who gladly clicked handcuffs onto the wrists of whomever they could grab, slapping their backs and leading them toward the jail with a firm hand on their shoulder.

I realized the only ones still hanging around the taverns on these nights were the most desperate. The women who had no other way to earn wages. The men who had already ruined their lives with too much drink. The jail was inevitable. They had nothing to stay home for. No reason to avoid the watchmen. My eyes welled up. If I told them, would that be enough for them to change their lives? What would the women do if they knew? Would they try again, in vain, to obtain work as a house servant or at the mill? If only those positions weren't already taken. If only there were more options.

I gripped Emmett's hand tighter. The anger started to rise again in my throat, and it threatened to erupt from the depths of my soul.

When we finally reached the waterfall, I screamed. It sounded of another world. It was high-pitched and full of pain. Emmett tried to comfort me, but I pushed him away. I picked up a rock and threw it into the river. Then another and another until my arm was sore. I finally fell into Emmett's arms and sobbed. He said nothing, only held me.

I cried hard. I thought of all the struggles. Of all the times we could have given up but didn't. I thought of my insignificance. My helplessness. The enormity of this hatred pushing upon me and everyone I loved. I cried until the tears were all gone. It was silent then, except for the steady sound of the water falling. My head throbbed but my thoughts, at least, felt more still. When I pulled away, Emmett wiped my cheeks, and although mine were dry now, his were not. My pain had touched him, even though he knew nothing of what caused it. I took his hand and led him to a large rock where we could sit.

"They aren't letting prisoners out early," I said.

"The guard was mistaken?" he asked.

I watched the water fall onto the rocks below. The moon was bright that night, and I could see the mist splashing back up like little clouds.

"In a way," I said. "He was mistaken when he guessed that the prisoners were being released."

I felt a lump form in my throat, threatening to hold my words in. I swallowed and looked down at my boots.

"They're being deported," I finally said. "They're sending them back to Ireland."

Emmett was sitting with his legs spread, his elbows resting on his knees, his hands clasped together. At first nothing changed. He stayed right where he was, still as the rock we sat on. But then, after a moment, he stood up and walked away from the waterfall, deeper into the wooded area, before I could even read the pain on his face. I heard some leaves rustling and then his own scream. A roar, really. I didn't go to him. I let him feel it. I looked up into the sky at the stars and said a little prayer. "Why are we enduring this?" I asked God. "Help me," I said. "Help all of us. We need help."

After many minutes, Emmett came back. He moved quickly and purposefully. He sat down and looked at me.

"You have to tell them," he said. I watched his leg bounce up and down as his stare intensified. "Paddy has to tell them."

"I'm not afraid," I said. And in that moment, I wasn't. I was too angry still to be afraid. "But what good will it do?"

"What good?" he asked with anger in his voice, too. "It will make them angry, like we are. It will keep them from going easily like animals to be slaughtered, dumb to their own fate. And perhaps, if there are even two Yankees who do not know, they will read it, and feel a touch of sympathy. Just a slight touch. Their opinion will matter, too."

I nodded but said nothing. Emmett held my hand.

"It's all right if you are afraid," he said. "You're right to be. Once everyone knows, those police officers, those politicians—their jobs are going to get much harder. They aren't going to like that. But I'm with you. I'm not leaving your side for a moment. If anyone tries to go after you, they'll have to get through me first."

I looked at him now. Searched his eyes for strength. It was there. That certainty. The same certainty that had assured me long ago that I would survive the journey across the ocean. It was here now, too, and it assured me.

"I know they will," I said. Emmett touched my cheek and kissed me. Our love felt immediate, and I didn't stop myself. We made love next to the waterfall that night, desperately and passionately. Every touch felt amplified. Every meeting of our lips, vital.

When we finally walked back home, the sun was about to rise. We couldn't quite see it yet, but the city was no longer hiding behind the complete blackness of night. The silhouettes of the buildings had a gray hue, and it was cooler than it had been all night. When I shivered, Emmett wrapped his arm around my shoulders.

I plodded through work that day, thankful that it was Saturday and we would be released early. I felt like a shell of a person. I tried to stay sharp and remind myself of the dangers of my position, but still, I worked slower than normal and received annoyed glances from the overseers.

"Are you sick, Rosaleen?" one asked me.

"No, sir," I said.

"Then move quicker," he said.

"Yes, sir," I said, but I barely changed my pace. I was only a few hours from the end of the day. I *would* get through it alive and with all of my fingers still attached.

I had an early supper that evening, and Emmett and I fell asleep before the sun was down.

I woke early the next morning, braided my hair, and walked down the stairs to fetch more firewood. After I piled on the logs and stoked the fire, I started to make breakfast.

I thought of Marie while I cooked. Of her long, nimble fingers gently cracking the eggs and gripping the knife that she used to slice the ham. Her warm smile. Her infectious —sometimes silent when something was particularly funny—laugh. I still couldn't understand how anyone could hate Marie. It hurt my heart to think that many people close to me did. My neighbors. Probably even people I called friends. Not everyone was vocal in their hate, but that didn't mean it wasn't there. Underneath the smiles, the hugs, it simmered. They couldn't understand that their hate was just as ugly as the hate aimed at us.

Emmett came up behind me and put his arms around my waist as I was finishing. He kissed my neck and said, "Mmmmm, that smells good."

I offered him a piece of cooled ham.

"Tastes good, too," he said. I smiled.

"Don't talk with food in your mouth." I dropped a piece on the floor for Cocoa, who had been waiting patiently. I gave her a slice of cheese, too, and a bit of fried potato. She wagged her tail.

I felt at peace that morning and didn't want to ruin it by

thinking of the task that lay ahead of me, so I didn't. I asked Mr. Joyce at breakfast to tell us a story about Kinsale and he did. It was about an old man who never spoke to anyone. He would be seen fishing on the rocks. Or drinking tea outside of his house. Mr. Joyce would say, "Hello," and tip his hat, but the old man just stared. He thought perhaps he was deaf. But one day the old man shouted to him, "Tie your boot!" Mr. Joyce looked down and saw that his boot was untied. He tied it and then yelled back, "Thanks, sir! I didn't know you spoke."

"My wife," the man answered, as Mr. Joyce walked closer. "She used to tell me that she'd never have any peace, me jabbering on like I always do. So when she died, I quit talkin', afraid that she'd haunt me. But my days are finally tiresome enough that I'd welcome a little bit of hauntin'!"

We all laughed.

"He became a dear friend after that," Mr. Joyce said. "Luckily, he died peacefully a year or so before the crops failed. I'm glad he didn't stick around to suffer. Don't believe he ever was haunted, either."

After breakfast, we all picked up our jackets and walked to Mass. The ground was hardening with the colder weather, and my boots no longer sunk in muddy spots or kicked up dust with each step. The air stung my cheeks, and I huddled closer to Emmett.

The church looked more commanding than usual. More somber. I knew it was just my eyes seeing it that way. Feeling the depth of everything. Feeling grateful for all that I had here. I looked all the way to the cross at the top of the tower.

What do you want me to do, God? I asked, silently. The wind blew, and we went inside.

We sat where we always sat, in the second pew, on the right side of the church, closest to the center aisle. Our friends came and took their spots, too. I glanced behind us and saw Nessa come in with her family. She smiled and waved. A pit formed in my stomach. I hoped Frank wouldn't be next.

I listened intently that morning. Especially to the songs sung in Gaelic. I hung on to every note. Every breath. Father Purcell stood in the wings overlooking his parish like a hawk stalking mice in a field. His eyes were intense. Searching. I looked at his fingernails. They were so clean. How did he keep them so clean? I looked down at my own. Traces of grease from the weaving machine wedged themselves into each and every crevice. I had washed my hands dozens of times since leaving work yesterday, but they were never as clean as Father Purcell's.

"A reading from the book of Hebrews," Steven Walsh said from the pulpit, snapping me out of my thoughts. Steven was only a few years older than Emmett, but he had learned to command a room well. Under the tutelage of Father O'Brien and Father Purcell, he was becoming a smart and comforting figure. "Let your manners be without covetousness, contented with such things as you have; for he hath said: I will not leave thee, neither will I forsake thee. So that we may confidently say: The Lord is my helper: I will not fear what man shall do to me."

A tingle ran up my spine. Another lesson in fear. Father Purcell replaced Steven and smiled at us all. He was taller, thinner, and only a bit younger than Father O'Brien. Three prominent wrinkles spread across his forehead. With one finger, he pushed his thick glasses closer to his eyes. He waited for the older woman to finish her song, and then he began.

"A reading from the holy Gospel, according to Matthew," he said. "'The disciple is not above the master, nor the servant above his lord. It is enough for the disciple that he be as his master, and the servant as his lord. If they have called the goodman of the house Beelzebub, how much more them of his household? Therefore, fear them not. For nothing is covered that shall not be revealed: nor hid that shall not be known. That which I tell you in the dark, speak ye in the light: and that which you hear in the ear, preach ye upon the housetops.'"

I was nearly breathless when I joined the parish in saying, "Praise the Lord Jesus Christ." I felt exposed, suddenly. It felt as though Father Purcell was speaking directly to me. I couldn't look up at him. Had God told me this in the dark?

"I saw a young mother the other day," Father Purcell said. "She was buying vegetables from the grocer. Before she paid, she tucked her rosary inside the front of her dress and did not speak to the grocer, but rather only smiled and nodded or shook her head."

I took a deep breath and looked at him. It felt safer, now that he was no longer speaking directly to me. I thought of the woman of whom he spoke. I couldn't imagine a priest catching me in such a state. He was not frowning, though. His face was calm and pleasant.

"When she saw me as she was leaving, her face turned red," he went on. "'Father, you must understand,' she said to me. 'They will charge me more if they know who I am. They will give me bruised, old fruit and vegetables.' I knew she was telling me the truth. I put my hand on her shoulder and instructed her to repent."

Was the woman here, I wondered. If so, she was certainly mortified.

"I am, in fact, instructing you all to repent," he said. "I have seen a change in this community. This hate directed toward us has caused much fear among us. But God tells us not to fear these men. If our fear causes us to deny our neighbors, our friends, our faith. To deny Him? Then we have cast our lot with the devil already. None of us can hide from the Lord. All is revealed to Him."

The church was silent. My breath grew steadier.

"Do not deny Him," he said. "Do not deny one another. The Lord will make us strong. Join me as we pray together."

I bowed my head.

"We pray for those who are lost. We pray for the tortured. We pray for the criminals. We pray for the poor. For the hungry. For those who are cold. For those who have no homes. We pray for the sick."

"Lord hear our prayer," we said.

I did not open my eyes right away. I would pray for them. And I would pray for the deported as well. But I wouldn't just pray. I would preach upon the housetops. I would preach the only truth I knew.

Chapter Twenty

After Mass, Mr. Joyce and Emmett went to the tavern for dinner but certainly not for drinks. I went home first.

"I'm going to let Cocoa outside for a bit and then I'll come," I told Emmett.

I needed some time to myself to think and to write Marie. I needed to write Miss Martha, too. I knew that once I told the Acre the truth and asked them to act, my life would be in danger in a new and immediate way. It felt important that she know what was happening.

I opened both our front door and the door to our room to let Cocoa wander off for a while. Then I sat with my pen and paper.

Dearest Marie,

Please tell me news of your temperance society. Have you gotten help with the planning and organizing? What initiatives are you working on? How is the community responding?

I adored Angel's response to my last letter. It made me smile on a dark day.

I have some news that I need for you to keep a secret for now. It isn't good. The Irish prisoners at the poor farm are being stolen from there and sent back across the ocean, to rid the city of its obligations to us. I would like to have better confirmation of these events, but my source is trustworthy. I believe him.

I feel despair and also the weight of knowing and possibly telling. I must make it known, and yet, I ask myself, then what? There is little we can do to stop it.

Pray for me that I will have the courage and clarity that I need. I miss you.

All my love,

Rosaleen

It felt reckless to put my intentions in writing, but I needed to. People outside of Lowell needed to know. My dear friends needed to know. I kept writing.

To Miss Martha:

I hope this letter finds you well. How is Ruth? And Mr. Collins? I have been so busy that I have not found time to write lately. But please tell Ruth that I will.

There is something that I need for you to know. I have reason to believe that the city is deporting Irish inmates at the poor farm here—criminals, paupers, and the insane. They are sending them back across the ocean.

I am fearful that any number of my friends could be next. A simple, and often unfair, arrest will have a person sent to the poor farm. They have lied before—about a person being drunk, or having previous arrests—and they will do it again.

If you have the time and could look into the legality of this, I would be grateful.

Please give everyone my love,

Rosaleen

I folded and sealed them both immediately. I thought of leaving them to mail later, but it felt unsafe to leave them on the table exposed. Even in my own home. I tucked them into my apron. I felt Angel's latest letter in there and pulled it out to read again. Lydia had written it. But I was certain that Angel had dictated every word.

Rosaleen,

Those poor ants! Can you imagine walking along, minding your own business, and suddenly, SNAP! You are eaten to pieces. If I was a plant, I would rather be one who makes its own sugar. Something to be proud of. Not like those mean plants. Lying so still and sneaky.

Write me soon about more things you know.

Love,

Angel

I smiled again, even though I had already read it many times. I would keep it there, in my apron, to read many more times. I put on my jacket and hopped down the stairs, leaving the door open behind me. Cocoa was sitting at the front door, waiting to come sit near the warm fire again. I let her in and left for the tavern once I saw her cuddled into her bed.

Emmett and Mr. Joyce had ordered me a meat pie, and I ate it hungrily. The tavern was warm, and a young woman played a sweet song on a harp in the far corner.

"Mr. Joyce," I said. "Do you think there will ever be a way for us to fight against the Know-Nothings? In a meaningful way?"

"Certainly," he said. "But it won't come from radicals. The most passionate among us cannot break through. We will need to be allowed to become successful. As serious business owners, police officers, teachers, politicians. That will take the humility of amicable people."

I felt color coming into my face. "People who will do what they tell them," I said. "That doesn't seem like power at all."

"Power is exerted through leadership," he said. "And leadership requires compromise. Sometimes that *does* mean doing what they want. But sometimes it means leading, convincing, and celebrating small but meaningful victories."

"What if they never let us?" Emmett asked. "Even when we are humble and amicable? They don't want us here. How will they ever let us into those positions?"

"We'll have to show them that we aren't going anywhere," Mr. Joyce said. "That it doesn't matter whether they want us here or not."

I looked at Emmett. He was right. This conversation with Mr. Joyce, with everyone who thought as he did, couldn't go on until I told them. But something was still pestering me. What if the old woman was wrong? What if this was all a rumor? I yearned for proof, but I didn't know how to get it.

~

I visited Nancy and Calvin the next night for tea. I still needed to talk to Calvin about the new personal liberty laws. I hadn't decided whether to bring up the deportations. I doubted Calvin knew it was happening, but if he did, it would have pained me to find that out. I wanted to believe that Calvin was helping us, not turning a blind eye to this horrific injustice. And then there was the letter. If I was going to write it, I couldn't expose myself first.

Nancy opened the door with a smirk. That same smirk. The one on her face when she'd assured me at our first encounter that not everyone was as happy as Sarah. I liked that smirk. It was comforting. She gave me a big hug. Her belly was big enough now that it had become a nuisance when hugging. The rest of her was still thinner than I expected, but her belly protruded out all on its own, as if that little baby inside couldn't wait to reach out into the world. Eager, like Nancy.

"Come in," she said. We sat in the parlor alone at first. She lay back on the couch, legs crossed, arms folded just above her belly. She looked at the ceiling.

"I've been thinking about your next lesson with the Catholic school girls," she said. Then she turned just her head and looked at me. "Paleontology."

"Paleontology?" I asked.

"Yes," she said, sitting up straighter and turning the rest

of her body to face mine. "The study of fossils. Have you heard of Mary Anning?"

I shook my head. Nancy's eyes lit up.

"She discovered all sorts of fossils from animals that lived long ago and no longer exist," she said. "The first flying creature. Giant reptiles. She was brilliant. And she was poor. Which means no one talks about her. But they should."

"Fossils," I repeated. "Are they bones?"

"Sort of," Nancy said. "She often found hers near the sea. The sand and the mud covered the animals' bodies quickly after they died, and that turned their bones and teeth into fossils. It preserved them. And then it becomes like a puzzle. Which animal did this bone come from? Sometimes these fossil hunters, these paleontologists, they only find one. But sometimes they find a whole bunch together. Almost a whole skeleton."

I nodded. "That's fascinating," I said. "I think they would like it. Do you have any books on it?"

She shook her head. "Just newspaper clippings about Mary. You can borrow one. But the library has some books. I stopped by the other day to check," she said.

"Thank you," I said. "I'll be sure to pick them up."

She smiled. She looked content. I wished we still lived together. I missed her even when she was right next to me. I wanted to tell her about what was weighing so heavily on my mind. But I didn't want Calvin to hear. I stood up.

"I'll go make the tea," I said. Nancy hopped up, too.

"I'll come with you," she said. "I've had so much energy lately. You probably think I'm tired, but I'm not at all. I was at first, but now I'm positively lively."

I laughed. "Positively lively," I repeated. "I'm not surprised. I wouldn't think that growing a baby would be very difficult for Nancy Parker. Something so small and innocent couldn't conquer you."

She smiled sideways at me. "I'm sure something will," she said.

Just then, I heard Calvin's footsteps coming down the stairs. I hung the iron kettle over the stove as Calvin came up behind Nancy and kissed her cheek.

"Hello, Rosaleen," he said.

"Good evening, Calvin," I said.

When the water in the kettle started to boil, I took it off the stove and poured it into a teapot.

"You two go sit," I said. "I'll bring the tea in."

Nancy didn't argue this time, and they both walked to the parlor. I found Nancy's serving tray and put the pot, cups, and sugar cubes on it. Nancy and Calvin were sitting on the couch. Calvin had his arm draped over her, and Nancy's foot bobbed up and down. She looked down at her hands resting on her belly, perhaps waiting for a kick or a nudge from the baby. Calvin watched her with love in his eyes and a faint smile on his lips. I set the tray down and sat across from them.

"Really, I could run through this whole town right now with all this energy," Nancy said.

Calvin chuckled. "And the neighbors would think you insane," he said.

"And then they would send you to the poor farm," I said.

Calvin raised one eyebrow. Before he could respond, I spoke again.

"Speaking of the poor farm," I went on, "I met a lovely young man there. A guard. Josiah Sallow was his name. Do you know him?"

"I can't say I do," Calvin said. "Once the prisoners leave the courthouse, they're no longer under my jurisdiction. The poor farm is run by a separate part of the city."

I nodded. He probably didn't know about the deportations, then. He wouldn't need to. "It's a shame," I said. "Such a nice young man. He wants to be a police officer someday."

Calvin smiled in earnest. "I hope he applies," he said. "We need good men. And he's already been approved by Rosaleen, our harshest critic."

I smirked. "I'm hardly your harshest critic."

I saw Nancy hide a smile.

"But I'm not here about that this evening," I said. "I'm here on behalf of the Lowell Anti-Slavery Society."

"Is that so?" Calvin asked, looking truly surprised.

"Rosaleen has always been quite the abolitionist," Nancy said.

"That's . . . surprising," Calvin said.

I grinned. "I'm full of surprises," I said. "Have you heard of the personal liberty laws?"

Calvin nodded. "I have," he said. "I'm not entirely sure what exactly they entail. But I've heard of them."

I went on, "One of the things it says—the thing you and your officers need to be concerned with—is that local police are not to assist in catching runaways."

"Well, that goes directly against the Fugitive Slave Act," Calvin said. "That's bold."

"Yes," I said. "And very likely to pass. Do you think your men can do it?"

Calvin looked into his teacup, eyebrows furrowed.

"Most of them will be happy to," he said. "Those who are members of the American Party detest the invasion of these Southerners. And we know that this new Republican Party is the architect of the personal liberty laws. We have a few Democrats who may be sympathetic to the Fugitive Slave Act, but I'm confident they will do what I tell them. Perhaps you know one of them?"

"Who?" I asked.

"Mr. Sullivan," he said. "Officer Sullivan now. His first name is Quinn."

"You hired him?" I asked.

"I did," Calvin said.

"That's wonderful news," I said, surprised at how truly happy I was for Quinn. "I'm glad you did so."

"As you can imagine," he went on, "some of the other men aren't too happy about it. But I told them they could leave their position or they could work with him like the professionals I expect them to be."

I nodded. "Quinn is no radical," I said. "They should find him agreeable enough."

"His father was friends with Cummiskey," he said. "An original Lowell man. A friend of my grandfather's. A man with a vision for this city. I trust him."

I sipped my tea. He was correct, of course. Quinn had been brought up to think in a way that would please Calvin.

"Well, if you have any questions about the new personal

liberty laws, please come to me," I said. "Or if your men do, they can ask me as well."

The thought of speaking to Officer Keyes again turned my stomach. I hoped that he would not come to me for anything, but I'd volunteered to do a job and I intended to do it.

"Thank you," Calvin said.

⁓

I thought all week about how to prove to myself that these deportations were truly happening, and on Sunday, I skipped Mass to wait outside of a different church on the other side of the Western Canal.

Reverend Edson was speaking with an older man as they exited the church through the front two red doors. The man had a cane and thick glasses and was hunched over, and the reverend had to lean in very close and speak directly into the old man's ear. Finally, the old man hobbled away, and Reverend Edson looked up and saw me waiting by a tree. He walked down the path toward me, looking around to see who else might be lingering.

I smiled as he neared.

"Walk with me," he said. We walked along the canal, both looking over our shoulders every minute or so. I wished the mills were running so the sound of the canal would have drowned out our voices.

"I'm glad to see your spirits have improved," he said.

"Oh, I'm still quite angry, Reverend," I said.

He nodded. "Yes, of course," he said. "I only mean that it appears you will no longer tear me apart because of it."

"Not you," I said, smiling. "There is just one more piece of information I would like."

"What is it?" he asked.

"What day do they pick them up?" I asked. "From the farm. Do you know?"

"Mrs. McDonough's son was taken on a Thursday, if I remember correctly. I only know because I was there on a Friday that week. She brought it up in passing, but I remember thinking it was awful late in the summer for him to leave. That Friday was much cooler than when I had last been there only five days before. Though, I don't know if they have a regular schedule or if it's consistent at all."

"Perhaps you could find out," I said. "Make a surprise visit."

He looked at me, concerned. "And what would you do with that information?" he asked.

I looked straight ahead as we turned a corner.

"I would see for myself," I said. "I need to. I need to see it. But I can't go to the poor farm every day, miss my shift, miss my wages, eventually lose my job. It would mean a great deal to me if you could give me an idea of when they come for the prisoners."

Reverend Edson was quiet. We walked for a minute before he spoke again.

"I will go on Thursday and I will see," he said. "But if you do this and if you are seen, it is likely they will throw you on that boat as well."

"I understand," I said. "But this is too important for me to doubt. And I *will* doubt. I need to erase any trace of doubt. Only then will I be able to do what needs to be done."

Reverend Edson stopped walking. "And what needs to be done?" he asked.

We were in front of a park now. Children giggled and shouted as they chased one another. I looked into the reverend's eyes.

"I'll come see you on Friday," I said. "Thank you."

Chapter Twenty-One

"I can't confirm that they come on Thursdays," Reverend Edson said to me when I went to visit him that Friday. "But I can confirm that they come on the second of each month. I asked the farm keepers."

I was sitting at his table, drinking tea, eating cherries, and swinging my legs back and forth with the anxious energy flowing throughout my body. I stopped.

"You asked the farm keepers?" I asked.

"Yes," he said. "They admitted that officers in a covered wagon come and take prisoners once every month. Although they aren't sure what happens to them after that. It seems likely that the rumors among the inmates are true."

My stomach was suddenly jumpy.

"I hope you take me at my word and believe what I have told you," he said. "I know how unsettling this truth must be, but please accept it rather than run around looking for more answers."

"And what would you have me do with it?" I asked. "With this truth?"

"I would have you pray," he said. "Perhaps petition the legislature."

"The legislature that is made up of Know-Nothings," I said.

"And other, decent men, too," he said.

"But you wouldn't have me tell others in the Acre?" I asked.

"What good will it do, Rosaleen?" he asked. "It can only cause unrest. More violence. You've said yourself the Irish have no power. Will it help your fellow man to rise up and respond in anger? Or will it only lead to more pain and suffering?"

"If he and she rise up in great numbers, perhaps we can gain power," I said.

Reverend Edson shook his head. "Power is not reliant on numbers," he said. "It is reliant on wealth. On social status. You see this in the South. In so many places, slaves greatly outnumber whites. But would an uprising be successful? Far from it. A slave uprising would be bloody and devastating."

"Fine," I said. "Not an uprising. But this can be motivation. If I petition the legislature alone it would surely mean nothing. If one hundred of my fellow men and women do, they may feel the need to listen."

"And who will control the anger of the masses?" he asked. "Who will funnel it into acceptable channels? Will it be you?"

I said nothing to this. It couldn't be me. Outing myself

as Paddy would undermine all I had worked for. Paddy's legitimacy lay in the presumption that he was a man.

"I'm asking you to think before you act," the reverend said in my silence.

I nodded. "You once told me," I said, quieter now, "that knowledge brings power. Knowing has to be the first step."

The reverend paced back and forth in front of the fire.

"When you write," he began to say, but then stopped pacing for a moment and looked at me, surprised he had said those words aloud. Surprised to acknowledge that he knew. We stared at one another for a moment before he continued. "Usually, at the end, you ask people to take action. That's the important part. Not everyone will listen, but we've seen that many will. Think hard about that part."

He walked closer to me and put his hand on my shoulder.

"Feel the weight of this responsibility," he said.

"I do," I assured him. I stood up and brought my dishes to the wash bin. I cleaned them and headed for the door. Cocoa got up from her warm spot by the fire—which she had gotten quite used to—and lazily followed me. I started to open the door, but stopped to look over my shoulder at the reverend. He looked older than I had ever seen him.

"Thank you, Reverend," I said. "You've shown me enormous kindness and respect. I know that being a friend to me upsets some in your congregation. But I appreciate it more than I can put into words."

His lips turned up in a smile and his chin lifted. His eyes relaxed.

"I am glad to hear it," he said. "You can always come to me. You are always welcome."

I smiled back at him, and Cocoa and I walked home by the bright light of the moon.

~

The week crawled forward slowly as I waited for November 2 to come. On Monday, I came home to a letter from Marie.

Dearest Rosaleen,

I am heartbroken for you. I know that fear. The fear of being taken from everyone you know and love and sent far away to a place of hopelessness. I wouldn't wish it upon my worst enemy, let alone a good friend such as yourself. Please stay safe. Stay out of the taverns. Go home early in the evening. And tell Emmett to do the same. Have you written to Miss Martha? If you haven't, please tell me and I will speak with her. I am going to the library soon. I will see if I can learn anything there.

My temperance meetings have grown. I have a number of women helping me now, and a few men, too. There is a nervous energy in the Black community because of the Fugitive Slave Act. We've all been looking for something to do with it, and so our meetings are lively and productive. We are working with the antislavery society to try to take on the school issue yet again. To get our children into Massachusetts schools. It will be a task.

I will be praying for you, hard. Write me often so I know you're well.

All my love,
Marie

If Marie had received my letter, Miss Martha must have as well. I hoped there was something she could do. I knew if there was, she was doing it. I fell asleep before I could write Marie back but promised myself I would do it later in the week.

On Tuesday after work, I stopped at the library to pick up the books Nancy had told me about. When I got home, Emmett and I flipped through them, marveling at the sketches of fanciful creatures and their skeletons.

"Don't let the nuns see these," Emmett said. "They'll have to repaint all the scenes of Noah and his ark, shutting these beasts out."

I laughed. "I think they would simply shun me instead. Maybe burn the books, too."

"So many acts of contrition after that," he said.

I laughed again. When we heard Mr. Joyce coming up the stairs, we put the books away quicker than we dressed ourselves on other nights.

Of all the dangerous and secretive things I had done since becoming Paddy, carrying those books with me to the girls' school the next day was awfully mild. Yet my heart still banged loudly in my chest, and it made me laugh at myself. The wrath of Sister Hunna was a fear I could not suppress.

When I finally sat down with the girls, they noticed my nervousness.

"Rosaleen, you look frightened," Alice said. Her hair had been pulled back into a bun, but it had slowly fallen during the day, and now, half of it was hanging in her freckled face. I smiled at her.

"Can I help you with your hair?" I asked.

She shrugged, and I took that as a yes. It was so dry and stringy, I could barely get my fingers through it.

"Alice, dear," I said. "What's happened to your hair? It feels like you took a bath in the dirt."

"I broke Ma's comb," she said. "We don't have money for a new one."

I grabbed the hair that I could and tied a ribbon around it. Then I took out some paper. *Buy Alice a comb*, I wrote before stuffing it into my apron and sitting back down.

She sighed loudly. I ignored it.

"All right, then," I said. "Get to work on those letters. I think you'll be quite surprised to see what I brought today."

They gave each other a sideways smile before starting on their letters. Ina finished first and tapped her pen on the desk as she anxiously waited for Alice. I noticed Alice's tongue poking out between her lips as she concentrated. I was sure the nuns punished her for that in class.

When she was finally finished, I took out the newspaper clipping Nancy had given me about Mary Anning.

"She's British," Alice said.

"She was," I said. "And poor. People disregarded her because of it. And because she was a woman. In fact, many of her discoveries have been attributed to men."

"What are fossils?" Ina asked.

"Animal parts that have been preserved," I said. "Bones, teeth, hair, footprints."

"And she found them?" Ina asked.

I pulled out the books with the sketches.

"Sometimes she just found one, but sometimes she found many," I said. "It's like a puzzle."

We flipped through the book, and I watched the girls'

faces transform from mild interest to awe. Their eyes opened wider. Their jaws went slack. Their mouths formed into long Os.

"What are these?" Alice practically whispered. I smiled big.

"Animals," I said. "Animals that used to exist but don't anymore."

"What happened to them?" Ina asked.

"I don't know," I said, looking back down at the book for answers.

"Do the nuns know about them?" Ina asked, in a true whisper now.

"I doubt it," I said. "I don't know if they would believe it. Do you girls believe it?"

They looked at one another for an answer, eyes still wide open in amazement. They both grinned and nodded vigorously.

"You bet I do," Ina said.

As I walked from the girls' school that night to the boardinghouse, I thought about what I had to do the next day. I thought of how many things needed to go right. To go just the way I wanted. Billy the horse needed to be available, probably for more than one day. If they were truly taking the prisoners to Boston, it would be a taxing ride. Billy couldn't make it both ways in one day. I would need to find a place at the farm to hide out close enough to see what was happening, but far enough, or hidden enough, to go unseen. If they did come and they did take the inmates,

I would need to follow closely enough to track them but far enough not to raise suspicion. I would pack myself food and would tell no one where I was going. This last point I couldn't completely see as settled. I wanted to tell Emmett. But if he thought it too foolish, he might try to stop me.

When I got to the boardinghouse, it was late. Nearly curfew. I tried to slip in, unseen, but Mrs. Durrand was right near the door, cleaning up the teacups and supper plates.

"Hello, Rosaleen," she said. I smiled apologetically.

"Good evening, Mrs. Durrand," I said. "I'm sorry it's so late. I'll be quick."

She shook her head. "I'm not worried about you being here," she said. "Just don't keep those girls up too late. And be quiet about leaving."

"Yes, ma'am," I said. I hurried up the stairs, hoping Sarah would still be awake. I knocked softly at her door. Nessa opened it, looking a little sleepy and surprised.

"Rosaleen, come in," she said.

"I hope I didn't wake anyone," I said, quietly, as I walked in.

Nessa shook her head. Berta was reading in bed. Sarah was at her desk, writing. Helen was kneeling next to the bed, praying.

I sat at the other desk and spoke quietly to Nessa while I waited for Sarah to finish.

"I heard that Quinn got the position as a police officer," I said.

Nessa frowned a little and nodded.

"You still disapprove?" I asked.

"I guess you could call me wary," she said. "He promised

me his intentions are good. Trying to change things from the inside and all of that."

"It's brave of him," I said.

She raised her eyebrows. "I suppose."

"It won't be easy," I said. "They aren't exactly going to welcome him."

She sighed and lay back, looking at the ceiling now.

"I know that," she said. "I guess I ought to be supportive."

"I'm sure he would appreciate it," I said.

Just then, Sarah turned around in her seat and smiled at me.

"Well, hello there," she said. I smiled back.

"Hello, Sarah," I said. "I know I don't look it now, but I'm going to be awfully sick tomorrow. Will you tell Mr. Harrison?"

She narrowed her eyes but kept smiling.

"You want me, Sarah, to lie?" she asked.

I grinned back at her. "Oh, you're right," I said. "Berta?"

Berta looked up from her book.

"Yes, Rosaleen?" she said.

"I'm sorry to interrupt your reading, but I need to ask a favor," I said.

She put her book down. "Go on," she said.

"Please tell Mr. Harrison tomorrow that I'm awfully sick," I said. "So sick that I might not be back at work until Saturday."

She nodded. "You do look terrible," she said. "Your skin is gray and green. Do get some rest."

I giggled. "Thank you," I said.

Sarah rolled her eyes. "Don't tell me what you'll be doing instead," she said.

"I have no idea what you're speaking of," I said. "I'll be in bed, sick, just like I said."

"What *will* you be doing?" Nessa asked.

"I wish I could tell you," I said. "But I can't just yet."

She frowned. "No fun," she said.

I touched her arm. "It's because I love you that I can't tell you," I said. "Now, Mrs. Durrand warned me that I can't keep you all up too late."

I stood up and so did Nessa. I kissed her cheek.

"Good night," I said.

"Good night." But she still looked a little sour that I wouldn't tell her my secret.

I hugged and kissed Sarah, too, and waved to Helen and Berta as I left.

On my walk home, I pushed away any lingering apprehension. I had decided that it must be done, and so I would do it. I took a deep breath and prayed.

Chapter Twenty-Two

I awoke early the next morning, before Emmett and Mr. Joyce. I packed a satchel with food—apples, bread, salted pork, and cheese. I tied my hair up quickly and gave sleeping Cocoa a pat before I slipped out the door.

The air was colder than I'd expected, and I was grateful that I had brought my warmer coat. I pulled it tight around myself and made my way to Mr. O'Neal's to inquire about Billy. I had brought a basket of biscuits as well. With six O'Neal children, food was always welcome. I noticed the steam coming from my mouth and wondered how much longer we had until the first snowfall. The trees had lost their leaves, and their bare branches reached out toward the street like long, nimble fingers. Women grabbed clothing from the lines. Men gathered firewood from beside buildings. No one looked at one another. It was too early and too cold for niceties. Occasionally, my eyes met another's, and they would nod quickly in recognition.

I knocked quietly on the O'Neals' door at first and then

louder after I received no answer. One of the older children came to the door, still rubbing her eyes.

"I'll get Da," she said. I nodded.

"Thank you," I said.

"Are you here about the horse?" he asked when he saw me. I nodded and handed him the biscuits.

"For the family," I said. "I baked them last night."

Mr. O'Neal raised his eyebrows. "That's quite generous of you," he said. "I'll put these inside and then we'll fetch Billy."

"I may need him for tomorrow, too," I said, certain now that this request was unfeasible. "I'm making a trip out of the city. I understand if it's too inconvenient."

Mr. O'Neal looked away in thought. "I'll be back in a moment," he said.

I rubbed my hands together while he was gone and then rubbed my arms. He came back a moment later with the empty basket.

"I do believe that should work just fine," he said. "I can't think of any previous arrangements I've made for Billy. And we must take care of him. If he needs to rest overnight, please make those arrangements."

"Thank you, Mr. O'Neal," I said. "I would never want to take your generosity for granted, and I would not have asked if it weren't a matter of importance."

He nodded and asked no further questions. He led me to the barn around the back, although I knew exactly where it was. He stroked Billy's nose and gave him a pat.

"When you bring him back tomorrow, do lock him up," he said, dropping the barn key into my hand.

"Yes, sir," I said. "Thank you."

He was already heading back to the house and lifted his hand in acknowledgment. I wrapped my satchel around Billy and led him to the street. People were starting to head to work now. Small, short conversations hummed throughout the Acre. A group of men walked toward me. One of them was Emmett. I hadn't left in time. Silently, I scolded myself. He looked at me in confusion and stopped to talk while Dennis and Patrick kept walking.

"What are you doing with the O'Neals' horse?" he asked.

I looked around. No one was listening to us. I couldn't lie to Emmett now. Besides, it was too late for him to change my mind. I had already skipped my shift.

"I'm going to the poor farm," I said, quietly. "And this is Billy." I put my hand on Billy's neck.

Emmett's eyebrows went up. He couldn't help but smile at Billy's name.

"Good morning, Billy," he said. "And why are you going to the poor farm on a workday?"

I looked around again.

"I'm going to watch them," I said. "I'm going to watch them take them. I need to see."

Emmett crossed his arms, looked at the sky, and sighed.

"You could've told me, Rose," he said.

"I didn't want you to try to stop me," I said. "I know it's a little foolish."

"Well, now I'm coming with you," he said. "Don't move."

He ran to catch up to Dennis and Patrick. As he spoke, they glanced at me. I saw them both nod, and then Emmett ran back.

"Told them I was sick," he said, breathing quicker from his short run. "Obviously I'm not. They suspect you."

I smiled. "As they should," I said.

"What have you got in here?" Emmett asked, already opening the satchel to look inside. "I'm going to need more than that. And we ought to bring a blanket. These clouds look like they aren't going anywhere."

I looked up now and noticed how dark everything still was. He was right. We couldn't know how long we might wait.

"We'll stop back at the house," I said.

"I know we've only just met, Billy," Emmett said, mounting the horse, "but I'll be in charge today."

I smiled and rolled my eyes as I accepted Emmett's hand and mounted behind him.

"He thinks he's in charge, Billy," I said. "But who knows the way there? You and I do."

Emmett pulled the reins to the right to turn Billy around. He obeyed but shook his head a few times after straightening out.

"You see?" I asked. "Billy knows who is in charge, and that's him."

"I suppose I *was* the last to know about this trip," Emmett said. "And so I am at your mercy. Won't you please show me the way?"

I smiled and pressed my face against his neck, smelling his hair. It smelled faintly of sweat but distinctly of Emmett. I enjoyed it. "We will," I said.

We stopped at the house. I dismounted.

"More food and a blanket," I said, confirming my tasks.

Emmett took off his jacket and handed it to me. His

wide chest and strong arms looked very bare in this cold weather with only a shirt to cover them.

"And my warm coat," he said. "It could be a long day."

When we got out of the city, I rested my head on Emmett's shoulder.

"Do you still want to bring a baby into this world?" I asked him. "Even with all of this worry?"

I felt him stiffen.

"Yes," he said, quickly. "Why? Are you expecting?"

"No," I said.

His muscles relaxed again.

"I think being a da and ma is going to be hard no matter," he said. "Even for Nancy and Calvin, and even for Ruth, if she chooses to have children."

"Their children will be able to do things ours won't," I said. "The possibilities for their children will be endless. Our child will have to do the same work as us, earn the same wages, live in the same house, and worry about all of the same things we do."

"Perhaps," Emmett said. "But perhaps not. I'm surprised to hear you being so cynical. I know it's hard to believe now, but people can and do change. Think about Lydia. Lydia was born a slave and now she has Angel, who can read and hasn't even turned five years old yet. Who knows what Angel will be able to do in the future? Who knows whose mind she'll change or whose heart she'll soften?"

"Angel isn't even allowed to go to the same school as

her white neighbors. Even though she is *so* smart. Even though she lives in Boston," I said.

"But her children might," he said. He was quiet for a moment, and when he spoke again, he sounded slightly frustrated. "If you let them take away our future, then you've given them everything."

A tear rolled down my cheek, onto his shirt.

"You're right," I said. "I'm not giving up. I'm just afraid."

"I know," Emmett said. "Calvin can't protect us forever. But he can give us some time to try to make this right."

I squeezed him harder, my hands joined at his chest. He put a hand on top of mine. We rode in silence for a while.

"Here," I finally said. "Turn right up here."

Billy turned and slowed.

"It's that house on the corner," I said. "The other houses are behind it."

"Across the street," Emmett said, pointing. "Do you see that tree?"

I looked. On each side of the dirt road, the land banked. Then the land flattened, and a large oak tree stood directly opposite the farm.

"That's perfect," I said.

We led Billy up the incline and tied him to a fat, strong branch. We sat at the base of the tree, and Emmett wrapped the blanket around my shoulders. Then he retrieved some food from the satchel. He brought me an apple and a few pieces of bread. I smiled at him. The clouds were starting to part just slightly. We ate our apples and our bread with our eyes focused on the farm. We saw the inmates spill into the field after their breakfast. We saw them walk up and down the rows, bending and standing, picking something up or leaving something on the ground, I couldn't quite tell which. The women pulled their shawls closer to their bodies every now and then. The children stooped to play in the dirt. In the distance, I saw men handling a donkey and hooking something onto its chest. Or perhaps it was a mule. It looked rather large. Even from a distance.

"There are children here," Emmett said.

"Came with their ma," I said, remembering what the reverend had told me.

Emmett didn't respond. The clouds parted a bit more, and I finally started to feel some warmth spread throughout my body. I kept the blanket on because I was comfortable. The inmates went back inside. I lay back and looked up at the tree. The leaves were still. A small gray bird with an orange chest landed on a branch. Her head jerked up and down and side to side with quick movements. She opened her beak and called to a mate before flying off again. I boosted myself up onto my elbows and let the blanket fall to the ground behind me. Then I turned onto my stomach and studied the ants. The way they never stopped moving. Their determined onward march. Lifting and climbing past obstacles.

"Rose," Emmett whispered in a stern voice, grabbing my arm. "A wagon just arrived."

I froze. My breath quickened, and my heart thumped in my chest. I was afraid. Somehow, I hadn't believed—up until this moment—that I would see anything at all. My stomach flipped, and a wave of nausea overtook me. I closed my eyes and took a deep breath. I willed myself to turn over and look. I sat up.

A wagon was stopped in the road. Three men walked away from it, toward the main house, and knocked. Two appeared to be wearing a uniform. A minute later, they were let in. I looked at Emmett, and he looked at me. I was sure he could see the fear in my eyes.

A wagon was stopped in the road. Three men walked

Chapter Twenty-Three

"Now we'll know," he whispered as we waited. "Now
we'll know for sure."

I didn't know if he was speaking to me or to himself. I
couldn't answer anyway. A lump had formed in my throat.
I could only watch.

We waited for many minutes for the men to come back
out. When they did, they led seven men, three women, and
one boy out of the house. Each was bound by their wrists.
The man who was not in uniform led the procession from
the house to the wagon. One officer walked to the side,
keeping an eye on the inmates, and the other walked
behind, doing the same. The inmates filed into the back of
the wagon, one at a time.

"They're going," Emmett said. "They're taking them."

The wagon started to move. Away from Lowell.

"And they aren't taking them back," he continued, his
voice sharp with frustration. He shook his head. "That's it,
then. We have our proof."

"No. I need to see where they take them," I said. "I need

to be sure of it. And what if one of them is Frank? We have to follow them."

Emmett's eyes shot up at me. "Do you think that could be Frank?" He didn't wait for me to answer.

He stood up quickly, untying Billy. I packed the blanket into his saddlebag. We both mounted, and Emmett quickly steered Billy in the direction of the wagon. We kept our pace far enough removed that we probably looked like a mere speck to the men driving the wagon. Certainly not close enough for them to hear us speak or for us to hear them. Yet, I couldn't say anything. Finally, Emmett whispered to me.

"Will they go all the way to Boston?" he asked, as if I knew. "How long will that take?"

"I've only been by train," I replied.

"Do you think Billy will be able to handle it?" he asked again.

"I asked Mr. O'Neal if I could keep him for the evening, if needed," I said.

Emmett said nothing. Perhaps he was sour at me for not telling him my whole plan. Or perhaps he was only thinking of the danger these inmates were in. Perhaps he was afraid for Frank.

I was getting hungry again, but we couldn't stop for fear of losing them. The road was fairly empty, but I wasn't sure what awaited us between where we were and Boston —if that was, in fact, where we were going. A few minutes later, my stomach growled.

"Quiet back there," Emmett joked. I giggled. I supposed he wasn't sour. I breathed a sigh of relief.

I looked at the sky. It was nearly midday, perhaps

slightly later, and the sun was out in full now. The road veered south. We could see a river to our right. I imagined it was the same one that flowed from Lowell, carrying the water from the waterfall and through the canals, although I couldn't be sure.

"That wagon is awfully large for eleven people," I said.

"Mmhm," Emmett said.

"It would be so cold on a boat," I went on. "Making that journey now. At this time of the year."

Emmett was quiet. We passed houses every so often. Farms that sprawled for as far as we could see. The people who worked them did not look up as we passed. When one woman, just a few years older than us, did, she smiled. Emmett tipped his hat. Finally, the wagon began to slow and then it stopped.

"What are they doing?" I asked, hoping Emmett could see better than I.

"I'm not sure," Emmett said. "But we'll stop, too. You can feed that pestering stomach."

We dismounted, and Emmett rummaged through the satchel. I squinted at the wagon, trying to see what they had stopped for. No one got out of the back. I saw the man in the front leading the horses to the river.

"They're giving their horses water," I said. "We should do the same."

Emmett handed me a few pieces of salted pork and a wedge of cheese.

"You eat," he said. "I'll take care of Billy."

Emmett led Billy through some trees toward the river. I kept staring at the wagon. A uniformed man exited the back. He took a deep breath, looked at the sky, and adjusted his belt. Then he turned away from me and spat his tobacco toward the trees. I backed further away, toward the river, where branches hid me from his sight. I nibbled on my cheese and watched him circle the wagon slowly, stretching his legs and kicking some rocks. A few minutes later, Emmett returned with Billy. He sat next to me and began to eat some of his food.

"If we are going to Boston," I said, "it'll be a long ride. I haven't ridden a horse this far since going to Cork."

"Which ride was worse?" he asked.

I laughed. "That one," I said. "No question. I have food now. And I'm with you."

"Who were you with for the other?" he asked.

"A man named Paul," I said. "He was a baker in our town and a schoolmate of my ma's. He sold oats. He had ways of processing them in his large bakery kitchen."

"Oats?" Emmett asked. "How did he have oats?"

"I didn't ask," I said. "But I knew he had to lie about them. Pretend he didn't have such a large quantity. I'm not sure if he grew them, too, or if he just processed them. He had to sleep with a knife on the road because of the thieves."

Emmett looked toward the wagon. He grabbed my hand and held it in his lap.

"Wouldn't it be wonderful if we could go back to a different Ireland?" he asked. "One that was even better than before? One where we could have our own land and grow and keep whatever we would like?"

I sighed. "I would go back with you if we could have that," I said. "But we both know we can't."

He shook his head. "Was the workhouse so terrible?" he

asked. I knew he was thinking of the inmates now. The ones huddled in the wagon just a bit ahead of us. What he truly meant was, "Will the workhouse be so bad for them?"

"Yes," I said.

~

Just after we started again, we passed through a town. There was a clothing store, a general store and post office, a bakery, and a shoe store. On a slight hill to our right, we could see a church, and farther back, houses scattered along a road. The wagon did not stop and so neither did we. Men sat outside of the shops or swept the porches. Horses ate hay from troughs next to the general store. One young man was leaving the clothing store. He looked up at me and smiled. He was quite handsome. It made me blush. I hugged Emmett tighter.

We passed a red maple tree that stood in stark contrast to the leafless trees lining the road. On the ground beneath it, only a few leaves had fallen. It was beautiful and jarring and I stared. With the bright sun shining through it, it reminded me of the color of Julia's hair. I thought of it laid out across her pillow at night. I missed her.

We rode for a long time in the quiet country. The road soon veered away from the river and toward the train tracks. Sometimes, the road crossed the tracks and then crossed back again. Billy awkwardly avoided the rails, doing a little prance to get to the other side. When a train was coming, Billy would get skittish and agitated. But once it passed, he was calm again.

We passed through one more town as the sun started to

set in the sky. Still, the wagon did not stop. This town was busier than the last at this later hour. Two women spoke to each other on the roadside. Music played from inside an inn. A man mounted his horse and passed us, going the opposite direction.

The land cleared once again, but only briefly before we began to approach a cluster of houses. In the distance, I could see Boston. To our left, three very large buildings sat on top of a hill, overlooking another river. The train tracks formed a barrier between the hill and the river, and next to them, a bridge brought travelers on foot and horse across the river.

The wagon finally stopped. And that's when I saw it. A line of people walking from the large buildings toward the wagon. They were shackled, too. Uniformed men jumped out of the wagon and held the flap open for the new passengers, who were now approaching. One by one, they stepped in. The uniformed men did not get back in, but walked to the front of the wagon where they disappeared from sight.

"There are more," I said. "It isn't just Lowell."

"No, it isn't," Emmett said. The anger in his voice was chilling.

A moment later, the wagon started to move again. We crossed the bridge. Things started to get more crowded along the road. Houses sat next to one another, nearly touching. Soon we crossed another bridge. Up ahead, I could see where the train tracks stopped. It was the Boston station. The end of the line. We were entering the city.

We followed the wagon as it turned onto Causeway Street. I looked to my right, realizing I knew exactly where we were. The inn was only a few blocks away, but the wagon was moving away from it, passing Lancaster, Portland, and Friend Street. We rode along the water, passing two more bridges on our left. Finally, ahead, I saw the looming ships. Emmett weaved in and out of the other horses and their carriages. The wagon turned at the pier. We turned as well and tied up Billy. Pilings lined the water, and I stood on one to see over the crowd.

The inmates were led out of the wagon, toward the dock, where a boat was being loaded with crates and boxes and barrels. I got off the piling and started to push my way through the crowd. Emmett followed but grabbed my hands and stopped me before I reached the dock. From behind, he pulled me close and wrapped his arms around my shoulders to keep me there. We watched.

An older woman was pleading with one of the uniformed men.

"My son," she was saying through her tears. "I need to say goodbye to my son! He'll be looking for me."

"Onto the boat," the man said.

"Please," she said. "My son."

"Your son is not here," he said. "It's too late. Maybe he should have thought of this before leaving you at the poor farm. Now get on the boat."

She looked down at her feet and sobbed. He grabbed her arm and pushed her up the ramp. She stumbled and fell. I wanted to look away. It was so painful. But I didn't.

I scanned their faces to see if Frank was among them. He was not. A man only slightly older than Frank was yelling at the other uniformed man.

"Where are you taking us?" he demanded.

I couldn't see the uniformed man's face, but I heard a small laugh.

"Far away from here," I heard him say.

"This isn't right!" the inmate said. "I have a child. I only had a month left in there."

"That's not my problem," the uniformed man said. "*You* committed the crime."

"I'm not going," the inmate said.

"Like hell you aren't," the uniformed man said, stepping closer to him. The inmate spit in his face. The uniform man swung at him, hitting him right in the side of the jaw. The man staggered a few steps before more men rushed him, men who worked at the docks. They tackled him and held him down. Were they Irishmen, too? Why were they helping these monsters?

"No!" the man yelled. "Let me go! They're taking me from my baby girl. Get off me!"

The uniformed man had found a chain, and he bent down and wrapped the inmate's ankles together. The inmate was brought to his feet and then pushed back down to his hands and knees.

"Get on the boat, you dog!" the uniformed man shouted. He kicked the inmate's side. The inmate didn't move. He kicked him again and again. Finally, the inmate began to crawl up the ramp.

The boy went next without a fight. I saw the fear in his eyes. The way they darted from man to man, hoping he could avoid that violence.

"Why is he all alone?" My voice cracked. The boy was only a bit older than Ronan and a bit younger than I was when I'd crossed the ocean. He put his head down as he scurried up the ramp.

The last in line was a woman my age. She had waited on the pier with the man who was not uniformed. Both of the uniformed men approached her.

"Time to go, Biddy," one of them said. She growled at them. As they got closer, she lunged and tried to bite one. He stepped back and laughed and then smacked her face so hard I could hear it from where I stood. She turned to run, but the other uniformed man grabbed her shoulders before she could take two steps. She looked up. Her eyes caught mine. She stared intently at me. I could see the anger but also the desperation. A single tear fell from her face. They dragged her the rest of the way, one man on each side. Her shoes came off and no one picked them up.

Chapter Twenty-Four

I could no longer hold back the tears. I turned to Emmett and sobbed into his chest. He held me tight, and I kept my head buried into his coat until I knew the boat, and all the people aboard, must be gone. But when I turned back around, I saw her shoes. Tattered, worn— barely shoes at all anymore. The dockhands moved about the pier as if those shoes were not there, so I walked toward the shoes, stooped down, and picked them up. Then I took them to the water and threw them as far as I could. They splashed in silently, lost amid the sounds of the boats. A man looked at me strangely but said nothing. I stood there and stared at the ripples. Was that woman insane? Had she been insane before they took her? Or was the idea of being torn away just too much? Was she crazed by the thought of the nothingness that awaited her on the other side of the ocean? Her eyes looked almost like an animal's, and I didn't think they would ever leave me.

Emmett gave me a moment alone before coming to me.

"There's my proof," I said, bitterly. "Nothing to doubt now."

He grabbed my hand and stared into the water. Behind us, the sun shone fiercely. It reflected off the water before it dipped behind a building and disappeared for the night. The water was dark now. Everything was dark now. So different from how it had looked only a moment ago.

"Tell them," he said. "Tell them exactly what we just saw."

"I will," I said with more anger than I'd meant to betray. "What else could I possibly do now?"

I looked at him.

"I am with you," he said. "Right here. Always."

My face softened. I hugged him.

"I love you so much," I whispered.

He brushed the hair from my forehead and kissed it. I knew we needed to stay the night at the inn, but I wasn't sure I could bear to see my friends just then. How could I put into words what I had just witnessed? How could I explain my mood? I had no words, only a deep sadness, and buried under that, an anger that threatened to erupt if uncovered.

We walked away from the ships but kept to the water, finding a place to sit out of the commotion of the docks and eat our remaining food. We sat there until we were cold. Until the boots walking the docks began to quiet. Until the streetlamps illuminated the fat rats, coming out of hiding to conduct their nighttime business.

"Will we go to the inn now?" Emmett asked. I nodded. "Do they have a stable? I don't remember seeing one."

I shook my head. "Miss Susan paid monthly to allow

our guests to use a larger one down the street. We can leave Billy there."

Emmett stood and took my hand. We left Billy at the large stable at the corner of Merrimac and Ivers and paid the stable hand. When we arrived at the inn, I felt regret for not coming sooner. It was too late to be disturbing Miss Susan. The doors were locked now. Still, I knocked quietly. To my relief, Miss Susan emerged from the kitchen. I had not woken her. She hurried to us with a look of concern.

She opened the door. "Rosaleen," she said, quietly. She looked down the street in each direction. "Come in."

We stepped into the silent inn. I imagined a few of the guests were still awake in the comfort of their rooms.

"Do you have room?" I asked her. "Just for tonight. We'll leave at dawn. We needed to give our horse a rest."

"Certainly," she said. "Follow me."

We walked upstairs on Miss Susan's heels, passing a few rooms before she creaked open the door to a small room facing the back alley. The sight of a bed made my eyes droopy. Suddenly, I felt exhausted, as if my legs might buckle underneath me.

"Are you in any kind of trouble?" Miss Susan whispered to me before leaving. She looked steadily into my eyes.

I shook my head. "I'm not in trouble," I said.

She nodded, seemingly satisfied. "I'll see you in the morning," she said.

I slept fitfully. My dreams were broken and incomplete. I saw the faces of the inmates, heard the older woman's sobs. The younger woman's growl. And then, distinctly, Ronan yelling. I sat up in bed, covered in sweat. Emmett turned over and reached for my hand. I lay back down and let a tear roll down my face. And then another and another until I was sobbing. Emmett held me there in his arms, and I felt his tears wet my shoulder, too. Eventually, we fell back asleep.

~

We awoke early, before the sun, and made our way downstairs. There was only one other man in the dining room, and Miss Susan promptly brought us coffee.

"Thank you," I said. Eileen came over next, bringing us a breakfast of pancakes and berries. She looked at me with curiosity.

"This looks wonderful, Eileen," I said, before she could ask me a thing.

"I'll tell Marie you said so," she said. "Miss Susan told us you were both here. Marie says you better come see her before you leave."

I smiled. "Of course," I said. Eileen lingered, waiting for more, but I simply didn't know what to say. *They're taking our people and sending them back to the wasteland that was our home?* No. Clearly, I could not tell Eileen what we had witnessed.

"We had a long day yesterday," I said to her. "Perhaps I'll tell you about it next time we're here. We must eat quickly, though. The ride on horseback to Lowell is not short."

"You took a horse?" she asked.

I nodded. "A friend's horse."

She finally looked about at the other tables that were

beginning to fill up. I could see her disappointment, but she smiled anyway and touched my arm.

"We'll talk next time, then," she said. She hurried back to the kitchen.

Emmett looked at me but said nothing. He understood, of course. We finished quickly. The pancakes were sweet and buttery, and Emmett sipped his coffee as I slipped into the kitchen.

Marie was putting the last of the pancakes onto the plates, and Eileen was swooping in and out, arms loaded with plates, back and elbows opening and closing the kitchen door behind her.

Marie wiped her hands on a rag and hugged me.

"Are you all right?" she asked.

"I am," I said. "I promise to write you and tell you about all of this." I paused and bit the inside of my cheek, realizing just how vulnerable and raw I felt. The emotions were threatening to spill out again, and my throat seemed to squeeze shut. Marie nodded and rubbed my arm. She could tell I was upset. I couldn't hide it from her.

"Please do," she said. "And if there is anything at all I can do . . ." She trailed off, knowing I knew the rest.

I couldn't speak, but I hugged her. She kissed my cheeks, and I hurried out of the kitchen. I slipped a few coins under my plate, knowing that none of the three would accept our money directly. If I couldn't pay the full price for the room, at least I could help pay for Billy's overnight board.

The ride back was quiet. This was real now. This was not merely a possibility anymore. It weighed heavily upon us. When we arrived back in Lowell that evening, Emmett went directly home, and I took Billy back to the O'Neals' barn. I filled his trough with hay and water and patted his neck. I kissed his nose and told him good night before locking the stable door behind me. Then, I slipped the key under the rug outside of the O'Neals' door.

I spent the rest of the evening sitting at the table in our room, trying to write. I sipped my tea as I looked at the page. *Friends and neighbors*, it said. And that was as far as I had gotten. I stood and walked to the window, where I watched neighbors beat rugs and take clothes down from the line. I went back to the kitchen and poured myself another cup of tea. I sat back down and tried to write again. This time I got about halfway down the page before I crumpled it up. I couldn't afford to waste paper, but it just wasn't right.

I went out with Cocoa for a bit and then came back inside and fell asleep.

The next day, after work, I sat and tried once more. *Friends and neighbors*, my new sheet of paper said. Occasionally, Emmett came and looked over my shoulder but patiently stayed quiet.

"I'll finish it soon," I said that night in bed. "It's always like this."

Emmett nodded and kissed me before rolling over and falling asleep.

I knew, though, that I wasn't ready. I had only anger and sadness, and I needed some clarity. Direction. I kept thinking of Reverend Edson and what he had told me. He said to think about what I was asking of them. What *was* I asking of them? I still didn't know.

~

The next day at Mass, my mind was still racing. Nothing felt adequate. My people needed something large. Something significant. I was still thinking of these things when we left the church. I was looking down at my feet, and when I looked up, my heart nearly stopped.

Standing at the fence, arms crossed, waiting, was Ronan.

I ran to him and gathered him into a tight hug. He didn't try to push me away. He let me hug him. When I did finally pull away, he said, "Don't be too excited. I'm not staying."

I looked at him, confused. "What do you mean?"

"They promoted me at the railway," he said. "My wages are higher now. But I didn't tell Aunt and Uncle." He smiled. "I'm saving it for myself. To do with it what I'd like. Come visit you sometimes."

I felt a stab of disappointment. But still. Ronan was here, with us, if only for a day.

"I'm glad you've come," I said, smiling.

Emmett and Mr. Joyce came up behind us. Emmett slapped Ronan on the back and shook his hand.

"Ronan!" he exclaimed.

"He's come to visit us," I said, so Ronan wouldn't have to explain again. "Just for today."

Emmett smiled big. "That's great news," he said. "Mr. Joyce is making his famous boiled ham. You'll love it."

Ronan nodded, still grinning. I hadn't seen him this happy in so long.

"I'm Mr. Joyce," Mr. Joyce said, reaching out his hand. Ronan shook it.

"It's nice to meet you, Mr. Joyce," Ronan said.

I put my arm around his shoulder as we walked home.

"Can I see the dog?" Ronan asked, shyly.

"Of course," I said. "Cocoa's getting big now. She loves everyone. And eats as much as a horse."

He smiled bigger. Suddenly, he looked like a child again. I wanted to make him see how wonderful life could be here, with us. I decided then that it would be my purpose that day. And maybe next time he came, he would stay for good.

We had dinner first. It was delicious, and Emmett and Mr. Joyce both told stories afterward, while we drank our tea. Ronan sat on the floor with Cocoa, who knew instinctively that Ronan was hers. I had been telling her about Ronan nearly every day since I'd claimed her, but it still made my heart swell to watch her fall asleep in his lap without hesitation. He stroked her head and stared at her sleeping face while he listened. Every so often he would look at the storyteller and laugh.

We put our coats on later in the afternoon and took Cocoa to the park. Emmett and Mr. Joyce intuitively understood the game I was playing and played along and played it well. Emmett bought Ronan a treat from the bakers. Mr. Joyce found sticks for Ronan and Cocoa to play fetch with. When Cocoa lay down for a rest, Mr. Joyce pointed out the different types of birds to Ronan and showed him where he knew a family of rabbits to live.

When the sun started to set and the sky started to

change colors, Ronan's face started to tense up again. He kicked at a weed in the ground.

"I've got to get back for supper," he said.

I nodded and tried to look as cheerful as possible. If I became sad, it would ruin the whole day, and he might not visit again.

"We'll walk you to the train," I said.

Ronan looked down. "All right," he said, quietly.

Cocoa was more obvious about her feelings. She walked close to Ronan on the way to the train and kissed his face eagerly when he bent down to say goodbye.

"I'll see you soon, all right?" he told her. "Be good for Rosaleen. I promise I'll come back."

Cocoa whined but wagged her tail slowly.

"Now I know you'll be back," I said to him as he hugged me next. "You can't lie to her."

"No," he said, laughing. "I can't."

Then he shook Emmett's hand and Mr. Joyce's.

"It was good to see you, Emmett," Ronan said. "Thanks for taking care of Rosaleen."

I hid a smile. He sounded so sweet trying to be grown.

"Anything for you, mate," Emmett said, grinning.

"Thank you for dinner, Mr. Joyce," Ronan said. "I had a wonderful day. Truly."

"Come back and see us soon," Mr. Joyce said.

Ronan nodded, turned, and boarded the train. Cocoa whined again and sat next to me. I patted her head.

"I know, girl," I said. "I'll miss him, too."

Chapter Twenty-Five

T hat night, I wrote another letter to Angel. I thought of what Emmett and I had talked about on our way to Boston. About how much Angel still had to learn about the world and how much she already knew.

Dear Angel,

Did you know that some animals used to live long ago, but they no longer exist? There are people who collect their old, preserved bones and study them. These people are called paleontologists. They try to put the bones back together, like a puzzle, so they can know how the animals looked.

One of these paleontologists was a woman named Mary Anning. She found a lot of these fossils (that's what the old bones are called) by the ocean. She was very good at finding them. I have some sketches that she made. I copied one below. It is believed to be the first flying creature. I hope you like it.

All my love,
Rosaleen

. . .

The sketch I included wasn't nearly as good as Mary Anning's, but it would do. I folded the letter and tucked it into my coat pocket to bring to the post office the next day.

I slept well that night, the joy of the day still inside me. I hoped it would stay with Ronan, too. I hoped it would power him through the week.

On my way to work the next day, I saw Nessa. She was grinning and giddy, and she ran to me.

"I have news for you," she said.

"Well, good morning to you, too," I said. "I see you're about to burst. Go on. Tell me."

"Quinn has asked to marry me!" she said.

My eyebrows went up.

"I know what you're going to say," she said, quickly, before I could reply. "But I'm turning seventeen next week, and Quinn is being paid very well now. It will be a relief for my family. My wages can go to them without them having to feed or house me. Quinn and I might even be able to buy our own house in a year or two."

She was right, of course. It would be a relief for her family.

"Well, it seems to me that you truly love him," I said. "If he treats you as he should, then I'm happy for you."

She linked her arm through mine as we waited to enter the mill.

"He does," she said. "He really does love me."

"Have you set a date?" I asked.

She nodded, excitedly. "January 30 of the new year," she said. "A little more than two months away. Ma wants me to wear her dress. Can you believe she kept it all this time and brought it here? I knew she was sentimental, but I'm appalled that she let us all starve before selling it."

I laughed. "There are quite a few of you McHugh children," I said. "Maybe she knew it would hardly help, even if she did sell it."

Nessa shrugged. "Perhaps," she said. "Will you go with me to the seamstress to get it altered?"

"I would love to," I said. "When are you going."

"Tomorrow," she said. "After our shift."

"I'll be there," I said.

She smiled and cheerfully hopped to the doorman, showing him her mill identification card.

Nessa's good mood rubbed off on me, and I spent the rest of the workday in relatively high spirits. When I got home that night, Mr. Joyce handed me a letter.

I ripped it open, hoping it was from Marie before realizing I'd forgotten to write her. I told myself I would after reading whatever was in my hands.

Dear Rosaleen,

Thank you for alerting me to this absolute atrocity. To think these people consider themselves humanitarians—and then do this! I am truly horrified. I looked into the matter, and it turns out this is not only happening in Lowell, but across the state. Something must be done.

I have already begun writing letters to the legislature and have encouraged my acquaintances to do the same. I am not sure if they will or not. Some are frankly too anti-Catholic for my liking, but I must keep them close for other reasons. If there is a more specific need you can think of, do let me know.

We will make them stop this nonsense. Don't lose hope.

Fondest wishes,

Miss Martha Collins

I sighed and folded the letter back up. Miss Martha's letters and those of people she knew certainly held more weight than mine. I was grateful, and yet, I felt it wasn't enough. I didn't know what else to ask her for. I wrote Marie.

Dearest Marie,

I can confirm the deportations are happening. I saw it with my own eyes, and it was terrible. That is why we were in Boston. That is why I was too overcome with emotion to say much of anything. I am sorry I couldn't speak of it then. Soon all the Irish here will know and my anger and fear will be shared.

Emmett, Mr. Joyce, and I no longer visit the taverns. We don't dare.

Next time I see you, we will have a long chat about it all. Pray for me. I know you always do.

All my love,

Rosaleen

The seamstress was located on the outskirts of town, south of the city. We crossed the bridge at the largest canal, the Pawtucket, and then passed the train station.

We passed the South Common and the grammar school. The River Meadow Brook flowed to meet our path behind the homes and shops at Thorndike Street. We turned just slightly right as Thorndike turned into Gorham Street. On the corner to our right sat a much smaller mill than the large ones along the river where we worked. This mill produced lumber and flour, and the surrounding area was still full of farms with only a dotting of stores. This must have been what Lowell was like before the streets became suffocated with people and large-scale factories.

"Why *this* seamstress?" I asked Nessa. "There are plenty closer. This is quite out of the way."

"Quinn's ma knows the owner," Nessa said. "Apparently she's the best."

The seamstress shop sat diagonal from the mill. A dry goods grocer was at another corner, and at the furthest corner, a family doctor. The seamstress shop was small. So small I might have thought nothing of it passing by. It was wooden and plain, and the sign—which simply said Seamstress—was only visible once you were right up at the door.

Nessa patted down her ma's wedding dress as I opened the door. Two women sat at two sewing machines, one on the left side of the room and the other on the right. The woman sitting to the left was nearest the door, and she was a petite, healthy-sized woman nearing forty years of age. Her skin was a deep, warm brown, and her round eyes regarded us with apprehension.

"Can I help you, ladies?" she asked.

"I need to have my ma's wedding dress altered," Nessa

said. Then she turned to the white woman, sitting at the far table. "Are you Mrs. Townsend?" she called loudly.

"One moment!" the white woman called.

The Black woman looked back down at her work, carefully moving the seam of a pant leg through the sewing machine. When she finished, she took the pants with her as she walked to the back of the room, folding them carefully onto a table. Nessa shifted her ma's dress to drape over her other arm.

The Black woman brought a dress back to her workstation. It was a beautiful scarlet silk. She used a needle and thread this time to work on some small imperfection on the sleeve. Nessa, meanwhile, was getting impatient.

"Can *you* help us?" she asked the Black woman.

"No, ma'am," she said. Then she stood up, took the dress and few more things with her, and left through a door in the back.

Nessa looked at me, confused. I shrugged.

"She looked awfully busy," I said.

Mrs. Townsend spoke up. "She is, and that's because she's excellent at what she does. Her name is Esther, and she doesn't work with Irish folks."

"Why not?" Nessa demanded, clearly offended.

"Because of how you all treat her," she said. "I don't blame her one bit. To tell you the truth, I rarely take Irish clients anymore, either. But I'll make an exception for Quinn's bride."

Nessa's cheeks got red. I couldn't tell if she was angry, embarrassed, or both.

"Thank you, ma'am," I said, to fill Nessa's silence.

I knew Nessa didn't want to be close with the Yankees,

but now that she was marrying Quinn, she at least needed to hold her tongue.

Finally, Mrs. Townsend stood up, folded the dress she was working on, and put it aside. She walked toward us, and I was surprised how young she looked. She had long, straight blond hair, pulled back at the nape of her neck, tied with a royal-blue bow. Her eyebrows arched high naturally, making her look permanently surprised. She pointed to a curtain at the back of the room, in the corner opposite the door Esther had walked through.

"You can change into the dress there," she said.

Nessa nodded and said, "Yes, ma'am," very quietly.

Mrs. Townsend crossed her arms and stared at me while we waited for Nessa.

"And you are?" she asked

"Rosaleen," I said. "I used to be Nessa's roommate at the boardinghouse."

She nodded. "Well, your hat is lovely," she said.

I smiled and touched it. "Thank you."

I thought about how guilty I had felt buying that hat the previous month. It was a deep purple bonnet with a simple gray bow. I had been eyeing it for quite some time. Every time I passed the store, I looked at it longingly. But I was not an extravagant person. I was practical, and I didn't need a new hat yet. Even still, one week after paying Mr. Joyce the small amount of rent he allowed us to contribute, I bought the hat. I would never have been able to afford it without Mr. Joyce's generosity. Mairead could never buy a hat like it.

Nessa stepped out from behind the curtain with the cream-colored dress hanging from her thin frame. The sleeves came to her elbows, and a blue bow was tied below her small breasts. Barely visible white flowers had been stitched into the neckline.

"It's beautiful," I said. Although she would be cold wearing that dress in January. Perhaps I would buy her a warm shawl, I thought.

Mrs. Townsend picked up some pins from her workstation and hurried over. First, she pulled some material from the top of the shoulders and pinned it. Then she worked her way down the back of the dress, pulling and pinning as she went.

"I'll help you get out of this," she said when she was done. Nessa nodded and the two of them disappeared behind the curtain.

I turned to look out the front window. The sun was nearly set, with only a faint hue illuminating the streets. I looked in each direction, up and down the street, but saw no lampposts. We would need to hurry home.

Nessa came out looking nothing like the happy bride I'd seen yesterday, but rather like she might start to cry. I grabbed her hand.

"Thank you, Mrs. Townsend," I said. "When should we be back to get the dress?"

"It'll be ready at the end of December," she said, carefully setting the pinned dress on the back table with the other clothes waiting to be fixed.

"We will be back then," I said, opening the door for Nessa. I kept hold of her hand as we started back.

"Are you all right?" I asked.

"I s'pose," she said. "I just hate how people treat Quinn." I couldn't see her face well, but she wiped her face and I believed she was crying a bit. "He's supposed to be grateful that they treat him like one of them. But they don't. Not really. He's to fall all over himself in gratitude over the scraps they allow him."

She paused again but I knew she wasn't finished. Just thinking.

"And now I have to act that way, too," she said. "I wish I could've gone to Mrs. Toole. She's a perfectly adequate seamstress."

"I know," I said. "It's difficult not to hate them back. But remember what Father Purcell said. Let it be *their* hate that eats at *their* heart and not at yours."

A few days later, Emmett came home from work in a rush. He looked upset and frantic.

"Patrick's been arrested," he said. "We've got to go to the jail and get him out."

I grabbed my coat right away.

"What for?" I asked

"Drunkenness," he said.

"I thought he knew not to go to the taverns."

Emmett only shook his head. I could see the anger in his eyes. We walked quickly to the jail. The air was getting bitter. The last few days had been particularly cold, and now the sun was setting.

I prayed that Abner Keyes would not be working that night, but he was. I could see the stupid sneer on his face as soon as we entered. As if he sat there all night just hoping that desperate Irish people would come storming in looking for a friend or family member. Tonight, it was us granting his wish.

Emmett looked as though he couldn't care one bit who was sitting there. If it were the devil himself, Emmett would have been prepared to negotiate something.

"Patrick Clifford," Emmett said to him, leaning forward with both hands on the desk. "We're here to bail him out."

But Abner Keyes wasn't looking at Emmett. He was looking at me.

"Rosaleen," he said. "It's so nice to see you. Something about those eyes. I can't forget them. It's almost like you come looking for me."

Emmett's face got red with anger.

"It's quite the opposite, I assure you," I said.

"So, it's your friends that can't get enough of me," he said. "But I knew that already. No respect for our laws. Our morals. Our way of life."

"We aren't here to chat," Emmett said.

Then Abner Keyes did look at Emmett.

"Is this your beau, Rosaleen?" he asked, looking Emmett up and down.

"Her husband," Emmett answered through gritted teeth.

A smile broke out across Abner's face.

"How lovely," he said. "Now, let me look here in this logbook for your Paddy. He isn't *the* Paddy, is he? Wouldn't that be a catch?"

My heart banged so loudly in my chest that it reached my ears. But Emmett kept his cool.

"Clifford," Emmett said again. "Patrick Clifford." He stood up straight and crossed his arms over his chest. He stared at Abner in disgust as Abner leisurely flipped through the logbook.

"Yes, cell three," Abner said. "That will be two dollars."

Emmett rummaged in his pocket and pulled out two notes. He slapped them down on the desk. Abner was still smiling as he collected the notes and stood up.

"You two wait here," Abner said.

"You know this man?" Emmett asked me when Abner left.

I nodded. "From the bridge. And from visiting Frank when he was here. He's everywhere. Don't you remember him from our wedding celebration? He was the one who closed down the tavern."

"No," Emmett said. "*They* all look the same to me. Nasty swine. Is he the one who threatened you, too?" I nodded and watched Emmett's jaw clench.

Abner reappeared a minute later with Patrick close behind, towering at least a head above Abner. His eyes and nose looked red.

"Thanks, mate," he murmured to Emmett.

We had turned to leave when Abner said, "Don't forget your court date, Paddy. Three weeks from yesterday."

I turned back around. "Court date?" I asked. "For drunkenness?"

"Oh, yes," Abner said. "If you end up here, then you'll end up there. Everyone has their day in court."

I looked at Emmett. They wouldn't sentence someone to the poor farm for one drunkenness arrest, would they? I wasn't about to ask, so I turned back around and we left.

"What were you thinking?" Emmett yelled at Patrick.

"Shona and I got in a fight," Patrick said. "A big fight.

She wants to get married, but I want to save up first. She thinks it's an excuse. We yelled. She cried. And I needed a drink."

"So come to our house," Emmett said. "Drink there."

"The company at the tavern is more . . ." Patrick started, trying to think of the appropriate word, ". . . comforting."

"Bloody hell, Pat," Emmett said. "You don't need that sort of company."

We were at Patrick's now. We stopped at the stairs leading to his door.

"I don't see what the big fuss is about," Patrick said. "The poor farm is supposed to be a treat, isn't it? A room, rent-free. A bed. Three meals."

Emmett looked like he wanted to hit him, but instead, he got real close to Patrick's face.

"Promise me you will not go to the taverns again," Emmett said, his voice shaking in frustration.

"Fine," Patrick said. "But that poor man Doyle is going to have to shut his tavern down. It isn't fair what they're doin' to him!"

I grabbed Patrick's arm.

"Say that again," I said.

Emmett and Patrick looked at me, suspiciously.

"About Doyle's?" Patrick asked.

"Yes," I said.

He glanced at Emmett before answering me.

"Gettin' us to avoid the taverns like this," he said. "They won't be able to stay open for much longer. It's wrong. That's their livelihood."

My face lit up with a huge smile.

"You're a genius, Patrick," I said. I kissed Emmett on the

cheek. "I've got to go," I said, before hurrying back to our house.

"What's with her?" I heard Patrick ask.

I knew now. I knew what I needed to ask of them.

First, I wrote to Miss Martha, hoping she could provide what I asked. Without it, I wasn't sure my plan would work.

I quickly folded it and addressed it. Emmett walked in as I tucked it into my apron.

"What was that about?" Emmett asked.

I nodded in the direction of Mr. Joyce, who was sitting at the table near the kitchen reading the newspaper and sipping tea.

Emmett walked closer to me. "Are you going to do it now?" he whispered.

"Yes," I said.

"Good," he said. "I can't stand to hear another friend talk of the poor farm as if it's a palace."

I stood up and kissed him and then walked to the kitchen to pour myself some tea. I paced as I sipped it, trying to gather my thoughts. Then I sat back down and started to write. The words flowed, and I let the anger I had buried bubble back up to my heart, down my arm, and out of my pen.

When I was finished, I reread what I had written. I looked up at Emmett. His eyes hadn't left me. I raised my eyebrows and smiled. He took my invitation and came over to read it, too. I watched his face as he read. His eyes narrowed and he nodded along. As he neared the end, a smile crept onto his face.

"I love it," he whispered. "But how?"

I took my letter to Miss Martha out again, unfolded it, and let him read that one, too.

"I hope it works," he said. "Are you ready for this?"

I stared into his eyes with a burning determination.

I said, "I'm ready."

Chapter Twenty-Six

F riends and neighbors,
    It is no secret that the city of Lowell denies the Irish our
dignity. They refuse us respectable jobs and fair wages. The
police round us up as if we are cattle, take us to jail, force
burdensome bail and false charges upon us, and then, sentence us
to hard labor at the poor farm. None of this is a secret.

THE SECRET IS THIS: They have been taking your loved
ones from the poor farm and forcing them onto ships. Ships that
take them back across the sea, back to Ireland. Where we left
only hunger and disease behind. Your fathers, daughters, sons,
brothers, and mothers are being sent to their deaths. Without a
penny in their pockets. Without a word to you. Never again to
return to your loving embrace.

The city of Lowell does not publicly acknowledge these sins.
They are done under a veil of secrecy. As our obedient feet
quietly shuffle to work each and every day to enrich this town,
they conspire against us.

We will not be cast out as lepers from the town that WE built!
March on city hall TODAY and demand that these unlawful

deportations stop NOW! Do not go to your jobs. Do not visit Yankee shops. Until this ends, we will force them to go without our hard work. Without our business. We will give them what they wish for: a Lowell without the fruits of Irish labor.

We will not be violent, but we will not be quiet. We will go to city hall today, and tomorrow, and every day until it ends! Stand with me!

Signed,

A Paddy

Two mornings later, Mr. Joyce sat back in his chair when he finished reading the letter in the newspaper. His eyes were wide, and he rubbed his chin in thought. Emmett and I ate our breakfast quietly, glancing occasionally at one another in anticipation.

"This is reckless," Mr. Joyce finally said. "There will be nothing to help these people while they lose their wages and go without. How do we know this is even true?"

I stared at the last bites of egg on my plate. I knew Mr. Joyce did not always support Paddy, but I knew that I needed his support now. And he was much more likely to support *me*.

"There's something I need to tell you, Mr. Joyce," I said.

"Yes?" Mr. Joyce asked, lowering the paper enough to look me in the eyes.

"We know that it's true," I started, looking down at my plate again, hoping to find some courage there. "Because we saw it happen with our own eyes." Then I looked up at him. "I am 'a Paddy,' and I'm sorry I've kept it from you for so long."

He studied me, concerned. His eyebrows furrowed. The room was silent. Chewing ceased. None of us moved.

"You," he said. "A Paddy." Then he looked at Emmett. "You knew?"

"Yes, sir," Emmett said.

Mr. Joyce slammed his newspaper down, stood up, and walked away from the table. He stood for a long time, staring at the wall, back to us. The silence was almost unbearable.

"My safety became a concern right away," I explained. "I only told who I needed to. But I should have told you, too. Can you forgive me?"

"You should have told me," he said. "But I understand why you didn't. I would have put a stop to it. It's irresponsible and foolhardy."

My face burned. I didn't like it, but I needed to take the scolding. And then I needed to convince him to help us.

"You are right," I said. "It is both of those things. But it is also necessary. I cannot stand aside while human beings are treated so poorly. Not when I have a perfectly good brain and hands that can write. It's all I can do—and I *must* do it."

More silence.

"If you had seen their faces at the docks . . ." I went on. "They were so afraid. So helpless. So beaten down. A boy not much older than Ronan was forced onto a boat all by himself. He was still just a child. He must have been terrified."

His shoulders rose and lowered as he took a deep breath. He turned.

"How do you intend to help these people who will be

without wages?" he asked. His eyes still pierced with disapproval, but his mouth was slightly more relaxed.

"Relief will come soon," I said. "I hope. I am anticipating support from Boston. Until then, perhaps Father Purcell and Father O'Brien will assist. We can expand the soup kitchen for a time. Ask for clothing donations from anyone who can give it."

Mr. Joyce looked at Emmett now.

Emmett shrugged. "Isn't she wonderful, Mr. Joyce?" he asked.

Mr. Joyce fought back a smile briefly, but then he started to laugh.

"I still do not approve," Mr. Joyce said. "But I bet Brianna would have been proud. Come on. We need to talk to the priests now."

We all grabbed our coats, and then I grabbed Mr. Joyce's arm.

"Thank you," I said to him. "I need you."

He pulled me close and hugged me.

"Julia would have been proud, too," he said in my ear.

She was, I thought to myself.

People were already crowding the sidewalk, newspapers in hand, talking loudly. I could feel the anticipation among us all as I walked by them.

Mr. Joyce knocked loudly on the church door. When no one answered at first, he knocked again. Father O'Brien came to the door, looking irritable. He motioned quickly for us to come in.

"Have you seen the Paddy letter, Thaddeus?" Father O'Brien asked.

"Yes," Mr. Joyce said. "We were just discussing it over

breakfast. I propose that we set up relief services here at the church. There is nothing we can do now about the contents of the letter. But we can plan for the inevitable. Once people act, they won't be receiving wages. They'll need food, perhaps clothing. Blankets. Firewood. Tools. Other necessities."

Father O'Brien was shaking his head.

"How long can we help?" he asked us, as if we could answer. "When will landlords begin demanding rent, evicting?"

"How long will it take them to stop this dreadful thing they are doing?" Mr. Joyce retorted. "What have these people done to deserve death sentences? It is barbaric, and I hope that the city will quickly reverse course. Besides, many of our homes are owned by the early Irish, and they will surely understand."

"We will pray that they do," Father O'Brien said.

Just then, Father Purcell appeared at the far end of the church. His robes swished as he strode briskly down the center aisle to put his hand on Mr. Joyce's shoulder.

"The church will help in any way we can," he said. "Put your mind at ease, Thaddeus."

"Yes, Father," Mr. Joyce said.

"We can ask Reverend Edson for the help of St. Anne's if we need it," Father O'Brien suggested. "Theodore has always been a good a friend to the Irish."

Father Purcell nodded.

"Will you be reporting to work today?" Father Purcell asked Mr. Joyce. Mr. Joyce shook his head.

"There will be too much work to do here," Mr. Joyce said.

I saw Father Purcell smile just a little before nodding again.

"We'll be back to help," Emmett said, excusing the two of us. We opened the door to leave. Outside, at least a hundred people had gathered, talking loudly to one another. I paused and turned back to Mr. Joyce and the priests.

"You should see this," I said. All three men followed us out the front door.

A man had climbed the stairs in front of the doors and was standing next to us. He addressed the crowd.

"How do we know these outrageous claims are true?" he shouted. "Where is this Paddy? Is he among us?"

There were murmurs throughout the crowd. I tugged on Mr. Joyce's sleeve and whispered in his ear.

"Tell them Mrs. McDonough's son wrote her a letter," I said. "He was sent to Liverpool and then Ireland. Please tell them."

He pursed his lips but spoke up.

"I've heard from one of our own that it happened to her son," he shouted. "Mrs. McDonough. He was sent back to Ireland."

The man turned to inspect Mr. Joyce.

"Are you the Paddy?" he asked.

Mr. Joyce shook his head. "I am not," he said. "Mrs. McDonough is old. Sometimes her mind is frail. I didn't pay it any mind until I read the letter this morning, like all of you."

Mr. Joyce was lying for me now, I thought. Although he likely did know Mrs. McDonough. He saw the paupers often when serving soup at the church. For many who frequented the soup kitchen, the poor farm was the next logical place to go.

"It's what happened to my ma, too!" Another man yelled in the crowd. We all looked at him. "It must have been! I went lookin' for her yesterday. I couldn't support her no more. She went to the poor farm a few months ago, and I visit her as much as I can. She wasn't there this time. No one would tell me where she was. The keepers told me people come and go all the time. But she wouldn't have left. Not without tellin' me."

More murmurs rippled through the crowd. Then a cry. A woman's loud sob rose above the rest of the noise. It came from a woman holding a child. Not quite a baby anymore. But very young. Another woman went to her and put her hand on her back.

"My husband," the crying woman said. "My husband!" She said it over and over again. A few more women went to comfort and hug her. One took the child, and I saw her small face for just a moment. Her eyes were his. The scene flashed in my mind again. The man who'd crawled onto the boat on his hands and knees. I thought I was going to be sick. Did she somehow know his fate? Or was she only overcome with worry?

"Listen," Emmett spoke now to the crowd. "We might not like what Paddy has to say all the time, but when has he lied to us?"

The murmurs died down. He had their attention.

"He's right about this," he went on. "If every single one of us shows up at city hall, if we refuse to work, if we refuse to purchase their goods and frequent their shops, they'll have to shut it all down. Everything. Father O'Brien and Father Purcell have agreed to help feed and clothe and shelter us all during this trying time. Tell your family and your neighbors that it's all right. They'll get their help. We can do this together. We'll take care of each other."

As I watched him speak, my heart swelled with pride. He was calming them. He was calming me. People were nodding now. Looking at one another with resolve.

"Let's do it, then!" the first man to address the crowd shouted.

"Aye!" a few more cried. Emmett's hand found mine and squeezed it. People began speaking excitedly and passionately to one another and many were hurrying back to their homes. I spotted Mairead coming toward us. I could see her face. It looked tortured.

"Rosaleen," she said, hugging me. "This is terrible. Those poor people! Being left in Ireland, all alone, with nothing? What an awful thing." She shook her head, and I saw tears forming in her eyes. "What if they take Frank?" she asked.

"I know," I said. "I know it's awful. It's a lot to bear. That's why we have to do this. So they can't take Frank, too. Let's put ourselves to work, then. Let's go see the nuns. I'm sure they'll need our help with something."

I put my arm through Mairead's, and we walked to the school together. When I looked back over my shoulder, I saw a small crowd of men forming around Emmett and Dennis, and I felt comforted by the sight.

∼

I could barely keep my eyes open on the walk home that night, but still, while I lay in bed, I ripped open the letter I had received that day.

Dear Rosaleen,

What a grand creature! I wonder what happened to them. Maybe their wings stopped working. This land is dangerous, but in the air, they must have been free. Or maybe that was the problem. Maybe they were so afraid to be trapped in the ark that they refused to come when Noah and God called. That would have been sinful, but I would understand. Please draw me another of these creatures.

Love,

Angel

I could not fight sleep for one more moment, and I fell into a dream that I was flying through treacherous storm clouds, barely able to see through the torrential rain, all while hearing someone calling my name in the distance. "Rosaleen," it called. "Rosaleen, come!" I awoke with a racing heart in the night. It took some time for me to fall back asleep, but when I did, I did not dream again.

On our way to the church the next morning, Patrick came running up to us, all out of breath.

"They've gathered at city hall," he said. "And now the police officers are there, too. Things feel uneasy."

"You go," I said to Emmett. "I'll come soon. I'm going to stop at the church first."

Emmett nodded and kissed me before following

Patrick. I walked briskly in the cold morning air, wrapping my arms tight around myself. I was rounding the corner when someone stepped in front of me. It was Fiona. Her eyes were sharp and focused directly on mine. She spoke in nearly a whisper, but her words were filled with hate.

"It's you," she spat. "I know it is. You're Paddy."

"I'm not sure what you're talking about," I said, trying to walk around her. She stepped to the side, staying with me through every movement I made.

"Here's what you're going to do next so that I don't tell everyone your little secret," she went on, as if she hadn't heard me. "You're going to get Frank out of that place. You're going to get him home to me so that we can be married and so that I won't have to cross the ocean to find him again."

"Fiona, it isn't me," I said. I looked at her. She had looked livid a moment ago, but now, she looked desperate.

"I don't care," she said. "I'll tell everyone it is anyway, and they'll believe me. They'll believe me because they know you're a traitorous slave sympathizer. Get Frank home."

"How do you expect me to do that?" I asked her.

"That part isn't my problem," she said. Her eyes grew wet a second before she stormed off.

Chapter Twenty-Seven

I closed my eyes and steadied my breath. It wasn't only the Irish I had to fear now if I were exposed. The Yankees' anger would be even greater. My head swam. Who would Fiona tell? And would they believe her? I opened my eyes and walked even quicker.

I reminded myself that Fiona had little more power than I. She could say what she wanted, but I had the support of many Irish. And Mr. Joyce and Emmett had already proved they would lie for me.

I felt calmer and more assured by the time I reached the church. Sister Celeste was helping Father O'Brien and Father Purcell address the needs of the community while the other nuns continued to hold class. With parents out of work, they had fewer children attending.

Sister Celeste hurried down the aisle toward me as soon as I entered. She was smiling.

"Good morning, Rosaleen," she said.

"Good morning, Sister Celeste."

"I'm so very proud of our community," she said. "They're doing just what Father Purcell asked of them. They're being proud of who they are. They are standing up to those who would paint them as less than human. It's evil what those city officials are doing. Leaving those people with nothing at all. All alone. Separated from their families." Her smile turned to a frown.

"It is evil," I said. "And we'll put a stop to it."

"Yes," she said, looking down at what she was carrying. It was a list. "I went from door to door last night and this morning asking people what they're worried about. What they will be needing for their families at this time."

"What did they say?" I asked.

"Food, of course," she said. "Coats. Plenty of families still haven't bought new coats. They're hoping their old coat will do. Or hoping the snow will hold off just one more week. Some women need laundry things. Lye soap, for one. The only producer of lye soap in Lowell is a Yankee. With winter coming and illness along with it, they'll be doing their share of scrubbing. Blankets, of course. Clothes for the growing children and babies. They want to know who is missing, too, but I'm not sure I can provide that."

I nodded along but felt my chest tighten. I was asking these people to give up so much at such a critical time.

"I'll see if I can find any donations," I said. "I know a few people on the other side of the city. Maybe they'll find it in their hearts to help."

Sister Celeste grabbed my hand and squeezed it.

"We'll do our best," she said. "And leave the rest to God."

I heard the crowd that was gathered at city hall before I saw them.

"We won't go!" they chanted. "We won't go!"

Emmett stood at the top of the steps, speaking to Calvin. The police officers stood on the outskirts of the crowd, waiting in anticipation for any sign of violence or destruction. Calvin's arms were crossed, and he was looking intently at Emmett, who gestured toward the crowd as he spoke. As I approached, Nancy ran up to me.

"You're not at the school?" I asked.

"Everything is chaotic today," she said. "The children's parents kept them home because they're afraid of violence erupting in the streets. And most of my Irish boys are at home, too."

I looked carefully at Nancy, trying to judge her reaction to all of this. She was watching the crowd, hands on her hips. This was the first time I hadn't told her what I was planning to write. I hadn't kept it from her for any particular reason, though. I wondered if she felt bitter toward me because of it. But then she flashed me a smile, and I knew all was right.

"This might be the most trouble you've caused yet," she whispered. "I'm proud. I'd like to think I had a hand in creating this monster."

I laughed. "A monster?" I asked, incredulously.

She nodded. "Out to destroy the worst and weakest among men."

"Tell your schoolchildren about me," I said. "The silent

banshee. Perhaps they'll fear me and grow up to be honest and just men."

"When did you learn about all of this?" she asked me.

"Only recently," I said, feeling that guilt start to creep back into my stomach. I never would have kept something like this from her when we both lived in the boardinghouse.

"I'm sorry," she said, sighing. "I do wish Calvin could help. I've talked his ear off about it. Asked him one thousand different ways what he could do. He assures me there's nothing. These policies come from people much more important than him."

"Does he see now why they have to stop arresting so many of us?" I asked.

Her gaze wandered back to Calvin and Emmett.

"I hope so," she said. "Sometimes he's difficult to read. He can be quite private in his thoughts. When I pester him about them, he sort of finds a way to disappear."

She looked back at me again.

"But I know he has a good heart," she said. "So I can only hope he finds the courage."

"How is this little one?" I asked, putting my hand on her large belly.

"A kicker," she said. "And giving me stomach pains."

I smiled at her belly and spoke to the baby.

"Quarrelsome like your ma," I said.

She snorted. "I can only hope she'll work with me and not crusade against me!"

I suddenly remembered my conversation with Sister Celeste that morning.

"Do you know of anyone who would be willing to donate some things to us while we wait for this to get sorted?" I asked. I looked around at the multitude of people who had just arrived, standing only feet away. Certainly close enough to hear our conversation. "Paddy asked these people to give up their wages at a most unfortunate time."

Nancy frowned in thought.

"What kind of things?" she asked.

"Coats, blankets, children's clothing, soap," I listed off.

"I'll ask the schoolchildren for old clothing and coats," she said. "They're always growing out of things. I'll make something up about where it's going."

I raised my eyebrows. "And when they see some Irish kid wearing it?" I asked.

She shrugged. "Not much they can do then."

"Other than put you out of a job."

She waved my concerns away. "Don't worry about that," she said. "I'll think of something. I'm clever, you know."

I smiled. "Thank you, Nancy."

"It's really the least I can do," she said. "I feel quite powerless. I can't understand how they hate you all so much. Isn't it exhausting? Haven't they got better things to do than worry that some poor, elderly lady is getting food and shelter from the city? I wish I held more sway. This," she said, sweeping her hand toward the crowd, "is quite smart, by the way."

"I can only hope it'll last long enough. That their will and spirit won't break," I said.

"I know it's difficult. I remember staring at the other mill girls when we would strike, questioning which of them would be the first to cave," she said. "You must trust them. It's the only way."

I nodded. Just then, Calvin and Emmett walked up to us. Calvin kissed Nancy's forehead.

"What are you doing here, darling?" he asked.

"I've come to see Rosaleen," Nancy said. "But already, baby is hungry. I think I ought to eat something. Will you come home for dinner?"

"I'm not sure I'll have time today," he said. He looked over his shoulder at the swelling crowd. "You go on and eat without me. Perhaps I'll be by the house later."

She kissed him and then turned to me. She hugged me the best she could, her belly bumping against mine.

"You can do this," she whispered in my ear.

For some reason, I started to tear up. In doubt or in confidence, I wasn't sure. I felt both and somehow neither. I wiped my eyes when she pulled away, and I watched her walk home alone, disappearing into the crowd and then reappearing again on the other side, where the streets of Lowell were clear and quiet. I looked back at the crowd. At the police officers, scowling at my people.

"Thank you for restraining your men," I said to Calvin. "I see the hunger in their eyes. So many Irish people in one place."

It was a bold thing to say. And yet, it was true. They looked as if they were only waiting for the opportunity, gripping their clubs tightly, scanning the crowd with intense determination. Shifting their weight from one foot to the other with an anxious energy.

"Well, your people are angry," he said. "That Paddy has caused quite a stir. I'm not sure my men feel safe."

I detected some anger in his voice, too.

"And shouldn't they be?" I asked. "If your family fell on hard times, would you want them sent back to wherever they came from?"

"My family came from right here," he said. "This very town."

"Then wherever your grandparents or their grandparents came from," I said.

He shook his head. "They came from here, too. Or the next town over. We're no immigrants," he said. "But I *do* know that I love this town. This is who I am. And I'll do what needs to be done to get it running peacefully again."

I pursed my lips. I knew that until he felt it in his heart, his efforts wouldn't be enough.

"We should be going, too," I said.

Calvin nodded. "I'll keep watch over the crowd, but any sign of violence or destruction and my men will have to act."

I looked at Emmett. He looked uneasy.

"I'll be back after I have some dinner," he said to Calvin. Calvin nodded once and walked back toward the building, back to where he could perch atop the steps and watch the crowd from on high. Emmett and I headed back to our house.

"What now?" he asked.

"I don't know," I admitted.

"We keep our neighbors from burning down the city," he said.

"It'll be easy," I said.

He laughed. "There's nothing too difficult for you."

He put his arm around me, and I leaned into him, already exhausted. We walked silently for a bit, but then I remembered my encounter with Fiona and stiffened back up. The worry washed over me again.

"What's wrong," he asked.

I looked around before answering.

"I saw Fiona this morning," I said. "She threatened to tell everyone that I'm Paddy unless I get Frank out of the poor farm."

We were at the house now. Emmett pulled away and looked at me.

"I told her that I'm not Paddy," I went on. "But she said she didn't care. She's convinced of it, and she'll tell them all anyway."

Emmett crossed his arms and closed his eyes. I saw his jaw clench. He opened his eyes again and sighed. "I knew how dreadful that woman was from the beginning," he said. "It wouldn't be the worst thing if the Irish knew. You're almost a hero today. But the Yankees. The Yankees can't know."

I nodded. "Good thing Fiona doesn't know any Yankees," I said.

He stared at me. I could see he was worried, but nothing else was said and we went inside. Mr. Joyce had a letter for me.

Dearest Rosaleen,

Ruth and I are coming with funds on Tuesday. Meet us at the rail station at noon. You've made a right mess this time. I trust

you, but I'm worried. I know God is guiding you. Don't do
anything stupid until then.
 All my love,
  Marie

I laughed with relief. Marie was coming. The funds were
coming.

Chapter Twenty-Eight

The next day, I left Emmett to deal with the rowdy crowd at city hall so I could meet Marie and Ruth. I was giddy with excitement. Miss Martha had pulled through! I got to the train station early and braided my hair as I waited for them. My hair was an unruly mess and needed to be washed, but I had barely had time to eat over the previous two days, let alone wash my hair. I tied the end with a ribbon and smoothed it down as I looked up and down the train tracks. Finally, in the distance, I saw the train approaching.

Marie got off first, and we embraced tightly. When she pulled away, I noticed her smile was strained. I held her hands and pulled her close again.

"Are you all right, Marie?" I whispered into her ear. She nodded. I wanted to ask her more, but Ruth was standing beside us, beaming. I turned and hugged her.

"Oh, Rosaleen," Ruth said, squeezing me tight. "It's so wonderful to see you!" Neither Marie nor I was short. And yet Ruth towered over us both.

"You as well, Ruth," I said. "It's been so long."

She looked me up and down.

"You look lovely," she said. "All things considered."

I smiled. "I look haggard," I said. "I've been trying to calm tempers around here."

She nodded and looked around to see who was listening. "Well, I hope what I've brought today alleviates some of that."

"It will," I assured her. "I can't thank your family enough. How did you do it?"

"You know Mother," she said, smirking. "She stormed right into a meeting of the Charitable Irish Society and told them that you all needed their help. And that if *you all* weren't Irish enough for them, then neither was *she*. And neither was her money! Their faces turned pearl white."

I laughed. "Your mother is a treasure," I said. "No matter how long I live, I'll never be able to repay her."

"Oh, stop that," Ruth said. "You know she doesn't expect that."

"I know," I said.

"So . . ." Ruth looked around again. "What should we do with the money?"

"I think we ought to take it to the church," I said. "I don't want to be responsible for it. They'll use it wisely. I trust them. How much is it?"

Ruth lowered her voice. "It's enough to last you all at least a month. Hopefully this will be sorted by then. If not, Mother will find you more. She's working diligently to sway the community. She's been writing articles. Talking about the recent attacks on the church. Reminding them of our duty to the poor of all nations. Now that's she's gotten the personal liberty laws to pass, she's entirely focused on this."

Words caught in my throat. I was moved that we meant so much to her. I nodded and managed to say, "Thank you, Ruth."

She squeezed my hand.

"Show me the way to the church," she said.

I took Marie's hand, too, and we made our way to the Acre. It wasn't every day that a Black woman, an Irishwoman, and a Yankee walked arm and arm through the Acre. Its inhabitants were dumbstruck. Words failed them at first, but the sudden quiet, the stillness that froze each passerby in place, was laced with hatred and disgust. The apprehension grew with each step until finally someone shouted at us. It was Fiona.

"Oh, look!" Fiona said. "It's Rosaleen's nigger friend! She doesn't look like anything special to me. Just like the rest of them. Useless. Dirty. Dumb."

That terrible woman. First threatening me and now taunting us. I turned and started toward her, but Marie gripped my arm and pulled me back.

"Don't," she said, sternly. "I appreciate that you would rip her head off. I see it in your eyes. But not today. You've put yourself in a load of trouble, and we don't need any more of it."

I looked around. People crowded around us, staring, blocking our way forward. It wasn't exactly a secret that I was an abolitionist. But this. This was bold even for me. I gripped Marie's hand even tighter.

"Please," I said, as loudly as I could. "Let us pass. These women have come to help."

A man in front of us spit on the ground. "Bollocks," he said. "No Yankee ever did care about an Irish person before. And we don't need *her* help. She needs to leave. Now." He raised a steady finger and pointed it at Marie.

I heard Marie's breath quicken next to me. I wanted badly to protect her. It hurt me that I had brought her into this. And worse, I hadn't thought about it first. I was too concerned with my own problems.

"No, sir," I said, trying to stay calm. "She won't. She's with me. We're just passing through."

Fiona walked up to us, sneering. "I'd like to see you try to pass through, *Biddy*," she said, quietly. Then she turned to the small crowd behind her.

"Make 'em leave!" she shouted. The people started talking amongst themselves. There were layers of people now. Mostly women, but some men scattered throughout.

"Get out!" a woman shouted from the back of the crowd. I looked at Marie. Her jaw was clenched. She scanned the people in front of us.

"We're only here to help!" Ruth shouted back. "Let us—" Then, something smacked Ruth on the side of her face, interrupting her. It was a dirty cloth. Her mouth opened in disbelief as she touched her face. A couple of boys ran away, giggling.

Suddenly, out of the corner of my eye, I saw another, much larger man walking swiftly toward us. It was Mr. Joyce.

"What is this about?" he asked, parting the crowd.

"Mr. Joyce," the man before me said. "I know this is your girl. Tell her we don't allow *these* kinds of people in the Acre."

"Let's go," Marie said, quietly but firmly.

"What?" I asked.

"Let's go," she repeated. "I can't stand here and wait for these people to attack me."

She took a step forward, head held high, practically dragging the two of us along with her. Past the men speaking. Past Fiona. I felt the hot stares, but no one touched us. I didn't hear the rest of the conversation. I didn't look back. None of us did.

I started to shake with anger and with shame. I wanted to say something. But nothing felt adequate. Ruth and Marie were quiet, too. Before we reached the church, Ruth finally spoke.

"That certainly could have been ugly," she said, finally taking the time to wipe her face with her handkerchief.

Marie laughed then. Ruth and I looked at her with surprise.

"I suppose I should have warned you both," Marie said. She shook her head. "It's not as if I would walk my Black face through the North End or through East Boston either."

"Marie," I said, nearly in tears. "I don't know why I didn't think of it. I feel like a fool."

She shrugged. "We made it. No one is hurt."

Ruth smiled, seemingly reassured. "Let's do what we came to do," she said as she opened the gate at St. Patrick's.

I watched my feet as we walked down the path. Of course Ruth didn't feel as I did. Ruth's loyalty was not with this community. Even though Irish blood ran through her veins, these were not her people. She couldn't understand them, and I didn't blame her. And Marie. Marie continued to love me even though these *were* my people. It made me feel sick.

~

Father Purcell was shocked when Ruth handed him the money.

"A gift from the Charitable Irish Society in Boston," she said, smiling sweetly.

He looked from the money back to Ruth, then to Marie and me.

"Th-thank you," he stammered. "This is . . . quite generous."

"We appreciate what you all are trying to do here," Ruth said. "It's plain wrong what they're doing with the inmates. We hope that this donation helps bring about change."

"We will use it wisely," Father Purcell said.

"Thank you, Father," I said.

We left the church, arm in arm again. We hurried out of the Acre, trying to ignore the grumbles and occasional shouts that were surely directed at us.

"I have an address here," Ruth said as we crossed the bridge toward city hall. "I'm to pay Mrs. Hopwell a visit. She wrote us a rather strange and somewhat funny letter about how surprisingly helpful you've been to the antislavery society."

I sighed. "She sure was surprised that I could be useful. It was a small thing. I only volunteered to be a resource for the police officers about the personal liberty laws and how they are to change because of them."

"Well, she certainly was not expecting that," Ruth said.

"Anyhow, mother would like me to meet her. Would you like to come?"

I glanced at Marie. "No, thank you," I said. "I would rather take a walk with Marie. Is that all right with you, Marie? Or were you hoping to visit Mrs. Hopwell?"

"We can take a walk," Marie said.

"Of course," Ruth said. "Just point me in the direction of . . ." She trailed off as she dug in her coat pocket to retrieve the address.

"Two hundred and twelve Tyler Street," I finished for her. "I remember it clearly because she was so reluctant to give it to me. It's in that direction." I pointed south, back toward the train station.

"Truly?" Ruth asked. I nodded. She rolled her eyes. "I hope she's not as dimwitted as she sounds. I'll meet you both back at the train station in one hour."

I hugged her before she walked away. Marie and I walked down Dutton Street, away from city hall, toward the mills. Neither of us said anything for a while. Finally, I spoke up.

"I'm so sorry, Marie," I said. "I should have known that bringing you into the Acre would be dangerous. Are you angry with me?"

She shot me an exasperated look.

"I'm not angry with you, Rosaleen," she said. "I'm sorry that you're upset. But this is my life. I have to be careful about where I find myself. Always. You might be hurt by what happened today, but I was not surprised one bit. I knew to expect it, and I came anyway. I wanted to see you. I wanted to help you."

I sighed. "How am I to work with them? How am I to forgive them?"

"Don't worry about them right now," she said. "The bears are your concern today, not the wolves. On the one hand, it is smart what you did. They'll be forced to address the deportations now. You were brave, and I'm proud of you. On the other hand, you've poked the bears. They'll be after you for this. Even after the deportations have stopped. They'll still be looking for you."

Her eyebrows were all the way up, and she looked at me intently to see if I understood.

"I had to," I said. "I watched them force those people onto ships. They'll never be able to come back. They'll never again see their families. They might even die."

"I know," Marie said, sighing. "I know. It happens to my people, too, remember? Every day. Gil thinks these personal liberty laws will protect him. I'm not so sure. Masters who haven't seen their slaves in years and years are itching to come up here and steal them. What if this new law provokes them even more? What if they want to test it? What if Gil's old master wants to test it? How can I even think about starting a family with him if he might get snatched away?"

I stopped walking.

"Are you thinking about starting a family?" I asked.

Marie smiled the first true smile I had seen from her that day. She nodded.

"But every time I even begin to think about it, to try to plan a wedding or find a home for us, I get knots in my stomach," she said. "True happiness is so close, Rosaleen.

It's within my reach. I've always wanted my own family. To be a mother. But now that it's here, I'm so afraid."

"I can't tell you it's going to be all right," I said. "I tried that once. I know you don't allow lies. Even well-intentioned ones."

"Huh!" she laughed.

"But marrying or not marrying Gil wouldn't make it hurt any more or any less if he did get taken," I said.

Marie looked down at her feet. "I know that," she said. "But if we have a child, that's another heart that will be broken. And it's no good to raise a child without their daddy."

I looked at Marie, standing in front of me, arms crossed, eyes down. She was biting her lip. Her fingernails pressed into her arm. I had never seen her so tormented. And I knew it had nothing to do with what happened that morning.

"What do you always tell me?" I asked her. "You have to do what's in your heart. And give the rest to God."

I watched a single tear fall from her eye and crawl down her cheek.

"It's going to take courage," I went on. "But you're the bravest person I know."

Chapter Twenty-Nine

I stood watching the spot on the horizon where the train had disappeared long after Marie and Ruth had left. I felt the weight of the last few days holding me in place. Anchoring me to this platform that allowed me to be in between. Not leaving and not staying. Nothing was expected of a person standing at a train station. I closed my eyes and tried to absorb some of Ruth's positivity, hoping she had left even a drop of it behind. Then I took a deep breath and started back toward city hall.

Emmett looked awful. I needed to give him a break. He had been the dumping ground for any and all concerns that day. Oddly enough, no one seemed to question whether he was Paddy or not. He was simply too likeable, I realized. People refused to believe that someone like him disagreed with them about anything. They gravitated toward him and hoped they were like him, too.

He smiled a big, tired smile when he saw me.

"How are Marie and Ruth?" he asked.

"The neighborhood didn't exactly welcome Marie," I said. "But we took the money to the church anyway."

"And there's enough?" he asked.

"There's enough," I said.

He looked relieved.

"Go," I said to him. "Go home. Have dinner. Sleep for a bit."

"I can't, Rose," he said.

"I'll stay," I said. "Your faithful and loving wife. They'll trust me in your place."

He looked out at the crowd. "I don't know," he said. And then a moment later, "All right. If you insist. Send Pat for me if you need anything at all."

I kissed him. "I can manage," I said.

He turned from me and disappeared into the crowd. My attention turned to the men and women. Some were chanting, some chatting with one another. Some were simply taking up space in this city. Forcing those passing by to notice them. At times, they sang. A few prayed together. It was nearing sunset when three men approached me.

"You're Emmett's wife, right?" one of them asked.

"Yes," I said. "That's right."

"We want to talk with the mayor," another one said.

"Or someone who makes decisions in this city," the first said. "We want to state our terms. Do you know who we can talk to?"

I looked at the three of them. They looked sincere and determined, but their clothes were torn. They stunk. The city would be disgusted to have to negotiate with these men. With any of us, truthfully.

"I'll see what I can do," I said.

Behind me, at the door to city hall, were two police officers. My eyes wandered to the edge of the steps. Two more officers stood there, level with the crowd. One was Quinn, looking rather nervous. The other was Abner Keyes. His eyes were scanning the crowd and caught mine. He had fire behind those eyes, and he smiled at me. It looked like a promise. It made me shiver. I turned away and hoped he would do the same.

I walked toward the doors of city hall. I recognized one of the police officers from the first time Nessa and I went to the jail to see Frank. He was leaning up against the wall, next to the door, reading a newspaper. The headline read: The Angel Gabriel Incites Riots in New York.

"Excuse me, sir," I said to him. "Some of the men here would like to speak with a representative of the city."

"And they sent a little lady to tell me?" he asked, still reading his newspaper.

"They'd like to state their terms," I said.

"Seems to me like this is between the mill owners and you all," he said.

"The city is what will make us go back to work," I said. "The city's policies are what we're concerned with."

The police officer shrugged. "The city isn't concerned with you," he said. "No one from the city wants to speak with any of you."

"You haven't even asked," I said.

He turned the page of his newspaper, ignoring me.

"Now this here," he said, "this is a Negro I like. The Angel Gabriel, they call him. He warned us about you Catholics and the trouble you'd cause."

"Who is the Angel Gabriel?" I asked, vaguely recalling hearing the name before.

"I suppose he's not a full Negro," he said. "One of his parents is white. Scottish, I believe. Anyhow, if he were an American, I'd say he could stay."

"Stay where?" I asked.

"In America, girl," he said. "Aren't you listening? But the rest, I'd send them all back to Africa."

"The other Black people?" I asked.

"Now you're gettin' it," he said.

"I thought you people were abolitionists," I said.

"I Know Nothing of who you speak," he said, smiling widely. "But I sure as hell am no abolitionist in the moral sense. Only in the economic sense. It goes against our way of life to allow Americans to own slaves. It's not what we believe in here. We honor hard work. A man should be able to get what he works for. Nothing more and nothing less. He shouldn't be gettin' rich off the work of slaves."

He stopped talking for a moment and spat a wad of tobacco onto the ground. It landed right next to my foot.

"But that doesn't mean I want to live with them," he said. "I'd put them on a ship and send them back to Africa. Back to where they came from. All of them."

Just like us, I thought. Then I thought of Marie. Back where she came from? She came from Philadelphia. And before that, Virginia. She hadn't come from Africa. She wouldn't know a single soul there. She wouldn't know their language or their customs.

"So you would treat them as property, too," I said. "Only confiscated property."

The officer laughed. "I like the way you think, Biddy," he said.

My stomach turned. I hated this man. If I had ever believed the Know-Nothings had even a drop of goodness in their souls, I didn't now. They were rotten to their core. I turned and walked away.

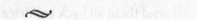

I stared into the pot of boiling water, watching the bubbles rise and pop and feeling the warm steam on my face. Emmett was interrogating me about the day. What had the men done? What did they say? What did I say?

"I told them that the city will arrange a meeting soon," I said.

"Did the city say that?" he asked.

I shrugged. "The officer wouldn't allow me to go into city hall," I said.

"Then why did you tell them that?" he asked.

"I have to give them hope," I said.

"Have you ever thought that hope isn't always yours to give?" he snapped.

My mouth fell open.

"*You're* telling me this?" I asked, disbelievingly. "You who urged me to write the letter? You who urged me not to lose hope?"

"Yes, me!" he shouted. "False hope is not helpful to them. To our friends! To our kin! What will you do when the city refuses to do anything at all? These men will think the city lied, which will hurt our efforts. You've asked our people to do this enormously risky thing. If you can't be honest with them, you should never have told them."

My heart started to beat faster with frustration. I tried to form words to rebuke him, but I was too exhausted and only blood rushed to my brain. I turned and stormed out, stomping loudly down the stairs.

"Ugh!" I shouted as I burst onto the street.

I didn't know where this was coming from. Maybe Emmett was as exhausted as I was. Of course I'd had to lie to the men. Of course I had to give them hope. I had decided to be their leader. If they couldn't deal with the truth of who I was, they couldn't deal with the truth of how impossible this situation was.

And *was* this situation impossible? What if Emmett was right about the city? What if the mills simply found workers elsewhere? Would anyone else work for such poor wages? I had convinced myself that we could force change. But what if we couldn't? What if they found a way around it? What if they threw us all into wagons and brought us all to the docks?

A new sensation started to rush over me: panic. I had no idea what the mills or the city was planning, how they were reacting to this. Who would know, and who would tell me? If Calvin knew anything, I doubted he would share it. He was professional and cordial. And from what Nancy had said, sometimes closed off to his own wife. I doubted I would be able to pry anything out of him but a perfectly crafted response.

I turned the corner and headed to St. Anne's. Surely Reverend Edson would have heard something from someone by now. Even though the mill owners disliked him, he always occupied the right rooms.

It was fully dark now, and the streetlamps were lit. The streets were oddly empty in this part of the city, and I remembered what Nancy had said. The Yankees were truly afraid of our violence. Would that make them more or less likely to meet our demands?

The light that hung above the side door of the church was lit, illuminating the dark wooden knocker. I knocked once, twice, three times, but no one came. The reverend must have been at home with his family. How was his family? I had forgotten to ask lately. I had forgotten about so many things.

I sat on the doorstep with my chin in my hands and elbows on my knees. I wished I had brought Cocoa with me. She would be drifting in and out of sleep now next to the warm fireplace, stomach filled with our supper scraps.

I looked down at a scuff on my left boot and tried to rub it away. It wouldn't come off. I closed my eyes and let the sadness and worry wash over me. I felt like crying. Emmett was supposed to be in this with me, but now he was angry with me. I didn't know what he wanted from me. How could I control their anger and their fears and also be honest with them? He was expecting too much of me.

When I opened my eyes, I noticed a man leaning against a brick wall across the street. He was smoking a pipe and staring at me intently. I froze. From his shiny shoes to his pristinely slicked-back hair, nothing about him said he was Irish. I couldn't look away. I was afraid to take my eyes off of him. He wasn't shy about staring either.

Finally, he tapped the side of his pipe, took one more drag, and then dropped his arm to his side. He tipped his hat to me before standing up and walking off. I searched for a door he might have come out of. A tavern or a smoke shop or a house. But the brick wall stretched for many yards and then only rounded the corner in each direction. There were no doors. Had he followed me? Was he there to watch me? My breath was shallow and still. I dared not move.

Chapter Thirty

I stayed on the step for a long time after he left. When I did eventually head home, I walked briskly, looking over my shoulder often and down every alley that I passed.

Mr. Joyce was fast asleep, but Emmett was still awake. I readied myself for bed and tried not to look at him. I was so hurt that he had scolded me. Especially at a time like this. The air was heavy with frustration.

When I crawled into bed, I pulled the blanket over my shoulders and turned away to look at the wall. I tried to count the cracks. Each one led to another, which led to three more. It was like a roadmap of heartache and desperation sprawled all over that home. Then, Emmett spoke.

"I've never told you about my aunt Emer," he said. "After all this time. I've told you the stories of my brothers and my da and ma. But talking about Aunt Emer has been too difficult."

He paused, and I waited for more.

"I've tried a few times, but I couldn't." His voice broke

with emotion. He cleared his throat a little, and I rolled over to face him.

"She was my world," he said. "She was Da's sister. And her presence more than made up for his absence. Aunt Emer was always right, and she knew it. Her stubbornness infuriated some people, but I adored it. I liked how she always stood up for herself. Even if she went too far sometimes, when she really *was* wrong. It was her only flaw. She was kind and loving and funny and caring. She had endless energy. She would challenge us to all sorts of games. She loved to see us sort out riddles or watch us find solutions to problems. We helped her do everything, because being around her was special. The feeling of a room changed when she entered it."

The tears flowed freely from his eyes as he spoke.

"She was fearless, too," he said. "I think that's why some of my uncles would get angry with her. She wasn't afraid to tell anyone when *they* were wrong. I thought she was untouchable."

I wiped his cheek with my thumb. He held my hand there as he tried to compose himself enough to continue.

"When the potatoes first failed, I would go on long walks with her to find eggs. She could walk all day and never get tired. We would search in trees or in small crevices in the wall along the road. I didn't like taking the eggs because I loved watching the birds, but I knew it was necessary and she assured me they would lay more."

I scooted a little closer to him.

"Then the visitors started to come," he said. "That was after the next season. Those who were already teetering on the edge of homelessness. The poorest ones. That second crop failure was enough to force them out. They might have been going south to Limerick. Or been on their way to family. Aunt Emer took them all in. Even the sickest ones. My brothers and I begged her not to. We had seen people starting to die. Neighbors, friends. But you couldn't tell that woman a thing."

He paused and took a few breaths. He closed his eyes for a few seconds and opened them again. "But she wasn't untouchable. The black fever came for her, too. My ma wouldn't let me see her. But I snuck in anyway. I tried to comfort her, but I could hardly hide my terror of what she had become. I told her she should have listened to us. If only she hadn't been so stubborn. And then she said to me, 'I don't mind. I don't mind dyin' this way. Because at least I helped. At least they weren't alone. None of this is worth it if we do it on our own.' She said, 'Imagine if I hadn't helped them but died anyway. We'll all meet our maker eventually. I want to tell him that I cared for his people, not only for myself.' It was the bravest thing she had ever said. I won't forget it."

He had been looking straight up at the ceiling but now turned to face me.

"I never thought I'd love someone more than Aunt Emer. But I do. I love you a thousand times more. Please, Rosaleen. Please take Aunt Emer's advice. Don't do it on your own. Don't make *them* do it on their own. Those men and women standing next to you out there—they need to be by your side. We can't do it without them. *You* can't do it without them."

I filled the last remaining space between us and rested my head on his shoulder.

"I'm afraid," I said. "I'm afraid of failing. All I've wanted since I started writing was to make some sort of difference. But I look back and can't find evidence of any change. If this fails, too, I'm not sure how I'll keep going."

"You need to trust them," he said. "That's how you'll succeed."

"I'm worried about Frank, too," I said. "And Fiona. A strange man was watching me tonight. A Yankee."

Emmett's eyes narrowed in concern. "What kind of strange man?"

"Dressed well," I said. "Smoking a pipe. He was staring. He tipped his hat to me. What if Fiona has said something?"

"Fiona wouldn't know a man like that," Emmett said.

"I suppose not," I said. "But who was he?"

"Perhaps he's an antislavery man," Emmett said. "You did call attention to yourself at that most recent meeting."

I took a deep breath and hoped it would help dampen my rising fear.

"I wish Mairead and I weren't the only Irish at those meetings," I said. "I know she is frightened to be there, and in truth, I am, too."

"I will come next time," Emmett said. "I'll protect you." He grinned, but I did not feel at ease.

"I already know you're an abolitionist," I went on. "I need *more* Irish. I need others. The rest loathe the cause. Today . . ." I stopped for a moment. Stopped myself from crying, too. I cleared my throat and started again. "Today,

Marie and Ruth and I were almost attacked. People blocked our way. They hollered at us. I thought they were going to hurt Marie. It made me so angry, and yet, I felt so helpless. I'm angry at myself, too. Not only for bringing Marie here, but for failing. Failing so horribly at what I've tried to accomplish as Paddy."

"They wouldn't have hurt her," Emmett said. "They're only afraid of what they don't know. And they're desperate. They're angry with the wrong people. They have nothing. Our people have nothing. How are they to help others when they can barely feed their families? Even if they felt as we do, how are they to act on that? How are they to prove themselves to you?"

"They can start by being kind," I said. "By treating Black people as fellow human beings. And you're wrong about not hurting her. If Mr. Joyce hadn't stepped in, things could have gotten much worse. Why haven't I been able to convince them that being treated poorly gives them no excuse to do the same to others?"

"You *are* convincing them," he said. "Slowly. The idea that Paddy is out there, that Paddy could be anyone, it has already stopped them spreading so much hate. These ugly things are only said in whispers between husbands and wives or the closest of friends. But every argument you make with that pen chips away at those lies, little by little."

I didn't want to hide the hate. I wanted to destroy it.

"Please, Rose," he went on. "You must give them time. You must give them a chance to learn to survive here. You must remember who our people can be. Not who they are now, during this desperate time. You wrote it before. We're a generous people. We love our neighbors. You must trust that spirit will show itself once again. Once they have wages and food and health and they aren't in danger of being shipped across the ocean."

"All right," I said, quietly. He took my hands and held them to his chest.

Chapter Thirty-One

E mmett held my hand again as I told the men the truth the next day.

"No one from the city is planning to meet with us," I said to the crowd as I stood on the steps of city hall. I peered over my shoulder at the towering structure behind me. At the agitated police officers. They wanted Irish blood, and they couldn't have it. Why were they still here if they couldn't kick a couple of us around? That's what their faces said. I turned back to the crowd.

"I'm not sure if or when they ever will," I went on. Emmett squeezed my hand.

"They will," he said, only to me at first. Then he said it again louder. "They will. If we stay the course, they'll have to. We won't give them a choice!"

The crowd cheered. I shook my head at Emmett but slyly smiled at him.

"The great Emmett Doherty bestows hope upon the Irish, but his far-too-proud wife must not?" I whispered. He laughed heartily.

"That was not the same," he whispered back. "I simply stated a future truth."

Now I laughed. A future truth. Only from my husband did such a nonsensical phrase make sense. I kissed his cheek and made my way down the stairs and through the crowd. Mairead grabbed my hand as I walked by.

"It isn't your fault, you know, that the city won't talk to us," she said.

I shrugged. I lowered my voice so those around us wouldn't hear. "Mairead, can I ask you something? You will understand. You're an abolitionist."

She looked at me curiously but nodded. She took my hand and led me a little ways away from the crowd. We sat at a bench, close enough to see the mass of people and hear the things they shouted, but far enough away that our conversation wouldn't be overheard.

"Do you think we'll always be the only Irish at those antislavery meetings?" I asked.

"Paddy's there, too, isn't he?" she asked. Was there a hint of sarcasm in that question? I couldn't tell, but I nodded anyway.

"I suppose," I said. "Is it mad to believe that one day there will be others?"

"Do you know what I think keeps plenty of people away?" she asked.

"Because they're unwelcome," I said. "I know this. And most of them despise the cause."

She shook her head.

"Perhaps some Irish despise the cause. Maybe most. But I don't think so. I think there are just as many Maireads in our community as there are Fionas," she said. "You can't honestly believe that you and Emmett and I are the only Irish people here who feel sympathy toward the slaves, can you?"

I sighed. "I guess not."

"And plenty are much braver than I," she went on. "They don't mind that they aren't welcomed. I think it's hard for any of us to call ourselves abolitionists while we work at the mills. We're touching that cotton every day. Maybe many didn't see it after that first letter from Paddy. They didn't make the connection. But after the fifth, sixth, seventh letter, once they learned more about what slavery was, they couldn't help but notice that we work with cotton every day. England is the enemy, but *we* are the accomplices."

She crossed her arms and looked over her shoulder at the church behind us. It was St. Anne's. She stared for a moment, perhaps marveling at its beauty.

"We need the mills. We need the cotton. Irish people don't want to stand up and say, 'I'm an abolitionist' on Tuesday evening and then wake up on Wednesday morning knowing that's an impossible path to walk. Even if their hearts feel one thing, their shame keeps them from expressing anything. We aren't afraid of the Yankees. We're afraid of being frauds."

She sighed and looked out at the crowd.

"The Yankees are no better," she went on. "They need the cotton, too. Even if they don't put their hands on it every day. That's why we're doing this, right?" She gestured to city hall with both hands. "Because they need the cotton, too. They rely on us: the Negro-haters. We'll touch the cotton. We'll spin it into money and houses and stores and anything else they need. And we don't mind, because we hate those Negroes anyway, isn't that true? That's what *they* think. Is that what *you* think?"

I looked up at her. She was staring at me with one eyebrow raised. I wondered in that moment if she knew who I was. Her question silenced me. Perhaps there was truth in what she was saying. Perhaps the loudest and angriest among the Irish *weren't* the majority.

"I . . . I don't know," I stammered. "I suppose not."

"You suppose not?" she asked. Now her lips were pursed in annoyance. She shook her head. "You can't see it, can you? When I say *we* touch that cotton every day, that includes *you*. Didn't you buy a lovely new hat not too long ago with your wages? Wages made from working the cotton picked by slaves? If you care *more* than the rest of us, oughtn't you leave the mills? Oughtn't you find work elsewhere?"

She stood up abruptly. "Perhaps in Boston you could live the righteous life of an abolitionist," she said. "But here? All of us benefit. Just because some of us aren't shouting in the streets, it doesn't mean that we don't wish we could help. But our hands are tied with yarn. And so are yours."

I didn't look at the faces on the street as I walked away. A lump formed in the back of my throat. I walked without thinking of where I was going. I tried to think of nothing at all. Not of Mairead's words. Not of her accusing eyes. I didn't realize where my body was taking me until I got there. Mr. Kittridge's bookstore.

It was quiet when I walked in. As it usually was. Sometimes, if there were enough people there, asking enough questions, it sounded like any other store. But usually it was quiet. Not because Mr. Kittridge ever asked any customer to lower their voice, but because everyone who came here recognized the importance of the place. Much like how people naturally hushed their voices when walking into a church. This place was sacred, too, to those of us who frequented it.

Mr. Kittridge stood at one of his printing presses with his back to me. He also sold empty notebooks, and occasionally, someone might pay him to print their own book. A family history, a collection of letters, of short stories they wanted to keep in good condition to pass along to their grandchildren. He took all sorts of odd jobs. He glanced over his shoulder when he heard the door open.

"Afternoon, Rosaleen," he said. "Can I help you with anything?"

"No, thank you, Mr. Kittridge," I said. "May I go up to the second floor?"

"Please," he said, continuing with his work. The staircase was in the corner and spiraled up to the second floor. I climbed them slowly, and when I reached the second floor, I looked around at the full shelves. There were so many books here that the shelves overflowed onto the ground. Stacks nearly reached the ceiling. But I knew I wouldn't purchase anything today. Mr. Kittridge was a Yankee.

I wandered to the area I knew contained romances and

mysteries. I tabbed through the books with my index finger, pulling out a few as I went. With my arms full, I brought the books over to the window seat directly across from the stairs. Brown velvet pillows sat along the platform, and I lay on them. With the books by my side, I closed my eyes. The sun was not quite in the highest position of the day and so it shone on me with all its might. Even with my eyelids closed, I saw not the usual black behind them, but a lighter brown. I inhaled deeply. The smell of the books calmed my soul. I turned away from the sun, opened a book, and began to read.

An hour or two later, after carefully returning the books to their rightful places, I walked to the church. The sun beamed down with determination. There were no clouds in sight. I squinted to see Father Purcell speaking to someone on the steps of the church. The other man's back was to me, but I would recognize his robes anywhere.

"Good afternoon, Father," I said to Father Purcell when I approached. At the sound of my voice, Reverend Edson turned to give me a warm smile and a discreet wink. He approved. A small weight lifted from my shoulders.

"Good afternoon, young lady," Father Purcell said. "This is Reverend Edson from St. Anne's church. We were just discussing what kind of assistance they would be willing to provide during our time of need."

"Hello, Reverend," I said. "It's very good to see you."

"Rosaleen and I know one another from the antislavery society," the reverend said. "She is a fellow abolitionist."

Father Purcell's eyebrows went up. Perhaps the word "abolitionist" provoked the same disgust in him as it did

Sister Hunna. I couldn't tell what emotions lay beneath the mild surprise he conveyed.

"Well then," Father Purcell said. "A happy meeting between friends."

"How is your daughter?" I asked the reverend. "She came to mind the other night, and I realized I haven't asked after your family in so long."

"She is doing quite well with her studies," he said. "Thank you for asking. My wife and she tell me often to vacation. I believe my fellow rectors at the church have persuaded them that it would be good for me. But I don't believe I could leave Lowell for any amount of time. Even for a short vacation."

"I must agree with your family," I said. "A vacation would be much deserved."

He smiled still but shook his head. Then he turned to Father Purcell.

"Please do let me know if those funds dry up," he said. "We will stand with you."

Father Purcell nodded once. "I am grateful," he said.

The reverend squeezed my shoulder before leaving. "Do come and see me soon," he said, quietly.

"Yes, Reverend," I replied.

As the reverend walked away, I felt Father Purcell's eyes on me. I looked at the ground for a moment, waiting for a question. It didn't come. When I raised my eyes again to meet his, I saw true curiosity there. I hadn't spent much time with Father Purcell. I doubted he would know me from the next young Irishwoman at a Sunday Mass. But he had seen me often that week. With Mr. Joyce on the first day, with Marie and Ruth delivering funds, and now as a friend of Reverend Edson's and an abolitionist.

"Rosaleen, is it?" he finally asked. I nodded

"You live with Thaddeus, is that true?" he asked.

"Yes, Father," I said.

"And your husband is Mr. Doherty?" I nodded again.

"I've heard he has done quite well managing things at city hall," he said. "Please give him my thanks."

"I will, Father," I said. "I've come to see the sisters. To see if there's anything they need."

"Yes, please do," he said.

"Thank you, Father," I said. I walked past him toward the door of the school and knocked. Sister Hunna answered.

"Come in," Sister Hunna said. "Rosaleen, tomorrow is Friday. I know you missed Wednesday's tutoring session, but Alice and Ina will still need help after school. Even with all of this going on." She swept her arm out and scowled as if I were to blame for it all, which I was. "Will you come tomorrow?"

"Yes, Sister Hunna," I said. "I will be here. Is there anything else I can do to help?"

"Your tutoring services will be sufficient," she said before turning on her heels and stomping away.

I couldn't let Sister Hunna's foul mood get in my way. I needed to do something. To be of service to someone. I looked around. Sister Celeste was rummaging around in a crate in the corner. I went over to her, and she looked excited when she spotted me.

"Rosaleen!" she said, clearly louder than she'd meant to.

She looked around and lowered her voice. "I've been meaning to speak with you."

"Is it about the girls?" I asked.

She shook her head. "We've been so busy these last few days, I forgot to mention it to you."

"What is it?" I asked.

"The Smelling Committee visited us the day before Paddy declared the strike," she said.

"The Smelling Committee?" I asked.

She nodded. "They're a congressional committee. They go around the state inspecting nunneries."

I narrowed my eyes. "For what reason?"

She shrugged and looked across the church. "The same reason the Know-Nothings here tried to break in," she went on. "Because they think we have something to hide. Luckily, a friend at a convent in Roxbury warned me. They visited their quarters first. We'd been expecting them some time, but we didn't know when they would arrive. They were awfully rude. Sneering at us. Asking the most ridiculous and degrading questions. Sister Hunna demanded a search warrant, which, of course, they did not have. The treatment was simply humiliating. They did not leave until they had searched our small home from corner to corner, window to window, under beds and inside of ovens."

"I'm so sorry, Sister Celeste," I said. She looked at me with a small smile.

"I half expected them to find some outrageous reading material from Sister Hunna," she said. "That would have been a show."

I laughed. "I shouldn't be laughing, should I?"

She shook her head but was still smiling.

"Isn't that what this country is supposed to protect? The reading of outrageous material? As much as Sister Hunna grates my nerves, she ought to be able to read whatever terrible things she wants. That's what these men say they believe in. But only for themselves, I suppose."

"Yes," I agreed. "Only for themselves."

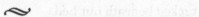

After leaving the church, I went home to make dinner. Mr. Joyce had scarcely been home except to sleep, and I wasn't sure if Emmett would go without food again.

As I walked home, I loosened my tight bun. The blazing sun and my strained temples were giving me a headache.

The Acre was noisy. Everyone had obeyed Paddy this time. I had yet to see even one person slip off to work. This time was different, and we could all feel it. But not everyone was at city hall. Danger hung in the air over there, strung from one person to the next. All it would take was one snap and the whole place could erupt into violence. Maybe half of the Acre went. Maybe less. The rest kept their distance, while still refusing to work or give the Yankees their coin. Staying home was safer, and so they spilled out onto the streets of the Acre. Children playing, women nervously chatting.

When I got home, I picked through the root cellar under the house before heading upstairs. It was sparse in there. A dozen potatoes at the most. A rack of salted cod. Some beans. A bit of rice. A lone tomato coupled with an onion. I sighed. We needed some meat. I decided to trek to the butcher's on Lowell Street, on the west side of the Acre.

Even though he no longer delivered straight to the board-inghouses, he was never idle. The animals were slaugh-tered and butchered, and then sat waiting for the line of hungry people who usually came at the beginning and end of each week.

I rummaged through my apron, counting my coins as I walked. I had forty cents still plus the two dollars at home, tucked beneath our bed.

The butcher shop was in a strange state. People wandered in and out. There was no line. With no wages this week, people came at whatever time suited them. Some families waited longer than others to spend their precious coin. The butcher looked worried. His eyebrows were furrowed. His lips pursed. He looked tired but also a bit jumpy.

"Hello, Mr. Fagan," I said. "How is business?"

He crossed his arms and shook his head.

"Usually, I know exactly when to slaughter the animals. But now, I don't. Today is busier than yesterday. But only a wee bit. I don't know when people will want their meat. Luckily, it's getting cold. The meat'll last longer."

"How about beef?" I asked. "Have you got any of that today?"

He nodded. "Slaughtered one cow yesterday." He turned from me and reached into a large container behind him.

"Chuck or round?" he called over his shoulder.

"Do they cost the same?" I asked.

"Twelve cents for round, eleven cents for chuck," he said.

"Chuck, please," I responded. I was only making a stew. "And a few bones as well."

He leaned forward, submerging the whole upper half of his body into the container before standing up again. He wrapped it in paper, weighed it, and handed it to me. I gave him twenty-five cents.

"I'm sorry about this week," I said before leaving. "I hope things go back to normal soon."

His lips were still pursed.

"As do I," he said.

I put the two pounds of beef under my arm and stopped one last time for a pound of flour before going home. I took the beef, flour, and bones straight to the kitchen. Then I went back down to the root cellar for a potato, an onion, and the tomato.

When I got back to the kitchen, I stirred the bone and tomato into a pot of water and brought it to a boil. I closed my eyes. The low rumble of the boiling pot calmed me. The smell of the broth made my stomach grumble. I sat at the table to wait. Suddenly, Emmett burst in.

"Rose!" he cried. I leaped to my feet.

"What's happened?" I asked, panic rising in my throat.

"It's good!" he said. "Sit, sit."

I clutched my chest. "You nearly gave me a bloody heart attack," I said.

"A man came to me this morning," he said. "Dressed real handsomely from head to toe. Clearly not Irish. He pulled me aside and said to me, 'Are you the one leading this?' I said, 'Not officially, sir, but I'm happy to speak for the men here.' I thought maybe he wrote for the newspaper. He said, 'I manage the mills. We want to meet with you. Just a few of you. Not too many. We've come to an agreement with the city. They've decided to stop the deportations.'"

My heart raced with excitement. I hadn't sat back down like he'd told me to.

"How do we know they'll do it?" I shouted at him with passion.

"That's what I said. I told him that's wonderful news but how are we to believe the city will truly do it?" Emmett accented each sentence with a heavy pant. From the run over or from excitement or both.

"Do you know what he said to me then?" Emmett asked.

"No!" I exclaimed, laughing exasperatedly. "Tell me!"

"He said that's what he wants us to tell them! He said, 'We don't want any trouble like this ever again. We shouldn't be involved in politics like this. We want it to go away for good.'"

Emmett dug into the pocket of his coat, which he hadn't taken off yet. He held out a small card.

"He wants us to meet him at this address in two days with an answer. The city will be there, too, he said."

I stared at the address in disbelief.

"He said no more than four people should come to represent the Irish," Emmett went on. "Me and you, of course. I want to bring my new mate, Baird. He's been helping me at city hall. He's a smart fellow. And he works at the dye shop. So that's another profession represented. Who else ought we bring?"

I thought of Nessa immediately. Would she be able to manage something of this magnitude? I hadn't seen her since the start of all of this. I wanted to speak to her.

"I'll think about who else to bring," I said. "But more importantly, what will we ask for?"

Chapter Thirty-Two

I slept soundly that night, dreaming of Ireland. Emmett was with me. We were at my cottage in Baltimore, and we were getting married again. It was only the two of us and Mr. Joyce. The wind whipped my hair around. I walked toward the water, avoiding black rocks jutting out of the ground here and there. The water was icy cold on my toes when I reached it, but I bent down, scooped a handful, and splashed it across my face. I closed my eyes and smiled and woke up in our bedroom on Fenwick Street.

After I ate breakfast with Emmett and Mr. Joyce, I kissed Emmett on the cheek and gathered my coat.

"I want to talk with Nessa," I said. "See if she'll come with us."

Emmett put his fork down.

"Nessa's awfully young, isn't she?" he asked.

I shrugged. "Younger than us," I said. "But unless Baird has a relative at the poor farm, she's the only one of us with someone to lose. She ought to be there. I think she can do it. She's smart. Let me talk to her."

Emmett thought for a moment and nodded. "I'll trust your judgment. You know her well." Then he turned to Mr. Joyce. "I wish you would come," he said.

Mr. Joyce shook his head. "I've too much to do at the church," he said. "You young folks can handle yourselves just fine."

"Goodbye!" I called before hurrying out the door. The list of things I needed to do that day was quickly multiplying.

The cold air stung my face immediately, and as I walked, I noticed the snow falling very slowly from the sky. Just small flakes here and there. But it had arrived. The first snow of the year. I enjoyed the first snow, but I also dreaded what it brought along with it. More and more snow. Impossible amounts of snow. For many months. The endless hauling of firewood. The fevers and coughs. I walked faster.

As I knocked on the boardinghouse door, I wondered who would be there. Only a few Irish girls lived at Mrs. Durrand's. Would they have stayed home? Would anyone else have? I shook my head and chuckled at myself. Yankees staying home for this. What an absurd thought.

Benjamin opened the door and smiled big at me.

"How is Cocoa?" he asked first.

"She is lazy, as always," I said. "She would crawl right into the fireplace if she had any less sense."

Benjamin giggled. "But you love her," he said.

"I love her," I agreed. "Isn't it school time yet?"

He shook his head. "In an hour."

"And you'll go today?" I asked.

He nodded. "Mother's not afraid of you Irish."

"Did any of the girls stay home yesterday?" I asked.

"Oh, sure," he said. "The Irish ones did. And Berta. Berta told me I better not grow up to be a disgusting pig like the rest of the men in this town."

My eyes grew wide. "She said that?" I asked. It was bold even for Berta.

He nodded. "Mother didn't hear her," he said. I shared a secret smile with him.

"That's good," I said.

He nodded again. "And I promised Berta to only grow into an honorable man."

I tousled his hair.

"I know you will," I said.

I found Nessa in her room with Berta and Helen. All three were readying themselves for the day. I pulled Nessa into the hallway.

"What do you think of all this?" I asked her, quietly.

Her nostrils widened. Her jaw clenched.

"What do I think about my brother being sent back to Ireland by himself? What do I think about my soon-to-be husband having to keep an armed watch over our people? I'm positively thrilled, Rosaleen." She rolled her eyes.

"Your brother isn't going anywhere," I said. Her eyes narrowed.

"How do you know?" she asked.

"I need you for a very important meeting," I told her. "You won't be able to tell anyone about it. Not your family, not your roommates, not even Quinn."

She nodded slowly. "All right," she said. "I can do that. What's it about?"

I leaned toward her and whispered in her ear. "The mills and the city want to make a deal with the Irish. They claim that they'll stop the deportations. We need to bring our terms, so they know we won't strike again."

Nessa looked confused. "We want them to stop," she whispered back. "Those are our terms."

I nodded. "But do you believe they will? Will we take their word for it? Even in writing? Or will we need something more?"

A look of understanding passed over her face, and she relaxed a bit.

"How do you know all of this?" she asked.

"They think Emmett is in charge," I said, smiling.

"Is he?" she asked.

I shrugged. "Not officially."

"Where is this Paddy?" she asked. "Seems like a coward to me. He has an awful lot to say on paper but then he hides. I'm grateful that we know what's happening now. But he ought to be out there doing what Emmett's doing."

Then she gave me a sharp look. "Is Emmett the Paddy?" she asked.

I scoffed. "Don't be ridiculous," I said. "Think about what we might want to ask the city for. I'll come back after supper, and we can talk then."

I went to leave, but Nessa grabbed my arm.

"Thank you for trusting me with this," she said. "You won't regret it."

I smiled. "Let's get your brother home."

Chapter Thirty-Three

I could have simply taught the schoolgirls their letters that week. I had enough else to focus on. We all did. But somehow, I felt that amidst all of the chaos and fear, it was more important than ever to take their minds far away from Lowell. So, I hurried to Nancy's, hoping desperately that she might have an idea for me.

The snow was still falling, and as I walked, I looked at the half-visible footprints along the sidewalk. Every snowflake that fell erased a small piece of each one. The flakes were bigger now. And falling faster.

Nancy's house looked quaint. The bushes in her garden, the tree in her front yard, the sloping ceiling, all peppered with snow.

She looked tired when she came to the door, but she broke into a big smile nevertheless. She let me in and pointed to a pile of clothes in the corner of the parlor.

"The donated children's coats," she said. "There are more upstairs."

"This is simply wonderful. Thank you," I said. "The

Irish children need coats every year. I wish the Yankees would donate willingly."

"Let's first stop them from deporting children," she said. "Then maybe we can move on to donating coats."

I smirked at her.

"I need a topic for this evening's tutoring session. Do you have any ideas?" I asked.

Her eyes twinkled. "Do I ever!" she cried. "I've been waiting for you to ask. Sit down, and I will go find it."

I sat on her green velvet sofa. It was so soft and clean. I didn't know how she kept it so spotless. Not a crumb or stray hair or a tea stain anywhere. I ran my hand along the arm of it.

Nancy walked into the study across the foyer, to a large desk pushed up against the far wall. From behind, I could hardly tell that she was pregnant.

"I keep misplacing things," she called over her shoulder. "This baby is taking more than just my food. It's as if she's erased half of my brain as well. At first, I blamed Calvin for moving things on me. He's been so distracted these days. Spending hours and hours with the mayor or going to meetings. And when he's home, he's either aloof or careless. Sometimes I wish he had never taken that position as city marshal. But I tell myself, better it's him than someone else. He won't be afraid to push back against the mayor. I just wish he were here more. His body and his mind."

She rummaged a little more. I heard drawers open and close. Books picked up and put down.

"Ah!" she exclaimed. "Here it is."

She spun around, revealing her round belly again. She was holding a magazine: *The Illustrated London News*.

"My oldest brother, Joseph, brought this back with him," she said as she sat next to me on the sofa. "You know he has that new position in Washington. They send him to England every now and then. This magazine is fascinating. It has illustrations!"

She flipped through the pages quickly. She knew what she was looking for. When she found it, she snapped the page open.

"This man," she went on. "Sir George Cayley. He invented a flying machine!"

I stared at the illustration on the page. It did indeed have wings, and there was, in fact, an illustrated man sitting in what looked to be the body of the apparatus.

"Does it work?" I asked, still inspecting the drawing.

"Yes!" she exclaimed. "It says here his poor coachman was strongly persuaded to pilot it. I'm sure you've heard of the giant, lighter-than-air balloons that brave, stupid people ride?"

I shook my head and laughed. "No!" I said. "I have not."

Nancy's eyes got wide, and she grabbed my arm.

"Oh, Rosaleen," she said. "You've got to get out of the Acre more often! Anyway, these people are carried off in these mammoth balloons. But they can't steer them! They're at the mercy of the wind. But this! You could steer this."

I scanned the article as she spoke.

"Not if you crash right way like this man did," I said.

"It wasn't right away," she corrected me. "I believe he flew a whole nine hundred yards. And next time it will be even further."

"Wow," I said, shaking my head. "Humans flying. This is something indeed. My students might not even believe it."

"Bring that with you," she said. "Prove it to them."

I looked up at her and smiled. "I miss you," I said.

"Come see me more, then," she said. She looked sad now. And seemed to be pleading. "I really am so lonely when I'm not with the schoolchildren. And soon they'll make me stop going to the school, too. When my big belly will no longer fit through the door."

Now I felt sad, too. Nancy loved to be around people. She loved to talk and to argue. She wasn't meant to be alone. Her eyes made me think of a withering flower deprived of the sun. I took her hands in mine.

"I will," I said. "I'm sorry I've been so busy."

She shook her head.

"I'm proud of you," she said. "And I understand. If you don't do something about these things, who will?"

I stayed at Nancy's later than intended. I told her about everything. About the meeting. About my conversation with Mairead. My fight with Emmett. The strange man watching me.

When I was done speaking, she said, "When we chose to speak up, we decided we wanted life to be hard on us," she said. "Fighting these companies, our city. It's dangerous and it's hard and most of the time we won't win. Be easy on yourself. This is an admirable outcome. You don't have to have everything figured out today. Just do the next thing that needs to be done. One thing at a time. Your people need you. And I know, in your heart, you *do* trust them. Otherwise, you wouldn't be risking so much for them."

I hugged her, and when I had to leave, I was reluctant to go. I stopped at home for a late dinner. Mr. Joyce must have been home earlier, because he'd left a plate of his boiled ham for me. Cocoa was sniffing for it when I walked in, her nose almost reaching the top of the stove.

"Not yours, girl," I said, patting the top of her head. She knew I would share. I sat at the table, and while I ate, I wrote a letter.

Dear Angel,

Your birthday is coming soon! You're going to be five years old! I hope your ma will get you a sweet treat. I wish I were there to give you one, too.

You won't believe what I learned today. A man has found a way for people to fly! His first invention only stayed in the air for a short time, but it worked! And the man inside the flying machine was just fine. One day, you might be able to fly just like that naughty flying creature that wouldn't come when Noah called.

Where would you go?

All my love,

Rosaleen

I took the magazine out of my coat pocket and tried to copy the drawing for Angel. It wasn't perfect, but it was decipherable. I folded the letter and addressed it. Then I wiped my mouth with a handkerchief and gave Cocoa my last cuts of ham and potato. After I wiped my hands, I took out another sheet.

Dearest Marie,

I am writing to relay some good news. Emmett and I and a few of our friends will be meeting with men from the city and from the mills to discuss ending the deportations—and with that, our protests. I am hopeful that the outcome will be good. Please pray for us.

I have been working with my people, hand in hand to coerce this change, and yet, I can't help but feel like a bit of a fraud. We both saw how they acted toward you. It was shameful. My only comfort is your old story about the bears. I must trust the other wolves and remember that I am one as well. That we are stronger together.

How is Gil? Have you decided anything yet? Please give him my love. Your sister, Zeke, and Miss Susan as well. I just wrote to Angel. It amazes me that she is only turning five. She is so far beyond her years.

Write me soon.

All my love,

Rosaleen

I gazed at my bed and longed to lie down. Tomorrow would be another long and trying day. Perhaps after that I could rest. I sighed, folded Marie's letter, and started toward the post office. I had a bit of time before tutoring started. The snow had slowed but had left the sidewalks and buildings covered with a thick layer of powder. My boots crunched through it, leaving distinct patterns behind. I thought of Henry. He had made these boots. That pattern was his. While I never missed Henry, I did feel a strange nostalgia for him. Life had been simpler at the inn. I hoped Henry had found happiness in his new position as shoe-maker—and happiness in another woman, too. I was sure he had. He was a kind man and certainly nice to look at. The thought satisfied me, and I pushed it from my mind.

The post office was busy. I waited behind a man reading a newspaper. The headline caught my eye: Smelling Committee Uses Your Tax Dollars for Alcohol, Lavish Spending.

I squinted at the article. I caught just a short bit of it before the man folded the newspaper back up and tucked it under his arm. It said:

Smelling Committee members have been reckless with their finances, indulging in excess alcohol spending, the finest hotels, and other rumored activities.

The Smelling Committee. Those were the Know-Nothings in Congress that Sister Celeste had spoken of. Rumored activities? If the Yankees were so concerned about spending their tax dollars on feeding the Irish, wouldn't this concern them as well? I looked around for proof of my theory. Did people look upset by the news? But that was a ridiculous expectation. This would only be the first black mark against the Smelling Committee. Still, an uneasy hope rose up in my chest.

~

The girls looked tired when I arrived for their tutoring session.

"Are you getting enough sleep?" I asked them. Alice nodded slowly.

"We're low on firewood at home," Ina said. "Da is trying to save enough for the next few weeks. So it's cold at night."

"Have you talked to the sisters?" I asked. "I'm sure they can help you with some firewood."

Ina said nothing and stared at her writing slate. It said, *For God so loved the world, as to give his only begotten Son; that whosoever believeth in him, may not perish, but may have life everlasting.* It was written seven times. At the eighth, it stopped at "perish." I sat down next to her and touched her hand.

"I suppose I could ask the nuns," Ina said, quietly. "But Da won't like it. He doesn't like askin' for things."

"I understand," I said. "I'll bring some over after this. Won't say a thing. I'll just leave it at your back door, all right?"

She looked at me and shrugged. "All right," she said.

"I brought something fun to show you girls," I said. "Should I save it for another time?"

Alice looked up at me with a small smile and hopeful eyes. But then she looked to Ina, her best friend and leader, to see if she would approve.

Ina shrugged again. "You can show us."

I brought out the magazine article.

"A flying contraption," I said, quietly. "For people."

Ina's eyes got wide. Alice's smile grew.

"People can fly?" Alice asked.

"Only for a couple of seconds at a time," I said. "But this is just the start. I'm sure they'll keep trying to build better ones. Now that we know it's possible."

Ina's face finally relaxed. "I would go somewhere warm," she said. "No. Somewhere hot. A beach where the sand will burn the bottoms of my feet right off."

Alice gave her a strange look, but I laughed.

"You're that cold, huh?" I asked her. "Would you ever come back?"

She shook her head. "Never," she said. "I'd live there alone. No one to bother me."

I looked at the bruise on the side of her neck. It was fading now. A sour green and yellow. But when I'd first seen it weeks ago, it was dark and mean and I knew it wasn't caused by an accident. When I asked her about it, she refused to answer. But I had heard about her da before. And I had seen the bruises on her brother, too.

"Maybe one day you'll make your own glider and fly it wherever you want," I said.

She sighed but gave me a weary smile. She was always trying to keep others at a distance. I hoped these lessons gave her even a little bit of hope. Even if I couldn't completely break down the wall that she needed to keep up. Perhaps one day she could dream of a life beyond this, a life where she could be free.

I let the girls read the article to themselves and then

whisper and giggle about it, huddled away in the corner of the room. I looked out the window and remembered I was to meet with Nessa after this. I would have rather given into my exhaustion, but then I thought about Ina over in the corner, shivering at night, afraid to ask for firewood in fear of her own father. She was somehow still here, learning, doing what was expected of her.

When it was time to go, I hugged Ina. "You know he's a coward, don't you?" I whispered in her ear. She nodded and squeezed me back. When she pulled away, the shoulder of my dress was wet with tears, but she was smiling.

Her sad smile reminded me of Ronan. These unthinkably strong kids. Adults had failed them. I felt more and more that I had failed Ronan. Every weekend that passed when he didn't show up, suitcase in hand, I felt I had failed.

I forced myself to push these thoughts away and think of what would come tomorrow. I would take Nessa home so we could talk with Emmett, too.

The other girls weren't back from their shifts at the mill yet, but Nessa had clearly been ready for me for some time. She greeted me at the front door of the boardinghouse and didn't even invite me inside.

"Let's go," she said.

"I'm going to take you to my house," I said. "We can talk with Emmett, too."

"I wish I could've brought Quinn," she said.

"You know why he can't be involved," I said.

"Yes, yes," she said. "I know. A strange thing has happened lately. I've come to trust his opinion more. And he's changing, too. He's seeing things in this position. Things that bother him. I think he's starting to understand how they truly feel about us."

"Is that right?" I asked.

"Before they start work for the day or for the evening, they meet at the jailhouse. Calvin usually comes to talk about what he would like them to do. Where he would like them to be. Most of them have been at city hall every day this past week. Well, after Calvin leaves, they always have some awfully rotten things to say about us—as you can imagine. Lazy, dirty, leeches. And they don't care that he's there, either. Sometimes they say it and stare at him. As if they're trying to provoke him."

"What does he say?" I asked.

"Usually nothing. He bites his tongue and goes about his business. But it obviously makes him angry. I've never seen him so angry as he was the other day. Sometimes, he wants to quit. It's been me talking him out of that. Can you imagine? But now that he's there, now that he's doing it, I'm starting to see why it's important for him to be there. I'm waiting for him to say something to them. I think he will. At first, he thought if they were just around him and saw how agreeable he could be, their hearts would warm to us."

She stopped talking and chuckled at the thought.

"Those old ideas are proving wrong," she said. She seemed almost excited about it. Excited to be right. We arrived at the house.

"You go on up," I said. "I've got something quick to do. I'll follow you in a minute."

I went to the back near the root cellar and gathered four logs of firewood. It was the most I could carry at once. Then, I crossed the neighbor's land behind our house and walked a little ways down Adams. Ina lived near the end, where Adams met Lowell Street in a solid block of tenements. I walked around the back and set the firewood down at the back door. Then I stepped back and found a small rock. I threw it at the window where I knew Ina lived. I prayed she would be the one to hear it.

When her face popped into the window, I breathed a sigh of relief. She nodded and disappeared again. I quickly hurried back home and hoped her da could be grateful and not infuriated. I trusted Ina to put on a good lie but prayed her da would be in the proper mood to believe it.

Chapter Thirty-Four

The four of us talked long into the night about our
strategy for the next day. Mr. Joyce tried his best to
stay out of "the politics of it all," but occasionally he
couldn't help offering his input.

Finally, I walked Nessa home quite some time after
curfew had passed.

"I'll explain to Mrs. Durrand," I told her before she
crept quietly inside. "I'll be back in the morning."

She nodded and shut the door behind her. I took in a
long breath of the icy air. It stung my lungs. Everything
was so quiet. I thought of that first year in Lowell. Of all
the nights I would sneak away from that same house to try
to find somewhere, anywhere, to put my letters. I had
gotten creative. Slipped them under window shutters,
leaving them flapping in the wind. Hung them on the
grocer's door handle. Tucked one under a broken, splin-
tered piece of wood on the barn door of the blacksmith's
shop. But eventually the hired guards were everywhere,

forming my own personal patrol watch. I'd felt hunted then by my own people.

I looked up at the sky and watched the stars twinkle. I'd never truly enjoyed the beauty of the night back when I was scurrying around the Acre at this hour. I was always too excited or nervous. But the stillness was comforting.

A small memory came to me then of Ireland. Of the stars one night. Ma and I were waiting for Da to come home after a longer-than-normal fishing trip. We sat on the grass facing the sea. I was lying on my back and naming all the stars for Ma. They had silly names like Oak or Cherry or Lily or Frog.

"You should name them after kings and queens and warriors," Ma said. "Those stars have lived even longer than people. They have seen the world all of its life. They have seen it all, and they are still shining. They'll never stop. They're special."

I thought about that. "Cherries are special, too," I finally said. "They're big and red and juicy, and when you look at them, you smile, and your mouth waters. They grow every year. Besides, some kings and queens are mean and awful."

Ma knew of whom I was thinking. She lay next to me.

"I will have to teach you of the great Celtic warriors, then," she said. "They are worthy of the stars."

Da came home that night. And many nights after. The night Da didn't come home, there were no stars. Only clouds and rain and wind blowing so hard I couldn't see a thing. We'd waited for Da inside that night. Huddled together. Afraid.

Ma never did get the chance to teach me about the Celtic warriors. The only Celtic warrior I knew was

Boudica, my old friend's namesake. When I thought of her, it still stung. Was she well? Was she alive? What horrible things had she endured? Perhaps her name had given her power. Perhaps she had prevailed after all.

Shivering, I headed back home, thinking of the task before me. The idea of walking into a room occupied by some of the most powerful and important people in the city made me nervous. I hoped our demands would hold up. I hoped our youth wouldn't cause them to dismiss us. Suddenly, I wished we had been able to convince Mr. Joyce to come instead of Baird. His presence demanded respect and attention. But I knew he didn't wish to be involved. I walked faster. I hoped Ina was warm enough tonight.

When I finally climbed into bed, sleep was hard to find. My body was exhausted. My head ached with a clenching feeling that only sleep could relieve. But my mind still reeled, imagining the meeting, anticipating our words, their words. My left side started to tingle and ache with numbness, so I rolled over to face Emmett. He was sleeping, his mouth slightly open and a quiet snore escaping his lips. I slowly and gently rested my hand on his chest and let his steady heartbeat finally lull me to sleep.

Emmett woke early, before the sun was up, pulling me out of a deep, dreamless sleep. He went to the fireplace and tossed another log on. Cocoa came up to me and sniffed my head. I could hear her wagging tail smacking the wall next to me. I smiled and sat up. Instead of thinking of my nerves, I tried to think of those Celtic warriors who Ma had said were worthy of the stars. If they were worthy of the stars, I was at least worthy of attending this meeting.

At breakfast, Emmett looked up at me. He gazed into my eyes and smiled.

"I love you, Rose," he said. He stopped eating and scooted his chair closer to mine. He grabbed my hand. "We're going to do this today, and we're going to save Frank. Save all of the inmates. They aren't going to send one more person from Lowell across that ocean. It's because of you."

I smiled back at him, blushing. I knew Emmett was a charmer. He always had been. He'd charmed me as soon as I met him. As soon as I'd accepted his hand and sat on that bed next to him. I was lost to him before I even knew it. And still, he could make me blush.

"And you," I said.

"A little bit of me," he said, grinning.

"And all our people," I said.

"I'm proud of you for trusting them," he said. "It's the right thing to do."

I leaned forward and kissed him. "I couldn't do it without my anchor," I whispered. "My rock. My dearest friend."

He cupped both hands around my face and kissed me again. "Let's make babies," he whispered back.

I giggled. "All right, but not right at this moment," I said. He gave me a mischievous smile.

"Are you sure?" he asked. "I think we have a few minutes. That's enough time."

I smacked him playfully. "With Mr. Joyce still here?" We both looked at him, snoring.

"I don't know if God could forgive that," Emmett said. "Later, then."

I winked. "Later."

Emmett and I huddled close as we walked toward city hall, and then we parted on the other side of the canal. I went to the boardinghouse.

"Mrs. Durrand," I said to her as she let me in. "It is entirely my fault that Nessa didn't make curfew last night. I wouldn't have kept her so late if it wasn't vitally important."

Mrs. Durrand raised one eyebrow and crossed her arms.

"Don't make a habit out of it," she said.

"Yes, ma'am," I said.

"Because next time it happens, I'll have to restrict your visits," she went on.

"I understand, ma'am," I said. "It won't happen again."

She sighed, but nodded. I heard Benjamin and Harriet laughing in the back room. Nessa came hesitantly down the stairs, no doubt expecting a tongue-lashing.

Mrs. Durrand glanced at her out of the corner of her eye.

"Rosaleen assures me it won't happen again," Mrs. Durrand said. "Go on."

Nessa smiled and hurried past.

"Thank you," I said to Mrs. Durrand. She nodded again and was off to make breakfast. I imagined she was growing tired of keeping track of all of these girls and all of their morals.

"You should eat first," I said to Nessa.

"I don't know that I can," she said. "I have too many nerves. Or perhaps I'm too excited."

"I know," I said. "But you ought to try."

"Fine," she said. She turned and went into the kitchen, coming back a moment later with a cup of coffee and a biscuit. She gulped the coffee down but only nibbled on the biscuit.

"I'm ready," she said.

"Are you sure?" I asked. Her eyes shone. She nodded.

Chapter Thirty-Five

We met Emmett and Baird at city hall, where we left Patrick in charge. As we walked to the address Emmett had been given, we passed stores hanging wreaths and selling pine branches and small fir trees. Christmas was only a week away now. It had approached quickly this year. I was glad I had mentioned Angel's birthday in my last letter.

Nessa's steps were quick, and I could almost feel her lively spirit radiating. I was glad now of my decision to include her. Although the walk was quiet, I could feel that we were ready.

The street that connected Water Street to Pleasant Street was an unnamed private street. That was where we were to meet the mill and city men. It was on the other side of the Concord River, where the river—which we'd followed on our way to Boston—met the canal. The Merrimack River bordered the city to the north. The Concord River cut into the city from the south. This small pocket of

Lowell sat in between the two, isolated from the city's daily happenings.

The house sat above the street, a short wall separating us from the grounds. We walked up a shallow but long set of stone steps. The house was an imposing, mostly square structure with small balconies attached to each towering upstairs window. A square, open-air foyer surrounded by circular columns greeted us at the front door. Emmett knocked, and as we waited, I studied our group. Baird was slightly taller than Emmett but not quite as broad and muscular. His hair was similar to Emmett's but lighter in color, like the inside of a log. He had large, round brown eyes and a wide nose, too. He looked like he could use a bath and a new pair of pants that fit properly. In fact, we all needed a good scrub and new clothes. Suddenly, I felt small. My confidence wavered. Emmett looked at me intently and nodded. The door slowly opened.

The man standing in front of us was familiar to me. I had seen him before. My breath caught in my throat. It was the same man who had watched me that night outside of St. Anne's. He noticed my reaction and smirked.

"Come in," he said in a low voice.

Inside, the house was immense. The hallway seemed to lead to an indeterminable number of rooms on the first floor. The ornate staircase wound to the second story like a massive coil, and I could just see the edge of the second-floor ceiling's marbled detailing. I felt my jaw clench, and I tried to breathe steadily. I looked at Nessa. Her mouth was hanging open, her eyes wide.

"Wow," she whispered. I reached for her hand and

squeezed, hoping it would remind her to pull herself together. She looked at me with that same shocked expression but quickly closed her mouth and nodded.

The man took our coats one at a time, holding them out between his thumb and forefinger as if they were rabid creatures. He hung them on a tall coat rack next to the door and led us through the parlor to the second room on our right. A large brass light fixture hung over a large oval table where four more men sat. Their hushed voices ceased entirely when we walked in. All but one stared at us. Some with curiosity, some with contempt. None of them stood.

"Please sit," the first man said, gesturing to the three open chairs on our side of the room. We all stared at them stupidly for a moment, counting them and ourselves, realizing we wouldn't all fit. Glancing around, Emmett quickly picked up a disused chair in the corner of the room and brought it to the table. He gestured for me to sit. Nessa sat next to me. Then Emmett, then Baird. The man who'd greeted us took his seat as well on the opposite side of the table. One of the other men rang a bell. A moment later, a young woman near my age entered. She had blond hair braided on each side of her head. Her eyes were green. And as soon as she spoke, I knew she was Irish.

"Yes, sir?" she asked.

"Tea for our guests," the man said. He was the oldest of the bunch. His white hair circled his head just above his ears in a fluffy band. He wore thin glasses perched on his nose. More fluffy white hair stuck out of his nostrils and ears. His frame was squished down, his neck nonexistent.

The Irish girl gave him a quick curtsy before leaving

again. My eyes darted to Nessa. Her lips were tightly pursed. Emmett spoke first.

"We are here because you've agreed to cease the deportations. Is that true?" he asked.

A different man sat forward wearing a somewhat amused, somewhat annoyed expression.

"Shall we introduce ourselves first?" he asked. It wasn't a question. But Emmett wasn't startled.

"I am Emmett," he replied. "I work at the machine shop. This is my wife, Rosaleen." He held his hand out toward me. "And this is Nessa. They work for the mills." Then he put his hand on Baird's shoulder. "This is Baird. He works at the dye shop. Thank you for inviting us."

The man sat back again. "I am Mr. Shaw. This is Mr. Baker." He pointed to the man at the end of the table who was gazing out the window next to him. "We are here to speak for the city. These three gentlemen—" He pointed to his right now, starting with the old man and ending with the one who had spied on me. "This is Mr. Morgan, Mr. Williams, and Mr. Phillips. They are here to represent the mills and the supporting operations. And we are all here because we have no other choice."

He growled the last part. I shifted.

Then he muttered to himself, "I told Ward this was a risky business, and what do we have now? Irish in our nice chairs." He shuffled some papers around. Mr. Baker still had not spoken.

The Irish maidservant entered the room again with a tray of tea. She set it down in the middle of the table and placed a cup in front of each of us. She poured the tea into all of our cups. Then she backed herself into the corner of the room to await further instruction. I looked at her, but her eyes were fixed ahead, staring at nothing in particular.

The old man had also been staring at some papers, but he looked up at the maid in the corner.

"You are dismissed, Ciara," he said.

She nodded and slipped from the room.

Despite the cold outside, I was beginning to sweat. My dress was looser than when I'd bought it a year ago, yet now it felt constricting and uncomfortable around the neckline. My mouth was dry. I looked at the other cups of tea. No one had touched theirs yet. I reached for mine anyway.

Mr. Phillips, the man who'd greeted us, spoke next.

"The mills are eager for the Irish to get back to work," he said. "The city has indeed decided to stop the deportations. We need to come to an agreement on how to assure you all that this is the case. We do not expect to face this problem again. It has cost us all quite a bit of money."

Mr. Shaw stared at us in a way that made me feel like a nasty beetle that he would rather crush under his boot.

"This city will employ us," Baird said, "to help guard and keep track of the money for the poor farm. We'll see to it ourselves that you keep your promise."

The room was silent. A chair squeaked. Finally, Mr. Phillips cleared his throat.

"Steven?" he asked, looking at Mr. Shaw, who let out a choppy, breathy laugh.

"That is utter nonsense," Mr. Shaw said. "Keeping track of money is a position of importance. You have to be familiar with mathematics, for goodness' sake."

I glared at Steven Shaw. I was getting annoyed with

him. "Sir," I said to him. "We know mathematics just fine. What we don't know is whether the city has the ability to carry out decent and honest policies."

He narrowed his eyes at me.

"I do not believe that I was speaking to you," he hissed.

"Guards might be doable," said a voice at the far end of the table. Mr. Baker was still looking away, but I was certain it was he who had spoken. We all stared at him waiting for more.

He said nothing else.

Mr. Shaw's face reddened. He huffed loudly.

"Our word in writing ought to be sufficient," he said, seemingly speaking to us all.

"It's not," I said.

He stood abruptly, looked at his colleagues, and then sat back down.

"Women!" he shouted at no one in particular. "They brought mouthy women!"

Nessa smiled at me and raised her eyebrows. I could tell there was something she was itching to say. I smiled back in approval.

"You seem like a very important man, sir," Nessa said to Mr. Shaw. "Far too important to be a clerk. A boring task, for certain. I am absolutely convinced that *you* weren't the one to approve city money be provided to the Smelling Committee during their most recent stay in Lowell. I would be entirely shocked if *you* had anything to do with the liquor or the prostitutes that were taken to Mr. Joseph Hiss's room at the city hotel." Then she lowered her voice to almost a whisper and the three men at the center of the table leaned in to hear her. "Irish prostitutes, from what I understand."

Mr. Shaw turned pale. I thought he might retch right there onto the table.

"Wh-who . . . who would say such a thing?" he managed to choke out.

I tried to hold in my laughter. Was she bluffing? How did she know of this?

Nessa sighed. "Don't fret," she said. "Now that I have had the pleasure of meeting you, I am most sure that you are not the type of man to be involved in such scandal. Although I'm not sure the *Lowell American* will make a distinction."

"Enough," Mr. Baker said. He finally turned to face us. "The two men are hired. You," he said, pointing at Emmett, "will be the clerk for the poor farm if you are able. Are you able?"

"Yes, sir," Emmett said.

"One woman, whichever one, will guard the women's quarters at the poor farm. The other man, will guard the men. That is all the hiring we'll be doing today." He stood up. "Mr. Williams, please write up the contract. Mr. Shaw and I will sign it. Then our guests can do the same, and we can all put this behind us."

He turned and left the room. I looked at Nessa. She shrugged at me and smiled again. I could see the satisfaction in her eyes. I wanted to ask her where she had learned of this scandal. Why hadn't she told us last night? But those questions could wait.

"I'd like you to have the job," I whispered to her.

"You're sure?" she asked.

I nodded. "You'll be just right for it. You're tender-hearted, like Josiah."

She grinned. "Now that's a great big lie, but I won't argue," she said.

The other men stood up, one by one, to smoke their pipes in the parlor. We were left with Mr. Williams, who was writing with some speed. I sipped down the rest of my tea. When Mr. Williams finished, he left as well and sent the two representatives from the city back to sign the papers. The four of us sat quietly. Ciara came back into the room. I wondered if she had heard our conversation.

"More tea, ma'am?" she asked me.

"No, thank you," I said. She gave me a small smile before gathering our cups and taking them back to the kitchen.

Mr. Phillips joined us as well. He did not seem to trust the city men. He pulled a chair to our side of the table but still kept his distance as he explained the contract and showed us where to sign. As soon as we did so, he escorted us to the door. Emmett held his hand out to shake Mr. Phillips's, who at first only stared. After an uncomfortable few seconds, he finally shook Emmett's hand.

"Thank you, sir," Emmett said. "We appreciate you being here."

"Well," Mr. Phillips said, "you all brought us into this."

Still, Emmett smiled at him on our way out.

We walked down the steps and onto the sidewalk before Nessa burst out laughing.

"You all looked as white as Mr. Shaw!" she said.

"Why didn't you tell us?" Baird asked.

"I knew when to use it," she said.

"How did you know about it?" I asked.

"Quinn," she said. "Things got awfully rowdy. He responded to the hullabaloo." She pointed to each of us. "But none of you can breathe a word about it."

Chapter Thirty-Six

Baird and Emmett stood on the steps of city hall. Emmett was whispering something in Baird's ear, and Baird was nodding. When Emmett turned to face the crowd, he was smiling. So was Baird, and so was Nessa, who stood a little to the side of the crowd with me. No one but us knew that anything was different about this day. Finally, Baird spoke.

"Attention!" he yelled. Some people stopped talking and looked up, but most continued on with their chatter and laughter.

"Aye!" he shouted, louder. "Shut ye mouths for once!"

Now people turned. Laughter rippled through the crowd.

"I have news from the city!" he went on. "There will be no more deportations!"

Audible gasps rose from the people. Most stood still, quiet, stunned.

"They've hired us—me, and Emmett here next to me—to work the poor farm. We'll be keeping track of the inmates now so we know they'll keep to their word!"

"Yea!" yelled a man with a strong, deep voice. Some of the women shouted and hugged one another

"It's time to celebrate!" Baird shouted. "And to return to work tomorrow. To return to wages!"

Cheers erupted now. I saw a woman crouch down, overcome with emotion. Tears streamed down her face, but she was smiling. I watched the surge of emotion overtake the exhausted crowd. It had been worth it. It was over. That's what their faces seemed to say. Then my eye caught someone at the edge of the crowd. A smaller person. A child, perhaps. He was walking toward me. It was Ronan! I ran to him and wrapped him in a big hug.

"Today is Saturday!" I exclaimed, pulling away, but still holding him at arm's length. "You aren't at work?"

He shrugged. "Told them I was sick," he said. "I've never been sick this whole time. At least not sick enough to miss work. I've gone every day for four years. Even with a cough and a fever." He looked around at the crowd. "I wanted to celebrate Christmas early with you and Emmett and Mr. Joyce. And some of the lads I work with were talkin' about all of this. I wanted to come see for myself."

"Of course we'll celebrate," I said. "That's what everyone is doing here today anyway. Come with me to see Cocoa, and we'll talk about it."

"The lads said you all refused to work or buy anything from the Yankees. And that you came to city hall every day to march and shout. They spoke about it so strange. They seemed a little afraid but excited, too."

I nodded. "The city was taking people from the poor

farm and sending them back to Ireland. Forever. They finally agreed to stop. Just this morning."

Ronan's eyebrows furrowed in thought.

"Do you think they're doing that in Boston, too?" he asked.

"Yes," I said. "I do. But I know my good friend Ruth and her ma, Miss Martha, are working hard to put a stop to it there. They're pretty influential people."

"What does that mean?" he asked.

"It means their opinion is important to powerful people," I said. "They're wealthy."

Ronan looked at me skeptically. "You know wealthy people?" he asked.

I laughed. "Only a few," I said.

"My friend Conor's da is at the almshouse for drunkenness," he said. "Do you think that's the same thing?"

"I think so," I said.

We were both quiet for a moment.

"It isn't fair," I finally said.

"Nothing about this place is fair," Ronan said with more bitterness than I'd expected.

I put my hand on his shoulder and pulled him close to me.

"Perhaps we can make it more fair," I said.

He scoffed and said nothing.

When we walked into our room, Cocoa jumped onto Ronan, her tail and entire backside wagging furiously. She covered Ronan's face with licks, and he laughed.

"I missed you, too, girl," he said.

"Are you hungry?" I asked. "I can make you some food."

"What's everyone out there doing?" he asked, looking out the window, trying to catch a glimpse of the crowd.

"Probably going to the tavern," I said. "We've all been avoiding it for so long because of the arrests. But we've cause to celebrate now. And there's nowhere else to do it."

"We should go, too, then!" Ronan said, excitedly. "I want to see Emmett. Will Mr. Joyce be there?"

"Perhaps," I said. "Will you stay with us tonight?"

Ronan turned to me and smiled. "I would like that," he said. "Aunt Maureen gets angry when I don't come home. But she gets angry at so many things. It doesn't much matter to me anymore."

"I'll take the train back with you in the morning," I said. "She can scold me if she likes."

Ronan giggled like the little boy he was. It surprised me to hear it.

"But you're a grown-up," he said. "That would be awfully silly."

"Exactly," I said. "Now, let's go to the tavern and get you something to eat."

Emmett squeezed Ronan so tight that he picked him right up off the ground.

"Ronan!" he cried. "We're so glad you've joined us on this happy day!"

I smiled at the two of them. Emmett let Ronan go and grabbed me next. I laughed as he took my face in his hands and kissed me. Then, he jumped on top of a chair and shouted to the whole tavern, "Drink up, friends! No one's gettin' sent to Dublin tonight!"

Men whooped and hollered and patted one another on the back. I took Ronan's hand, and we sat at a table.

"You should try the meat pie," I said to Ronan, looking around for a barmaid.

"All right," he said.

I spotted Mr. Joyce entering the tavern. I waved, but he didn't see me. Ronan jumped up and darted after him. Then, Nessa slid into the seat next to mine, pint in hand and grinning from ear to ear.

"You were great this morning," I said. "That's a well-deserved drink you've got there."

"Do you think?" she asked. "Do I deserve four drinks? This is my fourth." She giggled.

Just then, Ronan and Mr. Joyce joined us. Nessa cleared her throat and tried to sit straighter.

"Mr. Joyce," she said. "Wonderful to see you again so soon."

"Nessa," Mr. Joyce said, nodding. "You must have done well this morning. I've heard the good news."

Nessa beamed. "And who is this young man?" she asked.

"I'm Ronan," Ronan said, sticking out his hand for her to shake. She took it.

"Well, hello, Ronan. Such a handsome young fella. You should meet Harriet, Mrs. Durrand's daughter. She's a lovely girl. I think you would like her. Pretty too."

Ronan's face turned red, and I tried not to laugh. I took Nessa's arm and stood up.

"I'll be back in a moment," I said to Ronan and Mr. Joyce.

"Is Quinn here?" I asked Nessa as I steered her away from our table.

"No," she said. "Poor man. He's with those miserable bastards." She stumbled on a man's foot. She turned and touched his arm. "I'm awfully sorry!" she exclaimed. "Clumsy me!"

The man laughed at her and nodded. "Someone's enjoying herself!" he said, looking her up and down.

I gave him a tight-lipped smile and scanned the crowd for friendly faces. Was Mairead here? Or Helen? I didn't see them. I spotted Emmett at a table in the corner with Baird, Patrick, Shona, and Fiona. I took a deep breath and started to walk Nessa over. I didn't want to be around Fiona, but at least no one there would violate Nessa.

"Shona!" Nessa shouted in my ear before rushing over and hugging her. "Isn't it a wonderful day?"

Shona hugged Nessa back and smiled politely. She clearly had not had as much to drink as Nessa.

"Nessa," she said. "It sure is."

Then Nessa tried to focus on Fiona.

"I helped save my brother, you know," Nessa said to Fiona.

"And I'm supposed to thank you for that?" Fiona asked.

"Would be nice," Nessa muttered.

"She did," I said. "We couldn't have done it without her."

Nessa gave me a grateful half smile. Fiona tossed back a big gulp of beer.

"Guess I missed my invitation," Fiona said. "To whatever it was. Funny how Rosaleen here always finds herself in the middle of things. I wonder why that is."

"Oh, it's because she spends her time caring about people," Emmett said. "You ought to try it sometime."

Fiona rolled her eyes. Nessa turned to Shona.

"Can you believe the three of us get to work for the city now?" she asked. "I bet those will be some nice wages!"

"Three? You too?" Shona asked. "What will you be doing?"

"Guarding the women's quarters at the poor farm," Nessa said. "I won't start until after Christmas."

Shona's eyes got wide. "Some of them are insane, aren't they?" she asked.

"I suppose," Nessa said.

"The city calls them that, anyway," I added.

"Won't it be dangerous?" Shona asked.

Fiona laughed. "They don't let the insane ones do whatever they want, you know," she said. "They're probably chained up most of the time."

I hated how she spoke of those people like dogs. "They won't hurt her," I said. "Most of them are probably just incredibly lonely or sad. The mind and heart can only take so much hardship."

Fiona laughed again, but this time it sounded bitter. "Weak," she said. "Their minds are weak. *We've* all gone through hardships, and we're still standing."

"It must be exhausting," Nessa said, her words starting to slur.

"To be insane?" I asked.

"No," Nessa said. "To be her." She pointed at Fiona. "I bet you aren't like that to Frank," she said to Fiona. "You'd feel the back of his hand on your face if you were. I've felt it. We were kids, but still, it hurt then. It probably hurts worse now."

Fiona's eyes narrowed. "You know nothing of me and Frank," she replied. "And I plan on keeping it that way. You won't ever see him once we're married." She turned then and stomped off.

I looked back at Ronan and Mr. Joyce. They were talking and laughing.

"I'll walk you home, Nessa," I said.

"What?" she asked, incredulously. "I'm just getting started."

I smiled at her. "You won't want to be sick all day tomorrow," I said. "Come on. You can thank me later."

Nessa pouted but didn't argue again. She hugged our friends, and we left.

"Now we're both her enemies, aren't we?" I said once we had left the tavern behind. Nessa laughed.

"I wanted to like her," she said. "For the longest time. But it's impossible."

Chapter Thirty-Seven

I made Ronan a bed near the fireplace, and when he cuddled up with Cocoa and fell asleep in our home, my heart felt grateful. Emmett came stumbling home just after midnight, nearly as drunk as Nessa had been. He plopped down, face-first on our bed, still wearing all of his clothes and a dreamy grin. I sat at the foot of the bed and started to take his boots off.

"My lovely wife," he slurred into the bed, "givin' me a foot rub at the end of a long day."

"Wrong," I laughed. "Only gettin' your dirty shoes off our bed."

He rolled onto his back. "Worth a try," he said. I put his boots at the door. When I came back, his eyes were closed. I unbuttoned his coat. He nudged himself awake as I tried to pull his arms out. When I pulled the whole coat out from under him, he rolled to his side.

"Oh, Rose," he murmured. "Luckiest man alive." And then he was snoring.

I kissed his head and climbed over him to the other side of the bed. I lay there for some time, trying to allow myself to feel relief. To feel glad. I had plenty of reason to with our victory that day. But instead, I only felt unsettled. Like something, perhaps an insect, was crawling about inside of me, pushing various levers, making sure I was still paying attention. Perhaps it was my conversation with Mairead. I hadn't seen her since, and things felt uncertain between us. Or maybe it was Fiona. Maybe Frank was no longer in danger of being sent to Ireland, but he *was* still at the poor farm. He must have been nearly done with his time there, though, now that I thought of it. Did Fiona's threat still stand?

I tried not to think of it. I thought of Ronan by the fire with Cocoa. Ronan laughing with Mr. Joyce. I thought of all the people at the poor farm who wouldn't be taken away from their families anymore. Eventually, the insect stopped, and I fell asleep.

I left Emmett in the morning with fresh coffee and boiled, salted potatoes. He groaned, rolled over, and shooed me away. Mr. Joyce walked me and Ronan to the train station. Ronan held his hand out for Mr. Joyce to shake as he said goodbye.

"Remember what we talked about," Mr. Joyce said to him, smiling. Ronan smiled back and nodded.

"I'll see you soon, Mr. Joyce," Ronan said.

"I'm sorry I'm missing Mass," I said to Mr. Joyce.

"You have somewhere important to be today," he replied, looking at Ronan fondly.

Ronan and I gave our tickets to the railway conductor and boarded the train.

"Do you even like to ride these?" I asked him as we pulled out of the station.

Ronan nodded. "One day I'll likely be an engineer," he said.

"Is that what you want?" I asked.

"You think too much about what I want," he said. "A railway engineer is a good occupation. Good wages. I'd be lucky to have it."

I sighed. "You're right," I said. He smiled to himself, satisfied. We rode the rest of the way in a contented quiet.

The smells of the city hit me as soon as we disembarked. It was strange how Boston and Lowell smelled alike but still very distinct. The rusty, oily smell of the mills tainted Lowell's air, and the salty, fishy harbor smell tainted the air in Boston. But the smell of too many humans and animals sharing the space was the same.

I wanted to say goodbye again without pestering Ronan. I wanted to be there when he wanted me and not when he didn't. But I couldn't shake the image of him yesterday. Happy. Free of worry.

"Should I come in?" I asked him when we got to his uncle's house. "So your aunt can't scold you?"

Ronan looked up at the house apprehensively. "It won't matter," he said. "She'll scold when you leave anyway."

I tried to hold back, then, but I couldn't help myself. "Please leave them, Ronan," I said. "Please. Come to Lowell for good next time."

I saw the frustration contort his face immediately. His smile was gone.

"Stop asking," he said. "I'm not staying in Lowell. I know you make everything so perfect for me when I'm there. You think I don't love it?" He raised his voice. "You think that isn't the happiest home I can remember? Is that what you want to hear from me?"

He closed his eyes and wiped his sleeve across them.

"I want you to be happy and safe," I said. "I made a promise to your ma. I promised her I wouldn't leave you until you were safe. And I left you anyway. Where you weren't safe at all." Ronan's eyes darkened at the mention of his ma.

"You aren't the only one who made a promise to my ma," he said. "I made a promise, too. I promised I would listen to everything you said until we reached my uncle. And *then* I would listen to everything *he* told me to do. So that's what I'm doing. I'm listening to everything my uncle tells me to do, and I'm trying my hardest to do it. Because I also promised her I would find her a job and build her a garden. But I couldn't keep *those* promises."

He glared at me. He wasn't done.

"She was *my* ma. I won't carry the weight of a broken promise."

He sniffed and wiped his eyes again.

"I'm not special, you know," he went on. "You think I'm some sad story, but all the boys at the railway are my age or younger! Every year there are more who are younger. This is what people do here." He held his arms out to show me the reach of the desperation. He stepped closer to me, his chin pointed up so he could look into my eyes. "And you know what? If Ma had lived, she would have sent me there, too."

"Ronan, your ma did the most selfless thing a ma could

do when she let you go with me," I said. "I don't believe that."

"Well, you should," he said. "She wasn't special either. She was poor and hungry and sick. Like everyone else here. You and Emmett? *You're* the exception. Not me."

I wanted to hug him and cry on him. But that was a selfish urge, so I just took his hand in mine.

"I'm sorry," I said.

"It's not up to you to apologize," he said.

"I hope you'll come to Lowell as often as you can," I said.

He shrugged. "I'll see you around, Rosaleen," he said.

Then he turned and walked through the door, and my heart broke into thousands of pieces.

Chapter Thirty-Eight

Ronan's words burdened me like a tender full of wood as I walked to the inn. How could a young boy be so cynical? He was right, of course. I *was* the exception. Nothing around here was simple. People made difficult decisions every day in order to survive. I had Miss Susan to thank for my good fortune. I would make sure to remind her of that. Still, I hadn't done enough for Ronan.

As I left the North End, the streets became more hushed. The men were working in offices or shops. The women were also working or attending to household chores. The wealthier women were shopping and socializing. It was a quiet sort of bustle. As steady as a hummingbird's wings.

As soon as the inn came into view, I yearned to bury myself in its coziness and familiarity. I hurried to it. Miss Susan was cleaning tables when I entered, and she put her rag down and came to me. We embraced for just a moment.

"What a lovely surprise," she said. "You're in much

better spirits than last time, I see. Will you be staying tonight?"

I shook my head. "My train back to Lowell is this evening."

"You've missed Marie," Miss Susan said. "She left early for church this morning and now she and Eileen are likely at the market. You're welcome to wait for them."

"I will do that," I said. I spotted the broom behind the kegs and went to get it. Miss Susan didn't stop me from sweeping the dining room floor. We worked in silence for a bit before Miss Susan spoke up.

"I'm sure I'm not the first to ask, and if it's none of my business, tell me. But will you and Emmett be starting a family soon? I think you'd make nice parents."

I missed Miss Susan's way of saying exactly what she wanted to say. Nothing more. Nothing less.

"Thank you," I said. "We have been talking about it. I think I'm nearly ready. Emmett's been ready, but I wasn't so sure at first. Children change everything."

"I can understand that," she said. "I was never interested in starting a family. I always knew my family would be of a different sort. The people I choose to have close to me. I do love children. It wasn't about that. But having a man dictate what I do all day? How I spend my money? My husband, God rest his soul, could never have made a proper wife out of me."

I smiled. "Emmett doesn't tell me what to do," I said. "Thankfully. He advises me sometimes. But it's the way you would a friend. He knows I'll do what I want with that advice."

"You hold onto him, then," she said. "I hear more of

disgraceful husbands and unpleasant arrangements than of what you're describin'. You might not know this about Florence, but she used to have a husband, too. Florence is like me. A different kind of woman. He hated her for it. Said she was an embarrassment. He couldn't stand that she didn't worship him. He beat her awfully."

"That's horrible," I said. "What did she do?"

"She left him," Miss Susan said. "Took a train from New York City while he was at work. She showed up at this inn bruised and terrified, looking for a place to sleep. That's when I started to believe in God again. God led her here. I kept her hidden for months. And that bastard did come lookin' for her. He had friends lookin', too. Knockin' on doors all around the city. Never found her, though. I nursed her back to health."

Miss Susan's face rarely betrayed any emotion. But now I could tell just how special her relationship with Florence was. It was in the way she told the story. The pain in her voice reliving it.

"I'm glad she has you now," I said.

Miss Susan stopped scrubbing and looked up at me—trying to read me, perhaps.

"It's kind of you to say," she said.

I started sweeping again. I didn't want to make her uncomfortable.

"I'm glad we all have you," I went on. "Marie, Eileen, me. My life would be very different today if you hadn't taken me in. So would Eileen's. You truly changed our lives."

Miss Susan was quiet. My back was to her as I swept the corner of the room. Finally, she cleared her throat.

"Thank you," she said, quietly. Then she spoke a little louder, regaining her composure. "You are both excellent workers. It only makes sense."

Just then, the door to the inn opened, and Marie and Eileen came through carrying baskets of food.

Marie let out a little excited yelp. "Rosaleen!" she cried. "What are you doing here? I wasn't expecting you!"

I kissed Marie's cheek, then Eileen's.

"Surprise visit for the day," I said. "Here, I'll help you with those."

I picked a few eggplants out of Marie's basket and followed the two ladies into the kitchen.

"How's your beau, Eileen?" I asked.

Eileen rolled her eyes. "I'd kill him if I didn't love him so much."

I laughed. "Oh goodness. What did he do?"

"Applied for a position at a bloody newspaper," Eileen said. "He wants to learn how to use a camera and take photographs. Who has even heard of such a thing? I can't get him to stop talking about it. I told him no newspaper is going to hire an Irishman."

She heaved her basket onto the table in the kitchen and started to unload it.

"Would you believe it?" she went on. "He's found a fella whose parents are Irish and who works in the newspaper business takin' photographs. Damn him and his silly ideas. We're to be gettin' married eventually, you know, and he's off beggin' for a new position. Who knows what kind of wages this newspaper will pay!"

I looked at Marie, who was only half hiding a smile. She

shrugged. I put one arm around Eileen's shoulders and squeezed.

"Sounds exciting!" I said. "I think you ought to be proud of him."

She looked at me and raised an eyebrow.

"Whose side are you on?" she asked.

I laughed. "I saw a photograph once," I said. "I couldn't believe it. It was a man standing next to a cart. He looked so real. Like he might step off the paper any moment."

"Well, don't you get Eddie talkin' about it if you see him," she said. "He won't ever stop."

Eileen looked at what was left in her basket and then Marie's.

"I'll take the rest of these down to the root cellar," she said. "And then, if it's all right with you, Marie, I'll wash my clothes quick."

"Yes, that's fine," Marie said. Once Eileen was out of earshot, Marie grabbed my arm and pulled me closer.

"I've got news for you," she said.

"You go first," I said to Marie as we chopped the ingredients for the Sunday stew. I had told her that I had news, too. She didn't know yet about the meeting.

"Gil and I have decided to get married," she said.

I put my knife down and hugged her. She laughed a little and hugged me back.

"I kept talking to God like you said. He finally answered. He made me see that this is His plan. This is the time and place where He put me. Right here, in this country, where people are being hunted down and dragged back into a life in chains. I can't change what's happening today. But maybe I can change what happens tomorrow. Maybe my baby can change what happens in tomorrow's tomorrow. Fear can't help me. But hope can. Besides, I want a baby. I want it so bad in my heart. And Gil is already my baby's father. There's no one else out there. No other man —not even one who was born free—could take his place."

My eyes brimmed with tears, and my heart ached. This was courage. Marie and Gil and their determination to love one another. It was an overwhelming act of bravery. I dabbed my eyes with my sleeve.

"I can't wait to meet that baby," I said.

Marie grinned. "And come for the wedding?" she asked. "We're going to wait until it's a little warmer. Maybe in May."

"You know I would never miss that," I said. "For anything."

I kept chopping. Marie plopped ingredients into the broth, steadily plucking more from my pile as we worked together seamlessly.

"My news is good, too," I went on. "Our meeting went perfectly, Marie. The city of Lowell is stopping the deportations. Emmett will make sure of it, because he'll be managing the money for the poor farm."

Marie turned to me now, eyes wide. She hugged me again.

"That's wonderful news," she said. "You did it!"

I nodded. "We all did. All of the Irish in Lowell. And you and Ruth and Miss Martha."

"Are you worried?" she asked.

"About what?"

"About the people you've angered," she said. "They'll be looking for you."

My stomach seemed to roll over, and the worry I had been trying to suppress coursed through my body again.

"You think so?" I asked.

"Yes," she said. "Promise me you'll be more careful now."

"How?" I asked.

"Don't walk alone anywhere, at any time," she said. "Make amends with your enemies. Even if you still don't care for them. Make them believe that you do."

Fiona's bitter eyes came to mind. How could I even begin to make amends with her? But Marie wasn't talking about the Irish. She was talking about the Know-Nothings. I thought of all the Yankees I knew. I hadn't made enemies out of any of them. Except, perhaps, Abner Keyes. But he would have no way of knowing. Unless Quinn . . .

But I pushed that thought away, too. Quinn didn't know. And if he had found out somehow, he wouldn't tell those men. Nessa had told me how angry they made him. Surely his loyalty was with his own people over those men.

The only Yankee who knew my true identity was Nancy. And Nancy would take it with her to the grave. I knew that much.

"It's a serious thing that you've done," Marie went on as she sprinkled a pinch of spices into the stew. "You've interrupted their money-making. Their plans, their schemes, and in a big way."

"Yes," I agreed. "I have."

I sat down. I was quiet for a while, watching Marie stir and taste and add. Suddenly, I felt quite vulnerable. I needed to talk to Emmett. To Mr. Joyce. Could they protect me? Could anyone? Finally, Marie sat next to me.

"You did the right thing," she said. "I'm proud of you."

I smiled faintly. "How will I keep them away?"

She thought for a moment, biting her bottom lip, thinking.

"Don't write for a while," she said. "Just for a little while. And when you do write again, we'll think of a topic that won't make the Yankees so mad. Temperance, if you want." She looked at me sideways and gave me a sly smile.

Chapter Thirty-Nine

The day after I returned from Boston, I went to see Mairead. I couldn't have things between us so strained. Especially when I knew she was right. She had avoided me at work that day, and I felt a flutter in my chest as I knocked on her door. Dennis opened it.

"Rosaleen," he said. "Please come in. I'll go get Mairead."

"Thank you," I said. I sat on their sofa and crossed my arms. Then I uncrossed them. I felt uncomfortable, awkward. I sat on the edge of my seat, hands planted firmly next to my legs, bracing for something. Perhaps to run away when she didn't accept my apology.

She came into the room by herself, already looking irritated. I stood up.

"I'm sorry, Mairead," I said at once. "You were right. Everything you said. I've been a lousy abolitionist. And I've doubted my friends. It's why I've felt so awful lately. I know it."

She sighed. "You're a fine abolitionist, Rosaleen," she

said. "None of us have the luxury of leaving the mills. You do what you can. Maybe more than you should."

There it was again, another hint that she knew. I ignored it for now. But I would tell her soon. I would have to. She was too dear a friend.

"I can do better," I said. "If I can remember who we are as a people. If I trust the rest of you to have a brain and a heart. The Irish don't need to go to those meetings. We can help in other ways."

Mairead smiled now. "Wait just a minute," she said. "That last meeting was awfully fun. Promise me we can keep going."

I laughed. "All right, then," I said. "We'll keep going."

After work on Christmas Eve, I stopped on the way home to buy a holly wreath. The candles in our window were lit, and now I wanted a wreath with red berries that smelled of wet wood. The shop also sold small trees, and I thought of Henry's family decorating the one at their house. I gave the shopkeeper my coins and thanked him.

It hadn't snowed since the day before our meeting, but that night, it felt like it might. I breathed the clear air in. It was heavy. When I reached our home, I hung the wreath on the nail on the door. This was my first Christmas together with Emmett, as husband and wife, in our home. I couldn't help but to feel joy.

I bounded up the stairs, swinging the door open with a big grin on my face. Emmett was waiting. He smiled shyly at me.

"I tried my hand at cooking a Christmas meal," he said. "I think you'll enjoy it more than the cornmeal cakes I used to make."

I laughed and hugged him. "It's wonderful," I said.

"You haven't even tried it yet." He led me to the table and pointed to each item on the plate as he named them. "A roasted hen. Potatoes, onions, cranberries, bread, and cheese."

"I love it!" I said.

"I know this is a large supper," he said. "But I wanted to have our own special evening. Mr. Joyce is at Mass. I convinced him we would join him tomorrow."

I took off my coat and sat down at the table. The food smelled lovely. I cut into the hen and chewed very slowly to savor the juices and flavors.

"Mmmmm," I said. "It's been so long since I've had a roasted hen."

Emmett grinned. "I did a good job, then?"

"An excellent job," I said. "Can you believe in just a few days you'll be managing money for the city? This is a big deal for us. For all of us. The Irish have never held positions like this before, working for the city."

Emmett laughed. "Are you trying to make me nervous?"

I smiled. "No," I said. "I'm only proud of you."

"I hope I don't forget how to count," he said.

I laughed. "Even if you did, you'd still be better in that position than any Know-Nothing."

"Not the highest compliment I've received, but I'll take it," he said.

We ate quietly for a while. The sun was nearly completely set outside, and Emmett's face was half-illuminated by a kitchen lamp. I gazed at the scar across his cheek. He hadn't told me the story of it until last year. Perhaps because it wasn't anything particularly exciting. He'd raced his brother Steven down the hill toward the bog behind his house and tripped and split his cheek open on a sharp rock. The scar had been there for as long as he could remember. It was such a part of him that he forgot it was there at all.

I went to him and sat on his leg, tracing the scar with my finger. He wrapped his arms around my waist.

"I remember noticing this scar on the boat," I said. "I thought maybe you were a tough guy. A fighter."

He smirked. "And then you got to know me and realized I was just as afraid as anyone else on that ship."

I shook my head. "You never seemed afraid to me," I said. "You seemed like the bravest man in all the world." I kissed his scar, the place where his dimple indented, his lips. I kissed him slowly and gently. Then, I pulled away and whispered into his ear, "I'm ready to make that baby now."

He looked at me with hungry eyes, picked me up by my legs, and carried me to the bed. After, when he was still breathing heavily, he asked me, "Do you think we did it that time?"

We were both lying on our backs. I turned my head to him.

"It's likely," I said. "Mairead taught me how to track my cycle. Told me which days I'm most likely to become pregnant. Today was a good day."

"You promise you want this now?" he asked.

I smiled at him playfully. "I wasn't just trying to get you

into bed," I said. "Yes, I want this. I really want this. I finally feel like things might be moving forward for us. For all of us."

"What will we name her?" he asked.

"Julia," I said, without hesitation. He squeezed my hand. "And if it's a boy, Steven or James." I looked at him to see his reaction. He was quiet. His breathing was steadying. He stared at the ceiling. Finally, he spoke.

"If he's a little guy, James," he said. "If he's a big boy, Steven."

Then he looked at me and kissed my forehead before getting up to dress and put some tea on. I got dressed, too, and went outside to use the privy. The cold air felt nice on my flushed face. When I was done, I grabbed a log to bring back upstairs. That's when I saw Ina walking down our street alone.

"Ina," I called to her. She turned, just a few steps past our house.

"Happy Christmas, Rosaleen," she said.

"Happy Christmas," I said. "Is there anything you need?"

She shook her head. "Da's in a fine mood tonight," she said. "Sent me to fetch a cookie for my sister. Bakery's awfully busy."

I studied her face in the light of the streetlamp. I couldn't find much emotion in it. Certainly no joy. Still, I said, "I'm glad, and I hope your family has a lovely evening."

"Me too," she said. "Good night." And she turned to leave. I walked back up the stairs and was about to open the door when I heard footsteps. I spun around, clutching the log to my chest. It was only Mr. Joyce. The darkness had made me jumpy. He walked up the steps toward me.

"I'll take that log," he said. "Happy Christmas!"

He looked invigorated after Mass, as usual.

"Happy Christmas, Mr. Joyce." I gave him a kiss on the cheek and handed him my log.

"Who was that girl you were speaking to?" he asked.

We both looked down the street after her, a dark figure in the distance growing smaller and smaller.

"One of the students I tutor," I said. "Her name is Ina. We should say a prayer for her tonight."

The snow came down steadily during Christmas morning Mass. I watched it through the stained glass, the flakes tinted blue and green and purple and yellow. Father Purcell was sick, and so Father John performed the Christmas liturgy and homily. He read from Matthew and spoke of how good it was for Joseph not to cast Mary aside when he found her pregnant. Of how important Joseph's trust was in the Lord. I thought of how easy it must have been for Joseph to trust after an actual angel appeared to him. What about when God gives you no signs, no answers?

As we walked home from the church, the snow fell in large, wet flakes. Mr. Joyce lagged behind. He had been reluctant to leave without prodding the nuns for more information on Father Purcell's condition.

"Do you think if Mary lived today, she'd be called insane and sent to the poor farm?" I asked Emmett.

"Yes," he said. "She was probably called insane then. Only not by the people who wrote the Bible."

"Who must have had more faith?" I asked. "Joseph or Mary? Mary gave up her body to the son of God without even agreeing to it. I suppose they battled different emotions. But part of hers must have been anger."

Emmett only nodded.

"What about all of the women—since the beginning of time—who've been called insane, but who never had an angel come and tell their husband or their father otherwise?" I went on. "They all ended up at poor farms or almshouses or worse, I'm sure."

Emmett raised his eyebrows and looked at me.

"Who are you thinking of?" he asked.

I sighed. "Fiona called those women weak the other day. But I'll always remember that woman's eyes. The one on the boat. I'm not sure if she *was* insane, but they certainly treated her that way. She wasn't weak. The mother Mary wasn't weak."

"Fiona is a bit daft herself," Emmett said. "Have you thought of how you'll handle her threat?"

"Do you think it still stands?" I asked. "With the deportations gone and Frank's time nearly up?"

"As appalling as it is to do, you might want to talk to her," he said.

"If I must," I said. "But not on Christmas. I don't want to think about it on Christmas."

"Would you like to know what I'm thinking about on Christmas?" he asked.

"What?" I asked.

"Mr. Joyce's delicious boiled ham!" he said, turning to look over his shoulder. "Is he coming?"

I laughed. "I hope so."

I took Cocoa outside as soon as we were home. The snow fell on her eyelashes and her nose, and she shook her head to get them off. She dug her paws into the few inches of snow that covered the ground, one paw at a time, until she had dug a small hole. She stuck her nose in the hole, and her tail shot straight out in the air as she anticipated finding some small creature buried inside this mysterious, cold powder. I smiled.

Emmett had tea waiting when I came back inside. I set my wet boots by the fire to dry and hung my wet coat. Mr. Joyce stomped into the room a few minutes after me, trying to knock the snow off his boots.

"Father Purcell isn't allowing any visitors," Mr. Joyce said. "He must be quite sick."

"We'll pray for him," Emmett said.

"Do you need my help making dinner?" I asked.

"Please," Mr. Joyce said. He hung his coat next to the fire, too, and hoisted a sack of food onto the table that he had brought in with him. I took my place next to Mr. Joyce, and we worked quietly preparing dinner. I wondered if next year there would be a baby here, too. What a wonderful home for a baby, I thought. There would be no lack of love here.

After we had second and third helpings and all of the dinner was gone, Mr. Joyce pulled two letters out of his pocket.

"I brought these in for you," he said. I opened the first. It was from Angel.

Dear Rosaleen,

I don't know where I would go if I could fly. Anywhere, I guess. That's the fun thing about flying. That machine doesn't look big enough for Mommy and Daddy to come, too. I would miss them. Maybe they could each have one and we could fly together. Mommy's buying me a cake on my birthday, and Aunt Marie bought me a pretty new red dress. I think I'll wear it to church on Christmas. Tell me more about people who have made things that have never been thought of yet. Maybe I'll do that one day.

Love,
Angel

The second letter was from Ruth.

Dear Rosaleen,

Marie told me about your marvelous victory. I am so proud and pleased. I hope our contribution was helpful.

Mother has been hard at work convincing the legislature that the deportations across the state must stop. I do believe the tide is turning against the Smelling Committee—and perhaps against the Know-Nothings in their entirety.

We have done our part in convincing the most powerful and well-known abolitionists in Boston that the Know-Nothings are a harmful distraction to our overall cause. While they have no particular love for the Irish, they know that you are not the true enemy. The treasonous Southerners are.

I do hope to see you soon. Visit whenever time permits, and I will do the same. Merry Christmas.

All my love,

Ruth

P.S. – Mother cares not for talk of suitors, but Father has found a very handsome man that would like to court me. More details to come!

Chapter Forty

I met Nessa at the boardinghouse after work the day after Christmas. Frank was to be released from the poor farm that evening, and I'd promised to walk there with her.

"You ought to get a horse," I said to her as we walked, the sun starting to set. "You'll be walking this every day and every night soon. A horse would be nice. Isn't Quinn pulling in better wages now?"

"He is," she said. "I'm not sure he's pulling in *those* kinds of wages yet, but perhaps in a few months I can purchase my own. A horse would be nice."

We found Josiah in the same spot as our first visit. Right outside the men's quarters. His face brightened at the sight of us.

"I know you two from somewhere," he said. "I never forget pretty faces or pleasant company."

"We were here before to visit Frank McHugh," I said. "He's being released this evening, isn't that correct?"

"It sure is," Josiah said. "It's always nice to see an inmate released. Especially now that I know they truly are going home." He paused and scratched the back of his neck, looking down awkwardly. Then he cleared his throat. "Anyway, Frank should be finishing up supper right about now. Shall we go see?"

"Yes," Nessa said. "Please!"

Josiah let us inside, and we looked around at the men gobbling their food. Frank was eating the quickest. I worried he would choke. We went over to him.

"Frank!" Nessa shouted. He looked up at us and grinned. He stood and hugged Nessa. I watched him breathe in the scent of her hair. His eyes were closed, and he looked so happy. Then he opened his eyes and laughed.

"My baby sister!" he cried. "You've come to get me!"

She nodded vigorously. "Oh, Frank," she said. "You won't believe it, but I've got a job here! At the poor farm."

He looked confused for a moment.

"How did you pull that off?" he wondered.

"Have you heard that the deportations have ceased?" she asked.

"Of course," he said. "It was a real cause for celebration here, as you can imagine."

"I was part of that deal!" she squealed. Her excitement shone from her like a lamp in the dark. She stood tall, her chin lifted. Frank's eyebrows went up.

"You were?" he asked. "How?"

Nessa looked at me, waiting just a few feet away. "Rosaleen," she said. "Rosaleen arranged the meeting."

I shook my head. "They came to Emmett," I said. "But you should be proud of your sister. She saved the day."

Frank gave me a half smile before looking back at Nessa.

"And the position here was part of the deal?"

She nodded again. "We told them we needed to keep an eye on things here. Emmett's managing the poor farm's money. And Baird and I will be guards here. Baird is a man who came to the meeting with us. I'll be guarding the women and he the men. Rosaleen let me have the job. They said one of us women would be hired. She gave it to me."

Frank's eyes darted to me again and lingered. "Is that right?" he asked.

His gaze made me nervous. He stepped toward me.

"You and Emmett negotiated with the city?" he asked me.

"Yes," I said. "We couldn't let the deportations continue. We had to do something."

He stared at me for a long minute. Finally, he said, "Thank you."

I was shocked. "You're welcome."

"I know you and I haven't always gotten along," he went on. "But these last few weeks . . ." He trailed off, shaking his head. "There had been rumors for some time. We tried to ignore them. But when we heard of what you all were doing, we knew they were true. Every single one of us thought we would be the next one to go. I think I might have killed someone had they tried to take me."

His face was serious and pained.

"I'm glad it didn't come to that," I said.

Frank's mouth twisted into a smile. "Me too," he said. "I'm grateful to you and Emmett. I am." I smiled back. Nessa put her arms around her brother. "And my very own sister was a part of it!" He kissed the top of her head. "I couldn't be more proud, Nessa."

She looked up at him and beamed.

❧

I walked home alone that night. Nessa and Frank were to pick up Nessa's dress on their way home, and we parted soon after leaving the farm. I assured them I would stick to the roads where the streetlights would brighten my path.

I thought of Frank's face. About his relief. About Nessa's pride. I finally felt content. I felt a page was turning, a chapter ending. In a few days, Emmett and Nessa and Baird would begin their new positions. We would have a voice, even if it was a quiet one—and it would have an Irish brogue. I smiled.

But then a sound broke through my thoughts. Footsteps. I froze. The back of my neck prickled with gooseflesh. I spun around. No one was there. I heard nothing but the quickening of my breath. I continued walking, more alert now. My eyes widened in the dimming color of dusk. I tried to look behind each tree that I passed. My heart banged against my chest.

Suddenly, a jolt of pain behind my right ear made me cry out. Something had hit me hard. My whole head was drowning in a heavy pain. Within seconds, everything began to go black. Just before I collapsed, I felt hands under my armpits, dragging me away.

Chapter Forty-One

I awoke to the smell of urine and moldy hay. My eyes were slow to open and when they did, everything was blurry. I tried to move, but my feet were restrained. I tried to focus. Where was I? I was sitting up in a chair. I could see the chair's legs now and the rope tying them to my ankles. There was barely any light. I lifted my head as high as I could, but a yelp escaped my lips at the pain. I looked to my right, and as I turned my head, I felt sticky blood covering my hair and shoulder. I could see a lamp hanging on the wall next to a stall. I was in a barn.

Then I recognized a sound. A scraping. Of someone sharpening a blade. I turned my head to the left, but that side of the barn was shrouded in darkness. I went to wipe the blood from my face and realized my hands were tied together in my lap. There was a rope around my stomach, too, holding me to the chair. I pulled and twisted my hands in a panic, but they wouldn't budge. And then I heard a voice coming from the shadows. It made my blood turn cold.

"Well, well," Abner Keyes said. "If it isn't my favorite Biddy in all of Lowell. Just. Waking. Up."

I did not look up at him but watched his boots walk over to me. They stopped square in front of my chair.

"You know, I take that back," he said. "My favorite Biddy in all of Lowell is the one who led me to you. Wish I could remember her name. Handsome gal. All I had to do was promise to get her beau out of that farm. Too bad that's got nothin' to do with me."

He squatted down. My heart beat faster. He pressed the cold blade of his knife under my chin and lifted it so that I had to look at his face. He wet his thin lips with his tongue from corner to corner. They shone with spit.

"I was hoping to catch me a Paddy, and here you are." He laughed, then. An eerie, high-pitched laugh. "Didn't know you had the bollocks." He traced his knife down my neck, down the center of my chest, down my belly, and rested it between my legs. My face got hot with anger. I nearly spat in his face but stopped myself. I wasn't here to die. I needed to stay alive. *Stay alive, Rosaleen*, I thought. I tried to steady my breath, tried to think of something smart to say. Something to save myself. But I couldn't. All I could do was deny it.

"I-I . . . I don't know of what you're speaking," I stuttered.

"Don't be dense, girl," he said, taking his knife back. He picked under his thumbnail with it. "I told you. Your little friend betrayed you."

"It's not . . . it's not me," I said, tears streaming down my face. He stood up.

"That's enough," he growled. I stopped arguing. He paced in front of me.

"He's gon' be glad," he said. "Glad to have you taken care of."

"Who?" I asked, my voice much shakier than I wanted it to be.

"You'll meet him soon enough," he said. "I'm expecting him any moment now."

My shoulders began to shake. I was cold, but I knew that wasn't why I was shaking. Abner sat in a chair on the other side of the stall. His legs spread wide. He leaned between them, playing with his knife.

"I'll admit, that was some smart thinkin' you did with that last letter," he said. "Too bad it's the last one you'll ever write. But don't be too sad. You'll probably become a legend once you're gone. Because we'll make sure none of your kind ever does what you did. Ever. Again."

My gaze darted around the room, looking for something, anything to spark an idea. I couldn't give up. I needed to get out of this chair. Out of these ropes. I tried to ignore the pounding in my head. But it was making it nearly impossible to think.

I forced myself to focus. Abner was still speaking, but I no longer heard him. I closed my eyes and listened instead to the wind blowing outside. The mice shuffling through the stacks of hay. My own breath. I moved my foot slowly. The rope was loser down there. If I could only bend down, I was certain I could break my left leg free. But the rope around my waist was too high to bend that far. It was up near my chest, hugging my ribs. I couldn't try anything anyhow. Not with Abner sitting only feet away, watching.

I opened my eyes. Abner was smirking at something he had just said. He held his knife up in the air, rotating it around to watch it glimmer, admiring his sharpening work. Perhaps I could distract him. Have him turn his back to me for a moment. And what would I do with a free leg, then? Whatever I needed to, I told myself. I just needed to do something.

Water, I thought. *Water*.

"Water," I said. "May I have some water?"

Abner looked startled to hear my voice. He was in the middle of a story. Or perhaps he'd forgotten I could speak.

"You think this is a tavern?" he sneered. "There's no water for you here. Only for the horses. And I don't care enough to lead you to the trough."

The idea must have struck him as funny because he started laughing again. That awful, high-pitched laugh. But then another sound mixed in, nearly the exact same pitch. The squeak of a door.

Chapter Forty-Two

A bner didn't hear it at first, so caught up was he in his own joke—the vision of him forcing my head into a trough like a horse. But then the footsteps got louder and Abner stopped abruptly. He leaped out of his chair and stood to face the man in the shadows.

"There you are!" he exclaimed. "I know *the* Paddy isn't exactly *a* Paddy. But she's here. I got her. I checked my sources. I know we were expecting a man, but as you can see, she's not. But this is the writer. This is Paddy. I'm certain of it."

He stepped aside now so the man could see me. I squinted, but I could see nothing more than a vague figure.

"As I suspected," the man in the shadows said.

Sometimes, when a person focuses intently on one thing, on seeing or hearing or tasting a thing, they miss something quite obvious about it. And that's what happened to me at first. I heard the words but not the voice. It was only in the short silence that followed that it slowly occurred to me what I had just heard. A voice I had heard before. That I had heard many times. No. *No, no, no*, my mind said. It didn't make sense. It couldn't be. But I knew that it was, and my stomach rose in my throat. I turned my head and vomited toward the side that was not covered in blood. My eyes filled with tears. A sob escaped my lips.

"Father Purcell?" I trembled. The tears streamed down my face. "Why are you here? Why are you doing this?"

Father Purcell stepped closer, into the light. He stared at me and shook his head.

"How far astray you've been led," Father Purcell said, quietly. He sounded almost sad. But then his voice became sharp. "All of that nonsense about the mills, the Negroes, and now this."

"Please." I knew it was no use denying the truth to this man. He seemed to look into my very soul. "Please think about this. Father. I know the church doesn't always agree with Paddy. But *this* outcome—this time, it was a good one. Surely you can't be upset that the deportations have stopped."

Father Purcell's arms were crossed. His robes bunched at his armpits. His eyes looked solemn. He sighed loudly.

"I ought to be pleased that the Acre will once again be plagued with vice and sin?" Father Purcell looked down at me through his glasses as if I were waste stuck to the bottom of his shoe. "Those wicked and demented people were being punished, and He was glad for it. I was glad for it."

"And the poor?" I nearly whispered.

"I did what I could for them," he said. "The rest I must leave up to God."

He looked around the barn for a moment, his gaze finally landing on the chair Abner had been sitting on.

"Fetch me that chair, Abner," Father Purcell said.

This can't be, I thought. Father Purcell was the leader of our people. I shook my head. None of this made sense. Father Purcell sat in the chair, his back straight, still studying me.

"I've been searching for you for a while, you know," he went on. "Ever since I first arrived in Lowell and read your letters. I knew then that you were a problem. I knew I would need to deal with you."

He lowered his head and shook it.

"I mean, truly, girl, who do you think you are?" he asked, in a cutting voice. "Will the Merrimack River part and you'll lead your people out of Egypt? You're no prophet. You're only an arrogant, sinful woman."

"Fa-Father," I stuttered, my fear rising. I thought of every letter I had written that had been in opposition with the church. There were many. "What do you mean to do with me?"

One corner of his mouth curled upward.

"I mean to send you away," he said. "Just as St. Patrick did with the serpents in Ireland. You are the serpent of Lowell. You are poisoning this town. I mean to put you on the very last boat, leaving tonight. The deportations may have stopped, but I've been assured there is room for one more. It will get dark soon. And when the stagecoach arrives, it will take you to the docks, and you will be gone from our lives forever. It will take some time to scrub away the thoughts you have wedged inside of their heads. But if there is anything the Irish know to do, it is to trust in the church to lead them. And we will. I will."

I started to sob loudly now. Not another ship. Not Ireland. Not the workhouse. I had been angry before, but I had not been afraid. I'd had Calvin to protect me. But Calvin was not here. And this was not an arrest. The priest ignored my cries.

"The mill owners had a vision for this town," he started again, over the sounds of my anguish. "A vision of nice young women leaving their homes to be taken care of in a mill town like no other. The first and only of its kind. A place that would protect their integrity. Enforce curfew. Provide a place of worship. A place where fathers could send their daughters for a bit more coin to add to the family purse. Where they wouldn't have to worry about reputations being tarnished or modesty ruined."

I tried to think if there was anything I could say to stop this man. But my fear had overtaken me. The tears would not stop flowing. Father Purcell's face blurred. Warm urine ran down my legs.

"And *we* built it. The Irish built it. We are a proud people. When I heard, from my small parish in west Massachusetts, of what they had done here, I was proud," he said. "The Irish were living here peacefully, dutifully— until those boats came. Boats full of the lowest class of people. You all were a different kind of Irish. A sinful kind. You brought your fighting and your prostituting with you. You made it into just another filthy factory town. Ruining the hard work of those who came before you. How was I to save you all when you were so far gone? So, you can imagine how pleased I was with the deportations. They were the perfect solution. A blessing, truly."

He stopped speaking for a moment, and I could see the anger behind his eyes.

"Please, Father," I started, unsure of what I would ask of him. "Please. I can't go back there. I can't. There must be something I can do. Let me stay. I've a husband now. And Mr. Joyce. He cares for me greatly."

"I've thought of Thaddeus," he said, nodding, looking off in the distance. "He is a great man, and it will pain me to see him suffer. But he will move on. With God's assistance and with mine. He will pull through. Your husband, on the other hand . . ." His gaze shifted back to mine. "He is nearly as much of a nuisance as you. I'll have to find him a better wife to influence him in the proper way."

"No," I growled at him now, something fierce and hot pulling from inside my chest.

"Why, *yes*," he responded, standing up now. "What else is a man to do when his wife leaves him? Runs off without a word? He'll need to mend his broken heart with something. Or someone, I should say."

"You bastard!" I shouted.

Before I even saw him move, I felt the back of his hand hit my face. My head flopped to the side, and the searing pain flowed through my body again. I lifted my hands to my face. The blood was fresh again. I whimpered without meaning to. I heard Abner chuckling from somewhere in the shadows.

"You will not be forgiven for speaking to a priest that way," he hissed.

Then he turned from me and addressed Abner.

"Good work, Mr. Keyes." Father Purcell walked toward him. "I had my suspicions about this one. Your services are greatly appreciated."

I saw him hand Abner a purse. The same purse into which he had put the money from Ruth. The priest turned to me and smiled again.

"The church appreciates your donation," he said. "I have no doubt that this is exactly where the Charitable Irish Society had hoped their money would be spent."

The anger was building up inside of me, churning with desperation, creating a pent-up mixture that had no way out. No escape valve. I wanted to curse this man. I wanted to hurt him. I knew neither would help.

"Please," I tried again, trying to sound meek and agreeable. I needed to lie now. I needed to appeal to his pride. "It was wrong of me to write those things. Wrong of me to believe that was my calling. I see that now. I can be a good wife. A humble one. A loyal member of the church. I can change."

"Wrong!" he yelled. "You've had *years* to listen to my sermons. *Years* to see the error of your ways. I am not interested in your confessions now!"

Father Purcell turned his back to me again and spoke to Abner softly. I tried to make out what they were saying, but it was difficult to concentrate. My gaze darted around the barn. I tasted the salty tears falling down my lips. It made me recognize my thirst. My body begged for water. I wriggled, desperately trying to break free from at least one rope. I tugged at the one around my ribs and moved my hands back and forth with as much strength as I could muster. Everything was tied so tightly. And I was so tired.

And then I knew. I knew just what the woman at the docks had felt. I would do anything not to be taken to that boat. I would bite, kick, claw. I was not going back to Ireland. I would rip the hair from Father Purcell's head first. I would take his life. I was tired, but I would not stop fighting. I needed to wait. I needed to wait for the stage-coach. That would be my opportunity. I tried to breathe slowly and deeply. I tried to gather strength.

Suddenly, a crash came from behind me. Chips of wood flew through the air and landed on my shoulders and at my feet. I tried to turn my head to look, but all I could see was a door swinging back and forth, banging against the barn wall.

"Duck your head, Rosaleen!" a voice yelled.

Chapter Forty-Three

It was Quinn. I was sure of it. Despite being born right here in the Acre, Quinn's voice still had more than a slight brogue to it. I did what he said, putting my bound hands behind my head.

"Quinn, is it?" Father Purcell's voice rang out. I picked my head up just a bit to see that he was standing firm. Both arms bent at the elbows, holding his hands in the air as if giving a sermon. Abner stood next to him and slightly behind, a hand on his revolver.

"Don't move," Quinn shouted. "I'll shoot."

"You'd shoot a priest?" Father Purcell asked. "Surely not."

Quinn didn't answer.

"Come now, my son," Father Purcell went on. "Put that gun down and we'll talk. You must understand what this friend of yours has done. It is displeasing to God."

"I don't care what she's done," Quinn said. "You are not an officer of the law. You'll release her now."

Father Purcell shook his head. Abner's arm moved just a little, trying to release his revolver from its holster.

"Stop!" Quinn shouted. "Don't move! Abner. What is this?"

Abner chuckled. "What will it be, Quinn? Are you one of *them*, after all? This. This right here is the Paddy. Haven't we all been eager to find Paddy? Hasn't Paddy caused us nothing but problems? Well, we have her. Right here. Your priest knows what to do with her. Do you?"

"Release her," Quinn said again. "One of you will release her *now!*"

Father Purcell straightened up a little more.

"Shall we be rational about this?" he asked. "You won't be shooting anyone. I will untie her. But before we let her leave this barn, I need you to think, Quinn. Think about what she has done to your people. Think about how disappointed your father has been with all she has written. You know how harmful she is to the Irish. To everything we have been trying to accomplish in Lowell. We have a ship ready to take her away. So that we can right the wrongs that she has caused."

Father Purcell put his hands even higher into the air. "I'm going to walk over to untie her," he said.

"Go, then," Quinn said.

But as soon as Father Purcell took a step, Abner moved, too. He ran right at Quinn. The sound of a revolver going off pierced the air. I screamed. Wood came raining down again, this time from the roof. I heard a thump behind me and the groans of a struggle. Father Purcell took one last look at me and turned to flee.

I reached both hands out to grab him. I couldn't let him

get away. I pushed forward with all of my might but only grazed his robes before the chair tipped and I fell to the ground. I looked up to watch him disappear into the shadows.

"No!" I yelled. I tried the ropes again. I pulled and pulled at the one at my waist, and when it wouldn't budge, I leaned over as far as I could to try to release one of my feet. The rope around my ribs pinched my skin. I couldn't breathe. I clawed at the ropes around my ankles, but I was losing breath. I couldn't do it.

"Ugh," I groaned as I sat straight again, still tied to the chair. I was lying on my side now, facing Abner and Quinn. Quinn rolled on top of Abner and punched him hard in his face. Abner's head snapped to the side. Blood ran freely from his nose. He groped the ground next to him, searching for Quinn's dropped weapon. I saw the revolver only inches from Abner's reach. I swung my legs and the chair along with it to try to kick it away, but it was too far. I tried to scoot my body closer, but the chair was so heavy. The ground smelled of horse dung. I lay my face against it, trying to gather strength.

I watched Quinn punch Abner again. Abner's hand wildly smacked the ground. He was so close to that revolver. Another punch. This time, Abner's hand stopped moving. His head bobbed to the other side. I could see his chest rising and falling, but the rest of his body had given up. Quinn flipped him over but stayed on top of him. He gathered Abner's hands together and secured them and then did the same to his feet. He stood, leaving Abner face-down in the dirt.

Quinn's body heaved in and out with each breath. He looked around the barn.

"Where is Father Purcell?" he asked me.

"Gone," I said. "He's gone."

Quinn knelt next to me, still breathing hard. He took a knife from his pocket and cut the rope from my wrists. Then he cut the ropes from my ankles, walked behind me, and freed my waist. I scrabbled away from the chair, away from Abner, and sat with my back against the stall. Tears began to flow freely from my eyes again. I rubbed my wrists where the rope had been and started to sob.

Quinn sat next to me, facing Abner.

"It's all right, Rosaleen," he said. He took my hand and squeezed it. "You're all right. You're safe. You aren't going anywhere."

I nodded but couldn't stop the noises coming from my mouth. We sat there for only a minute, Quinn letting me cry while he held my hand, assuring me that I wasn't alone. Abner began to stir. Quinn quickly grabbed his revolver from the ground and stood up. He pointed it at Abner.

"Rosaleen," he said. "I'm going to need you to do something for me. Do you think you can help me?"

"Yes," I said. Of course I could help him. He'd just saved me.

"I can't bring Abner to the jail alone," he said. "The other officers. I know where their loyalties lie. And it isn't with me. I need you to get Calvin. He might be the only one to believe us. Can you do that for me? Can you get Calvin?"

I stared at him for a moment, blinking.

"What about Father Purcell?" I asked. "Will we just let him go?"

"He's already gone," Quinn said. "Like you said. We can look for him tomorrow. We can worry about him then. I need you to get Calvin right now."

I nodded. "All right," I said. "I can help you. I can get Calvin. I can do that." I was speaking as much to myself as I was to Quinn, because I wasn't sure yet that I could. My legs felt numb. My head tingled.

"I know you're hurt," Quinn said. "But I can't leave Abner alone."

I shook my head now, trying to shed any other thoughts or doubts.

"I can do it, truly," I said. I stood up, a bit shaky at first. Abner groaned.

"I'll hurry," I said. Quinn nodded and smiled.

"We've got this bastard," he said. "We've got him."

Chapter Forty-Four

I was still dazed leaving the barn, but after a minute, I started to run. The blood was flowing through my legs again, and although I was dizzy, I ran as quickly as my body would carry me. I ran through empty streets until I reached the yellow house. I nearly cried again at the sight.

I banged on the door as hard as I could.

"Nancy!" I yelled. "Calvin! Please, open the door! I need help!"

But neither Nancy nor Calvin came to the door. Emmett did.

"Rose," he gasped, sweeping me into his arms. "Rose!" He squeezed me tight. When he pulled away, he noticed the blood. His eyes went wide as he touched it gently.

"What happened to you?" he asked.

Nancy came up behind him.

"Where is Calvin?" I asked them both. "I need him."

Nancy's eyes were huge with shock. She grabbed my hand and pulled me into the house. Calvin was coming down the stairs, buckling his belt. He was already dressed in uniform.

"Rosaleen!" he said. "I was just about to send out a search party. Where have you been? Emmett's been worried sick." He hurried over to me. "And you're bleeding."

"We need you. Quinn is at a barn near the gravel pit. Do you know where it is?"

"Yes," Calvin said. "I know it."

"He has Abner Keyes there, restrained," I said. "He needs your assistance."

Calvin straightened up. His head moved backward like a turtle retreating into its shell. His eyebrows furrowed.

"Abner?" he asked. "Why?"

"Because he kidnapped me," I said. "He did this." I pointed to the wound on my head. "He knocked me out and dragged me into the barn and tied me up."

"That piece of shit!" Emmett growled. He took a step toward the door, but Calvin stopped him.

"Let me handle this, Emmett."

Emmett's hands were balled into fists at his sides. He was fuming. Calvin crossed the room in a few strides and grabbed his gun from the drawer of his desk. Then he walked to the door, stepped into his boots, tied them, and took his hat from the coat stand. He placed it firmly on his head, kissed Nancy, and was gone.

I sank into the couch. Nancy and Emmett sat on each side of me. At first, they both seemed afraid to touch me. Afraid

I would shatter into pieces. Finally, Emmett gently brushed my blood-crusted hair behind my shoulder. I leaned back and rested my head on the soft cushion.

"He had help, but the other man escaped," I said.

"Who?" Nancy asked. "You should have told Calvin." She was standing up now, hurrying to the door.

"No," I said, as loudly as I could. "Don't tell him."

She stopped and turned. "Why not?"

I looked at Emmett now. He was waiting attentively.

"It was Father Purcell," I said. "Our priest."

I watched Emmett's face turn from red to pink to an almost gray color.

"Father Purcell?" he whispered.

I nodded. Nancy walked back over to me and sat down again.

"Oh, Rosaleen," she said, lightly touching my shoulder.

Emmett looked down now at our hands, shaking his head in disbelief. He looked like he might be sick.

"He found out who I am," I said. "*Fiona* told. He was going to send me on a ship back to Ireland. He said I was a problem. That I think I'm a prophet. That he's been looking for me for years."

Nancy rubbed my back now but stayed quiet.

"I'm so sorry, Rose," Emmett said, quietly. "We knew the church didn't approve of what Paddy wrote. But still. I never thought they would do something like *this*. And Fiona." He swallowed hard. "I always knew her to be wretched. But this is unthinkable. I told you to trust our people, and they betrayed you."

I touched his cheek.

"No," I said. "You *were* right. Quinn saved me. Keyes and

Father Purcell both tried to convince him not to. They both reminded him of how horrible and dangerous I was. But he wouldn't listen. Father Purcell . . ." I trailed off. I thought of the way he'd spoken of us. Of those of us who'd suffered the most. Who'd come here in desperation. Who'd seen things he would never have to see. ". . . Father Purcell is *not* our people. And Fiona. Fiona is a demon. She's not even human, let alone my kin. She belongs in the depths of hell, where she came from."

Emmett was still shaking his head in disbelief. The only noise was the ticking of the clock in the kitchen.

"You can both stay tonight," Nancy finally said. "We can get you cleaned up. I have a bed upstairs."

I shook my head. "Thank you," I said. "But I want to go home."

She nodded. "Can I get you anything?"

I turned to look at her. "Something to drink, please," I said. She rushed to the kitchen. Emmett's grip on my hands hadn't loosened.

"I can't understand how Father Purcell could be working with Keyes," Emmett said. "After they tried to raid our church."

"He paid Keyes, too," I said. "Paid him with the funds Ruth and Marie brought."

The color was rushing back to Emmett's cheeks. His shock fading. His anger rising again. Nancy came into the room with three cups of tea.

I sat up and drank mine down greedily. Nancy sipped hers and then held it cupped in her hands. Emmett didn't touch his. He stood, finally letting go of my hands, and paced. I understood his rage. But I was too tired to feel it with him. I had used every last drop of feeling tonight. I felt only exhaustion now. I set my empty cup on Nancy's table.

"I'm so tired. I'm going to go home," I said to Nancy. "Thank you for the tea. Please tell Calvin how grateful I am when he gets home."

She put her hand on my back and helped me to my feet.

"You know I will," she said. I smiled faintly at her. Emmett came to my other side. He nodded at Nancy.

"We are grateful to you both," he said. "Good night."

Chapter Forty-Five

I leaned heavily on Emmett as we walked home. We were both quiet. I, too tired to speak, Emmett, too indignant. As soon as Mr. Joyce saw me, he rushed out to retrieve bandages from the church's medical wing.

Emmett helped me into the tub and gently washed the crusted blood from my head, my neck, my shoulder, my back. My clothes would be soaked next. I gazed into Emmett's eyes. I saw pain in them, behind the anger.

I touched his hand. "I'm all right," I said. "I'm here."

I saw something inside him break. His eyes filled with tears.

"I feel responsible, Rose," he said. "I should have seen the danger. I should have protected you. I promised to protect you."

"None of this is your fault," I said.

"I should have taken Fiona's threats more seriously," he said. "I dismissed her when I shouldn't have."

"And what would you have done?" I asked. "Followed

her around day and night? Locked her in the cellar? Killed her?"

He shook his head. "I don't know, Rose. I don't know. But I should have done *something*. And to believe I trusted that man with my soul. With my confessions."

"None of us could have guessed the evil in him," I said. "None of us could have known that he felt such hatred toward us all. Please, don't blame yourself."

"Toward us all? What did he say?" he asked.

"That we were a different class of Irish that came from the famine. Sinful. That he was grateful for the deportations."

Emmett shook his head. "A different class of Irish. Damn him." He closed his eyes.

"He could use a lesson from Aunt Emer," I said.

"Hah," Emmett grunted, opening his eyes, a half smile forming across his face.

"But we got Abner," I reminded him.

"So, one Know-Nothing in jail, only hundreds more to go."

"He was the worst one, though, wasn't he?" I asked.

Emmett sighed. "I suppose."

He helped me out of the tub and wrapped me in a towel. A chill ran up my spine, and I started shaking.

"I almost went back there," I said, quietly, thinking of how lucky I was to be at home. "He almost sent me back. He told me he was going to find you a better wife once I was gone."

Emmett laughed now, heartily. He took my face in his hands.

"I would never find another wife," he said. "You're the only one for me. Now and forever. I would have gone after you. I would have swum to Ireland. You'll never be rid of me."

I buried my face into his chest and breathed him in deeply.

～

Father O'Brien had provided Mr. Joyce with just a bit of laudanum. I heard Emmett and Mr. Joyce speaking in hushed tones as I fell asleep, unable to fight my exhaustion or the effects of the medicine any longer.

I awoke early the next morning but stayed in bed for some time, relishing the feel of the soft blanket against my skin and the heat of Emmett's body next to mine. I wouldn't report for my shift that day. Someone would tell the mills. But I needed rest.

When Emmett woke, he turned to me and brushed his thumb across my cheek.

"Good morning, beautiful," he whispered. I took his hand and kissed his palm. He stood, put his clothes on, and went to get a log to add to the fire. Mr. Joyce was stirring as well. I took my time getting up, my head still throbbing. I closed one eye as I sat up, careful to do so as slowly and gently as I could. My brain felt jostled by even the smallest movement.

Mr. Joyce hurried around once he realized I was awake, boiling the tea, cooking the breakfast. Emmett came back up with the logs and tossed them onto the fire.

"Emmett told me what happened," Mr. Joyce said, his voice a bit shaky. "I hope that man goes straight to hell. I know he will. He belongs with the devil. It's a terrible thing he's done. *Terrible*."

Mr. Joyce was still staring at the breakfast he was cooking. His knuckles went white gripping the handle of the pan. The blood rushed to his face. Then he looked up at me.

"Whatever things I have said about Paddy . . .". Mr. Joyce shook his head. "I would never agree with that man. You know that, don't you, Rosaleen?"

"Of course, Mr. Joyce," I said. I stood gingerly and began to walk to him, but Emmett came to my side and made me sit at the table instead. Then he went to Mr. Joyce and took the spoon from his hand.

"I'll do this," Emmett said. Mr. Joyce nodded and came to sit in the chair next to me. He took my hands in his. I saw the same pain in his eyes as I'd seen in Emmett's last night.

"To think that he would take you from me, too . . ." Mr. Joyce said. "After everything. I couldn't have continued on. You and Emmett are my world now. My family." His voice was breaking.

I began to tear up, too. Mr. Joyce cleared his throat.

"I will not let this go unpunished," he said. "The church must know who that man truly is. Father O'Brien must know."

"But he *can't* know, Mr. Joyce," I said. "He can't know I'm Paddy. He might not put me on a boat like Father Purcell wanted to, but he also can't accept Paddy. Not after all of the things Paddy has said. The church can never accept Paddy."

"Then I won't tell him that part," Mr. Joyce said. "No

matter who you are or what you've done, Father Purcell's actions were those of a deranged man. Father O'Brien must know who *he* is. He must never be welcomed back to St. Patrick's or back to Lowell at all."

I was hesitant. It felt risky. But I also trusted Mr. Joyce. He would never do anything to put me in danger.

"If you must," I said. "Tell him what you need to, but nothing about Paddy."

Mr. Joyce nodded. "Nothing about Paddy."

Chapter Forty-Six

I awoke that Sunday feeling famished. It was still dark, and I crept across the room slowly to nibble on some bread. I sat at the window and watched the sleeping city. A cat scurried across the street. A man walked, head down, with his hands deep in his pockets. The moon was bright and reflected off the cobblestones.

I had promised Mr. Joyce I would attend Mass. He had spoken to Father O'Brien, who was horrified.

"I won't have you angry at God," Mr. Joyce had said the night before. "I need you to see the difference between Him and the devil. Father Purcell was doing the devil's work."

I reluctantly agreed, although I assured Mr. Joyce that I was not angry at God. No matter what Father Purcell had meant during that sermon about fear, he unwillingly delivered a message to me that I'd needed to hear. A message that led to the end of the deportations. A message that saved Nessa's brother.

When I arrived at the church, though, fear took hold of

my chest. My breath became shallow. We sat in our regular pew, and I couldn't look up. I stared only at my feet and my shaking hands. Mr. Joyce grabbed my hand and held it tightly. I looked up at him. He stared into my eyes and nodded slowly.

I listened as Father O'Brien told the people of St. Patrick's church that Father Purcell was not well. He had left Lowell. He would not be back. Instead, Father O'Brien's older brother, Father Timothy O'Brien, would be taking over the church. He would arrive within the next few weeks. Wouldn't we all welcome him warmly?

My eyes stung and tears threatened to form. These people would never know what Father Purcell had thought of them. But I knew. I thought of Sister Hunna, then, with a bitter taste on my tongue. She felt the same way, and she was still here. I had to hope that Father Timothy was a good man. A man who might correct Sister Hunna's hate.

Quinn and Nessa waited outside the church for me. I hugged them both. Mr. Joyce and Emmett showered thanks upon Quinn with such force that I thought they would smother him. Finally, the air quieted, and we all stood looking at one another. Quinn spoke first.

"It's too bad that they can't know the truth about Father Purcell," he said.

I looked at him and knew that he understood. Certainly, he had told Nessa my secret, but he would tell no one else. I smiled at him.

"I am so grateful," I said. "For everything you've done for me, Quinn."

Nessa looked at him in admiration.

"I'm curious," I went on. "How did you know what was happening? How did you know to come?"

"I was on patrol. A girl came running up to me," Quinn said. "She said to me, 'You know Rosaleen. Please go save her. She's been attacked.' And then she told me exactly where to find you. She said her name was Ina. I had no idea what I was walking into. I thought it would be an insane person. A criminal. I suppose they were both of those things."

Quinn looked at someone behind me and stood up straighter. He smiled and cleared his throat.

"Chief Parker," he said. "Nancy. It's lovely to see you both."

I spun around, and Nancy gave me a long hug.

"How are you feeling?" she asked as she pulled away. "You look much better."

"I feel all right," I said. "Still sore."

"We have come to check on you," Calvin said. "And I have come to ask something of you."

He took off his hat and ran his fingers through his hair. "I'd like you to come work for me at city hall. I'm sure you've heard from Nancy about how busy I've been. It's really become too much for me. The handbooks, the meetings, the writing of notices and letters. I need a clerk. I'd like it to be someone I trust and someone who I know will work hard and diligently."

I looked at Emmett. We were both shocked. "Truly?" I asked Calvin.

Calvin put his hat back on. Nancy was gripping his hand and grinning at me from ear to ear.

"Yes," he said. "Truly. Will you accept?"

"I will," I said, laughing a bit. "Thank you, Calvin."

"Good," he said. "You'll start on the first of the year."

Emmett shook Calvin's hand.

"Thank you, Calvin," Emmett said. "Thank you."

Calvin nodded. Nancy kissed both my cheeks.

"You'll be wonderful," she said.

～

I arrived at the school that Wednesday for tutoring. The following day would be my first day as Calvin's clerk. I had no lessons planned for the girls. No news of the bigger world. No inspiration. I had only my presence. I hoped it would be enough.

Ina looked glad to see me but was even more withdrawn than usual. She was a child who had witnessed what was surely a frightening scene. Who had been checking in on her since? No one.

"Alice, would you like to work on your letters for a bit while I talk to Ina?" I asked.

Alice bit her lip and nodded. I led Ina away, and we sat on a burgundy rug at the back of the room. I took her hands.

"You saved my life," I said to her. "I'm forever grateful to you. You were so brave. So incredibly brave. What were you doing over there?"

"Looking for Da," she said. "He works over there, mining the gravel. He didn't come home. I checked the taverns first, but he wasn't there. Ma doesn't care where he is. She avoids him the most. She gets the worst from him, too. Sometimes, when he hits her, I don't think she'll get back up. She always does, but sometimes, for just a moment, I think he's killed her. But our family needs his wages, so I kept looking. Who else would make sure he showed up to work tomorrow? So I went to the pit next. I didn't know where else to look. I was sitting there, in the pit, watching the rats scurrying. Trying to think of where else to try. Then I heard a thump and a yell. I looked over the top of the pit and saw that man dragging you. You were so limp. I thought you were dead. I ran as fast as I could. When I saw that police officer, I recognized him. I trusted him, because I knew he was one of us."

Her lip started to quiver, and a strand of hair fell in front of her face. I brushed it back.

"Thank you," I said. "That must have been very scary. Please, tell me how I can help you. With anything at all."

She took her hands back and sat on them. She looked down at her dress.

"They haven't found him," she said. "We don't know where he is. Ma's looking for a job. She'll have to bring my siblings here to the nursery if she finds one."

Then she looked up at me.

"I don't miss him," she said. "How could I? But still. I feel terrible. Like I ought to miss him. Like it's my fault he's gone, and with him, his wages. I must have done something to make him angry. He always says it's my fault. That I'm too surly. I give him headaches. I'm glad he's gone. But I don't know how we'll get along now."

"You'll get along just fine," I said. "The church will take care of you all. You don't have to hide it anymore. You tell them exactly what it is that you need."

She sighed. "I wish I could work," she said.

"No," I said. "Not yet. You're still a child. You leave that to your ma. The nursery here is wonderful. I've even heard that Yankees are asking to be admitted. And neighboring communities outside of Lowell. But your siblings will get a spot first. The nuns take care of our community. You will all be just fine without him and his wages."

A single tear fell from Ina's eye. "I hope he never comes back," she said. "Never."

Chapter Forty-Seven

I arrived at city hall before Calvin. I simply walked through the front doors, climbed the stairs, and stood in front of the door to his office. I thought of how I'd sat in that office months ago, trying to make the most of the few minutes I would have to bend his ear. Now I would have many minutes during many days. It was dizzying the amount of time I would have to see for myself the inner workings of city hall. It gave me flutters in my chest from both excitement and nerves.

I had spent some time thinking the last few days: Why me? Why had Calvin chosen me for a clerk? He could have had any young woman in Lowell. Any man, for that matter. I thought about who Calvin was. Who I had known him to be. I knew him to be even-tempered. Professional. Certainly never rash. He seemed proud of his ability to stay levelheaded and think clearly. I had rarely seen much emotion in him. Only when he looked at Nancy with love.

Calvin wanted to be better at his job. That was the simple answer I had come up with. He had hired Quinn to make better decisions on the streets. To act as a counter to the other patrolmen, who, knowingly or not, treated the Irish differently. Treated them unfairly. Oftentimes, treated them as less than human. Quinn was there to remind the others of our humanity. To be fair when he patrolled the Acre. To step in when his fellow officers let their hatred take over. It was a lot to ask of one man, but in time, there would certainly be more.

I was here to bring that same counter to Calvin's decisions. He'd hired me to speak up. To tell him when he wasn't seeing something because he was Calvin. Because his family had been in Massachusetts for generations. Because sometimes, he wanted to be so fair that he was unfair. He had blind spots, and he knew this. Hiring me was his way of admitting there were some things he couldn't accomplish on his own. The Know-Nothings had finally proved to him that they were truly dangerous. And maybe he'd hired me, too, because he recognized my willingness to do the work. To be patient and persistent.

He knew I would accept, because he knew I could see the opportunity in this position. I would be in rooms with people who could snap their fingers and change a policy. Who could utter a few words and change the outcome of a vote. The kind of people who never even thought about the power they wielded, because they had never lacked it. The kind of people who would never even notice my presence. I would be recording information that was only spoken about in hushed tones, over a glass of whiskey and a tobacco pipe. I could be the eyes and ears of my people, and as Paddy, the mouth.

Calvin arrived precisely at 8 a.m., hat in hand, hair combed perfectly to the side, boots shining.

"Good morning, Rosaleen," he said. "I hope you're ready to work today, because I certainly have a lot for you to accomplish."

"Yes, sir," I said. "I'm not sure I've ever been so ready to work."

He smiled as he searched for the key to his office in his coat pocket. He unlocked the door, and we both entered. He had pushed a small table and chair against the wall. A stack of papers sat on one corner of the desk, a pen and ink on the other. I stood in front of it, staring. My desk. For me only. Calvin brushed past and sat at his own desk. His mind was already spinning ahead, unaware that this moment was anything other than ordinary.

"I'm to meet my men at the jail soon," he said as he flipped through his notebook. "I've got a couple of letters for you to write, so listen carefully to what I need them to say."

"Yes, sir," I said, quickly sitting on the edge of my desk chair, poised to work. I dipped my pen in the ink and listened.

Middlesex County House of Correction
  DEAR INMATE #79463:
  This letter is to inform you that you've been relieved of your duties as a city of Lowell police officer effective immediately. You have been charged with kidnapping, bribery, inappropriate use of a city-provided weapon, and lastly, with neglecting your duties to serve and protect the citizens of Lowell. Your trial will be held on

the second of February. I, City Marshal Calvin Parker, and my colleague Officer Quinn Sullivan will both be present to testify. If convicted, you will never again be eligible for service with any city, state, or local police force within the state of Massachusetts. The minimum sentence to be served for these crimes is fifteen years at the Middlesex County House of Correction.

May God have mercy on your soul.

City Marshal Calvin Parker
  On Behalf of the City of Lowell

Chapter Forty-Eight

The night before Nessa and Quinn's wedding, I took the long way home. My mind danced with excitement for them. But it was restless for another reason, too. Abner Keyes's trial would be held in only three days.

What would Keyes say? Would he expose me as Paddy? Surely he would. And then what? Would the jury, void of Irish bodies, see him as a madman or a hero of the law? And what would their decision mean for me, for Paddy?

These questions turned my stomach upside down, so I walked and walked, despite the freezing temperatures, pushing my nerves down to my legs and out my feet. I wiggled my fingers inside of my gloves to keep them from aching with chill. Then, I heard something in the distance. Voices. Like a faint buzzing of bees. I rounded the corner and saw a light. The only light shining unapologetically at this hour. It came from a large barn that was used as a tannery. The voices drew me closer.

I heard one man's voice rising clearly above the others.

He was speaking to them from atop a large box. I stopped at the edge of the doorway, listened closely, and watched from the shadows. The barn was filled with Irish, their backs to me, their attention focused on the speaker.

"We were promised a life here," the speaker was saying. "A chance to provide for our families. A chance to escape starvation and disease. Instead, we were met with hate. With people who would spit on us and give our jobs to Negroes!"

Murmurs of agreement rippled through the crowd. The speaker had a heavy brogue but looked cleaner than the rest. More polished. His clothes fit. His hat had never been dented. He looked familiar, but I couldn't decide where I had seen him before.

"We arrived here by chance," he went on. "Our ships landed in Boston or in Canada or in New York. But it's not where we truly belong. We aren't wanted here."

He looked intently at the crowd, and his eyes betrayed both anger and exhaustion.

"We need to go to the South. The great Irish patriot, John Mitchel, has moved to the South," he went on. "Like us, he came to the North first. He lived in New York for only a short time before he recognized that we could never be great here. They will always prefer the Negro. We will never earn their respect. We haven't yet, and we won't. John Mitchel and more of our kin are thriving in the South. And we can, too!"

I scanned the crowd for a reaction. Wives looked to their husbands with hopeful eyes. Men crossed their arms and rubbed their chins in thought, or nodded in agreement, looking down at their feet, which they shuffled in place.

"I will be taking names of anyone here tonight who is interested. Don't worry about the cost of gettin' there. It's been taken care of. Thank ye all," he finished.

I watched a swarm of bodies crowd the speaker right away. Others stayed put, talking to one another in hushed tones. Only a few turned and left, passing me on their way out.

And then I saw Frank. Fiona was holding his hand. Anger rose in me at sight of her. I hadn't seen her since the kidnapping. In truth, I'd been afraid to. Afraid that Emmett or I would kill her with our bare hands. And here she was. I could do nothing but retreat even further into the dark of the night, shaking with frustration. The people at this gathering were not my friends. This was not the place for me to confront that miserable hedge whore.

They walked toward the speaker together, Fiona gripping Frank's upper arm as if he might run off. She steadied him, directed him. Fiona was leaving, and she was taking Frank with her. She was probably trying to leave as quickly as she could to avoid the trial that hung over us both like a storm cloud. She knew Frank would be convinced by this rhetoric. By this vile argument.

Cowards. And in that moment, I hated them both. Fiona, of course, but Frank, too. After all we had done for him. After all Nessa had done for him. He was choosing Fiona. He was choosing her needs, her hate, her anger. Everyone in that barn was a coward. We were finally making progress, and they couldn't see it. The frustration I felt toward those people rose like bile in my throat. Fine. Let them leave. I had done all I could, and still their hearts were heavy with spite. We didn't need them in Lowell. Traitors.

I turned to leave before I made a wrong decision. Standing only inches away, blocking my exit, was Mr. Phillips. The mill man from the meeting. The one who'd spied on me. I gasped.

"I didn't see you there, sir," I said, breathless with shock.

He chuckled. "I suppose not," he said. He was dressed more handsomely than I had ever seen a man dressed. Why? At this time of night, in the alleyways of the outskirts of the Acre, it felt obscene, uncomfortable. "Rather strange finding you at a meeting like this," he said. "Weren't you fighting so the Irish could stay in Lowell? What's this now about leaving?"

"I didn't mean to be here," I said. "I was only passing by."

"Yes, I know," he said. His expression turned from amused to firm in only a moment.

"I know quite a lot about you, in fact," he went on. "Walk with me."

He offered his arm. I hesitated. This was the man who'd been disgusted to take our coats. And now he was offering his arm? I took it, too curious to resist.

We walked away from the barn, toward the heart of the Acre.

"It seems to me as though we have a new problem, wouldn't you say?" he asked.

I said nothing.

"You must feel like you've failed those people. Failed to make them see the light. Hmm?"

"I'm not sure what you mean," I said, my heart beating quicker.

"No need to play dull with me, Rosaleen," he went on. "My job is to know things. And my job is to fix things. I do it quietly and effectively. You may not know where I am or what I'm doing, but I can assure you that I know where *you* are and what *you're* doing. The same goes for any other influential person in this town. Irish or not."

He paused for a moment and looked at me, very serious. My mouth was dry. Did he expect some sort of confession? I wouldn't do it. I only stared back.

"Fine," he said. "You're smart. Nothing needs to be said. But something needs to be done. The mills cannot lose hordes of Irish to the South. They simply won't. And so, you and I will find a solution to this new problem of ours."

I looked at my feet as we walked.

"You're good at what you do," he said. "But I can help you become better. I can help you accomplish the things that you've always been reaching for. Because," he paused again and stopped walking, too. I had been so consumed by what he was saying that I hadn't noticed where we were. Only feet from my front door. "I know things. Things that you don't know. Think about it. Here's where you'll find me."

He slipped me a note, folded in half. I stared at it.

"You're worried about the upcoming trial. Don't be. I took care of it." I looked up at him. He was smiling out of the corner of his mouth. He tipped his hat.

"Good night, Paddy," he said, before disappearing once again into the dark.

I breathed steadily, staring at the place he had just occupied. I watched the steam my breath had made. Behind me, I heard the Irish who had stayed behind at the barn coming home. I heard their soft whispers, their quick footsteps. I didn't turn to look at them. I felt frozen in place.

Good night, Paddy, his voice echoed in my head.

"Good night, Mr. Phillips," I whispered into the night.

Author's Note

I would first like to thank my fantastic beta readers for their time, their honesty, and their dedication to this book's success. I appreciate every single one of you: Faith O'Connor, Latia Sanders, Megan O'Connor, Helen Preston, and my amazing husband, Tim Boyle.

While most characters in this book are entirely fictional, some did exist, including: Anthony Burns, George Moore, Mary Anning, Sir George Cayley, Hugh Cummiskey, Kirk Boott, Reverend Theodore Edson, Father John O'Brien, Father Timothy O'Brien, John Orr (also known as "the Angel Gabriel"), Joseph Hiss (member of the Smelling Committee), and Frances Ellen Watkins Harper (referred to only as "Frances," a friend of Marie's and leader of the temperance movement). The nuns were inspired by the real-life sisters of Notre Dame who came to the Acre with nothing and built a school for the Irish girls that would grow rapidly through the years and become a place that was respected by citizens of all religions. To my knowledge, none of them were as hateful and bitter as the made-up Sister Hunna.

The American Party, better known as the "Know-Nothings," were also very real, as were their anti-foreigner beliefs, and between 1855 and 1857, Lowell, MA, was governed by a Know-Nothing mayor. Across the country, the Know-Nothings would claim more than one hundred elected congressmen, eight governors, a controlling share of six state legislatures—including Massachusetts—and thousands of local politicians.

The opening scene of this book is taken from history, and occurred during Lowell's summer of 1854. Every day after their shifts ended, the Irish came to defend their church from an enraged mob of Know-Nothings who wanted to raid the girls' school. As described, an Irishwoman threw a member of that mob over the bridge and into the canal.

The deportations are another true-to-history event. According to Hidetaka Hirota, author of *Expelling the Poor: Atlantic Seaboard States and the Nineteenth-Century Origins of American Immigration Policy*, Massachusetts deported fifty thousand people between the years of 1840 and 1870. Building upon a seventeenth century law that allowed "beggars" to be banished from the colony, Massachusetts adopted harsh and very subjective methods of controlling immigration. The Know-Nothings in particular made it a clear and vocal part of their policy that they were in favor of deportations for Irish and Catholic immigrants and frequently called the Irish "leeches upon taxpayers." One prominent Know-Nothing from Boston said that it was a known fact that the Irish "will not work while he can exist by begging." Deportees were taken from almshouses, poor-houses, and poor farms, so while records do not specify how many of the fifty thousand were Irish, records do reveal that the overwhelming majority of those residing at almshouses, poorhouses, and poor farms in Massachusetts were born in Ireland. In Lowell, it was observed that no more than eight inmates out of 130 were "native poor."

The protest to stop the deportations is entirely a product of my imagination. In reality, the deportations continued until the Know-Nothings were voted out of power, political priorities began to shift, and hate directed toward the Irish and Catholics began to dissipate.

In Lowell in 1850, there was only one Irishman who was identified as a "watchman." This one watchman inspired the character of Quinn. There is no documented evidence of police misconduct that occurred in Lowell, MA, at this time. However, in the year 1848, almost every person arrested for "drunkenness" in Lowell was Irish. Though Irish people made up less than 30 percent of Lowell's total population, 92 percent of all drunkenness charges were of Irish people. By the early 1850s, Lowell had disbanded its old constable and city watch and created a professional police department tasked with cleaning up what many in Lowell considered a crime problem caused by the influx of Irish immigrants. Yet, drunkenness seemed to be the main crime the Irish committed. "Drunkenness remained a particularly Irish problem. The only other major crimes in Lowell around 1850 which were committed by them were assault and battery and larceny, and these were usually alcohol-related," observed Brian C. Mitchell, author of *The Paddy Camps*.

Most of my research was done through the online resources of the University of Massachusetts Lowell, the Library of Congress's online archives, and Digital Commonwealth's online collection. I also read *The Paddy Camps: The Irish of Lowell, 1821–61* by Brian C. Mitchell, *Battle Cry of Freedom* by James McPherson, and *The Immortal Irishman* by Timothy Egan.

About the Author

Lisa Boyle has been writing stories for as long as she can remember. Born and raised in Finksburg, Maryland, Lisa received bachelor's degrees in journalism and international  affairs from Northeastern University in Boston, Massachusetts. As part of her college program, Lisa traveled the Middle East and spent two months reporting on political and human-interest stories. She has been published in various online magazines, and has held many different jobs over the years from cheesemonger, to educator at the U.S.S. Constitution Museum. Lisa and her husband Tim live in North Carolina with the best daughter in the world and a goofy-looking mutt named Lloyd.

Sign up for Lisa Boyle's newsletter for the latest updates: lisaboylewrites.com

Did you love this book? Don't forget to write a review!